The
WITCH'S
KIND

LOUISA MORGAN

www.orbitbooks.net

ORBIT

First published in Great Britain in 2019 by Orbit

1 3 5 7 9 10 8 6 4 2

Copyright © 2019 by Louise Marley

Excerpt from *The Sisters of the Winter Wood* by Rena Rossner
Copyright © 2018 by Rena Rossner

The moral right of the author has been asserted.

All characters and events in this publication, other than
those clearly in the public domain, are fictitious
and any resemblance to real persons,
living or dead, is purely coincidental.

A CIP catalogue record for this book
is available from the British Library.

ISBN 978-0-356-51256-3

Printed and bound by CPI Group (UK) Ltd, Croydon CR0 4YY

Papers used by Orbit are from well-managed forests
and other responsible sources.

Orbit
An imprint of
Little, Brown Book Group
Carmelite House
50 Victoria Embankment
London EC4Y 0DZ

An Hachette UK Company
www.hachette.co.uk

www.orbitbooks.net

In memory of my grandmother,
the painter Elizabeth Lucinda Morgan Campbell,
who understood that art is life.

1

June 30, 1947

It was a long summer evening, the sun reluctant to sink beyond the Olympics, the shy stars holding back until the last possible moment. I lingered in my garden, sidling between my careful rows, tying up pea vines and pinching back tomato leaves. I ran my hands through the blueberry bushes that grew against the back fence, searching for a few more ripe berries to add to the baskets waiting in the pantry. I had a dozen ready to sell at the market. I expected to get ten cents apiece for them. I had eggs to sell, too, and several fat heads of butter lettuce.

It was a good harvest for early summer. I would be able to pay my electricity bill, my share of the party line, and have enough left over to buy scratch for the hens and flour and sugar and coffee for myself.

I scooped the berries into the front pocket of my overalls and straightened to gaze up into the twilight. These were lonely moments on my isolated farm, but I found beauty in them. Tatters of cloud shone silver against the violet sky, shimmering in the night wind. The breeze rippled the leaves of the apple trees clustered between my place and the shore of Hood Canal, and it tinged the air with the scent of salt water.

I felt the pull of the canal as a physical sensation. Its tides seemed to resonate with the tides of my own flowing blood, its life calling to the life in my veins. Sometimes the pull was so strong I had to drop what I was doing and go to the shore, driven by a need to touch the water, to feel its cool, salty texture on my fingers or washing over my bare feet. I felt the tug that night, the water beckoning to me, but the sky was beginning to darken, and the field between my house and the canal was pocked with holes and tangles of tall grass. I told myself I would go in the morning, as I often did, perhaps fish for flounder from the half-submerged dock or just ramble along the beach in search of sea glass.

I liked holding the glass fragments in my hand, bits of brown or blue or clear glass worn smooth by the water. I tried to imagine what they had once been part of—a milk bottle, a medicine vial, a jelly jar, perhaps even a glass dish that had at one time rested in some housewife's kitchen cupboard. I told myself stories about how the glass had ended up in the water. The milk bottle might have been thrown overboard from a ship. The glass dish might have slipped out of the housewife's hand and shattered on the floor. The jelly jar might have belonged to a child, who meant to catch polliwogs in it but had dropped it into the creek with small, water-slick fingers. I kept what I collected in a mason jar on the kitchen windowsill, where the sun could shine through, splashing the counter and the floor with prisms of light.

When a coyote yipped, somewhere to the north, I started from my reverie. I hurried through the garden to the house to call Willow in from the darkness. One coyote wouldn't be a problem for a dog of her size, but a pack of them could. We had lots of coyotes on the peninsula.

I had hung an iron bell on my back porch, an artifact salvaged from some derelict ship. I pulled the leather cord to strike the clapper, sending its hollow clang rolling out into the dusk. From beyond the orchard, Willow barked in answer, and I went to the side gate to hold it open for her.

She was hard to see in the dimness, but I could make out her pale silhouette as she loped through the apple orchard and trotted across the empty field toward the garden. She rubbed her shoulder against my leg as she came through the gate, and I scratched behind her ears. We walked side by side toward the house, my hand on her head, her rangy body warm and muscular against my thigh.

My aunt Charlotte said nobody calls a dog with a bell. I didn't know if that was true. I didn't know much about dogs except for Willow, and she always came when I rang the ship's bell. She did it from the very beginning, even when she was so small I could hold her in my two hands.

I had never intended to have a dog. The previous June, Charlotte had paid me a surprise visit, rolling up my dirt lane in her big Studebaker, churning billows of dust as she swung the auto into the space by my yard. She hadn't bothered waiting for the dust to settle; she had climbed out onto the running board, one gloved hand waving, the other clutching something small and beige and fluffy. I had come out onto the front porch to greet her, and I had squinted through the haze, trying to see what she was carrying.

"Barrie Anne!" she cried. "Brought you a present!"

No one uses my full name anymore, not since my parents died. Will never did use it. Charlotte likes it, but I really think she uses it to remind me that she's family. That she knows me better than anyone.

She climbed off the running board, leaving the Studebaker's door open, and came toward me wearing a wide, scarlet-lipsticked grin. I started down the steps to the yard to meet her, but when I saw what she was carrying, I froze.

I wasn't afraid of dogs, or of any animal. I catch my own fish in Hood Canal. I chase away the deer who stretch their necks through my fence to nibble cherry tomatoes and snap peas, and I shout and clap at coyotes who threaten my henhouse. I even shot at one, although I hated doing it so much I never did it a second time.

But a puppy of my own, one I might fall in love with, worry about, and one day, inevitably, lose—that frightened me.

No. I kept my hands at my sides. "Aunt Charlotte. I can't."

"Yes, you can, kiddo," she said. With the puppy in her arms, she swept past me in a swirl of scarves. "You need her. Trust me."

I knew better, of course, than to argue with Charlotte. She knew things. It was always wise to heed what she said.

I crossed the yard to close the automobile's door against the dust before, resigned, I went back up the steps to follow my aunt into the house.

She was waiting in the living room, standing with her back to me. The puppy's wide eyes and comical ears were just visible above her shoulder. One ear stood up, its tip pointed at the sky. The other, darker than its mate, fell to one side like a wet brown leaf. The puppy's smooth little head begged to be stroked. Its liquid eyes gazed at me with innocent curiosity.

Charlotte heard my steps behind her and turned, holding out the puppy. Reflexively, my hands reached for it, and at the same moment, the hard pain of remembered sorrow pierced the center of my chest. Instinctively, I cuddled the puppy over the ache. It nestled there, warm and soft and vibrant with life.

"Where did you find it?" I asked, already knowing I could never let the little creature go.

"Not it. Her. And by the lagoon," she said. "Actually, I didn't so much find her as she found me."

"Oh, my gosh, Aunt Charlotte. Were there other puppies? Did someone dump a litter?"

"Not that I could find. I looked, but this was the only one I saw, and she was a mess. Muddy, wet, shivering. She was hiding under a willow tree, and the moment I came down the path, she ran straight toward me." She reached out a hand and stroked the little dog's head with her forefinger. "It's no accident, of course. This puppy was meant for you."

"Why do you say that?"

She winked at me and reached into her pocket for her cigarettes. "It's the family thing. I just know."

I held up the puppy so I could look into her dark eyes, fringed with ridiculously long black lashes. Sweet puppy breath wafted across my face, and her little heart thudded under my fingers so that I felt as if I had a hummingbird cupped in my two hands. I was in love with her even before I returned her to my chest and cradled her there. The warmth of her tiny body seeped through the bones of my rib cage to caress my sore heart, bringing sudden tears to my eyes. "Oh, Aunt Charlotte," I choked. "She's—She's just—"

"Perfect. Of course she is." Charlotte lit her cigarette and held it in her teeth as she smiled at me. "She needs a name."

I didn't even stop to think. I didn't have to. "It's Willow."

Charlotte laughed. "That was quick! Suits her. She'll grow into that name."

I pressed my cheek to the soft little head and whispered into her crooked ear, "Willow. That's you, little one. Do you want to be a farm dog?"

The puppy twisted her neck to lick my face and then relaxed in my arms with a long sigh. Charlotte said, "I think that's her answer."

Charlotte proved to be right, as she invariably was. I needed the puppy. More to the point, I needed *that* puppy. Willow kept me connected to the world when I was tempted to give up on it. She seemed to know what I was thinking or was about to think. She followed me everywhere, her tail eager to wag, her pink tongue quick to loll with doggy laughter. If I went out without her, she knew the moment I turned for home, and waited by the door for me to appear. She filled the empty spaces of my life with her bright spirit and lively presence. I came to feel that she reflected me, in an uncanny way, as if she were the canine version of myself.

By the time Willow and I reached my postage stamp of a back porch, full darkness enveloped the peninsula. Even my hens had settled into their coop with a little chorus of drowsy chirps. I took a last glance back over my sleeping garden, then past the ragged line of trees along the canal, and on up into the reaches of the spangled sky.

The day was over. It was time to go inside, into the lighted kitchen, to pour a glass of lemonade for me and fill a bowl of water for Willow. It was later than usual for our dinner, and I planned to go to bed early to be ready for another long day in the garden.

I was about to tell Willow all of that when a glow flared beyond the tree line, directly in my field of vision.

I thought the light might have come from a falling star. I loved seeing them. They invited me to consider the immensity of the universe and the insignificance of one twenty-five-year-old human being. I imagined this one making its brave journey through the infinite darkness, coming from Mars, or the rings of Saturn, or some even more distant place, only to plunge into the cold waters of Hood Canal, setting the dark waves sparkling ever so briefly.

If my invented life story of the meteorite was right, the light should have died swiftly. It didn't.

I moved to the edge of the porch, leaning forward to see past the rosebush at the corner of the house. A waxing moon, nearly full, had risen above the Cascades to the east, fading the stars around it and lighting the empty field and the apple orchard, but it didn't lessen the glow coming from the canal.

I couldn't resist the urge to know, to see. At my knee, Willow whined as she gazed out toward the canal, and her expressive tail trembled.

"Come on," I whispered to her. "We have to go find out what that is."

It wasn't a prudent decision to go out into the night with only a dog for company. I should have at least dug the .30-30 out of the closet, but I was afraid if I took time for that, the glow might fade, whatever it was. I didn't want to miss it.

I set out at a trot, pausing only to close the garden gate to keep the critters away from my hens. With Willow beside me, I hurried across the field. The moonlight showed me the molehills and stones that lay in wait, and we moved quickly.

In minutes we reached the orchard. I had to be more cautious there, feeling my way between the trees and over the roots that arched above the ground. The light, fainter now, drew me on, and in a few more moments I emerged onto the shore. I stopped at the crest of the bank, steadying myself on the low branch of an apple tree as I gazed, rapt, into the water.

An unlikely and unfamiliar light bloomed there, as if someone had turned on a lamp. It shimmered and shivered beneath the waves, reminding me of the way a full moon might look behind shreds of windblown cloud. I couldn't make out a source for the light, but the surface of the water glistened with it as if the peaks of the waves had been painted silver. I arrived just in time to watch it fade. Its glow thinned and spread and dissipated into the darkness.

I had no idea what I had seen. It was gone in moments, leaving only an ordinary night on the peninsula, a bright moon and a sprinkle of white stars in an unremarkable black sky.

I clung to my tree, searching for some trace of the phenomenon, but it had vanished as if it had never been, leaving only the glimmer of stars on the shifting waves. With my heart pounding, I let go of the tree, and shuffled forward to the edge of the bank.

I felt a powerful urge to climb down the cut to the beach and plunge my hands into the water. It seemed to my awestruck mind that perhaps I could catch some of that mysterious light, gather it up in my fingers like a shred of seaweed borne in on the tide. Willow nudged me, encouraging me to do it, to go to the water.

At that moment, I heard the coyote bark again. Another sounded, not far away, and was answered with a chorus of yips. A pack, hunting. Willow stiffened and growled, and I knew I had to get her back inside the safety of our high fence. The temptation to engage with the coyotes might overcome even Willow's usual good sense. I took hold of her neck to keep her with me.

I backed away from the bank and into the orchard. I kept a firm hold on Willow's ruff as I blundered my way through the darkness of the trees. I had to keep my hand on her as we crossed the open field. It wasn't like her, but that night she kept turning back, resisting my direction, which made me anxious.

With the aid of the moonlight and the lights from the house

as a guide, I led her home as swiftly as I could. My heartbeat didn't settle into its normal rhythm until we were through the garden gate, with it locked behind us, and inside the house, the door firmly closed. The dog whined and scratched at the door once I had locked it, another thing she never did. It made my belly crawl with nerves.

As I hastily fried bacon and scrambled eggs for our belated meal, I pondered the phenomenon. I knew about algae bloom and the bioluminescence that could result, but I had never observed it. I had a feeling the color was different, but I would have to go to the library to research that. There could have been an oil slick from one of the big fishing boats, but how could that have been so bright, bright enough for me to see the corona from my back porch? And surely the light had come from beneath the water, not floating on the top as a spill of oil would.

Willow resisted me again when it was time to go to bed. I had to tug at her to get her to come upstairs, and once there, I closed the bedroom door to keep her in. She finally surrendered, sprawling in her customary position across the foot of the bed. I lay down, pondering the mystery. If the coyotes had not stopped me, I might have had an answer. As it was, I had only questions.

A huge, cracking yawn overtook me. I knew there was nothing more I could do that night. I hoped there would be other witnesses to the event, explanations from people who knew more than I. I turned on my side, consigning the questions to the morning, and fell into the solid sleep of someone who had worked outdoors for all of a summer's day.

Willow woke me at five, pawing at my shoulder beneath the blankets. I thought she must need to go out. Blearily, though I could have slept longer, I got up. In my housecoat and bare feet, I opened the back door for her, then switched on the RCA Victor on the kitchen counter. I listened to the combination of news and music as I filled the percolator and took a loaf from the bread box. I listened for some report of the strange light the night before, but the announcer didn't mention it, which was strange. The war was over, but we were all still wary, alert to any activities out of the ordinary.

The war had changed the peninsula. Japanese farmers, friends and neighbors born and raised on the Olympic Peninsula just as I had been, had been interned in Idaho, and their farms seized. One of the dairymen, a Norwegian immigrant, had lost both his sons, one in Italy and one in the South Pacific, and in despair, he sold his land to a company that bought it for the timber. Dr. Masters, up in Port Townsend, lost his only boy, Herbert. He went on practicing, but I never saw him laugh again.

Some of the changes were for the better. The coast guard improved the roads to the coast guard stations, hung telephone wires, and built radio towers. I didn't care much about roads, since my pickup was as rough to drive on pavement as it was on dirt. I didn't use my telephone much, either. The other people on the party line always picked up when they heard a ring, as if they didn't know the three-ring pattern was mine. I did like listening to the radio, though. There were days when KXA, which broadcast from Seattle, was my only link to the world beyond my little farm.

I trotted up the stairs to pull on a shirt and my overalls, leaving my feet bare. In the kitchen, I scrambled eggs again and scraped half of them onto a plate and the other half into Willow's bowl. Charlotte teased me about that, but Willow had always eaten what I did, from those very first days, and eggs were one thing I had in abundance. I set her bowl on the mat beside the range, stuck a slice of bread in the Toastmaster, and went to the back porch to ring the bell. I stood there for a moment, tasting the summer air.

Living alone had made me sensitive. When Will was still at the farm, I didn't differentiate the scent of wild fennel from that of slowly ripening blackberries or notice how cloud patterns changed from season to season. I didn't scan the sky to anticipate the weather or feel the air with my fingertips to decide whether to hang washing on the line. Sometimes I thought I might be acquiring some of Willow's talents. When she put up her muzzle into the breeze, her nostrils fluttered as if she were riffling the pages of a book, learning secrets carried on the wind. It seemed to me I sensed almost as much as she did.

The morning sky, so bright with stars the night before, had turned grumpy and gray. Patches of fog puddled in low spots in the field and in the curves of the lane. Such weather would slow the ripening of my tomatoes but make for a good morning at the market. With luck, I could sell my things early and get home in time to repair the shed roof, which had started leaking in the May rains.

I rang the bell and propped open the screen door for the dog while I went back to my breakfast. I was buttering toast when I realized Willow hadn't come in. Her bowl was untouched. Recalling my unease of the night before, I dropped the toast and the butter knife and dashed to the back porch.

There was no sign of a plumy beige tail or a sleek head, not in the garden, not near the henhouse. I scanned the field and squinted toward the apple orchard. Nothing.

The old pain was never far away, and now it seized me anew, making me press my fist to my breastbone. Thinking of the coyotes, I banged the ship's bell, yanking hard on the leather strip. The clapper produced a furious sound that made my ears ring. While the echoes died away, I ran back into the house for my father's old Winchester .30-30, stored behind the winter coats in the closet under the stairs.

Carrying the Winchester at the ready, I trotted along the path through the garden, the stubs of weeds biting at my bare soles. I was unlatching the gate when I spotted Willow weaving through the orchard. The pain in my chest released all at once, like a bubble bursting, leaving a giddy spot of relief in its place. I lowered the gun and called, "Willow! Come!"

She was coming, but there was something wrong. Usually she loped easily through the sparse yellow grass. Now she walked slowly, as if she had been hurt. I closed the gate to keep the chickens in and started out to meet her, wincing at the scratches on my feet, wishing I had put on my boots.

Within a few steps, I could see Willow wasn't injured. She was carrying something.

Willow had always lugged things home. Most came from the

shore, a child's bucket; the ruins of a straw hat; several pieces of driftwood, sculpted by the sea, now serving as garden art. Other treasures were less savory—a rotted crab, a beer bottle crawling with bugs, a filthy pair of men's undershorts.

This was something completely new.

Willow paced past me, balancing every step. Her burden was an awkward-looking shape. It swung from side to side in the grip of her jaws, a dark, mottled color in the gray light. She climbed the steps to the porch gingerly, taking one tread at a time, and settled the thing gently to the floor. It seemed to be a blanket, wool or cotton or felt, folded over on itself, the ends tucked in the way you might tuck in a pillowcase.

Willow put her nose inside the folds, and a sound emerged from it, a sound that rocked me with memory.

My infant son had lived only a few hours. Scottie had been barely strong enough to breathe, let alone cry, but he had made that sound, a mewing such as a kitten might make, or a raccoon kit, even a coyote pup. Some sort of animal. Something that didn't belong on my porch.

"Willow?" I whispered.

She drew her nose out of the bundle and cocked her head at me, then sat down with an air of having completed her job and expecting me now to do mine.

I spun to face the empty field, lifting the .30-30 as I moved, slipping my finger inside the trigger guard. I fully expected some fierce maternal creature to come racing toward the house in search of her offspring. I felt as if danger lay in front of me and behind me at the same time.

My heart hammered in my ears, blurring the whisper of the wind. I scanned the field, the orchard that stood between my farm and the canal, the scraggly stand of pine trees on the west side of my property. I clutched the gun and tried to remember if there was a shell in the chamber.

I didn't see anything. The sound came again.

With shaking hands, I laid the .30-30 on the bench beside the door. I took one more look over my shoulder before I approached Willow's offering. I bent over it, but my thighs tensed, ready to spring away in an instant.

I heard it a third time, a faint, questing whimper.

Warily, I extended a bare foot toward the bundle and tried to open it with my toes.

The material was wet, as if it had been lying on the beach. I could see now it was flannel, gray, with a pattern of red threads running through it. The fabric was soft, and it moved easily under my foot. I put out my hand, but tentatively. My fingers tingled with anticipation, ready to pull out of the way if something in there had teeth, claws, a fighting instinct.

At my touch, the folds fell apart, opening to show the thing within. I stopped breathing as I stared, struggling to believe my own eyes.

There was a small pale face, paper-white strands of hair plastered to a little skull, and closed, delicate eyelids. I saw hands curled into fragile fists like tiny nautilus shells, and toes like pearls peeping out beneath some sort of garment. I saw all those things, but my mind refused to translate them, to sort them, to organize the disparate parts.

My need for air roused me, and I sucked in a noisy breath. Willow jumped to her feet, her tail waving, her eyes fixed on my face. With the rush of oxygen, my brain assembled the bits into a whole, and I moaned with the shock of it.

It was an infant. A baby. And it was sopping wet.

With trembling hands, I reached for it. As my fingers slid beneath its ribs, its eyes opened to reveal a shade of green as vivid as a shard of sea glass. My breath stopped again at their unexpected beauty.

When I lifted the baby to my shoulder, I expected the smell of wet diaper. Instead, I recognized the scent of the sea. The little thing was drenched in salt water. I wrapped my arms around it, fearing it must be chilled. It didn't shiver, though the gown it wore—more unfamiliar fabric—was soaked. The infant settled itself against my chest, its wet head tucked under my chin, not unlike Willow had done when I first held her, and it repeated its tiny whimper.

My experience of mothering had been so brief that I had learned almost nothing in practice. Now I had only my instincts to draw on. I held the baby close with one hand and opened the door with the other. I snatched a towel from the rack beside the sink and spread it on the kitchen table.

With difficulty, I wriggled the sodden gown off the little body and laid the naked baby on the towel. A girl. The delicate tracing of veins in her head and throat shone blue against her translucent skin. She had fat little legs and arms and perfect miniature fingernails. I used my fingers to brush the seawater from the silky strands of her hair. Her eyes followed my movements as I dried her and wrapped her in a fresh towel from a kitchen drawer. Her cheeks were plump and smooth and as rosy as the inside of an abalone shell.

My own newborn's face had looked crumpled, as if he had been born at the end of his life instead of at the beginning, an exquisite, wrinkled little man. I had kissed his forehead over and over as he struggled for breath, and I hugged him close to me long after he gave up trying. Even when he grew cold, when I understood that I couldn't will life back into his frail body, I had held him against my chest. Those terrible hours came back to me as I cradled the foundling. I felt the thump of my panicked heart against her own.

During the war, someone had abandoned a baby boy in a back pew of the Presbyterian church up in Quilcene. It was a newborn, wrapped in an army blanket and tucked into a wicker shopping basket. I never heard what became of the poor little thing, but at least his mother had left her infant where he would be found and taken care of.

But this baby! This baby had been left in the dark, exposed to the cold and the waves. The coyotes could have found her, or any other predator. The tide could have swept her into Hood Canal to drown.

"You saved her, Willow," I murmured. The baby stirred at the sound of my voice. Willow nosed my thigh, and without thinking, I lowered the infant so the dog could see her. Willow licked the baby's scalp with her long, gentle tongue. The little girl's eyes widened, and she gave a tiny gurgle.

I paced the kitchen with the baby in my arms, wondering

what I should do. The slender telephone directory lay on the kitchen counter, but I couldn't bring myself to pick it up. My neighbors were kind people, but despite my having lived among them for nearly two years, they still regarded me as a curiosity. They had liked Will better than they liked me, and now that he was gone, my last hope of respectability had vanished. I knew I should have tried harder to be sociable, but I seemed to have lost the knack for small talk.

Mr. Robbins, the dairyman, had lectured me at the market, saying it wasn't proper for a young woman to live on her own, three miles from the nearest neighbor. He said I should move into Brinnon, a proper town, where people could watch out for me.

What he really meant, and which I understood, was that I needed a man. A man to tell me what to do, and how to do it, and when, too. Probably a lot of the folks in the town and at the market agreed with him. And now, if I were to pick up the telephone, that line everyone listens in on—

No. Who could I call? How would I explain the discovery of an abandoned baby? Mr. Robbins would call the police. Mrs. Urquhardt, who had seven children of her own, would call Social Services. The Millers were religious and very sweet. They'd probably send out their pastor or something.

They'd all have a thousand questions about where the baby came from. Who would believe my dog carried her home? They might even think I had stolen an infant to replace my lost one.

For that matter, *I* had a thousand questions. Was there a woman in trouble, down at the shore? Had there been a boating accident? Should I call the police myself so they could search?

I couldn't leave the baby. I couldn't care for her, either. I had nothing for her to eat. No idea what to do next.

I needed Charlotte.

2

May 28, 1939

My parents caught Spanish flu in 1928, when I was six. My father's sister came to Port Townsend from New Mexico to nurse them and to take care of me. Both my parents died. My aunt Charlotte never left.

I asked her once if she hadn't been afraid she would catch the illness herself. "No, I was sure I wasn't going to get sick. In any case, no point being afraid," was her answer. "We're all going to catch something. If we're lucky, it's old age." It was a very Charlotte thing to say.

In order to stay with me, Charlotte gave up her art studio in Taos. She supported the two of us by doing illustrations for medical texts and journals, creating frightening, oddly beautiful diagrams of arteries and capillaries, nerves and muscles and bones. The cups and bowls around her drawing board bristled with red and blue and gray pencils, fine-pointed pens, small pots of colored ink. She spent most of every day on her commercial assignments, and then, usually late in the evening, she turned to her original work.

Charlotte painted vast canvases studded with squares of color. She created patterns out of the squares—swirls and pyramids and mazes—sometimes in primary colors, sometimes subtly developed pastels. I often got up for school and found her still at it, her ashtray overflowing with lipstick-stained butts, her hair spattered with paint or her face smudged with chalk. She wore canvas smocks when she was painting. The rest of the time she wore trousers.

I pled with her once, after she sold one of her paintings, to buy a dress with the proceeds.

"Why?"

"The other ladies in Port Townsend wear dresses."

"I'm not like the other ladies in Port Townsend. You've probably noticed."

"Well, true. But, Aunt Charlotte—"

"You have to choose your role models wisely, Barrie Anne. Miss Katharine Hepburn wears trousers. Miss Amelia Earhart wore trousers."

"Mrs. Eleanor Roosevelt wears dresses."

That earned a belly laugh. "I purely love Mrs. Roosevelt, kiddo, but if I had her figure, I'd wear dresses, too. Those bosoms!"

Blushing, but giggling, too, I subsided. Aunt Charlotte went on wearing trousers.

I didn't really mind the trousers all that much, but I had always been aware that, as a family, we were different. The mothers of my friends wore dresses, with bib aprons over them whenever they were at home, which was most of the time. Their fathers went out to work as plumbers or accountants or salesmen, and when they returned, dinner was waiting for them. The mothers removed their aprons, combed their hair, even put on lipstick before their husbands came home.

Sometimes I was invited to stay for dinner in my friends' homes. I loved sitting at a lively table, with chatter and laughter and arguments and all the normal racket a family makes. Such moments, in my childish mind, diminished our own quiet dinners. When we sat down in our kitchen nook, Aunt Charlotte often was still wearing her painter's smock. Her hair was usually covered with a bandana, and her fingers were always stained with paint and tinged yellow by her cigarettes. She was invariably preoccupied, whether by work or by her latest painting, I usually didn't know. We ate, as a rule, in silence.

None of that was bad. I don't remember ever complaining. It was just that we were...different. In my secret thoughts, hidden away so as not to hurt my aunt's feelings, I longed to be normal, to be part of what I considered a normal family, with a father to watch my tennis matches or my swim meets, and a mother who spent her days cooking and cleaning, sewing or knitting.

I'm afraid I yearned to be like other people. Regular people. I'll always be grateful I never said such a thing to my aunt Charlotte.

The day before the end of my junior year of high school, Charlotte allowed me to drive in Port Townsend for the very first time. She had been teaching me in her seven-year-old De Soto, taking me out on the easy roads around Fort Worden or through the tiny town of Chimacum. On that sunny spring day, I steered the De Soto anxiously along Water Street. As I negotiated the traffic, my palms perspired with nervousness inside my white gloves. Despite my best efforts, I ground the gears as I turned up Monroe.

Charlotte said, "You have to let the clutch out gently."

"Yes, sorry."

"It's all right. You're doing fine."

I managed to get us to our destination, the post office, with no further mistakes. Charlotte patted my shoulder and pointed to a parking spot. I pulled in, only bumping the curb a little bit.

While Charlotte climbed the brick steps, I stepped out of the De Soto. I lounged against the hood in the sunshine, trying to pose the way the *Life* models did, tossing my head back, ruffling my hair with my fingers.

It didn't work very well. The metal of the hood was too hot to lean on, and my hair stayed stubbornly straight, despite the hours I spent tying it up in rags every night. I was trying to earn enough money for a cold perm, working afternoons and Saturdays at the dry goods store, but Charlotte was strict about how that money would be spent. Books first, she said, the ones I would need for college the following year. Then a perm if there was money left over.

I knew she was right, but I was seventeen. I wanted more than anything in the world to look like Hedy Lamarr.

As I was trying to coax a strand of my hair to curl around my finger, one of my classmates emerged from the post office and came leaping down the steps two at a time. "Barrie Anne

Blythe!" he cried, charging toward me. "Only one more day
in the creaky old schoolhouse, right?"

"Hello, Herbert," I said. My voice cracked embarrassingly.
My cheeks burned in a most un–Hedy Lamarr fashion.

Of all the boys who might have appeared, it had to be Herbert Masters, the boy I was hopelessly sweet on. He wore a
University of Washington sweater and saddle shoes. His
slicked-back hair glistened with Brylcreem. He was terribly
handsome, a perfect match for Hedy. Or for Rose Mahon, the
girl he had taken to homecoming. Not for me.

I was hopeless in social situations. I was at ease on the baseball field or the tennis court or the swimming pool, places
where my long legs and broad shoulders were an asset. I loved
sports. I hated small talk. I didn't go to dances. That is, I didn't
go to dances after the first one, when I had stood awkwardly
beside the refreshment table the entire evening. I was too tall,
too unfashionable, too shy. It was no comfort that I wasn't the
only wallflower, that there were half a dozen other girls who
didn't dance, who slouched in chairs or hid in the bathroom.
The whole thing made me miserable, and I never tried again.

It seemed to me, young as I was, that Herbert was as close
to perfect as a boy could be. He was a year ahead of me, and
one of the few in my school who was taller than I was. He was
a football star. President of his class. The doctor's son, a catch
for any girl. From my lonely distance, I yearned after him,
or someone like him, someone who would make me feel I
belonged. Make me feel pretty. Popular.

I wanted to talk to him, to laugh with him, to toss my hair

and smile up at him the way I saw Rose Mahon do. I also wanted to sink into the earth and disappear. It was agony.

If Herbert noticed my flaming face, he spared me any comment. He gave me a white-toothed smile that made my stomach quiver. "Is this your auto? Spiffy!"

If only I could toss off a comment like "Spiffy!" with such insouciance. Instead, I stammered, "Well, not exac—No—I mean—It's my aunt's."

"Keen! Do you drive it?"

"Y-yes. Sort of."

"Take me for a spin, then. I'll buy you an ice-cream soda!" He pulled a worn porkpie hat from his pocket and clapped it carelessly on his head.

I tried not to look down at my three-year-old pleated skirt or the fraying lace on my shirtwaist. Herbert could look dashing in a wrinkled hat, but it was different for boys, especially boys like him. I never seemed to achieve anything remotely fashionable. I might just as well have worn a pair of Charlotte's trousers—at least that would make some sort of statement.

I came to wish I had conquered my self-consciousness that day. Just three years later, Herbert Masters would die in the first battle of El Alamein. In retrospect, he and his friends, with their up-to-date clothes and abundant pocket money, were more like me than I realized, but at the time they seemed to inhabit a different world from my own.

"S-sorry, Herbert. My aunt is in the post office, and I have to wait—That is, I—"

"Oh, too bad!" He cuffed me lightly on the shoulder. My

heart fluttered at his touch, offhand as it was. He said, "Another time, maybe. See you in the funny papers!" Before I could think of a response, he was off down the street, gay, confident, the very picture of a young man about to burst upon a fortunate world.

"Friend from school?" Charlotte was at the passenger door, tipping up the brim of her hat to watch Herbert's jaunty progress.

"Just someone in my history class."

"Doesn't that count as being your friend?"

"Not with a boy like Herbert."

"Ah." Charlotte eyed me across the roof of the De Soto. "Are you all right?"

I shrugged and looked away, swallowing an urge to cry.

Charlotte sighed. "Come on, kiddo. Let's go to the soda fountain."

"What about your work?" She had brought a package out of the post office that was even thicker than the one she had carried in.

She opened the back door and laid it on the seat, saying, "It can wait. Nothing better for boy trouble than a soda with a friend."

"It's not really boy trouble," I said glumly. I got into the driver's seat as Charlotte climbed in on the other side. I spread my palms on the steering wheel. It was too hot for my fingers, even through my gloves. "Herbert is one of the popular boys."

"You don't think you're popular?"

"Girls like me are never popular," I said with bitter conviction.

"You mean smart girls."

"They call me a tomboy, too."

"I've always liked that about you."

A wave of irritation swept over me, though I knew none of this was Charlotte's fault. I complained, "My hair is hopeless, and my clothes . . . and I never know what to say to boys."

"Boys probably don't know what to say to you, either," she said.

"I'm afraid it will be just the same at college."

Charlotte said gently, ignoring my cranky tone, "It's going to be okay, Barrie Anne. Come on. Let's go drown our sorrows with a Green River."

I blew out a breath, pressed the De Soto's starter, and gingerly let out the clutch. As I shifted and backed out into the street, Charlotte took a battered pack of cigarettes from the smoker's vanity and tapped out the last one. "It's not true what they say, you know."

"What's that?"

She touched the car lighter to the tip of her smoke. "They say boys don't like girls who are smarter than they are. Or better at sports. They're wrong."

I didn't agree in the slightest, but I was too busy watching the road to argue the point. I drove cautiously downtown to Baker's drugstore. I ground the gears twice and made the handbrake squeal when I set it, but Charlotte only arched one penciled eyebrow and didn't say a word.

The two of us went in to sit at the counter. I propped my chin on my hand as I watched the soda jerk mix green syrup into fizzy water. "Aunt Charlotte?"

She rotated her stool to face me. In the powdery slant of sun-shine, I noticed faint touches of gray in her hair. Her eyelids had begun to sag a little at the corners, a detail that gave me a jolt of anxiety. She crushed her half-smoked cigarette into a painted metal ashtray. "Do you want to ask me something?"

I was on uncertain ground with my question, but I needed to know. I spilled out the words in a rush. "Did you love some-one who died in the Great War?"

She laughed, which made her cough and cover her mouth. When the cough subsided, she said, "No, kiddo. Nope. I did not love someone who died in the war. Why?"

"I just wondered. I guess because you never got married."

"Lots of people never get married."

"But usually there's a reason."

"Is there?" Our sodas arrived. Charlotte picked up a straw and stuck it into the glass. "I'm not the marrying sort of woman, Barrie Anne. Never was."

"You never fell in love?"

She took a long sip of green fizz, then pulled a fresh cig-arette pack from her trouser pocket. "There was someone I cared about," she admitted, as she peeled foil from the pack. "But marriage wasn't possible."

"Why not?"

She stuck the cigarette between her lips and spoke around it. "None of your business, young lady."

"He was married!" I dared.

She laughed, gripping the cigarette between her front teeth. "Nope."

"What then?"

Charlotte struck a match, put it to the cigarette, and drew. "I can't explain it to you, so I'm not going to try. We're supposed to be talking about you, in any case."

"Nothing much to talk about." I took a sip of Green River and wrinkled my nose against the tickle of the bubbles.

"You know, Barrie Anne, I don't think any young person thinks they're popular."

"Were you?"

"I didn't think so then, no. I see it differently now. I had lots of friends."

"Boyfriends?"

She blew out a thin, lazy stream of smoke, like an extended sigh. "I was friends with boys, sometimes, but... It was a long time ago. Things were different when I was your age. Before the war."

"How were they different?"

"We were chaperoned. Always. A girl might be sweet on a boy, but only from a distance."

"Were you ever sweet on a boy?"

She chuckled, but there was something guarded about the sound. She took another drag of her cigarette and settled it into the ashtray. "No," she said. "I wasn't." She tucked her straw between her lips as if that was the end of it.

"No, tell me! You were never sweet on a boy? Ever?"

Charlotte sucked up a mouthful of bubbles, savored it, and swallowed. "I never was. I suppose that's why I'm not a marrying kind of woman."

"But wait! You said you cared about someone..."

"That's different."

She didn't look at me again, which meant I could study her profile and try to understand what this odd conversation meant. I knew her well enough to know she wasn't going to say anything further, though I wanted more. There was something about the set of her shoulders and the tuck of her chin that seemed mournful to me. Solitary. It jarred me out of my self-absorption.

We weren't demonstrative, the two of us. I had barely known her before my parents' illness, nor had she known me. She had no idea how to behave with a young child. She was never strict. She was kind, in a distracted way. I don't remember a lot of hugs or kisses, but Aunt Charlotte was there, day in, day out, ready with tea or food or a bit of extra money if she had it.

And she knew things. Secrets, sometimes. Predictions. Other people's thoughts.

I didn't think much about it. She was an unconventional woman, and her hunches were an everyday part of our lives, like the little square house we lived in and the unusual way my aunt made a living.

What I did think about, and what began to worry me for the first time that day, was that Charlotte had no one but me.

I drank the last of my Green River and ventured to ask one more personal question. "Aunt Charlotte," I said, "will you be all right when I go to college next year? When you're all on your own?"

She lifted her head and flashed me her crimson grin. "Barrie Anne Blythe, you silly girl." She touched my hand with her fingers. Her glove was damp from the soda glass. "Are you worried about that? Me being alone?"

"Well—yes."

Chuckling, she patted my hand. "Not to hurt your feelings, kiddo, but I'm looking forward to it."

Foolishly, I suppose because I wanted to, I believed her.

3

July 1, 1947

I laid the foundling on the divan and covered her with an age-softened crocheted blanket I kept there for occasional naps. The moment I straightened, those startling eyes opened, and she began to whimper. It was a tremulous little cry, full of anxiety. It made me snatch her up again, blanket and all, to cuddle her against my shoulder.

Willow had whimpered exactly like that on our first night together. Charlotte had brought a basket for the puppy. I put it on the floor next to my bed and settled Willow into it, but the moment I left her to get into bed myself, she began to cry. Five minutes later, she was snuggled into the curve of my arm. She slept there all night, a node of warmth and comfort tucked beneath my chin. As she grew bigger, she moved to my feet. The basket lay on the floor, unused. She always slept on my bed.

It chilled me to think of this baby lying alone on the beach, sending her hopeless little cry into the darkness. How frightened she must have been! If puppies were terrified of being alone, I could only imagine what it must feel like to an infant.

I went to the wall phone. I tried to lift the receiver gently, but it emitted its telltale clank as it always did, announcing to everyone on the party line that someone was making a call.

"Number, please?"

I spoke Charlotte's number, then leaned against the counter as I waited to be connected. The baby's soft weight warmed my shoulder and the side of my neck. Beyond the window, the marine layer was beginning to break apart, and patches of sky gleamed here and there, the blue promise of a warm summer day. It was the sort of day on which Will and I first saw this place, strolling around the neglected garden, walking on the creaking boards of the porch, peeking in the windows to fantasize how we would modernize the kitchen and the bathroom. None of those things had happened.

"Hello?"

I started. "Oh! Aunt Charlotte. It's me."

"Barrie Anne. At last."

"What do you mean, 'at last'?"

Before she could answer, we both heard the click that meant someone else on the party line had picked up. She said, obviously choosing her words carefully, "I had a—a feeling—you might need me. Everything okay?"

The Blythe talent at work. I should have known.

Cautiously, I said, "Yes, Aunt Charlotte. Everything's okay. It's just that I was hoping—" I searched for the right words, the ones she would understand but my neighbors wouldn't. "I was thinking perhaps—you could come for lunch?"

There was a pause in which I heard someone breathing. Not Charlotte. Her smoker's wheeze was easy to distinguish. I wondered which neighbor it might be. Mrs. Urquhardt was the most likely. With all those children, she was almost always at home, and I was sure she listened in on party line calls just to alleviate the tedium of her housebound life. Mrs. Miller was another possibility. She seemed to have an eternal cold and always breathed like a kettle on the boil.

Charlotte gave a small cough, and whoever the breather was moved the receiver away from her mouth. "Lunch," Charlotte said speculatively. I listened to her draw on her cigarette. She exhaled with deliberation before she asked, "Am I bringing it?"

Her little jest broke my tension. Like a balloon jabbed with a pin, I sagged against the counter, weak-kneed with relief that Charlotte would soon be there to help. The baby wriggled in my grasp, and I said hastily, "Yes, please. And I need goat's milk."

My eavesdropper drew a surprised breath at the same time Charlotte snorted a laugh. "Goat's milk!"

"Yes."

There was another pause while she considered this. "Well. Goat's milk, yes. I'll be there as soon as I can. I'll pick it up on the way."

"Thank you."

In a wry tone, she added, "Thanks for the invitation."

When I heard her break the connection on her end, I banged the receiver onto its hook for the benefit of my eavesdropper. Charlotte understood, of course, about the party line. We never spoke of anything private over my telephone, not since Will vanished and people began to whisper about me.

The great irony of the war's aftermath was how eager menfolk were to resume their belief in the fragility of women. It was fine for women to build bombs and work in shipyards, to carry the mail or run a dairy, as long as there weren't enough men to do those things. But now, the men who had survived were home. They wanted their jobs back. They took it for granted that this was the right and proper way of things, that women should retreat to their kitchens and nurseries. I thought that, too, once upon a time, but my convictions had changed.

I'm not proud to admit it, but there were times when I couldn't help thinking how much easier it would have been for me if Will had died in the Pacific. War widows were respected. They could hang a gold star banner in their front windows. They received government money. They had their community's sympathy and support.

I had nothing but my shame.

The baby in my arms stirred and whimpered again. The sound made my empty breasts contract, and the sensation brought fresh memories. Scottie, in his brief hours of life, never nursed, and for two weeks after he was gone, my breasts ached with unspent milk. Nothing helped, neither cold water nor warm, not wrapping my breasts, not even the soothing poultice Charlotte made with mint leaves. It had hurt, but still, I was sorry when the aching eased. It had seemed right that my body should hurt as much as my soul.

Holding the baby in one arm, I went to fill the kettle and set it on the range. At least I could boil water, perhaps spoon a little into her mouth after it cooled. While I waited for it to simmer, I opened the icebox, though I knew perfectly well what was in it. Eggs, what was left of a pound of butter, a piece of salmon, and a bottle of Mrs. Urquhardt's homemade root beer. Nothing that would help.

I hummed to the baby and paced through the kitchen, around the table with its mismatched chairs, on to the front room, then back again. Willow, who had emptied her bowl, sat and watched me, her head to one side. The clouds burned away as I waited, revealing the hot pale blue of the July sky. My chores waited outside, undone. My uneaten breakfast had gone cold on the counter. The market was forgotten.

I glanced at the Bakelite clock resting under the telephone, a little pink-and-green Art Deco thing Charlotte had given me to take to college. Three quarters of an hour had passed. The goat's milk would have to come from the Chimacum market, and we were another hour's drive past that.

I tried teaspoons of water, but they dribbled uselessly down the baby's chin. I paced in irregular circles, crooning to her, my own stomach grumbling in response to her hunger. Willow rose and followed, turning when I turned, looking up at me whenever I paused. I was in the front room when the Studebaker appeared at last, boiling up the dusty lane at a blistering pace. I waited, the crochet-wrapped child against my shoulder, and braced myself.

Charlotte leaped out of the car, one hand on the fedora she had recently taken to wearing, the other holding a string bag. She kicked the car door shut with her foot and strode up to the porch. She opened the door and came straight in.

She stopped when she saw me and looked me up and down. "You're really all right?"

"Yes."

"Good. But there's something, isn't there? Something's happened."

I blew out a breath, pulled down the blanket, and pivoted so Charlotte could see the infant's head of spun-sugar hair.

"My God." Charlotte took one step and stopped again. "That's a—That's a baby!"

"It's a baby."

Charlotte's hand trembled so that the jars in her string bag rattled together. She seemed to have trouble getting her breath. "Barrie Anne," she finally croaked. "What have you done?"

I spoke above the child's head. "It wasn't me. It was Willow."

"Willow!"

"Willow found her, on the beach, I think. Carried her here."

"On the beach?" Her gaze met mine, suddenly sharp.

I held the baby tighter. "It seems so."

"How did Willow carry her?"

I gave her a weak smile. "Like she carries everything. Gets her mouth on it and lifts."

Charlotte took off her hat and tossed it onto the divan. She approached, bent to look into the baby's face, and gasped. I knew those luminous green eyes, with their long, fair lashes, had opened.

"Where's her mother, for heaven's sake?"

"No idea in the world. I need to go look for her, but—I didn't want to leave the baby, and I didn't want to take her with me in case..." I shrugged my free shoulder. "What I might find—I doubt it's good."

"Such a tiny baby! Newborn?"

"I would guess a month or so, wouldn't you?"

"She smells like salt water."

"I know."

"She was in the canal!"

"She must have been. She was soaking wet." I led the way to the kitchen, with Charlotte following. "See that little mound of flannel? She was wrapped up in that."

Charlotte walked past me to crouch beside the fabric. She stripped off her gloves, and her artist's hands investigated it, touching, stroking, testing a fold between her thumb and forefinger. She got to her feet, frowning. "It looks like an old blanket."

"That's what I thought. She was sort of—well, swaddled in it, I suppose."

"Was she abandoned?"

"I don't have any answers. I couldn't think what to do with her, so I dried her off and then wrapped her in this thing."

"And called me," Charlotte said, with a twist of her lips. I had caught her unprepared. She wasn't wearing her usual lipstick, nor were her eyebrows penciled.

"I don't have anyone else I can call."

"The police come to mind, Barrie Anne. A lost baby!"

"I thought of that, but—people around here already think I'm weird. What if they thought I stole her?"

"Nonsense."

"Even you—what was the first thing you said? 'What have you done?'"

"I spoke without thinking. I know perfectly well you wouldn't steal a baby."

"Besides, Willow brought her to me. Me. That means something."

"I would certainly say so."

"And Willow found her by the water, Aunt Charlotte, as if the sea brought her, served her up just for me. If I call the police—" My voice shook, and I had to swallow. "If I call the police, they'll take her away." The baby stirred against my shoulder, mewing her little cry.

"No doubt they would."

"I don't want them to do that. I-I *can't* let them do that."

"That's a strong feeling, Barrie Anne."

"I know."

Charlotte gazed back at the infant. "Why goat's milk?"

"I heard Mrs. Urquhardt gave her twins goat's milk when she couldn't produce enough herself. She was pretty old when they were born, I think."

"You're lucky I trust you. I knew something had happened—was going to happen—but I didn't know quite what. And that was the oddest request I've ever received." Charlotte set her string bag on the counter and bent to take a saucepan from my cupboard. "The milk came from that little goat dairy in Quilcene. It's fresh, but I think we're supposed to scald it. Do you have a bottle and a nipple?"

It was a simple question, and I had an answer. I wanted to

answer. I opened my mouth to do so, but then I couldn't say the words. My throat had closed tightly around the old pain, and I couldn't speak past it.

Charlotte looked up in question. When she saw my rigid expression, her face softened, and our shared grief throbbed in her voice. "Kiddo. Did you keep everything?"

I pressed my trembling lips together and nodded my assent.

Charlotte said, "Nursery?"

I managed a tight "Mm-hmm."

She took the stoppered bottle of goat's milk from her bag and poured it into the saucepan. I lit the burner, then stepped back to keep the blanket away from the flame while Charlotte trudged up the steep stairs.

Charlotte had been as thrilled as I had been by my pregnancy, and she plunged into preparations with typical enthusiasm. She helped me choose baby clothes. She painted the nursery ceiling to look like a blue sky with white clouds. She insisted on taking me up to Port Townsend for visits with Dr. Masters, though Will kept proclaiming this was a waste of time and money, that his mother had borne her babies at home, with only her sister to help.

Dr. Masters thought everything was fine. If Charlotte suspected anything was wrong, she never said so. It wouldn't have helped, in any case.

After Scottie died, it was Charlotte who packed up everything—the layette, the cradle, and the new *Common Sense Book of Baby and Child Care*, which I had read from cover to cover. I couldn't bear to look at any of the things we had so carefully chosen, leaving Charlotte to lug everything up the stairs herself, which meant she knew right where things were stored.

Just as the milk began to steam, she returned from the nursery with a never-opened package of baby bottles and rubber nipples. She rinsed a bottle, filled it, and settled a nipple and ring over the top. I sat down at the table, and when the milk was cool enough, I put the bottle to the baby's lips. She fixed those sea glass eyes on my face and immediately began to suckle. A powerful emotion rippled through my belly, and I closed my eyes, helpless against the intensity of it.

Charlotte said, "Tell me what happened."

I opened my eyes to find the infant still gazing at me, her miraculous pink mouth working and working around the rubber nipple, her cheeks growing rosy with the warmth of the milk. I smiled down at her and snuggled her closer in my arms. When the bottle was half empty, her eyelids began to droop. The lashes were as fair as her hair, as wispy as dandelion fuzz.

"I don't really know," I murmured, in answer to Charlotte's question. "Willow came up from the beach this morning, carrying that bundle. I heard a little sound, and I was afraid it might be an animal of some kind. Once I worked up the courage to look—there she was."

The baby sighed, sinking into sleep. The nipple slipped from her mouth, leaving a small, shining bubble between her lips. I set down the bottle and lifted her to my shoulder, patting her back until a tiny burp escaped her. I couldn't resist pressing my cheek to her soft head. I whispered, "Look at her, Aunt Charlotte. Such a miracle. A perfect, healthy little girl."

"Oh, Barrie Anne. Sweetie."

"That's not all, Aunt Charlotte. There was something strange last night, this light from the canal."

"A light?" She frowned. "What was it like?"

"I could see it beyond the orchard, as if it was just beyond the trees. It was late, but I wanted to see what it was, so I went to the beach."

"In the dark? Barrie Anne, you promised me you'd be careful out here on your own."

"I was! I took Willow with me."

"And the gun?"

"No," I admitted. "I was in a hurry. I was afraid I would miss it, whatever it was. I almost did, too."

"And what was it?"

"There was light under the water, glowing, sort of shimmering. It faded so fast, I couldn't tell what it was."

"Did you put your hand in the water?"

"I was going to, but the coyotes started up, and I needed to get Willow inside."

"So you don't have any idea."

"No." I shook my head.

"I wish you had, Barrie Anne. Put your hand in the water, I mean. As long as you were there."

"Have you ever seen anything like that?"

"Not in a long, long time. Years."

"You never told me about it."

"No. I'll tell you some other time. Right now we have to think what to do."

"You mean, about the baby." I didn't raise my eyes, because they had filled with tears.

"You need to figure out whose she is. Find out what happened."

"I know. I do know that." I was a little ashamed of my reluctance, though of course she was right. What I wanted, really, was to sit where I was, hold a warm, sleeping baby, and pretend that nothing else mattered, that there was nothing else I had to do.

Charlotte moved to the sink to run water into the milk pan, giving me a moment to recover myself. When the saucepan was clean and the rest of the milk stowed in the icebox, she put her back to the counter, her arms folded. "We need to be practical. What if her mother is out there somewhere, injured, needing help?"

"If you'll stay with the baby, I'll go look."

"I'll bring the cradle downstairs."

"I can do that later." I stood up and carried the baby into the front room. Once again, I laid her on the divan. This time, her eyes remained closed. I thought she was too little to roll over on her own—I had learned all about that from Dr. Spock—but I wedged her in with an extra cushion just the same. "I'll take Willow with me."

"As if she would let you go without her."

"I know."

"Take the gun."

"I won't need it," I said.

"Be on the safe side." Charlotte took one of the high-backed chairs from the dining table and carried it into the front room, where she set it beside the divan. She settled onto the chair and leaned forward to smooth the crocheted blanket with her hand. "Odd things have been going on around here." She straightened and pulled a cigarette pack from her pocket.

"Some strange men are going up and down the peninsula, asking questions."

"What kind of men?"

"Government, we think. They're talking about it at the Mercantile."

"What do they want?"

"They won't say. They showed up after that incident with the Boise pilot."

"What incident?"

She tapped a cigarette out of the pack, shaking her head. "You should read a newspaper once in a while, Barrie Anne."

I shrugged. I used to read newspapers all the time, but in the past year, nothing they had printed seemed important.

Charlotte flicked her lighter with a paint-stained thumbnail. "It was in the *Trib*. He claims he saw weird things in the sky, some kind of aircraft, I guess. Saucer-shaped, of all things. Near Mount Rainier."

"Military," I said. We had gotten used to seeing airplanes of all kinds, odd-looking craft that flew out of Ault Field on Whidbey Island. During the war, I often heard their propellers growling through the clouds. Sometimes, when I wasn't working at Tibbals Hill, I ran outside to stand in the dark to try to catch sight of them, but there was little to see. I had to be content with only the faint gleam of starlight on their wings. I imagined them as airborne leviathans, enigmatic and ponderous, like the whales that swam in the waters around the peninsula.

Charlotte said, "Well, maybe."

I started toward the closet beneath the stairs. "I haven't seen any government men out here, but I'll take the rifle."

"Be careful," Charlotte said, as I pulled out the .30–30 and dropped two shells into the pocket of my overalls.

"I will." I wasn't sure what I was being careful of, but it was easy enough to promise.

As I opened the screen door, she called, "I mean it, Barrie Anne. There's something strange going on. I have a feeling."

Willow followed me down the porch steps and along the path to the side gate. I let her run ahead as we crossed the field. The gun was cool and solid in my hand, and I decided I was glad to have it with me.

I knew better than to ignore Charlotte's feelings.

4

August 31, 1939

To celebrate the last day of my summer job at the dry goods store before college, Charlotte announced we were going out to dinner. We didn't often have restaurant meals, but she had just completed a big job for a gynecology textbook, and the publisher had paid her the moment she shipped off the illustrations. My tuition was paid for the year, and at Charlotte's insistence, I had saved enough money for my textbooks. We felt rich. It seemed the shadows of the Depression might be receding at last.

Charlotte was waiting when I emerged from the store. She leaned against the hood of the De Soto, a cigarette dangling from her lips, both hands in the pockets of her trousers. Her hat was pulled low over her eyes against the late-afternoon sun. "Hey, kiddo," she said, squinting through a haze of smoke. "Said your goodbyes?"

"Yes. Mr. Hansen gave me an extra ten dollars."

She straightened and took the cigarette from her mouth. "Generous of him! I'm sure you said a proper thank-you."

I grinned. "I think I overdid it. He practically pushed me out the door."

Charlotte laughed and opened the car door. "Hop in. Tonight we deserve a cocktail!"

I was too young for a cocktail, of course, but I knew what she meant. My aunt had a weakness for gin rickeys. She was fond of saying she broke only one law in her life, Prohibition, but that she broke it a thousand times. The day the repeal passed, Aunt Charlotte celebrated with three gin rickeys in a row, all from her private stash. She toasted President Roosevelt with each one, then fell sound asleep on the chaise in her studio.

At the Central Café, Charlotte ordered her gin rickey, and I ordered a Green River. We ate oysters and grilled salmon and talked about me, about the friends I would make in my freshman year, the things I needed for my dorm room, and the classes I would be taking, English and psychology and my favorite, physical education. I ate a dish of vanilla ice cream while Charlotte smoked a cigarette, and we drove home replete with good food and the sense that all was right with the world.

It was strange to get up the next morning with nothing to do. The dormitory wouldn't be open for another two days, and I had already folded my pleated skirts and carefully ironed shirtwaists into my valise. I lazed my way downstairs, looking forward to having coffee with my aunt and wasting an entire day reading or walking on the beach one last time.

Our house, built by my father just after the Great War, was a perfect box shape, two floors stacked on top of a basement.

Charlotte said it was called a Foursquare. I had grown up in it. I had slept in the small upstairs bedroom since my childhood. Charlotte used the big bedroom that had been my parents' and had turned the third bedroom into her studio. There was a dining room downstairs, but we never used it. We ate all our meals in the kitchen nook, with its banquette seating around a small table. We liked it because it nestled against a window and gave us an eastward view of Kah Tai Lagoon, down the hill from our house. We both loved watching the light of different seasons play across the still water, gleaming in summer, shimmering in autumn, as gray and dull as old pewter in wintertime.

I found Charlotte there, seated in the nook. She was bent over the *Times*, a cigarette burning in the ashtray by her elbow. "Good morning."

She glanced up. "Morning, kiddo."

"Anything in the news?"

"Afraid so."

I had picked up the percolator, but I paused in the act of pouring coffee. "Afraid? What's happened?" She smoothed out the newspaper and turned it so I could read the headline. "Poland? Oh, dear. That's sad."

"It's more than sad."

"Why? I mean, I'm sorry for the people, but…"

"France and England are Poland's allies. This is war."

"Not war for us, though."

"It will be." Charlotte drew on her cigarette, and when she exhaled, she said, "I feel it."

I set my full coffee cup on the table and reached for Charlotte's to refill it, then stopped.

She had plunged her forefinger into her cup, though steam still rose from her coffee. Her finger was submerged to the knuckle, and her eyes were distant, peering at the lagoon through a spiral of smoke.

"Aunt Charlotte! You'll burn your finger!"

She blinked and looked down at her hand. She lifted her finger, letting it drip into her cup. It had gone red, but I didn't think it had blistered.

"Silly," she muttered, and thrust the finger into her mouth.

"Silly!" I cried. "More than silly! Why did you do that?"

She didn't answer my question at first. She looked troubled, and not just because she hadn't yet done her eyebrows or her lips. Her cheeks were sallow, and deep creases dragged at her mouth. "I have a feeling about this war." She glanced up, and her mouth curled at one side. "Oh, never mind, kiddo. You know I get these feelings sometimes. I don't like this one at all."

Uneasily, I said, "I'm not sure what you mean." I slid into the banquette opposite her, but I didn't pick up my coffee cup. I watched her, hoping for an explanation. I knew from experience that if I asked too many questions, Charlotte was likely to shut down, to change the subject. She liked to talk about me. She rarely talked about herself.

She looked past me, waving away the smoke so she could see the lagoon through the window. "They're not all so dark, but this one—this one is like a shadow," she said, in an absent way, as if she were speaking to herself. "Like a cloud bank rolling in from the bay. Gray and cold. Frightening."

"Like fog? I never find fog frightening."

She looked at me then. She exhaled a long breath and crushed out her cigarette. "It was a bad analogy." She took the newspaper back and folded it so the headline didn't show.

I wrapped my hands around my cup, struggling to understand. I felt as if I were missing something important. Something I should already have known.

I said, "So this feeling—is it like the time you told me not to drive down Lawrence but go all the way to Monroe? And then there was an accident on Lawrence?"

She gave me a wry look. "You remember that."

"Of course I remember. Two people went to the hospital."

"That was a little different, because it was useful."

"And you said not to worry about that junior picnic, when everyone was wearing fancy clothes and I was the only one who didn't have a date."

"Did I?" Charlotte smiled. "I don't remember that one."

"You said, 'Don't worry, there won't be any picnic anyway,' and there wasn't. A thunderstorm came up."

Charlotte chuckled. "Pretty ordinary stuff."

"I've never thought about it much, other than—well, you know things. That's just the way you are."

"Yes. Just the way I am."

"Why did you never talk about it before?"

"It never seemed important." She creased the newsprint with her thumbnail. "I should probably tell you, though. The talent—knowing things—it runs in the family."

"It does? Our family?"

"Yes, the Blythe family. Well, the Blythe women, specifically."

"Not my father?"

"No men seem to have it. I've always thought it's because they don't trust anything they can't measure and analyze and control. You can't control this."

"Oh."

"Scott—and the other men, my father, his father—laughed it off as women's nonsense. None of us likes to be laughed at, so we kept things to ourselves." She sighed and pushed the paper to one side. "You could say we have premonitions, although we never used that word when I was young. Grandmother Fiona always referred to it as her little talent."

"But I don't have it."

Charlotte slid out of the banquette and stood up. "Not yet, anyway."

"Do you think I'll have premonitions someday?"

"Maybe not. The talent, the knack, whatever it is, seems to be dying out in the modern age. Now that we have the telephone, the telegraph, the radio...we know a lot of things already, and a lot faster than we used to. Maybe we don't need it anymore."

I frowned, trying to grasp what she was saying. I wasn't entirely sure I believed any of it, but I didn't want to ally myself with the men who made fun of it, either, men who dismissed it as nonsense. Clearly, Charlotte didn't think it was nonsense, and my aunt was one of the wisest people I knew. I strove for something neutral to say, and settled for, "That seems kind of a shame."

"Does it? Sometimes I wonder. It can be painful to know what's coming." She tightened the sash on her housecoat.

Curious, though still not quite convinced, I said, "Like knowing there's a war coming?"

"Like that, and worse." Her shoulders hunched as she buried her hands in her pockets. Her voice grew rough with emotion. "I knew my brother was going to die. And your mother. I knew before I left Taos. I was taking a bath after I packed my bags for the trip, and I knew."

"Oh, poor Aunt Charlotte!" There was no doubt of the sincerity in her voice and in the darkening of her eyes. A faint tremble of anxiety began in my belly. "How horrible for you."

"It was. All the way, on the train, I felt as if I could barely see for the cloud around me. I couldn't eat, couldn't sleep—I was a wreck. Then, when I reached Port Townsend and saw how terribly ill they were—"

The tremble crept up into my chest. "Oh, no. That's—that's so sad."

"Yes. It was terribly sad."

"But I'm not sure I understand why a newspaper article should upset you as much as—" I broke off, hardly knowing where this conversation was taking us.

She gazed past me, through the window of the nook and out to the shimmer of the lagoon. She said, "I remember what it was like when the war started in Europe. Everyone kept saying it wasn't our fight, and we didn't have to worry, but in the end, we got dragged into it just the same, and it was awful."

"But we won, didn't we? The war to end all wars?"

"That's how they sold it." Every one of her thirty-nine years showed in her face at that moment, lines around her mouth, dragging at the corners of her eyes. "Every generation has its war, I suppose. I'm afraid mine will have two of them." She blew out a breath and started toward the stairs. As she put her foot on the bottom tread, I heard her whisper to herself, "I don't know if I can face it."

I wanted to run after her, to comfort her, but I couldn't think of what to say. It didn't seem right to argue with her. I wanted to know more about this weird Blythe talent. I wanted to think about all the times, when I was growing up, that she knew things, silly things that didn't seem to matter much, and which I had never asked her to explain. All that mattered to me then was tennis, and swimming, and my school friends. The odd things she knew were trivial, easily explained away, like when a check would come in the mail or when rain would cancel a baseball game.

I knew I would have to find the right moment to persuade her to tell me the family history. Beyond cards and letters from scattered aunts and uncles and cousins I had never met, I knew almost nothing. Why was that?

It wasn't until Charlotte was already up the stairs and in the bathroom that I realized she hadn't explained why her finger was in her hot coffee.

I pushed it all out of my mind as best I could and spent the day as I had planned. I organized my things, talked to a high school friend on the telephone, wandered along the beach below Chetzemoka Park. I picked some blackberries for our dinner on the long walk back to our house, and when I got there, sunburned and sticky with perspiration, Charlotte's usual pragmatic mood had returned. She praised the berries and sent me up to have a cool bath before dinner. We ate baked halibut and a salad and talked about the ferry schedule for the morning. The newspaper had disappeared into the bin beside the woodstove.

I went to bed early to finish my library book so Charlotte could return it for me. I was reading *The Sun Also Rises*, recommended by my English teacher, but I didn't like it much. I pitied Jake Barnes and, in my naïveté, thought Brett was a horrible woman who deserved to end up alone. I skimmed through the final chapters and closed the book with a feeling of disappointment.

I turned off my lamp and lay back on my pillow. I wondered if Charlotte counted as one of the Lost Generation. She had been my age when the Great War ended. Had she turned to drink and sex the way Hemingway's characters did? Somehow I couldn't picture that. She had always been the epitome of discipline—well, except for the gin rickeys.

My eyelids were just beginning to droop when something clattered downstairs. Wide awake again, I scrambled out of bed and went to open my bedroom door.

Across the hall, the light was on in Charlotte's room, but the door stood ajar. I crossed to the top of the staircase and saw a glow from the kitchen. "Aunt Charlotte?"

She appeared in the kitchen door, her housecoat untied and her hair erupting in all directions. "Oh, damn. I woke you. Sorry about that. Dropped a saucepan."

"I was awake. What are you doing up? You're not painting?"

"No." She pulled back inside the kitchen, but I heard her mutter, "Worrying."

I padded down the stairs. The only light was the one on the stovetop. The can of cocoa powder rested beside the range, and the saucepan, half-filled now with milk, steamed gently in the dimness.

"You might as well join me." Charlotte went to stir the cocoa into the milk and added sugar from the canister with a generous hand.

"You're still thinking about the newspaper," I said.

She wheezed a sigh. "I was remembering things. Can't get them out of my head."

I chewed on my lip for a moment. I wasn't used to Charlotte being vulnerable. She was the strong one, the leader, but it occurred to me that perhaps it was time for me to be an adult, too. I said uncertainly, "I don't know whether to distract you or let you talk about them."

"That's sweet, kiddo." She chuckled and ran her fingers through her rat's nest of hair, as dark and straight as my own, though half as long. "You might not appreciate me putting these memories into *your* head."

I went to the cupboard for the china mugs. They were thick white ones with blue rims, and they'd been in the kitchen as long as I could remember. I had a hazy memory of seeing them in my mother's hands when I was small. They always reminded me of coming home from school on chilly winter afternoons. I set them on the counter beside the range.

Charlotte poured the cocoa, and we settled ourselves into the nook in our usual places. In the gloom, starlight glimmered in the side of the icebox and the glass fronts of the cupboards. It was cozy, the two of us sitting together as we had so often, but the summer night throbbed with a sense of impermanence. It made me ache with nostalgia, for childhood, for tradition, for the comfort of what was familiar. We had sat this way so many times, talking about school, about my plans, about what I wanted from life. Had we ever talked about what Charlotte wanted? I couldn't remember.

I knew little about her life outside of her years in Port Townsend with me, though I knew she had come from Taos when my parents were ill. Occasionally she received a letter with a New Mexico postmark, but she never told me who wrote to her. She had friends in Port Townsend, but no close ones that I knew of. Her family—our family—was scattered across the country, the Midwest, mostly, I thought.

She reached into the pocket of her housecoat for her cigarettes, and as she shook one out, she said, "Any thoughts on a major yet, kiddo?"

"We're not going to talk about that." I pushed the ashtray close to her elbow. "We're going to talk about you."

She put the cigarette between her lips and dug through another pocket for a matchbook. "Nothing you need to know, Barrie Anne. My life is all history now."

"We're all history eventually."

Charlotte laughed and coughed. "Sounds like something I'd be likely to say."

"I probably learned it from you." I smiled, feeling grown-up at that moment. It had seemed the perfect thing to say, and I was proud of it.

She struck a match and grinned at me above her glowing cigarette. In the low light, and with no cosmetics, she looked younger and, just then, merrier. I found myself wishing I had known her when she was a girl.

"I think," I said, "that you should tell me about your memories. Get them out."

She flicked ash and took another drag. "Learn that in high school, did you?"

"A book I read. Sports psychology. Talk about what you're afraid of."

"And what do you have to be afraid of, pray tell?"

"Going off the high diving board," I said without hesitation. "It terrifies me."

"Ah. I sympathize—I who can't swim at all. I suppose just not doing it isn't an option?"

"Not if I'm going to be a phys ed instructor."

"You've decided!" She lifted her mug in a toast. "Congratulations! What helped you make up your mind?"

"Aunt Charlotte. You're changing the subject."

Charlotte's grin subsided into a half smile, an expression both resigned and peaceful. "I'll tell you a little bit about me, if you really want to know, kiddo."

"I do." I leaned forward over my mug. "I don't know why I never asked before."

"Natural for children to think about themselves," she said, looking down into her mug and turning it in circles on the tabletop. "You know I never expected to be a parent. Not that I'm your parent—"

I interrupted. "You are, though! You're the only parent I have, and you've been wonderful." She lifted her head, and I saw that her eyes were shining as if with incipient tears. I doubted that. Never, in the years we had spent together, had I seen my aunt cry. If she wept when my parents died, she did so in private. She occasionally sniffled in the movies, but only at points when I was mopping copious tears from my face. Even when she had pored over the newspaper that morning, looking as forlorn as I had ever seen her, there had been no tears. I supposed it must be the starlight, and the dimness of the kitchen, that made her eyes shine that way.

"Have I never thanked you, Aunt Charlotte? What would I have done without you?"

"I don't want you to thank me, kiddo. I never needed that." She pushed her cigarette into the ashtray, shaking her head. "It's all so complicated. I hope your life isn't as complicated as mine has been."

I couldn't think of a reply, so I drained my cocoa. When I set down the mug, I fixed her with as expectant a look as I could manage.

She chuckled. "Stubborn," she said. "Like your father."

"Like you."

She chuckled again. "Granted. Okay, I'm going to tell you some of my story. You should probably be in bed, though. You don't want to be exhausted for your first day of classes."

"Classes don't start till Monday. I'll be okay."

"More cocoa?"

"I'll get it."

I got up to fetch the saucepan and tipped the rest of the cocoa into our mugs. A quarter moon had risen over the peninsula, and it shone through the kitchen window. I flicked off the range light, and we sat together, my aunt and I, in a silver wedge of moonlight.

She linked her hands beneath her chin and gazed out into the moonlit garden through half-closed eyes. Beyond it, the center of the lagoon shimmered, but its coves and shallows were dark. In a husky voice, Charlotte said, "I was going to be a nurse. You didn't know that."

"No, I didn't. You never told me." I wrapped my hands around the warm mug and watched her. Her face went soft with memory as she looked back down the years. As she spoke of her youth, the pitch of her voice rose, giving me an idea of how she might have sounded before beginning her cigarette habit.

"There were soldiers everywhere when I started nursing school. By the time I was halfway through my first semester, we had a military hospital on campus, and the nursing students were expected to volunteer. My very first feeling—hunch, premonition, whatever you want to call it—came when I was walking up the steps into the hospital. It was raining, these fat, cold raindrops, and I stretched my hand out from beneath my umbrella to feel them.

"Suddenly I *knew*. It swept over me as if I had stumbled into a waterfall, and it made me shake so badly I had to sit down on the stairs. My friends thought I was afraid of what we were going to see, but it wasn't that. It was that I knew perfectly well what we were going to see. I knew it as if it had already happened." She gave her head a shake. "I still remember how those bricks felt, cold and hard and wet, catching at the material of my skirt.

"I pulled myself together, of course. No other choice. Went into the hospital and did what I was told, as we all did." She reached for her cigarette pack and pulled one out between her fingernails. "A lot of the patients had been gassed by the Germans. The treatment was scopolamine, mostly useless. Oxygen worked for a while, but only if you kept it up, and we couldn't keep it up." She paused to light the cigarette. Smoke curled in ribbons of gray and white, sparkling in the moonlight. She waved her fingers through the tendrils and watched the wisps drift apart. "Sometimes I think I smoke because it makes my breath visible. Proves my lungs are working. Theirs were ruined, you see. Anoxemia. We had to watch them suffocate."

"That's awful."

"Ghastly." She drew another mouthful of smoke. "Long time ago now, of course. Poor devils are all long dead."

"But it still bothers you."

"What bothers me is that I knew what it was going to be like but couldn't do a damn thing about it."

"But why did you know? What brought on the premonition, or any premonition? Do they just—just come out of nowhere?"

Charlotte's face grew vague with memory, and I had the urge to put my hand on hers. I didn't. It was too easy to distract her and have her pack me off to bed. "It was raining," she said softly, and stopped.

I waited a moment for her to go on, frowning. "Raining?" I finally prompted.

"Yes. Raining. Water."

"Water?" I breathed, not understanding but not wanting her to stop talking. The rhodium clock set into the stovetop showed me the hour was already far gone into the morning. It was cold in the kitchen, and I tucked my bare feet up under my housecoat to warm them. I should have gotten a sweater or the afghan from the sofa, but I didn't want to get up and break my aunt's train of thought.

"Yes. It's always about water." She drew on her cigarette and breathed out a thin, silvery stream of smoke. Her voice grew soft with memory. "My grandmother Fiona used to confound the housemaid by dabbling her hand in her mop bucket every morning. To 'see what's coming.'"

"She knew what was coming? That's what you do!"

"Yes, sometimes. Grandmother Fiona did that every day. Frightened the maid so much she eventually quit."

"What was she afraid of? The maid, I mean."

"Oh, the silly girl," Charlotte said with a chuckle. "She grew up in some village in the Highlands, and she said she couldn't work in a 'heathen house where there was water witches and such.' She marched right out one morning while Grandmother Fiona's hand was still dripping. Mother was furious."

"Water witches," I repeated, disbelieving. "She thought Grandmother Fiona was a witch?"

"Well, a water witch."

"I thought those were people who dowse for wells and so forth."

"That's one kind. It's a different talent."

"But Grandmother Fiona couldn't have been a witch...."

Charlotte blinked and crushed out the stub of her cigarette. I knew she was coming to the end, and I still wanted more. "Is that what you think your premonitions are, Aunt Charlotte? Witchcraft?"

She laughed. "Of course not!" She rubbed her eyes, and I was afraid she was going to say she was tired. "This is the twentieth century, after all. No one believes in witchcraft."

"Then what is it?"

She didn't answer my question. She said, yawning in a pointed fashion, "Good lord, look at the clock."

I knew what the clock said. It was nearly three, and the sky would begin to lighten within the hour. "We can sleep in," I said.

"You'll be exhausted in the morning."

"I don't care. You've told me so little about the family, about your past. I want to know."

She had been about to rise from the banquette, but she settled back again, though she raised one warning finger. "Just ten more minutes, and we're off to bed."

"Okay." I pushed the ashtray close to her hand. An extra cigarette sometimes worked.

She didn't respond to that, though. She turned her head to the window, to the starlit darkness of the summer sky. "I don't know what to tell you, Barrie Anne. There's no good answer. Grandmother Fiona told some strange stories about her relatives back in Kinloss, not just Blythes, but Campbells and Stuarts and others. I remember her whispering things to my mother, but only when my father couldn't hear."

"Why?"

"The men made fun of her, the poor old thing. Even my mother was inclined to smile behind her hand when Grandmother Fiona was telling stories about the women of her family and what they could do. Some of her tales were pretty wild, I have to admit. Some of them went as far back as the eighteenth century."

"Like what?"

"She said there were women who knew things. Wisewomen, she called them. Some of them knew the sex of a baby before it was born. Some knew whose husband was stepping out on his wife. There was a story from a long time ago about a girl who had disappeared, and everyone thought she fell from a cliff into the sea, but an old woman claimed she had run off with a tinker. No one believed the old woman, until the girl came back with two babies and no husband, and then they knew she was right."

Charlotte sighed, her fingers now groping for her cigarette pack while her eyes remained fixed on the window. I held my breath, not wanting to interrupt the flow. I had never heard her talk about such things, and it was fascinating.

She drew out a fresh cigarette, lit it, and blew a cloud toward the window. In a ruminative tone, she said, "Some women knew whether a person was going to recover from an illness or not. Grandmother Fiona said those were the ones in danger, the ones who knew if people would live or die. Those women would put their hand in the burn near their house or even in a cup of water the sick person had drunk from, and then they would know."

"Water," I remembered the coffee cup and Charlotte's

reddened finger, and a thrill crept over my arms and my neck, bringing up gooseflesh.

She seemed not to hear. "That frightened people. Once the men of the town tried to drown a woman who predicted a death, and when she didn't drown, they were even more afraid of her. A whole legend developed, that the woman—a Stuart, she was—could breathe underwater. They drove her out of town, exiled her, called her a witch. A water witch. She had to go live in a hut by herself."

She smiled, following her memory back through time, her burning cigarette forgotten in the ashtray. "I loved that story. I even gave the witch a name. I decided she was called Morag— I think I read the name in a book. Unlikely story, of course, and probably exaggerated over the years, but I loved the tale of Morag, and I made Grandmother Fiona recite it to me over and over. My mother tried to get her to stop, but Grandmother Fiona was like a freight train when she got going. She stopped for no one."

"I wish I had met her," I murmured.

"She was a force of nature, my grandmother. Your great-grandmother. She always said if you were like Morag and knew who would live and who would die, you were better off keeping what you knew to yourself."

"But still she swished her hand through the maid's wash water!"

"Every morning. I suppose she thought that wouldn't scare anyone." She gave a faint, reminiscent chuckle. "My mother never forgave her. She said she had enough trouble keeping help without Grandmother Fiona scaring away superstitious girls."

"But it was just superstition. Not really—witchcraft."

"Grandmother Fiona said it was 'just a little water magic.' I always liked that."

"Did it ever do any good?"

"Sometimes. She talked one of my cousins out of going to San Francisco in '06, and then the earthquake happened. She said her own grandmother threw a fit one day when her son—Fiona's father—wanted to go fishing for salmon in the firth. She pestered and pestered him until he changed his plans, and it was a good thing, because there was a big storm, and three other boats that went out never came back."

"Did you believe in all that? The water magic? Morag?"

"Well, I was young and impressionable. I wanted to be like Morag, to breathe underwater, to know if people would live or die. Then as I got older, in my teens, I decided my grandmother was just dotty. A dingbat, your father said, though he was too nice to say it in her hearing. Then when I started having my own premonitions—Grandmother Fiona was gone by then—I wished I could ask her more questions. About our family history. About Morag. About our kind."

Our kind. I liked that. It made me feel like one of a select few, even though I showed no sign of any particular talent. I said, "Couldn't your mother have answered your questions?"

My aunt's lips compressed, making two sharp lines appear beside her mouth. She reached for her cigarette and took a furious drag. "You realize, of course, that my mother is your grandmother. Whom you never met."

"I know." I watched her curiously, wondering what had

caused her sudden change of mood. "I just thought it was because she lived so far away. Iowa? Kansas? Someplace dry."

"Yes. Kansas. No ocean, no big lakes. Dry." Her voice roughened, as if the lungful of smoke had made her suddenly hoarse.

I wondered why we had never spoken of this before, not even when the letter arrived, informing us my grandparents were dead. "She never came to visit before my parents died?"

"They went to visit her once. I think Thelma was expecting you at the time. But no, Mother never came here. She avoided places with a lot of water. She was afraid of discovering she was the same kind of woman as her mother."

"So she believed in it, too."

"She never told me if she did. I had to guess." She ground her cigarette butt into the ashtray with an angry movement. "She was a hard woman, your grandmother," she said, in that rough tone. "She and I didn't speak or write for years."

"Why?"

She glanced over her shoulder at the clock on the range. "Good lord, Barrie Anne. You need to sleep."

"Wait! Was it because of the water witches?"

"No. It wasn't about that. Now we're going to bed."

"But, Aunt Charlotte—what about your premonitions? What do you think they are?"

She was already on her feet, clearing the mugs, setting the saucepan in the sink to soak. "I mostly think Grandmother Fiona was right. It's just a little water magic."

Slyly now, too tired to be cautious, I said in a mock whisper, "Does that make you a water witch, Charlotte Blythe?"

She cast me a pretend scowl. "It does not. I don't breathe underwater. I have enough trouble breathing air. Now, off to bed with you."

"Wait—"

"Nope. You've listened to an old lady talk too long already."

"You're not an old lady."

"Old enough."

I persisted. "Please sit down again, Aunt Charlotte. I want to hear more stories. I want to know these things. Why did you never tell me before?"

"Oh, Barrie Anne." Her scowl relaxed, and she leaned back in her chair. "I've always been afraid you'd think we were weird, we Blythes. You have a conventional streak, you know."

"I do?"

"Oh, yes. Wanting me to wear dresses. Wanting me to be like your friends' mothers."

I felt a tinge of compunction because she was right. "I like you the way you are, Aunt Charlotte."

She chuckled. "That's a very sweet thing to say. Very diplomatic."

Encouraged, hoping to wrest more history from her, I prompted, "So you were going to be a nurse, but you didn't like it?"

"They closed the school when the influenza hit, brought home by all those poor boys."

"They didn't close the school forever!"

She opened the tap and filled the sink with water. The roughness in her voice had eased, but she sounded tired. And sad. "I just never went back, kiddo."

"Why?"

She hesitated, and I sensed she was choosing her words with care. Creating an answer that would be no answer. She said finally, "Someone taught me to paint. I liked that better than nursing."

"Who taught you?"

She turned back to the sink and began rinsing the cocoa pan. "I don't want to talk about it just now, if you don't mind."

I wanted to press, but I could see these memories upset her, and she had already told me more in one night than she had in years. Reluctantly, I said, "Okay. Thanks for the cocoa."

"Sleep tight, Barrie Anne."

"You, too."

I trudged up the stairs, my jaw stretching with a huge yawn. I was asleep moments after I fell into bed, but I didn't rest well. I dreamed of war surrounding our peninsula, bombs and guns and breath-stealing gas. As Charlotte had warned, I was exhausted in the morning.

5

July 1, 1947

I headed out across the empty field with Willow trotting beside my left thigh and the .30-30 cradled in my right arm. I felt a tremor of anxiety, recalling Charlotte in the moonlight eight years before, describing her premonitions. She had another one when I brought Will home to meet her. She told me about it at the time, but I was blind with love. I didn't listen.

But now, with a strange infant sleeping on my divan, and the possibility of something terrible awaiting me on the shore of the canal, I knew better. I had learned that Charlotte's little feelings should never be discounted.

Nor should mine, for that matter.

Willow and I waded through long dry grass under the high sun. The shade of the apple orchard was welcome but brief. We emerged on the other side, where Willow leaped and I skidded down the cut in the high bank and onto the gravelly beach. To the right was the ancient, moldy dock, doing its best to wriggle loose from its pilings. One crooked bollard survived, though it was rotting at the bolts. In the distance I could make out two rowboats with men fishing, their long poles invisible against the glare. I didn't own a boat of any kind nor had I ever seen one moored here.

The tide was coming in, flooding the dock with every wave, threatening the roots of vegetation that formed the bank. I suffered a fresh spasm of horror at the understanding of what might have happened to the baby if Willow hadn't found her. The thought of it, of a wave sweeping that beautiful infant into the water, made my heart pound and my hand on the Winchester shake.

Willow, untroubled by imagination, trotted off along the shore to my left. I followed, but my mouth was dry with dread. It was a distressing activity, searching for something I didn't want to find, like looking for spiders under the furniture but hoping even as you crouch down to peer into the darkness that you don't see any. I made myself take the greatest care despite my reluctance. I lifted up the lowest branches of brush to look beneath. I squinted into the shadows of the evergreens that lined the bank. I scanned the sun-bright water until phantoms danced before my eyes. Nothing.

Willow moved purposefully, leading me on until she reached a snag of madrona. Its tip was submerged by the water now, but a low tide would expose several yards of beach beneath it. Willow nosed the trunk where it rose above the water and pawed the wet sand at the waterline. I hurried to see what attracted her. Again, nothing. She backed away and sat down in the sand, tilting her head at me in question.

"Was this the place, Willow? Did you find her here?"

She whined and lay down with her head on her paws, her eyes fixed on me.

I bent, waiting for a wave to wash toward me. When it did, I dabbled my fingers in the cool saltwater. It told me nothing.

Of course I wasn't as adept as Aunt Charlotte. I didn't know if I ever would be.

I had to climb over the fallen madrona to check the beach on the other side. I worked my way up the bank as far as I could, fighting trailing blackberry vines. I climbed on top of the snag and shaded my eyes against the water's glare, but except for the fishing boats and the gulls squawking overhead, we were alone.

With a mixed sense of relief and worry, I jumped back down to the sand. My heart settled into its normal rhythm, or as normal as it was going to be on this strange day. I touched the dog's head and said, "Come on, Willow. There's nothing here."

I started back down the beach. Willow followed, but she lagged behind, disappointment obvious in her drooping tail and flattened ears. I waited for her in the shade, and when she reached me, I stroked her silky head. "I know," I told her. "Something sad happened. Something bad that we can't fix. We'll probably never know what it was, Willow, but you did well. You saved the baby."

Her lopsided ears twitched, and she licked my hand.

The midafternoon heat had risen sharply by the time we left the coolness of the orchard with its clusters of green apples just beginning to show streaks of red. I hurried through the field, impatient to get back to the house, to see the infant again, to make some sort of decision.

I stowed the rifle safely back in the closet, drawing the coats over it so it wasn't visible. I tiptoed into the front room and found the baby sleeping sweetly on the divan. Willow padded after me and took up a post next to the infant. She lay down with her head on her paws, but she watched everything I did, and her ears twitched at every small sound the baby made.

Charlotte had brought down the unused layette from the nursery and was unfolding tiny nightgowns, pristine diapers, a baby's bath towel with a miniature hood. She and I had ordered everything from the Sears Roebuck catalog, poring over the pages of baby things for hours. We had chosen an enamelware basin with a pink rim and tiny blue flowers painted on the sides, and I had been delighted with it when it first arrived in the parcel post. I recalled tracing the flowers with my fingers, imagining my baby splashing and gurgling at bath time. There was a blanket, soft blue flannel printed with white teddy bears. I remembered lifting it out of the box. I had no presentiment then, no premonition. Perhaps that had been a blessing. There had been enough pain without anticipating it.

This wasn't a moment for such reflections, though. Charlotte stood up, gathering the bits of the layette into her arms. "I gather you didn't find anything."

"No."

"What shall we do now?"

It was so like Charlotte to link us together that way, even though this situation wasn't her problem. As with the difficulty with Will, my aunt never shrank from sharing my burdens, though I was now more than old enough to carry them alone.

I gave her a grateful look. "The first thing is a bath. So the little thing won't smell like seawater."

"When she wakes up."

"Right. I'll go up and get the cradle while she's still asleep."

Charlotte lifted one nearly invisible eyebrow. She didn't comment, but I'm sure she had realized, when she discovered a year's worth of dust in the nursery, that I hadn't set foot in it once in all that time.

I gave her a lopsided smile before I went to face my memories. I climbed the stairs with as steady a step as I could muster and paused for only a heartbeat before I set my jaw, opened the door, and went inside.

The room wasn't as dirty as I had feared, just hot and stuffy from being closed up for so long. It still smelled faintly of paint. I glanced up at the sky ceiling Charlotte had created and ran my fingers over the top of the pretty blue bureau. They came away gray with dust.

The cradle was in a corner, covered with a sheet. When I pulled off the sheet, I saw with a pang the pink-and-blue-plaid quilt I had so carefully tucked in around the tiny mattress. The cradle was white, with a tiny scene of rabbits and chicks painted on the miniature headboard. For a moment I couldn't breathe, my chest paralyzed with the sadness over this tiny, pretty thing lying unused and neglected all those long, empty months.

I could have cried over it, but there was no time for tears. I was needed now. I made myself take an unsteady breath and swallowed to release the constriction in my throat. I picked up the cradle and carried it downstairs in my arms, taking care on the bumpy staircase.

The baby began to stir as I set down the cradle beside the divan, and Willow jumped to her feet, watching her. Charlotte went into the kitchen to run water into the enamelware basin. I lifted the infant, and those wonderful eyes opened to fix their solemn gaze on my face. "Hello, little one," I murmured. "We're going to give you a nice warm bath. You'll like that."

Charlotte called, "Ready, I think, but you should test the water."

I carried the baby into the kitchen. I laid her on the counter to peel away the crocheted blanket. I dipped my elbow into the warm water before settling her into the basin. Her pink mouth opened, and she cooed, a high, small sound as sweet as birdsong. As I sluiced water over her shoulders with my palm, one little hand rose above the water like a tiny pink starfish, then splashed down, sending droplets over her face and my arms. She cooed again, and Willow, watching every movement, wagged her tail.

I glanced across at Charlotte. Her face had gone oddly pale. She was holding her dripping hands over the basin and staring into the water, her lips a little apart, both eyebrows lifted high.

"Aunt Charlotte?" I said. "She's awfully slippery. Maybe you could wash her head while I hold her."

Charlotte blinked, and her eyebrows lowered, but she didn't look up to meet my gaze. She bent over the basin, scooping water into her palms. She dribbled it cautiously over the baby's scalp, then rubbed gently, combing back the strands of pale hair with her fingertip, as the baby's eyes followed her movements.

I said, "Peaceful little thing, isn't she?"

Charlotte's voice trembled slightly when she spoke. "She seems to be."

"Are you all right, Aunt Charlotte?"

She didn't answer at first. She ran her long, sensitive fingers down the baby's head and around the occiput. "Such a lovely shape," she said in an oddly thin voice. "When I'm doing an illustration, I always think how elegant the human skull is, the arch and curve and—"

She broke off and straightened, her hand still cupping the baby's head.

"What is it? What's the matter?"

Charlotte blinked again, the action of someone trying to steady her nerves. Her voice grew even thinner, no more than a breath of sound. "Barrie Anne. Look. Her ear—there, behind the auricle—She—"

"What?" I looked more closely. The baby's ear curled close to her skull in miniature translucent whorls. "Is there something there?" I secured my grasp under the little wet body, and with my free hand I lifted the teardrop of skin that was her earlobe. It flexed easily beneath my finger, revealing what lay beneath.

I gasped.

Beneath the ear, and just behind it, was a delicate fan of skin, so thin it was almost transparent. As I gaped at it, it moved, ever so slightly, shivering like the wing of a resting moth. It lifted just enough to show the tender opening beneath, then settled. I didn't dare touch it. It flexed again, and I released the little earlobe as if it had burned me.

"Look at that," Charlotte began, and stopped, staring at me.

I stared back. "Good God. What *is* it?"

Charlotte stepped away from the basin, holding her hands away from her as if they were contaminated. The last color had drained from her face. The pupils of her eyes swelled until they nearly drowned the irises.

"Aunt Charlotte?"

"Barrie Anne," she whispered. "You know what it is. You recognize it; you just—you can't—"

"I *don't* know," I said, but I trembled with uncertainty. "Is it maybe . . . a birth defect?"

"I don't think it's a defect."

"But it could be. It could go away, too. Heal up, or—"

"I don't think that's going to go away."

"But you must have seen—I mean, all those medical illustrations—Surely you've seen—"

She brushed her hands against her trousers with short, anxious movements. "No," she whispered. "No, I haven't."

"But they say, when babies are—When they're not fully formed—"

Charlotte blinked and crossed her arms, gripping her elbows. "It's not true. Sometimes there's a vestigial tail, yes. Not this."

"I'm sure I've heard . . . somewhere . . ."

She shook her head. "Old wives' tale."

I looked back at the baby, the wet jewel of an infant, her face and hands and toes more beautiful than any of Charlotte's illustrations. I slid my hand down her back, searching for that vestigial tail Charlotte had mentioned, but there were only the tiny bumps of her spine, like beads on a necklace, leading down to the smooth curve of little buttocks.

"You *do* know," Charlotte repeated.

I did.

One of the ways I kept Willow and myself fed, especially when I couldn't afford beef or lamb, was by fishing. In the canal, I caught Chinook or Coho salmon, depending on the season. Sometimes I caught halibut or flounder. There was nothing sophisticated about my fishing. I used an old pole of my father's, with worms or grasshoppers or bits of leftover meat for bait, but I knew fish.

Gazing down at the wet baby in the basin, looking into her emerald eyes, I shuddered to think how I brought those fish home. Usually I cut a branch, something thin and flexible. I stripped the leaves from it, so I could thread it through the mouth and out the gills of whatever fish I had caught.

Gills. Gills like the ones tucked behind this baby's ears.

I had to swallow a surge of nausea. "Oh, my God," I breathed.

Charlotte said, "Dry her, Barrie Anne. Let's get her dressed before she takes a chill."

"You're sure it's not true that babies—fetuses—sometimes have gills?"

"I'm positive. It's one of those myths that gets passed around."

"But that's what those are."

"More or less, I would say."

She had begun to sound like herself again, and that helped me, too. My stomach settled as I lifted the infant out to the waiting towel. I dried her feet and legs, her bottom, rubbed her chest and her back. I used a corner of the fabric to gently scrub at her hair and dab at the folds of her neck. I didn't touch her ears.

I diapered the baby, awkwardly, needing practice. Charlotte

held out a nightgown, and I wriggled it over her head. As I held her to my chest, her head turned toward my breast, pink mouth working, seeking.

"She's hungry again," I said.

"Of course she is." Charlotte turned to the icebox, brisk now, and took out the goat's milk. "You were always hungry after a bath."

We did what needed doing. I fed the baby. Charlotte helped me tuck her into the cradle. We never thought about lunch, though Charlotte smoked two cigarettes, standing over the sink in the kitchen. Charlotte stayed with the baby while I went out to water the garden and spread scratch for my hens.

It was a long, weird day. We didn't speak of the mystery again. In fact, I spent a lot of energy avoiding it. I brought in some romaine, and Charlotte washed it for a salad. I took a piece of salmon out of the icebox, but neither of us could look at it. I put it back, and we settled on tomato sandwiches for supper. The baby woke, and I changed and fed her again. She settled peacefully back to sleep as we ate, and after we had cleaned the kitchen, we watched her in silence, listening to the twitter of birds in the long summer twilight. Willow lay beside the divan, alert to every sigh and rustle that came from the cradle.

At last, as the slow darkness stretched over the woods and the fields, Charlotte spoke. "Have you decided what you're going to do?"

I answered with no hesitation. "I'm going to keep her." The quiet thump of Willow's tail on the floor applauded my announcement.

Charlotte was more cautious.

"You should think this through carefully, Barrie Anne. You don't know what she is."

"She's a baby."

"Yes. But she's something more."

"That's not her fault."

"I didn't say it was a fault."

I gazed at her familiar, weary face. "Aunt Charlotte, I have a baby. After all that's happened, it's a miracle to me. I don't care if she's—well—different. Everyone is different in her own way, isn't that true? She's beautiful. Perfect. I love her already."

Charlotte spread her hands. "Kiddo, I'm with you, whatever you want to do. I just want you to understand what you're taking on."

"I was ready to have a baby. I'm prepared to raise a child."

"Alone?"

"Lots of women do that." I grinned, my heart suddenly light with hope and happiness. "*You* did it, Aunt Charlotte!"

She gave no answering smile, but she patted my shoulder, saying heavily, "That's why I know how hard it is."

6

August 1942

The war shadowed everything about my junior year at the University of Washington. Supplies ran short, redirected to the war effort. Boys in our classes enlisted, or were drafted. Often, they disappeared from school without warning. Several of my professors also enlisted, showing up once or twice in uniform and then, like their students, vanishing. It was an unsettled, uneasy time, not least because I had met Will Sweet.

I stayed on campus for summer classes that year, one of a diminishing number of students. It was a lonely place, with half-filled classrooms and understaffed faculty. Even the maintenance of the buildings suffered, as men left for the armed services. Those of us who remained wandered the depleted campus with an increasing conviction that we should be doing something different, something more patriotic. Something adult.

My tuition for the summer term was paid, so I forced myself

to stick it out, though I was restless, eager to get on with real life. After final exams, I rode the ferry across the Sound, then took the bus up to Port Townsend. Charlotte greeted me with her usual casual affection, and I ate her crab dinner with gusto, despite my anxiety about what I had to tell her. It was good to be back in my own bed, at home in our cozy square house. I slept soundly despite my nervousness.

The next morning dawned bright and hot, a perfect summer day. Charlotte and I carried our coffee out into the garden. Still in our housecoats, we sat on the faded wooden bench beneath the plum tree. Its branches sagged beneath a burden of ripening fruit, and with my bare toe, I pushed at a fallen plum. Its skin split, revealing the rich flesh inside.

"Wasted that one," Charlotte said.

"Sorry." I kicked it under the rhododendron bushes that edged the garden and told myself to get on with my task.

I gazed past the shrubbery to the morning sparkle on the lagoon, where the bufflehead ducks dived for insects, their webbed feet paddling the air with comic intensity. I watched their antics as I tried to gather my thoughts. Charlotte's quizzical, patient gaze tingled on my cheek. She knew something was up. I sipped some coffee, cleared my throat, and blurted, "Aunt Charlotte, I'm leaving school."

Her eyebrows flew upward. "Barrie Anne, no! Why?"

I had rehearsed this moment in my mind, but the words I had planned fled in the face of her surprise and disappointment. She hadn't finished college herself. I knew how much she wanted me to complete my degree, and I had thought out a complete argument so she would accept my decision, but my clever approach evaporated under the summer sunshine.

I struggled for a way to explain. "Aunt Charlotte, you know how—that is—how the war has changed everything. People are leaving school—"

"You only have a year to go!"

"I know, but—I'm going to go back once the war's over. Really, I am. And they say it can't last more than a year."

Charlotte sighed and slumped against the back of the bench. I felt her defeat as a weight in my heart, and I knew I was crushing her dearly held ambition for me. I felt tears start in the back of my throat, and my belly grew tight with the effort to hold them in.

My aunt reached into her pocket for a cigarette. Bitterly, she said, "You know, Barrie Anne, they always say things like that. No more than a year. Home for Christmas. The war to end all wars. I don't believe any of it."

"You have one of your feelings, I suppose."

She put the cigarette between her pursed lips, avoiding my eyes. She flicked her lighter and took a drag before she said, "I don't need one to know that this is a bad war. All of Europe, Japan, China, Australia, now the United States. That sort of conflict doesn't resolve easily. Certainly not in a year."

"But we have to win."

She squinted at me through the smoke. "Be sure you understand why that is. What the stakes are, and how it will affect all of us."

I sniffed the spicy smell of cigarette smoke in the fresh air and the pungence of the crushed fruit beneath my feet. War seemed terribly far away from that tumbled garden, with its unpruned roses and unruly grass. I settled the mug of coffee into my lap and focused on its iridescent surface. There was nothing for it but to get it out in the open.

I blurted, "The thing is—I've met someone." I lifted my head to face her directly, and it felt like turning toward a firing squad.

She stared at me for a moment, narrowing her eyes against the stream of cigarette smoke. I did my best to keep my face still. It was something she herself was good at, freezing her features, masking her emotions. It wasn't so easy for me.

At last, she spoke, and her voice was gravelly with emotion, though her face revealed nothing. "That's what this is about, then. You've met a boy, and you want to quit college to—what? Get married?"

I quailed, even though I had prepared for this. I looked back into my coffee cup to steel myself. "Yes. To get married." I took a mouthful of coffee.

Before I could swallow, she said, "Are you pregnant?"

That made me choke and splutter coffee over my housecoat. "No, no," I said hastily, when I recovered my voice. "Of course I'm not pregnant!"

"Hmm. And how long have you known him?"

"We met in my Physiology class." My cheeks stung with self-conscious heat. Charlotte knew my class schedule as well as I did.

"So you've known him about six months."

"Yes."

She tipped her head back and blew a smoke ring into the clear air, deceptively casual. "In other words, you don't know him at all."

"I do, though! I know all about him."

"Really? You know his parents, his plans, his background?"

"I love him. And he loves me. That's all I need to know."

Charlotte tapped ash onto the ground. "Barrie, that's the easy part. The rest—"

I broke in, erupting into the admission I had meant to explain in a grown-up, reasonable fashion. "He's enlisted in the navy. He's shipping out in October, and I can't bear it!"

Charlotte let a beat pass, smoking, her eyes turned up to the evergreen canopy above us. "I gather you think you have to marry before he goes."

My throat dried, making my voice thin. "Aunt Charlotte, what if he gets killed? Herbert Masters got killed in Africa, did you know? Boys are getting killed all the time. I couldn't live with myself if...if he died, and we hadn't—"

"Your quitting school won't stop our boys getting killed."

"I'll join the women's auxiliary or something. Do my part for the war effort."

"Do it after you graduate."

"Aunt Charlotte, I want to marry him." I gripped my mug, focusing on the pearly swirl of coffee and cream. I had sworn to myself I wouldn't be talked out of it. Even more compelling, I had made a solemn promise to Will that I would stand my ground. That I would be a grown-up and decide my own life.

Charlotte fell silent for a long time. She finished her coffee and lit another cigarette. I drank the rest of my own coffee, which meant I needed to go to the bathroom. I made myself wait, to give my aunt a chance to speak her mind. She said at last, "You're nearly twenty-one."

"Yes."

"Your mother was younger than that when she married my brother."

"I know."

"But it was a different time." Charlotte bent to crush out her cigarette on the ground. "We've come a long way since the first war. By that I mean, women have come a long way. You don't have to do this."

"Sorry?"

"You don't have to get married if it's about sex."

"No! It's not that! I mean—" My face burned anew.

Charlotte put up a hand. "Don't tell me. I'm not asking."

I didn't have much to tell her, in truth. These weren't things we talked about. No one in my circle of friends did, either. Our ideas of love were distilled from movies, Hollywood ideas. In my secret thoughts, I cast myself as glamorous Hedy Lamarr, carrying a torch for Randolph Scott. I thought Will was just like Randolph Scott, handsome and mysterious and strong. I didn't think of Hedy or Randolph as sexual. They were romantic. It wasn't the same thing at all.

I leaned back against the bench. Now I really needed the bathroom, but I couldn't leave with her thought hanging in the air. I crossed my legs and bounced one foot. "Aunt Charlotte, it's not about sex. At least, not just about sex."

"Okay."

"Will is pretty straitlaced, though. Catholic."

"So it *is* about sex."

I blew out a long breath and decided to make a clean breast of the whole thing. "It is for him. I said I didn't care, and I told him I don't want him to go off to war without... Well. He won't sleep with me if we're not married. I love him for it, for respecting me. For knowing I'm not that kind of girl."

Charlotte's lips twisted. I couldn't tell if she was about to laugh or cry. "You said—"

"I said I didn't care. And I don't." That was Hedy being heroic. I couldn't admit I was glad Will hadn't taken me up on my offer—and that was his being Randolph, wise, masterful, stronger than me. When I was with him, I wasn't the tomboy, wallflower, overlooked tall girl. I wasn't awkward. I didn't feel plain. I felt as if I belonged, the way I was sure all the popular girls in my high school felt.

What I wanted was for my old schoolmates to see us together, to see that Barrie Anne Blythe was as popular as anyone.

And I wanted a family like my friends had. A whole family, husband and wife, children, all together in a home like everyone else's. I would leave that unspoken, of course. It wasn't my aunt's fault I hadn't grown up that way. I would never hurt her feelings by telling her I longed for something different.

Charlotte picked up her cigarette pack and looked into it. It was empty. She folded it in two and creased the cellophane with her fingers. "You surprise me, kiddo," she said in a conversational tone. "I always thought you were a conventional girl."

I didn't want to explain to her that I wasn't, really. I said, hoping I sounded like an adult, like someone who had learned a few things about life, "I used to be conventional, I think. I've changed since I went to college. And then of course there's this stupid war."

"Wars do have a way of shaking things up."

"You're not shocked."

"God, no. Sex is nothing. What shocks me is that you would leave college when you're so close to your degree."

"A whole year to go!" I cried.

"Which will go by in a heartbeat." Charlotte tilted her head and gazed at me.

I couldn't take it anymore, so I jumped to my feet. "I know we're not done talking, but I really have to use the bathroom."

"Well. I do, too." Charlotte got up more slowly and gathered our coffee mugs, stuffing her empty cigarette packet into hers. "You go first. I'll meet you in the kitchen."

When I came back from the bathroom, Charlotte had a fresh pot of coffee started and had taken eggs and butter from the icebox. "Be right back," she said, and disappeared up the stairs.

I took a bowl from the cupboard and began breaking eggs into it, though I wasn't sure I could eat anything. I was just dropping a thick pat of butter into the cast-iron skillet when she returned. She poured another cup of coffee and went to the kitchen nook. "Come and sit. We'll have breakfast in a minute or two."

I refilled my own cup and followed her. From beneath my eyelashes, I stole a glance at her face. Her eyelids looked heavy, and new lines weighted the corners of her mouth. Doubts assailed me. How could I disappoint her?

But how could I break my vow to Will?

I remembered so clearly the moment I had made it. He and I had been standing in the shade of the giant maple tree beside the Suzzallo Library. The brick facade behind us glowed with sunshine, and the sky was a heartbreakingly clear blue, the color of hope and happiness. The world seemed absolutely perfect at that moment, with Will's arms around me and his lips against my hair. He whispered, "Promise, Barrie! Promise you won't let me down. I want you to be my wife, and as soon as possible. We're going to be the perfect couple!"

The feel of his lean body against mine made my belly soften with an unfamiliar ache. I saw other students glance at us and smile. I felt I could see us through their eyes, a handsome pair, tall, fit, fair hair and dark—I felt like a movie star. I was Hedy Lamarr in that moment, and Will was Randolph Scott, caught in the flash of cameras, glamorous, enviable.

I couldn't have made myself say no even if I wanted to—and I didn't want to.

Now, as Charlotte had asked, I slid into the banquette with my coffee cup and braced myself for what came next. Charlotte slit open a new pack of cigarettes, then gave me a wry smile. "All right, kiddo. Tell me about him. Tell me about this Will."

A flood of relief at being able to speak about him made my cheeks flush and the pitch of my voice rise. I sounded like a child, but I couldn't help it. "Oh, Aunt Charlotte! He's just—he's just *wonderful*!" In my enthusiasm to make her understand, I didn't notice her response to my gushing. I imagine she was amused, but she hid it well.

"He's going to be a doctor," I said, speaking too fast, eager to explain his perfections. "He's from this tiny town near Spokane, nowhere, really, and his folks grow apples. He came to the UW on a scholarship. The dean didn't want him to leave, but he said he really wants to serve, to do his part. He's going to be a medic on a navy ship, and when he comes back, when the war is over, we'll both finish school, and then he'll be a doctor and I'll teach physical education."

I had to stop for breath. Charlotte was smoking, gazing out the window as she listened. When I paused, she said, "A doctor. That's good."

"He's so smart. Brilliant, really. The smartest one in our Physiology class."

"Hmm. And this smart boy thinks it's a good idea for you to quit school?"

"Well, he has to go to California for training—boot camp—and he wants me to come with him. A lot of the sailors are doing that. It's the war—"

"I know it's the war. I know you feel you have to cram everything you can into your life, as quickly as possible. I understand it. I still don't like it."

I took my courage in my hands. "I can't change my mind now."

"Of course you can. A little separation for the two of you—"

I slid out of the nook. Looking down at her, feeling that the moment of acceptance, of understanding, had passed, I blurted, "Will's coming here. This weekend."

She stared up at me. "Barrie Anne, slow down. Consider. This is too big a step to take in a hurry."

I cried out in desperation, "I'm going to marry him, Aunt

Charlotte! I'm going to, whether you like it or not! I just—I just *have* to!"

I spun away and started out of the kitchen. At the doorway, I looked back. She was standing up, her cigarette dangling from one hand, the other hand gripping the front of her housecoat. She looked utterly stricken.

"Oh!" I cried, stamping my foot. "Oh, I just wish you'd been in love at least once, Aunt Charlotte! Maybe then you'd understand how I feel!"

The look in her eyes was unreadable.

Will arrived in Port Townsend three days later. He parked his bright red jalopy in front of our house and jumped out, jamming a straw boater onto his head and straightening his jacket. I was watching from behind the drapes in the little entryway, wishing my friends from high school could see my tall, lanky college man coming to call.

Will's resemblance to Randolph Scott was uncanny, at least to my dazzled eyes. He had the same honey-brown hair and clear-cut chin. He wore horn-rim glasses that made him look grown-up and intelligent. Just watching him wend his way through our unkempt garden made my heart flutter. I dropped the curtain and dashed to the front door, pausing there to smooth my hair with my hands as I waited for him to ring the bell.

I heard Aunt Charlotte come out of her studio to stand at the top of the staircase. When the bell rang, I counted to ten before I opened it. I think Charlotte gave an amused snort, but I didn't glance back to see if she was laughing.

A moment later, I was swept into Will's hard embrace, my face buried against his canvas jacket. He smelled of sunshine and sweat and bay rum, and when he kissed me, I felt the sweet prickle of an incipient mustache against my cheek. I drew back to look at his face, haloed by summer sunshine, and thought my heart might burst with love.

Being in love is a special kind of insanity. It's as if the mind gives way under some primal drive, a need to touch, a compulsion to possess, almost to devour. I felt that way about Will, wanting to clutch his hand, circle his lean waist with my arm, tie him to me with whatever bind I could discover. The passing crushes of high school—even my half-hearted yearning for poor Herbert Masters—faded to nothing before this driving desire.

Charlotte came down the stairs, and I introduced them. Will snatched off his hat and put out a hand to shake hers, saying, "So nice to meet you, ma'am. Barrie has told me wonderful things about you."

I beamed with pride at his courtly manners. I remember now that Charlotte's smile was perfunctory, but at the time I barely noticed. I saw nothing but Will.

The next days went by in a hot haze. Will and I talked, kissed, touched at every opportunity. Charlotte tidied her studio so Will could sleep on the chaise there. She cooked meals for us, and we ate them, though I couldn't have said what they were, and I'm sure I didn't taste a thing. I took Will to the beach and to the fort and strolled with him along Water Street, hoping everyone would notice my handsome beau. We took long drives in his jalopy, my hair wrapped in a scarf against the wind, his arm around my shoulders.

It was an idyll, romantic as any film, made poignant by our awareness of war news. Will did most of the talking. He made all the decisions, but I didn't care. I felt precious, beloved, and beautiful. It felt right and proper that Will should decide where we should go, what we should do when we got there, where we should stop for lunch. This, I believed, was how marriages worked. This was the way it was supposed to be, just like in the magazines and in the movies. I felt no qualms about letting him plan our future.

It would be a short war, he said. I was sure he would come home covered in glory and medals, and he chuckled when I said so. He assured me I would finish college while he started medical school, and then I could teach during his internship and residency. He told me it would make his mother happy if I converted to Catholicism before babies started coming. I was touched by his concern for his mother's feelings, and I promised I would.

I was so absorbed in him that I barely noticed Charlotte's expression growing more and more grim. When I did notice, I thought it was just because of my leaving college. I told myself she would get used to the idea, especially now that she could see for herself how wonderful Will was. She would come to understand the urgency of my feelings and the rightness of my choice.

As he was getting ready to leave on a bright, hot morning, I ran back into the house for a thermos of coffee for his long drive. When I came back outside, he was standing beside his jalopy, his boater tilted forward against the glare of the sun. Charlotte stood just inside the open gate, her back to me. Her shoulders were hunched, and her fists were buried in her trouser pockets. I couldn't see Will's eyes, but his neck jutted forward at a sharp angle, and his lips were compressed into a hard, angry line.

I caught a startled breath at the uncomfortable tableau the two of them made. I hurried forward in time to hear Charlotte say, "It's unforgivably selfish."

If I hadn't been watching when he spoke, I wouldn't have recognized Will's voice as he grated, "I think I know what's best for Barrie."

I reached them then, out of breath, clutching the thermos with both hands. "What's wrong?" I cried.

Will pushed back his hat, and I stumbled to a halt. His face, despite the heat, had gone dead white. His mouth was pressed so tight it nearly disappeared, and his eyes blazed violet with fury. Even three steps away from him, I saw the throb of his pulse above his shirt collar.

Charlotte turned to me with a deliberate movement. "I've spoken my mind. Your fiancé has spoken his." She nodded in Will's direction. "Good luck to you." Stiffly, she turned her back to us and stalked up the overgrown path to the house.

Trembling, I said, "Will? What on earth...?"

He said, "I won't have that—that—*woman*—telling me how to live my life."

An icy feeling bloomed in my chest and spread into my arms and my belly. The thermos slipped from my fingers and crashed to the flagstones. I heard the shattering of the glass liner and let it lie where it fell. "Don't you mean *our* lives?" I whispered.

He didn't answer me. The door to the house closed with a cracking sound. Will said, biting off every word, "You do know what she is, don't you?"

"Who? Do you mean my aunt Charlotte?"

"Yes, your aunt Charlotte!" he snapped.

"Will," I protested. "I don't know what you—"

"Oh, never mind, Barrie!" He twitched his shoulders, as if impatient to be off. "I suppose it's to be expected you wouldn't understand, a girl like you. We'll deal with that later." He readjusted his hat brim. "I have to get out of here."

I might have been less surprised if he had slapped me. After three days of sweet talk and charm, this harshness was a shock. I didn't move beyond the fence, standing where I was, staring at him in dismay.

He glared at me across the gate. "Are you going to come and kiss me?"

I should have said no. I should have told him if he wanted a kiss he could take the three strides to where I was standing. I didn't say that, though. I didn't even think it.

I made my shaky legs move. I stepped out through the gate and obediently held up my face to receive his cold kiss.

Moments later he was gone, his tires spitting gravel every which way, his engine roaring and then fading swiftly as he spun away down the street. He didn't wave, and he didn't look back. Hurt and confused, I leaned against the gate and sobbed into my hands.

I didn't see Charlotte as I fumbled my way back into the house and up the stairs to my bedroom. I sat down at my dressing table, wiping my streaming eyes with a handkerchief and trying to grasp what had gone wrong. I recalled standing in the kitchen, pouring coffee into the thermos, adding just the amount of cream Will liked before screwing on the cap. I remembered glancing at my reflection in the hall mirror as I went out, fluffing my hair so it would look its best as I said goodbye. Only half an hour before Will and I had been planning our courthouse wedding in Seattle! What could have happened in the meantime?

I moved from my dressing table to the bed so I wouldn't have to watch my face turn mottled and ugly with crying. I lay on my back with tears running down the sides of my face and into my hair. The abundant sunshine pouring in through my window couldn't lighten my black mood. The trill of the song sparrow in the cedar tree beside the house mocked my misery. I had expected to cry when Will left, but this—this ugly parting was a blow.

The day was half gone when Charlotte knocked gently on my bedroom door. "Barrie Anne? Are you all right?"

I got up, straightened my dress, and crossed to the door. When I opened it, Aunt Charlotte gazed at me, frowning. "Oh, kiddo. Your eyes are all swollen. Let's get you a cold compress."

I brushed back my hair with my fingers. "I don't want it, Aunt Charlotte. What happened? Why was Will so angry?"

"It's going to be hard to explain."

"I need to know, though."

"Yes, you do." She sighed and turned to cross the hall. "Come on, I want to show you something," she said. Listlessly, I followed her into her studio.

I had always loved Charlotte's studio. Despite the open windows, it smelled richly of paint and chalk and cigarette smoke. Piles of medical texts jammed a scarred credenza and an ancient drafting table. She tended to work on several things at one time, so the room was crowded with easels. I had always marveled at her intricate, detailed illustrations. In a bookcase that lined one wall were editions of the textbooks and journals she had worked on. As a young girl, I used to trail my fingers over their spines, admiring the long, technical names. They were a visual history of her career, and I was proud of them and of her.

Charlotte was at work on a large canvas of her own, an enormous thing in varying shades of gray and black and silver. It caught my eye, something new to me, a painting she must have started while I was away at school. It made me think of the waters of Puget Sound in the evening, shiny as silver, still as moonlight. I sighed, wanting to compliment it, but I was unable to shake off the torpor of my mood in order to speak the words.

Charlotte crossed to a small pine cabinet in the corner of the room and bent to open the bottom drawer. She pulled out a square object wrapped in brown paper and tied with twine. She ran her hands lovingly over the package, as if her sensitive fingertips could see through the paper to what was inside.

I said, "What is that?"

"It's a picture."

"You mean a painting?"

"No. A photograph." She tugged at the twine. The knot loosened stiffly, as if it hadn't been undone in a long time.

"Why do you keep it in that drawer?"

She pushed the twine aside and opened the stiff folds of paper to reveal a slender gilded frame in the Arts and Crafts style of a quarter century before. "I've kept it in a drawer because I don't know how to explain it to you." She lifted her face, and her drawn expression startled me. She had tied back her hair with a bandana, and the sunlight was harsh on her skin. No tears glistened in her eyes, but her lips looked soft and vulnerable, as if she could weep if she allowed herself to.

I felt tightness in my throat, my tears returning in response to her distress. "Aunt Charlotte! What's wrong?"

"Nothing's wrong, really. Not now, in any case. It's an old photograph, and it all happened a long time ago, but..." Her voice faltered, and she looked down at the picture in her hand. "I told you once I was never sweet on a boy, and that was true. But it's wrong to let you think I've never been in love. I was in love once. I was just your age." She drew a tremulous breath as she held out the framed photograph. "This is who I was in love with."

I took the picture and looked down. The face gazing out of the frame was young, with wide eyes and a big smile. A pale bob framed round cheeks, and a Victorian cameo, held by a ribbon, nestled at the base of a slender throat.

I said, "I don't understand. This—this is a girl."

"Yes. A girl."

"But you said you were in love..." I frowned in confusion. I felt as if comprehension was just beyond my grasp, like an idea I had once had that wouldn't come back to me. My left hand rose, fingers outstretched, as if to seize it, but it eluded me. I felt a stab of embarrassment at the slowness of my mind. I repeated, "I don't understand, Aunt Charlotte. This is a *girl's* picture."

"That's right, Barrie Anne," she said in a gentle voice, as if explaining something difficult to a child. "A girl. She's the only person I was ever in love with."

I fumbled my way to a stool and sank onto it, lost in the jumble of my thoughts. Charlotte's revelation was simply outside of my experience.

She said, bitterly now, "You see why I hid her photograph."

"I don't—Do you mean—" I was helplessly inarticulate. I was vaguely aware that such things existed, but only in the abstract. In the sense that there were odd things in the world, things I knew little about, things I never questioned or worried about. Things that had nothing to do with me.

Charlotte pulled up another stool and sat down at a little distance. "I loved this girl just as you love Will. I know it's strange to you, but there are lots of people like me. They hide their natures, as I do, because it's dangerous."

"Dangerous?"

"Oh, yes. My kind of love is considered a crime in a lot of places. To say nothing of the churches saying it's a sin."

I shifted my shoulders, trying to take this in. My aunt

Charlotte, a criminal? It wasn't possible. I looked back at the photograph of the pretty, fair-headed girl and tried to imagine it. I couldn't. None of it seemed real.

It's embarrassing to look back at my younger self and realize how naive I was, how unworldly I and all my friends were. I thought of how it felt to kiss Will, how my body flamed when he touched me. I tried, briefly, to imagine such a connection between Charlotte and the girl in the photograph, but my mind skittered away, unable to comprehend the possibility.

But she was my aunt Charlotte. I loved her and had a thousand reasons to respect her. I couldn't think anything bad about her.

I struggled for something to say, finally asking, "What was her name?"

"Georgia. Everyone called her Georgie."

"Did—did my parents know?"

"That I was a homosexual?" I flinched at the word. I don't think I had ever spoken it. "No, Barrie Anne, they didn't know. My mother did, but not Scott and Thelma. I doubt they would have allowed me to be your guardian if they had."

"Why?"

She shrugged and dug in her pocket for her cigarette pack. "It's the way people think about someone like me and like Georgie. That is, some people. Enough people to cause us trouble, to make us hide. My family, for example. When I left school to go to New Mexico with Georgie, they stopped speaking to me. Grandmother Fiona answered my letters, but only until my mother found out and intercepted them."

I pondered that for a moment. "So...what happened to her? To...to Georgie?"

"I left her behind in Taos when I came here. I meant to go back, but then..." She gestured with her unlit cigarette.

"But then my parents died." Suddenly I could see it, understand what had happened to Charlotte and the decisions she had made. "It was Georgie, wasn't it? Georgie who started you painting. Who took you to Taos."

There was real pain in Charlotte's voice when she answered. "We left college together and went to New Mexico. It was strange, being in such a dry place, but that's where I learned medical illustration, to make some money while we studied art. I'd had physiology classes already, in my nursing course, so that was a good start."

"How long were you there?"

"Well, let's see." Charlotte put her cigarette between her lips and lit it. There was something defensive about the action. "Almost ten years, I guess. Taos was an interesting place in the twenties. Musicians, sculptors, poets...it was an easy place to live. Accepting. Of course we knew, if Georgie came here with me, to Port Townsend, people wouldn't understand. Or, worse—" She gave a bitter laugh. "They *would* understand and make our lives miserable. I couldn't ask Georgie to do that."

"You stayed because of me."

"I stayed because I had promised my brother and my sister-in-law. Because you needed me, and because, above all, I wanted to be here with you. And of course, there's water all around us, and that—" She broke off, waving away that thought, then extended her hand to take back the photograph. She gazed down at it and said, "I've missed her, but I made the only decision I could. I've never regretted it."

"You could go back now, though," I said tentatively.

She turned her head to blow her stream of cigarette smoke toward the open window. Not looking at me, she said, "Georgie passed away while you were in high school."

"Oh, no! Oh, my God." I looked into the photographed face again. I imagined, if this were Will's picture, and he were gone, how devastated I would be. "I'm so terribly sorry, Aunt Charlotte. You had to grieve alone. You never said a word."

"Thought it better to keep it to myself. Now, though . . ."

"Now? Does this have something to do with Will?"

Charlotte kept her back turned. Her shoulders were hunched again, but I could see the tremor in the hand that held the cigarette. I said, "Aunt Charlotte? Did you tell Will all of this?"

"No. He guessed."

"What? How?"

She took a long, slow drag of smoke and blew it out. "Some people are good at that."

"Is that why he's angry?"

"No." She tapped her cigarette into an ashtray and gave me a sideways look over her shoulder. "No, kiddo. I told him he shouldn't marry you until he gets back from the service. That's why he's angry."

"Oh!" A wave of relief made me press my hands to my chest. "Oh, but he said—"

"I have a feeling, Barrie," Charlotte said.

"A feeling—"

"Yes. This is a bad one."

"No! You're just saying that because you don't want me to quit school!'"

"No, Barrie Anne. That's something I would never do. I might make a mistake once in a while, but I know better than to deliberately misuse the talent."

She held my gaze, and the chill began to creep through my chest once again. "Aunt Charlotte, I promised him."

"I asked him to release you from your promise. He refused."

"He—he loves me."

Charlotte's lips twisted, and I thought she would remark on that, but instead, she exhaled a long, wheezy breath as she ground her cigarette into the ashtray.

I said, "We're getting married next week."

"I wish you wouldn't, but you're an adult now. I can't stop you."

"I was hoping you'd come."

There was a long, miserable moment of silence before she said, her voice scraping in her throat, "I can't, Barrie Anne. Not after—Well, I just can't."

"Aunt Charlotte..."

She spun on her stool and stood up. We avoided each other's eyes as she walked past me, carrying the photograph in her hand. When she reached the door, I jumped up. "Aunt Charlotte. I'm really sorry about Georgie."

She paused in the doorway, nodded, and crossed the hall to her bedroom.

I married Will a week later in a civil ceremony at the King County courthouse. Charlotte didn't come. Will's parents didn't attend, either, or any of our friends from the university. There were no flowers, no cake, no champagne—not even a real wedding dress. Our witnesses were courthouse employees. Someone snapped a single photograph and took my address to mail it to us. Before I knew it, almost before I could catch my breath, it was done.

Two days later, we were off to San Diego Naval Repair Base on a train jammed with a hundred other hastily wed couples. Will never spoke another word about Charlotte until he returned three years later.

7

July 12, 1947

Charlotte and I decided to call the baby Emma, in honor of her emerald-green eyes. Emma, unexpected and utterly surprising, slipped into the vacant space of my life as if she had been created to fit it. She tended to be awake in the dark hours and asleep during the day, so we left the cradle in the front room, where she could nap in the sunny warmth. Charlotte had a woven basket we decided to use as a bassinet upstairs. I padded it with flannel sheets and the blue blanket with its pattern of white teddy bears. I set it beside my bed where I could put out my hand when Emma woke in the night. Sometimes I could pat her back to sleep. If she was really fussy, I got up, warmed a bottle of goat's milk, and snuggled her next to me as she suckled. More than once the two of us fell asleep that way, the baby nestled on my chest, her head beneath my chin.

Sometimes I found my aunt watching us, Emma and me, with an odd expression, speculative, sometimes doubtful, often worried. I tried to pretend I hadn't noticed. I was happier than I had been in a long time. My broken heart was healing, slowly, surely, miraculously.

"I should take my things from the house in town and move down here," Charlotte announced one hot morning. "You're going to need the help."

I suspected it was more than my need for help that prompted this decision, but I was grateful for it, and didn't ask. I said, "Only if you're sure you want to do that, Aunt Charlotte."

She chuckled through the smoke of her morning cigarette. "You couldn't keep me away."

"I'll empty out the storeroom so you can set up your studio."

"Perfect. That room has a nice southern-facing window. The light should be good." She poured coffee from the percolator and crushed out her cigarette. "Now, Barrie Anne. I want to talk to you."

"Oh, so serious!" I was smiling. It was hard not to, with Emma sleeping like an angel in her cradle and sunshine bathing my garden, promising a bounty for the farmers' market. I felt deliciously warm myself, as if I had taken a chill and finally recovered from it.

"Yes, I'm quite serious." Charlotte glanced from the kitchen to the front room, her face softening as she gazed at Emma. I followed her glance, comforted by the small, clear puffs of the baby's breathing. Willow, curled next to the cradle, sensed our regard and thumped her tail. Charlotte said, "You need an explanation."

"You mean, for the . . ." I waved my hand. I didn't want to

say it. Both of us avoided speaking the word aloud, but she knew what I meant.

She gave me a lopsided grin. "There *is* no explanation for those, I'm afraid. What I meant is a lot simpler. How did you, a woman on her own, come by a baby?"

"Surely there are lots of orphans needing homes since the war."

"Sadly true, but you'll need specifics. A history. Provenance."

"You make her sound like a piece of furniture."

"We do sort of catalog people, don't we? Who you are, where you came from, how you got to this place. Just the same, you're going to need a birth certificate for Emma."

I grinned above my coffee cup. "I think I know an artist who could manage that."

Charlotte laughed. "I accept the commission. But where should she be from?"

"Elsewhere." I reached for the percolator. "Who's going to track down whatever details we create? Everyone's busy with their own problems."

"Do you have a map?"

I paused, the coffeepot poised over my cup. "Map?"

"Map. Of the state."

"I'm sure there's one somewhere."

"Let's find it. We'll pick a town, someplace obscure. Emma can be from there."

I went in search of a state road map Will had left behind, and I eventually found it on the floor of my bedroom closet in a forgotten knapsack. As the kitchen warmed in the July sun, we spread out the map on the table so that the whole state of Washington lay before us, a tangle of roads and cities in black, a smattering of blue rivers and lakes, assorted islands and peninsulas in shades of gray and green. We found a hamlet in the farthest corner of the state from us, a tiny place that merited only the faintest dot of cartography.

We dug out my own birth certificate as a model, and Charlotte looked it over. "This will be easy," she said. "You'll be fine as long as no one comes looking for her."

"That won't happen," I said with confidence. Charlotte lifted her eyebrow.

The government men came that afternoon.

Charlotte wasn't there when they arrived. She had decided to start the moving process that same day. "It's going to take a few trips," she said, as she pulled on her hat and smoothed her gloves over her hands. "I'll try to hurry. I know you have work to do in the garden. Feed chickens and so forth."

"I'm okay for today."

"Good. I'll load up the car. Be back by supper."

I cradled Emma on my shoulder and waved goodbye from the front porch, watching the Studebaker swirl away in a brown plume of dust. I realized it had been days since I started up the International. I would need to do that, or the battery would be dead. It was a cranky old truck, a prewar model, and it might be dead already. I decided I would try it after lunch, while Emma was sleeping.

I gave her a bottle and then settled her in the cradle while I made my own lunch. Charlotte had gone to the Chimacum store the day before for bread and cheese and butter, and some of my own lettuce was crisping in the icebox. I made a thick cheese sandwich and dropped some lettuce and cheese into Willow's bowl. I was just sitting down when I heard an engine coming up the lane.

I jumped up and went to the front window, worried Charlotte had developed engine trouble or something, but it wasn't the Studebaker. It was a late-model Buick, maybe even a brand-new model, longer and lower than Charlotte's car, with sweeping front fenders and chrome everywhere. It slammed to a stop in front of the house, as if the driver had decided to brake at the last minute. Two men got out before the roiling dust subsided. They brushed at their clothes with fretful motions, as if the dust had surprised them.

My first thought was that both men must shop at the same store. Their fedoras, which had to be too warm for the summer heat, looked identical. They wore them at the same angle. Their ties were unfashionably skinny and solid black, with no dots or squares or any of the patterns I expected on men's ties. One of them was taller than the other, but their wide-shouldered black suits appeared to match. They wore pristine white shirts and black wingtip shoes that had probably been shiny when they first put them on in the morning. Now they were hazy with dirt. One man carried a briefcase. The other had a small notebook in his hand.

They stood for a moment, eyeing my house, then shading their eyes to look past it to the garden, bursting with pea vines and tomato plants, busy with chittering hens, then on to the empty field. I knew that from where they stood, they could catch a glimpse of the canal beyond the apple trees. It had to look inviting, cool and blue and fresh, to two men wearing such unseasonal clothes.

My next thought was that they had come for Emma. As they started up the path to the front porch, I hurried to pick up the sleeping baby. For a frantic instant I cast around for some way of hiding her, but there was no time. In any case, the front room was full of baby paraphernalia, a dead giveaway that there was an infant in the house.

They knocked. I pulled the blanket over Emma's head, hiding her face. And her ears. I muttered, "Willow, here," but she was already at my side.

I opened the door no more than six inches. At the sight of the two men, Willow's hackles rose, and her tail slung low. I said, "Can I help you?"

The taller man looked uneasily at Willow as the shorter one spoke. "Are you Mrs. Sweet?"

"Who are you? Do you need something?"

"If you're Mrs. Sweet, we need to ask you some questions."

"Why?"

The taller man, though he obviously wasn't happy about Willow's wary stance, said, "Can we come in?"

I hesitated. Willow was no ordinary dog. Like my aunt, she knew things. She didn't like the men, so I didn't, either. "You haven't told me who you are," I said.

"I apologize." The shorter man shifted his notebook to his other hand and dug in his pocket. He held out a wallet, open to what looked like a badge, though he closed it before I got a good look. "We're with the federal government. I'm Mr. Harrison. This is Mr. Woods."

I didn't move, and I kept my left foot wedged securely behind the door. I wasn't as tall as either of them, but I was strong, a farmer, an athlete, a chopper of wood and hoister of fence posts. I trusted my ability to slam the door in their faces. I said, "What branch?"

"What?"

"What branch of the federal government?"

Harrison's mouth quirked to one side as if he was resisting a patronizing smile. "Information," he said.

"That's not a branch." I braced my foot more securely. "The FBI is a branch. The War Department is a branch."

His smile faded. "Ours is called CIA. Central Intelligence Agency."

"I've never heard of it." I pushed my foot against the door, and it closed an inch.

He braced the door with the flat of his hand. "It hasn't been announced yet."

Woods said, "We won't keep you long, Mrs. Sweet. If we could just sit down, make a few notes..."

Willow's lip curled, and Woods took a step back. Good, I thought. Afraid of dogs. For the thousandth time, I felt a rush of gratitude toward my aunt for insisting I accept the gift of Willow.

So many things had happened in the last twelve days that I had forgotten all about the government men supposedly going up and down the peninsula. Suddenly it came back to me, along with the story in the *Trib* about a pilot spotting strange aircraft. I thought hard and fast. If I acted suspiciously, would that make the situation worse?

I wasn't certain, really, that there *was* a situation. They had barely glanced at the baby in my arms. It seemed it was the field they were interested in, or perhaps the canal beyond it. And, I suspected, the sky above it.

They were more weird than scary. If there had been only one man, I wouldn't have thought much of the whole thing. It was just odd that they came in a pair, like boots. And there was Willow's reaction, which made me wary.

Willow obliged me at that moment by beginning to pant, flashing her long white canines, demonstrating the impressive size of her open jaw. Woods visibly flinched, and as I repressed an amused smile, I decided. Between the two of us, Willow and I should be able to manage if things got nasty.

I stepped aside. The men came in, wiping their shoes ostentatiously on the braided rug inside the door. They removed their hats as they gave my shabby little house a perfunctory glance.

"Thank you," Harrison said. "Okay if we sit at your table?" He nodded toward the kitchen with its dented and scarred table and mismatched chairs.

I said, "Yes," and closed the door with my foot. "Willow, here," I added. Obediently, she padded close at my side. Her hackles had lowered, but her tail still signaled her disapproval. I kept Emma in my arms, her white-blond head hidden by the blanket. She slept on, her light, steady breaths tickling my neck.

As we sat down, Willow took a place beside my chair, her eyes shifting between the two men as if they were two sheep to be herded.

Woods opened his briefcase and lifted a sheaf of closely

typed pages onto the table. Harrison brought a fountain pen from his pocket, uncapped it, and opened his notebook. In a self-consciously conversational way, he said, "New baby, Mrs. Sweet?"

"A few weeks, yes."

"Congratulations. Your husband must be proud."

I didn't answer. I had no idea what these men knew about me. The question felt like a trap, and I wished I was free to simply order them out of the house. But there was Emma.

I blinked, dropping my eyes and drawing a shuddery little breath, as if the question caused me pain. I said in what I hoped was a girlish voice, a vulnerable voice, "Can we just get to your questions? I have work I need to do while my baby's napping."

Woods cleared his throat, and it sounded like a reproof to his superior. They exchanged a brief glance. Harrison swept a palm across the table as if he were looking for crumbs and then laid his hat on it. Woods followed suit, though without checking for dirt. Harrison pulled his pocket square from his breast pocket and wiped perspiration from his brow. He said, "Yes, of course, Mrs. Sweet. I'm sure you have a lot to do, with a new baby and all, so we'll get right to it. We're trying to track down reports of citizens seeing some strange aircraft over the past month."

I tried to hide the relief I felt. I said innocently, "Aircraft? No. I haven't seen anything out of the ordinary. Just the ones out of Ault Field. Some from Boeing Field. Less since the war, of course."

"Do you know much about airplanes?" he asked.

I'm afraid I gave him a sour look, despite my efforts to seem like an innocent female. I suspected he knew quite well what I knew about airplanes and was trying to trap me. "I was an army observer at Tibbals Hill."

"Ah, the station out at Fort Worden. What was that like?"

"You can go see it for yourself. It's still there."

"Can you tell me what you saw? Aircraft, ships...?"

"No." It gave me satisfaction to say that, and to say it firmly. I was on certain ground now. "I'm sure, Mr., uh, Harrison— I'm quite sure you know I can't tell you that. I signed a secrecy agreement with the army."

Woods cleared his throat again. I wondered which man was really the superior.

"I was just curious," Harrison said, but Woods leaned forward, interrupting him.

"Let's talk about now," he said. At his movement, Willow jumped to her feet. Woods leaned back into his chair with a little hiss of indrawn breath, and Willow sat down again. Woods resumed, but he kept a nervous eye on the dog. "You have a good view over Hood Canal."

"A slice of one."

"Right. So. What we're asking people," Harrison put in, pressing his notebook open with his palm, "is if they've seen anything strange recently. In the skies. In the water."

"In the water?"

"Or in the skies."

I drew a little breath of relief at having skipped over the question about the water. "In the skies," I repeated. "You mean like that pilot from Boise? Like he did?"

"Right," he said. Harrison eyed me more closely. "You heard about that?"

I said, "It was in the paper, that's all. I haven't seen anything like strange aircraft, at least not since the war."

Woods also fixed me with a searching look. His eyes were a sort of dull gray, I noticed, managing to be cool and hard at the same time. "Did you see strange aircraft during the war, Mrs. Sweet?"

"Sure. Didn't you?"

Harrison said, "Did you report them?"

"To whom?"

"Your superiors. You were working for Army Artillery."

"These were our own aircraft, coming from Ault. Why would I report them?"

"What did they look like?"

It was Woods who asked that question. I looked directly into those flat, gray eyes. "Mr. Woods." My pretense of a fragile feminine voice evaporated as I spoke with confidence and a touch of temper. "It was a world war. We still have enemies. If I had seen experimental American planes, I certainly wouldn't describe them to two perfect strangers who showed up at my door and asked me a lot of odd questions."

Woods blinked but gave no other sign that he had taken in my insult. Harrison cleared his throat and fiddled with his notebook, but he didn't seem to know what to say next.

Emma stirred against my shoulder. I stood up, not wanting them to have a glimpse of her unusual hair. Willow came to her feet, too, her shoulder hard against my thigh.

Woods pushed back from the table. "Where's your husband, Mrs. Sweet?"

My back was up by then. If I had possessed hackles like Willow's, they would have bristled. I wished I could curl my lip as she had and show long, sharp canines. Tension tightened my belly and hardened my voice further. "That's a rather personal question, don't you think, Mr. Woods?"

"Well," he said, with feigned concern, "a woman alone, on an isolated farm . . ."

Harrison stood up, too, putting his pen back into an inside pocket. He said, "And with a baby. That can't be easy."

In what I thought must be a serendipitous stroke, the Studebaker chugged up the lane at that moment and came to a dust-roiling stop beside the Buick. "Oh, good," I said. "My aunt is here." They turned as one to eye the Studebaker and the trousered woman climbing out of it. "You see, I'm not alone. She's come to help me with the baby."

Harrison said quickly, as if certain Charlotte's arrival would interrupt him, "Do you know anything about the incident on Maury Island?"

"Where's Maury Island?"

Woods, gathering his papers and stuffing them into his briefcase, said, "Never mind." Both men picked up their hats, and we started toward the front room as Charlotte was climbing out of the Studebaker and opening the trunk. At the door, Woods said, again with that unconvincing friendliness, "I'd love to see your little one, there. I have three of my own."

I took a step back and felt Emma squirm beneath my tightening grip. I said, "Sorry. I don't want to wake her. It took forever to get her to sleep."

The two men glanced at each other and then back at me. The tension in my belly grew into an ache. I don't know if I grew pale or flushed, but they stared at me as if I had done something suspicious. I blinked, trying once again to look guileless. To look like a tired young mother with things on her mind.

Harrison said, "If you see anything, notice anything, you should call us."

It was hard to maintain the innocent expression in the face of this blundering command. "You mean, Mr. Harrison, at this agency that doesn't yet exist?"

Harrison's mouth opened, but Woods spoke before his partner could. "I left a card on the table, with the number."

I snapped, "Long distance, no doubt."

"We would reimburse you, of course."

Charlotte had reached the porch by then, a bulky box in one arm, her handbag dangling precariously from the other as she reached for the door handle. Harrison pulled it open before her hand could touch it and stood aside to let her enter. Both men touched their hat brims, said, "Ma'am," and then were out the door and off the porch as if the last thing they wanted was to be introduced. Willow, stiff-legged, watched them go.

Charlotte dropped the box on the divan as I shut the door with my foot. "Government men," she said.

"So they claimed."

"I came as quickly as I could."

"You knew?"

She didn't say she had had a feeling, but her shrug told me it was true.

"I guess it was our turn," I said.

"I don't like the look of them."

"I didn't like anything about them. Neither did Willow." The dog, relaxed now, thumped her tail on the floor and smiled up at the two of us, her tongue lolling with satisfaction that the threat had left. "They knew a lot about me."

"What did they want?"

"Wanted to know if I'd seen any strange aircraft."

"What did you tell them?"

"I told them the truth. I haven't."

Emma began to squirm in earnest and emit her mewing cry. I pulled back the blanket, smoothed her head, and started toward the kitchen to warm a bottle. Charlotte followed, lugging her carton to the dining table.

"Did they ask about the baby?"

"They asked about Will, which made me feel like they were asking about Emma."

"They've probably spoken to your neighbors."

"I guessed that."

She folded back the flaps of her box. "Well. Looks like I was right."

"About the government men?"

"That, yes, but I meant about the birth certificate. I had a hunch I'd better get that made before I did anything else." She pulled out a heavy yellow sheet of paper and held it up for me to see. It was artfully done, with straight lines, a convincing-looking seal, all the spaces properly filled in. "I thought it would be best if Emma's birth mother wasn't married, so I didn't list a father."

"Simplifies things." I tested the bottle on my wrist and gave the nipple to the baby, who began suckling with gusto.

"Yes. So, as it happens, Emma was born out of wedlock to one Agnes Laurence of Malden, Washington. It was a home birth, and a Dr. Neal filled out the certificate. Poor Agnes died not long after. I should probably do a death certificate, too, but I'll need one to copy."

"That's a good story, Aunt Charlotte."

"I know." Charlotte grinned and dug out her cigarette pack. "I should write novels, maybe, instead of illustrating body parts!"

"I suspect the body parts pay better." We laughed. Emma joined in with a milky gurgle, which made us laugh harder.

I was settling Emma into her cradle when I remembered the last odd question they had asked. I went up the stairs to the room Charlotte was arranging as her own. "Do you know anything about an incident on Maury Island?"

She was taking things from a suitcase and folding them into a bureau drawer. She straightened and gave me an odd look. "They mentioned Maury Island?"

"Yes. I don't know where it is."

"It's north of Mount Rainier, in Puget Sound."

"Why do you know that?"

"I stopped at the Mercantile for cigarettes. Someone cut out a newspaper article about it and tacked it up on the bulletin board behind the counter."

"What did it say?"

"Some harbor patrolman says he saw something under the water around Maury Island. The story they're telling is that one of the airships crashed into the water."

"Oh." I had a sudden sinking feeling, as if my blood pressure had dropped. Faintly, I repeated, "He saw something under the water."

"Yep." Charlotte dropped the blouse she was holding into the drawer. "I don't like this. If those men come back, I don't think you should let them in."

"I don't know if I can stop them."

"You should try." She shook her head, scowling. "They think they know what they're looking for, but they don't. They don't have any idea. Not that I would tell them that. Nor would they listen to a woman's point of view if I did." She turned back to her suitcase. "They think science explains everything."

"I suppose some things can never be explained."

"I suppose." Charlotte closed the bureau drawer with a decisive click. "But it's all connected. Everything is connected."

8

August 2, 1947

It was obvious that goat's milk agreed with Emma. In those first weeks she grew like a proverbial weed, very like the swiftly growing ones I spent hours yanking out of my garden. Emma's legs and arms lengthened, losing some of their plumpness. Her candy-floss hair grew thicker, with a tendency to curl around her forehead. She smiled and gurgled at us, and we both chattered baby talk at her. She loved Willow, reaching for her whenever the dog was near. I was cautious about this at first, but it was soon clear that Willow regarded Emma as her personal charge. She sat near her cradle and followed us when we carried her up the stairs or out to the garden. She blocked the curious hens from poking the baby with their beaks, and they soon lost interest. She seemed to know when Emma was going to be hungry, or when she was sleepy. More than once I found Willow resting her head on the baby's leg, enduring the unsteady little pats of those starfish hands.

Watching this one sunny morning, Charlotte said, "That dog is an amazing babysitter."

"I know." Emma was sleeping under Willow's watchful eye while I pinned wet baby things onto the clothesline at the side of the house. Charlotte had come out to lounge against the porch railing and smoke a cigarette. She breathed out a puff of smoke into the clear hot air as I dug two wooden clothespins out of my pocket and pinned a diaper into the flapping, bleach-scented row of them.

Charlotte nodded toward the diapers and gowns clipped to the lines. "You're going to need bigger gowns. And more diapers, or you'll be doing this every day."

"I know. I have a bit of money in the silverware drawer, from the last market."

"Let's go to the Mercantile."

I felt a shiver of anxiety. "I don't know, Aunt Charlotte. I'm not sure I want to take her out, not yet."

"I think you should, kiddo. The longer you keep her hidden, the more curious folks are going to be." She straightened, smiling down at the sleeping infant in her basket. "Adopting a baby is perfectly normal, Barrie Anne. If you'd gone through the usual channels, you wouldn't think anything of it."

"But people will want to look at her. Hold her. What if they see?"

"I have an idea about that."

I finished hanging the laundry while Charlotte carried the basket and Emma into the house. By the time I went back inside, my empty laundry basket on my hip, Charlotte had warmed a bottle and was settled into the rocking chair with the baby in her lap. She had wrapped a slightly worn white satin ribbon around the baby's head and over her ears and tied it with a bow at the top of her skull. Fluffs of Emma's pale hair curled around it. "Baby chic," Charlotte said.

"Where did you find the ribbon?"

"It was tied around some old letters," she said.

I recalled seeing the bundle when she was moving in. She had tucked it under a pile of scarves and stockings in her bottom drawer as I was putting fresh sheets on her bed. I didn't ask whose letters they were, nor did she say anything, but I could guess. They were Georgie's.

I said, "She looks sweet."

Charlotte nodded. "I think we're ready, Barrie Anne. Let's get this over with."

I had been dreading this moment, but I knew she was right.

There had been a little boy in my grammar school who was born with a withered hand. Children haven't learned the trick of pretending they don't see something embarrassing, and when he first arrived, everyone stared at that poor little hand with its shriveled-looking fingers and grayish skin. I remember how he pulled his sleeve down to cover it and how he wore his jacket all the time so he could hide his hand in the pocket. We all got used to it eventually. It was different but no longer shocking. In time, he stopped hiding it, and all of us stopped noticing it.

But gills...Emma's particular difference would be much harder to explain.

The rippled surface of Port Townsend Bay glittered like crushed sapphire in the August sun. The bricks of the downtown buildings glowed russet, and the whole town shimmered with summer heat. Emma slept the whole way in the car, and her cheek was rosy where it had rested against my shoulder. She was still asleep as we climbed out in front of the Mercantile. I checked the ribbon and shaded her face with my hand as we walked inside.

As if no time had passed, I saw the same faces I had seen the last time I shopped there. Nothing seemed to have changed except me. Tina Rogers stood behind the counter, her hair a little grayer, her hips a little wider, but otherwise the same as the last time I saw her, when I was still working at the dry goods store. Two housewives whose faces I knew, though not their names, were mulling over saucepans. They smiled when we came in, the way women do when a baby appears, and they paused in their shopping to coo over her.

"You're Barrie Anne Blythe, aren't you?" one of them asked.

"It's Barrie Sweet now," I said. "I married during the war."

"Your baby is adorable," the other one said. "Congratulations."

"Thank you."

"How old is she?"

"Two months."

"Oh, my goodness! Are you getting any sleep?"

It was such a traditional conversation, the sort of chat between mothers I had expected to have when Scottie was born, that I began to breathe more easily. No one asked to hold her or offered to touch her, which was a relief.

Charlotte and I spent a delightful hour poring over knitted rompers and tiny socks, lacy caps, even a shelf of baby toys. We spent all the money I had and some of hers, buying two rompers, two new nightgowns, four pairs of socks, a little pink cap with a ribbon to tie under Emma's chin, and a celluloid rattle with a painted bunny face.

We stopped at the lunch counter, taking a booth so we could manage the baby. She woke as we slid into the banquette, but she didn't whimper. Her eyes were wide with wonder at the sights and sounds of this new place. Charlotte assured me she still had money in her pocketbook, so we ordered hamburgers and malteds.

The waitress was a girl who had been a year ahead of me in high school. "Gosh, Barrie," she said, as she wrote down our order. "It's been a long time."

"Hi, Rose. I don't think I've seen you since the war ended." Self-consciously, I adjusted Emma's position on my lap. Rose had been one of the popular crowd, a cheerleader and a homecoming princess. She had dated Herbert Masters all through high school. We'd never exchanged more than a few words.

I felt a stab of sympathy for her. She must have grieved when she heard Herbert had been killed, but I didn't know her well enough to say anything about it.

She tugged at her uniform, a pink nylon dress with a short white apron, as if it embarrassed her. "Is this your baby?"

"Yes. This is Emma."

"She's darling. I love the ribbon."

"You remember my aunt Charlotte?" The two nodded at each other, and Rose disappeared behind the counter to clip our order onto the cook's spindle. She made the malteds herself and carried them on a tray to our booth, smiling again at Emma.

"How old is she, Barrie?"

"Two months." Emma's carefully constructed birth certificate listed her date of birth as May 20. We thought she might be a bit older than that, but it seemed as good a guess as any. Who was there to argue about it?

Rose set the silver shakers down on the table, with tall glasses and paper straws, then stood back with her empty tray propped against her hip. "Didn't I hear, Barrie—I mean, not to pry, but—didn't you have a little boy just last year?"

I didn't have to pretend the pain that still could make my throat ache and my eyes glisten. Charlotte stepped in swiftly. "Barrie Anne's boy passed away," she said quietly.

Rose's face reddened. "Oh, my God, I'm so sorry. I didn't know that." The cook rang the ready bell behind her, and she turned to see that our order was up. She said, "I'll be right back," and went to get our hamburgers.

When she returned with them, she said, "Barrie, I'm really sorry about your baby boy."

I had recovered myself by cuddling Emma to my heart. "Thanks, Rose. It was hard."

"So sad. But you already have another one!"

It was gauche and bordered on rudeness, but it was what we

had expected, though we hadn't known who would be first to broach the subject.

Rose slid our plates into place but stayed beside our table, avid for gossip.

Charlotte was ready. "Emma is adopted. Her mother died when she was born, and a family friend knew Barrie Anne had lost a baby, so she put the two of them together."

"Oh, golly!" Rose clutched her tray to her bosom. "Oh, I see! Golly, that's just so sweet!" Someone at the counter cleared his throat. Rose, with obvious reluctance, tore herself away from us in order to serve her new customer.

Charlotte and I gazed at each other for a moment in silence. Her lips curled without mirth as I stroked Emma's cheek with my finger. "That went well," she said. "Everyone on the peninsula will know the story before the week is out."

Emma put up her hand to touch my cheek. I kissed her tender palm, and she gurgled like the miniature charmer she was.

I laid out one of Emma's new nightgowns that night and filled the enamel basin so she would be clean when she wore it. August evenings on the peninsula were long, the sun lazing down the western horizon as if it had all the time in the world to go to its rest. The peaks of the Olympics turned rosy under its lingering glow. We kept the windows open to hear the birdsong and occasional bass notes of bullfrogs from the creek on the far side of the field. Emma had drunk a full bottle

of milk and seemed to be looking for more sustenance. Charlotte and I talked about making some applesauce and a puree
of carrots to supplement the goat's milk.

I lowered the baby into the basin, laughing as she gave her
little crow of delight. Charlotte, pausing on her way upstairs to
paint, said, "That child loves her bath!"

"I know." I held Emma with one hand and gently splashed
her with the other. "Maybe she'll sleep tonight!"

"Maybe, kiddo," Charlotte said, grinning. She started up
the stairs. "You were a night owl, as well, your mother said.
Until you were about two."

"Two! Good grief. I'll be exhausted!" I didn't mean it,
though. When Emma woke in the night, wanting me, I felt
a rush of satisfaction. Of happiness, and well-being, and gratitude for being needed.

Charlotte went upstairs, and I rubbed a tiny bit of Ivory soap
into Emma's fluff of hair, careful not to let any drip behind
her ears. I was looking down at her, smiling at the vividness
of her eyes, when she suddenly grinned in response, opening
her mouth wide to show perfect, toothless gums and a curl-
ing pink tongue. She startled me, and my hand slipped from
beneath her wet shoulders.

She bent sharply backward, flinging out her arms as if she
meant to do a back flip. Her bottom slid along the bottom of
the basin, and her head sank beneath the water.

I gasped and reached for her, then stopped, my shaking fingers outstretched.

Emma's sea glass eyes were wide-open, unblinking, fixed
on mine through the clear bathwater. Her smile grew, and

I watched, frozen with horror, as bubbles streamed from her mouth—*and from behind her ears.*

I called hoarsely, "Charlotte! Come quickly!"

Emma, lively as a polliwog in a creek, paddled with her hands. She kicked her little feet, rippling the bathwater, and more bubbles erupted around her. By the time Charlotte reached us, clattering down the stairs, Emma had been underwater for at least thirty seconds, and I had never seen her look happier.

Charlotte said, "What is she—oh. Oh, lord."

She shouldered me aside, staring at Emma. The baby's eyes glimmered through the water like their namesake emeralds, and she wriggled with undeniable delight. Bubbles flowed around her, iridescent in the fading light. She smiled through them, as if she had created them on purpose for their perfect shapes and rainbow colors.

I put out a forefinger and lifted the earlobe closest to me. Charlotte blew out a long, meaningful breath.

The gill, that small, vulnerable organ that should not have been there, tucked so neatly beneath the mastoid bone—that little opening, as delicate and precise as an eyelid—flexed gently, steadily.

Charlotte said, in a choked tone, "Definitely not a defect."

I couldn't answer. I also couldn't take it anymore. I snatched up the baby into the safety of the air, drawing a frantic breath myself as if I could provide oxygen to her little lungs. I clutched her to me, and she dripped water over my shirt. Emma kicked her feet, gave a joyful squeal, and spat a mouthful of water that dripped over my chest and down the front of my shirt.

Above the baby's wet head, I stared at my aunt. She spread her hands, and though my own face was frozen in shock, hers split into a huge grin. I gasped, "Why are you smiling?"

She said, with a chortle that seemed not to fit the situation at all, "I'm just wishing Grandmother Fiona were here to see this!"

"Aunt Charlotte! Emma was—She was under the water, and—"

"Yes, she was. She was *breathing* underwater." She was still smiling, raising her eyebrows at me, waiting for me to understand.

"But—why—Aunt Charlotte, what are you smiling about?"

"You've forgotten the legend, Barrie Anne. The one about Morag, the Stuart woman the villagers in Kinloss tried to drown. The story Grandmother Fiona used to tell."

Water was dripping down into my overalls now, so my thighs were wet. I began to shiver, but more with shock than with the cold of the bathwater. Shock, confusion—denial. I said in an unsteady voice, "Are you talking about the water witch story? But you said—you said it was exaggerated, a legend, that your grandmother was—was dotty, I think was the word."

I shivered harder, and my knees felt weak. I'm ashamed to admit I was feeling a little woozy. I blinked hard against the cloud of spots before my eyes and took one unsteady step backward, toward the rocking chair.

Charlotte, with a little exclamation, snatched up a towel and took the baby from me, wrapping her swiftly and then, with Emma on her shoulder, guiding me the rest of the way to the chair. "Here, sit down, Barrie Anne," she said. Her grin had faded, and a worried frown creased her forehead. "You feel faint?"

I nodded. Speech was beyond me just then. I put my head on my knees and drew deep breaths through my nose, trying to settle the thrumming in my ears. I had never fainted in my life, and I had no intention of starting now. I drew one more long, long breath and held it as I lifted my head and sat up straight in the rocker.

"Better?" Charlotte asked.

I nodded again, but I didn't try to get up. I felt odd, looking up at Charlotte and Emma, as if they inhabited some world different from my own. There was a space between us that seemed to yawn deep and wide, though it could be measured in inches. It was an unbridgeable gulf, created by a reality I couldn't bring myself to recognize, a reality I couldn't reconcile with the one I had always known.

I breathed again, swallowed, and croaked, "Aunt Charlotte. She breathed underwater. *Underwater.*"

"Yes. I saw." Charlotte hooked a low stool with one foot and sat down close to me, turning Emma to face me. She sat on Charlotte's lap like a little towel-robed Buddha, bright-eyed, rosy from the bath, smiling her gummy smile. "You seem more upset by this than by discovering she has gills."

"Gills! Those could be—just—I don't know. An anomaly. But this is—this isn't possible. It isn't *scientifically* possible!" I had my breath back, and as I blinked, my disorientation eased. I put out my hand to touch Emma's foot, but grazed Charlotte's knee instead. Her flesh, muscle, the bone of her knee-cap, were as solid as ever. As much a part of my world as ever. I slumped back into the rocker, feeling as if I had just completed a long run. Or a high dive.

Charlotte nodded acknowledgment of my recovery, and her face relaxed. "Kiddo, I know enough science to know that it doesn't explain everything. We have so much still to learn. We don't know how the brain works, for example. We don't know why some people have brown eyes and some have blue. We've only just learned about antibiotics and vaccines. We don't know if there are people on other planets, although I'm pretty sure that's what those government men are trying to figure out."

I grimaced at the thought of the government men.

Charlotte went on. "I know this for sure: what people don't understand, they fear. Frightened people are dangerous people, as Morag's story demonstrates." She rubbed Emma's fluff of wet hair with a corner of the towel, then combed it with her fingers, musing, "I wonder how many others there have been."

"Others? What others?"

"Others like Emma."

"You think there are others?"

"It makes sense, doesn't it? That she wouldn't be unique? There could be others who hid their difference out of fear. Out of caution."

"But, Aunt Charlotte—where do they come from?"

"Where did our Emma come from?"

It was the question I had consciously avoided. "We don't really know, do we?"

"We know she came from the water. That Willow found her by the water."

"But—" Again my throat dried, and for an instant my vision swam. "But, surely not—not *under* the water."

"Why not?" Charlotte spoke without inflection, as if she were discussing a grocery list. "Add that to the list of things modern science has not yet figured out. There could be civilizations under the water. In outer space. Beyond our solar system, even."

"Now you're thinking of the saucers."

"There are universes we know nothing of, Barrie Anne. Under the water. Beyond the sky. We live in a world of mysteries."

I had nothing else to say, but I thought that Emma—my Emma—was the greatest mystery of all.

9

The War Years

The train to San Diego, where Will would attend navy boot camp, was jammed with soldiers in uniform and young men in ill-fitting suits heading to various military bases. It was made even more crowded by the throng of wives and girlfriends who couldn't bear to be left behind. The rattle of voices was a constant tumble and roar of sound, an ear-numbing blend of treble and baritone voices. The train was so crowded many people had to sit on laps or on suitcases that blocked the aisles, and a fug of tobacco smoke, perfume, and sweat clogged the air.

Despite these discomforts, the journey felt like a party. In our car, someone played a banjo, and someone else had a ukulele. The music only stopped very late at night. Everyone seemed giddy with anticipation, sure that what was coming would be a great adventure. If there were doubters, or if any of the men were afraid, they kept their thoughts to themselves.

Will and I found ourselves crammed into a corner of our car, five people sharing a bench seat meant for three. Opposite us were two other couples, the Ormundsens and the Walls. Peggy Ormundsen had red hair, cinnamon freckles, and a cheery grin. She was small and plump and pregnant, the roundness of her belly just beginning to show beneath her maternity smock. She sat on Henry's lap for most of the trip, and when there was space for her to move to a seat, the two of them held hands or dozed in each other's arms.

Sally Wall was a gaunt girl, with thin hair and a beaky nose. Her husband, George, was a head shorter than she, and so shy he was nearly tongue-tied. He watched Sally constantly, his hands lifting whenever she moved, as if she were about to fall or shatter to pieces before his eyes. Once I found her crying in the ladies' room, and when I put my arms around her, she sobbed that she was afraid of leaving home, terrified of her husband going away, dreading the prospect of being alone. I stayed with her, patting her shoulder and handing her bits of scratchy toilet paper to wipe her eyes. Half an hour passed before she recovered herself. When I walked back with her to our compartment, George gave me a grateful look. He didn't say anything, but he kept his arm around her narrow shoulders all the rest of that day.

I couldn't help thinking that my husband was the best-looking man in our whole train car. Despite the lack of privacy and complete lack of shower facilities, he managed to hold on to his Randolph Scott charm. Once or twice I saw other girls watching him and then watching me. I wasn't feeling particularly put together myself—not at all like Hedy Lamarr—and I hoped they weren't wondering how a tomboy like me could have married such a dreamboat.

He did seem like a dreamboat, too. The wedding had been quick, and the honeymoon just one night in an inexpensive Seattle hotel, but I was sure it was all the beginning of a great romance. Our plans hung before us like stars on the horizon, full of promise. Everything and anything seemed possible. I thought of Charlotte once or twice, with a pang of regret at having disappointed her, but I forgot her quickly enough in the excitement of the moment.

Only officers and their wives were allowed to share quarters on the naval base. Will and the other enlisted sailors were required to live in barracks, and the wives who traveled to San Diego with them—part of a horde of women following their men around the country—were forced to find their own accommodations. When we reached San Diego, I tracked down Peggy and Sally in the giant arrival hall to suggest we find an apartment to share. They were both enthusiastic about the idea, and Sally wept tears of relief. We kissed our husbands, saw them off on rusting, noisome buses to the base, then walked together into the unfamiliar city.

We stayed in what my aunt would have called a fleabag hotel for three days while we searched for an available apartment. By the time we found one, a shabby one-bedroom on the third floor of a building with no elevator, our roles in the unlikely friendship were established. Peggy was always ready to laugh, to joke about even the direst situation. Sally was shaky and uncertain, depending on anyone who would make decisions for her. I was the strong one, physically and emotionally. I was the one who could lift suitcases and lug boxes, was willing to barter with our cranky landlady, and happy to stare down catcalls and wolf whistles from the boys in uniform crowding every street.

I didn't mind, really. The city sported a festive air, with bright-eyed boys filling the cafés and bars, laughing, swaggering, heedlessly spending their money. Vivid posters urged us to buy war bonds, warned us that "Loose lips might sink ships," and reminded us to "Do the job *HE* left behind."

It was a relief to leave the run-down hotel, even though our new place smelled of mold and mothballs. It was fun shopping for a few things to make it feel like home. We pooled our cash to buy a secondhand Motorola radio, and we found a thrift shop selling old but clean sheets to make up the lumpy couch. I thought Peggy, her belly swelling more each day, should sleep in a real bed. We agreed Sally would share with her and leave me to sleep on the couch in the sitting room.

Will was the first of our men to receive a pass. I met him on the street to show him the way up two flights of stairs to our apartment. Sally and Peggy were already in their hats and gloves, headed off to see the new Veronica Lake picture. I stood aside so they could admire my tall husband, looking dashing in his whites. The navy had clipped his hair nearly to his scalp, making his horn-rims seem enormous, but his lean jaw and cool blue eyes still made my belly quiver.

He nodded to my roommates, and they clattered down the stairs, calling goodbyes as they went. I shut the door and took his hand as I gestured to the dingy walls and stained floor.

"Welcome to the palace!" I announced, with what was meant to be an easygoing smile.

My smile faded as he scowled, taking a long, appraising look at the dinky kitchen space, the worn couch, the small, square enamel-topped table. He said, "Only one bedroom?"

"It was all we could find that we could afford. All the apartments are full of girls just like us."

"You can't have looked very hard."

"Will, we searched for three days. Gosh, you should have seen the hotel! This is a great improvement."

He pulled his hand free of mine and went to set his cap on the table. "Barrie, I'd rather you found a place of your own."

Hurt and confused, I struggled for a response. Finally, lamely, I asked, "Why?"

He gestured at the place, describing a dismissive arc with his arm. "Look at it! I wouldn't stable a horse in here."

I had planned our evening in great detail: a supper of pot roast and asparagus, with fresh rolls from the corner bakery. I was wearing my favorite sweater set and pleated skirt and had done up my hair in a victory roll. I had even washed the sheets on the bed, in case. . . .

A flood of resentment swept over me. I took a step back, putting distance between us, when an hour before I had been longing to be in his arms. I said stiffly, "It won't be for long."

"Who uses the bedroom?"

"Peggy's expecting. She needs to sleep in a bed."

"What about Sally?"

"They share. Sally gets too nervous to sleep alone."

"Those girls are taking advantage of you. It's fine for them, maybe, but this isn't the way I want *my* wife to live."

I took another step back, startled and furious at the tears that stung my eyes. Will had a canvas sack over his shoulder. He unslung it and threw it on the couch. "Clothes," he said offhandedly. "You'll have to keep them. They won't fit in my seabag."

I stalked past him, my face averted, crossing to the range to make an unnecessary check on the pot roast. I knew it was done, but I looked at it anyway, then shut the oven door with a bang. I stared at the red-and-white salt and pepper shakers in their stovetop niche, blinking through a haze of tears.

It was my second big mistake with Will. I wish now that I had tossed my head and announced that if he was going to be unpleasant, he could just go back to the base. I had, after all, left school to be with him. Hurt my aunt in order to do what he wanted. Taken on responsibility for two girls who now looked to me to solve every problem that came our way.

But I didn't say any of that. I crossed my arms over my solar plexus, gripping my elbows, sniffing away the angry tears. I told myself he was going off to war. That he was tense because he was afraid. That his world, too, was turned upside down. I was his wife. It was my duty to comfort him. To make him happy.

I had an unworthy impulse to tell him that if he were an officer, we could live together, but that would have been spiteful. I quashed the thought before the words reached my lips.

I took an apron from a hook behind the door and tied it over my skirt. As I started whisking flour and water together for gravy, I said, "There's nothing I can do about it now, Will. Let's just enjoy our evening. There's a bottle of beer in the icebox." I didn't look at him, but I heard his sigh as he bent over the little icebox to take out the beer. Without looking up, I handed him the church key. He levered off the cap, took a long swallow, and belched.

I felt composed enough then to face him. Apparently his bout of temper had subsided. He lifted the bottle in salute and gave me the heart-melting smile I had fallen in love with, the corners of his eyes crinkling charmingly behind his horn-rims. "That smells good, Barrie," he said. "I'm so glad you can cook. Chow at the base is awful."

"Dinner will be ready in a moment. Do you want to sit down?"

The table was already set, adorned in its center by a utility candle stuck in a saucer. I scraped a long match and put its flame to the wick. Will settled into one of the rickety wooden chairs, frowning again as it rocked on its uneven legs. I turned back to the gravy to hide the gritting of my teeth against a fresh spurt of temper.

I went through the motions that evening, struggling to recapture the honeymoon feeling. When I said goodbye to Will, I smiled and kissed him and waved as he walked away up the street. Peggy and Sally had been watching for him to leave, and they rushed up the stairs after he was gone. I told them what they wanted to hear, a happy account of a romantic evening, but when I curled up on the uncomfortable couch that night, I wept unspent tears into my secondhand pillow.

I didn't act on Will's preference for me to live alone. We couldn't really afford it, and I assumed he had figured that out, since he didn't bring it up again.

I liked sharing an apartment with the two girls. I spent hours helping Peggy plan a layette and accompanying Sally on long walks when her nerves threatened to overwhelm her. We knew we wouldn't be in San Diego long enough to take jobs. Any employer would know we weren't going to stay. Girls like us cycled through the city in waves, like the recruits they followed.

We clung together, the three of us. We laughed and gossiped, sang along to the radio, cooked penny-wise meals, and laid plans for when the war was over and we were all settled in picket-fence houses with babies coming every year.

Henry came to the apartment the most often, as if he knew his wife was counting the hours. Like Peggy, he was cheerful, grinning, cracking corny jokes and pretending to try to kiss all of us at once. Sally and I hurried out to a café to give Henry and Peggy the apartment, and they were in each other's arms almost before we were out the door.

Sally's George, though so colorless and silent, showed up for every visit with chocolates for all of us or a nosegay of flowers for the table. He always insisted Peggy and I didn't need to go out, but we did anyway. We wandered downtown, window shopping, sometimes going to the pictures or stopping for a sandwich before making our way back. One such evening we arrived home to find that George had run down to the corner store for root beer and ice cream and was waiting for us to return to make root beer floats while Sally beamed with pride over her little husband's kindness.

When Will visited, he brought me his laundry and once a pair of shoes for me to clean. He gave me his letters to mail home, saying it was easier than mailing them from the base, and somehow it became my task to write to the University of Washington for his transcripts to speed the process of his becoming a hospital corpsman. He was irritable and impatient as we waited for the papers to arrive, and nothing I could say improved his mood. He hated the barracks, he hated boot camp, he even complained about the relentlessly sunny Southern California weather.

There were a few times, though, when he was all charm, when he played the part of the young man I had fallen in love with. At those times I doubted myself and wondered why I allowed myself to have such confused feelings. When he was accepted into the corpsman program, he hugged me and thanked me for typing letters and filling out forms. Once when his parents sent him a bit of money, he took me out for dinner.

He was a perfect gentleman that night. He held my chair for me. He asked what I wanted to have from the menu, then ordered it for me, calling me "the lady" as he spoke to the waiter. He ordered a bottle of wine and urged me to try a glass.

We toasted each other, and he said, "This is the way our life is going to be, Barrie. Perfect. The best of everything for the doctor and his beautiful wife."

I returned to the apartment that evening buoyant with hope that my romance was real after all, that everything would be exactly as he said. That everything would be perfect.

That hope died a slow, painful death. Will knew nothing of how I spent my days while he was at the base, and he didn't ask. He wasn't interested in what Peggy or Sally were doing. If I mentioned Aunt Charlotte, the narrowing of his eyes and the tightening of his mouth stopped me from going further.

I started waking up in the night with a feeling of being unable to breathe. I would throw off my hand-me-down blanket and thrift store sheets and go to stand at the window, looking out on the lights of the busy city and longing for my own cool, quiet peninsula. I had to admit to myself that this wasn't at all what I had expected. I tried thinking up reasons—excuses—for Will's bouts of temper, for his criticisms, for his self-absorption. I tried not to think about how sweet plain little George was, or how funny and personable Peggy's Henry always seemed to be. Peggy and Sally were too considerate to comment on Will's coolness or his patronizing glances, but I couldn't help wishing he just would stay at the base. His behavior embarrassed me, but I didn't know what to do about it.

I didn't write these feelings to Aunt Charlotte, but I admitted to myself, in the wakeful small hours of the night, that she had been right. I should have stayed in school. Will and I should have waited. The war was the reason I made this mistake, and the war was the reason I couldn't undo it now.

Peggy and Sally and I went together to see our husbands embark on the USS *San Diego*. War news was all around us, and it wasn't good. We knew little about where they were going, except that their ship was heading to the Pacific Theater, where the fleet at Pearl Harbor had been destroyed, and where the battle for Guadalcanal now loomed in all its bloody horror.

The ship was new and daunting, a gray monster looming against the blue California sky. The sailors, mustered in long, straight lines, looking heartbreakingly young and fresh and eager. I watched the ceremony with Peggy and Sally, standing with the other wives and girlfriends, waiting for the men to be set free to say their goodbyes. Peggy, her maternity smock stretched over her growing belly, clung to Henry until the last minute, smearing his cheek with Victory Red lipstick, then tearfully trying to scrub it off with her handkerchief. Sally wept, too, trembling, while George manfully tried to comfort her.

Will wore his hospital corpsman's insignia, the caduceus gleaming in the bright sunlight. His cap, angled just so on his cropped hair, made him unbearably handsome, and at that moment, surrounded by dozens of couples saying their farewells, I experienced all the emotions a wife was supposed to have. I felt love, and devotion, and a poignant anxiety for my husband's safety.

They were good feelings, relieving me, however briefly, of my guilt over the simmering confusion and resentment that had marred our time together. As we said goodbye, I clung to those good feelings, those *proper* feelings. I could believe, in that instant, that I was doing something right.

When the bosun's whistle sounded, the sailors broke free of their families and friends and trotted toward the ship as if they couldn't wait to be gone. Peggy and Sally and I stood close together, a wartime trio of friends, waving our handkerchiefs and calling goodbye. I kept my free arm around Sally, and Peggy gave her a shoulder to lean on, though Peggy herself was crying so hard she wasn't much more stable than Sally.

I didn't feel like crying. I pretended to myself I had to be strong for my friends, but the truth was less honorable. What I felt, as Will's lanky form disappeared among all the other sailors in their whites, was relief, and weariness, and some other, less clear emotion that made me peer after him and wonder who, after all, I had married.

Just as I caught a last glimpse of him, moving up the ramp into the ship, I shivered, physically, despite the heat. I narrowed my eyes, peering after him. What had just happened? What had I felt?

I had no time to ponder it. Peggy and Sally were mopping their eyes, clinging to each other and then to me. We had to stand there until the last sailor had boarded, and all the other friends and families had begun to leave. I couldn't think for the broken sobs of my two friends filling my ears, their tears dampening my blouse. Once we were finally set free, my still-hiccuping roommates dragged me away to drown our sorrows in an ice-cream soda and plan our next steps. By that time, my brief moment of presentiment was all but forgotten, and I did my best to mirror my friends' misery over parting with our husbands.

We three had things to do before we could leave San Diego. We had a week left on our rent, and we spent it packing, writing our first V-Mail, clearing out leftover condiments and perishable food, laundering bed linens and towels. I washed my thrift shop sheets and donated them to the cause of whoever would come after us in that dismal apartment.

Sally's mother came to accompany her home to Oakland on the bus, and I was glad to relinquish responsibility for my high-strung friend. Peggy and I took the train together to Portland, where she changed for her home in Bend while I continued on to Seattle. We promised each other we would write, that after the war we would visit.

As my train clanked its way north, I gazed out at the gray Pacific Ocean washing the sea stacks and rocky beaches of Oregon and Washington and pondered the friendships generated by war. Peggy, Sally, and I had nothing in common besides sailor husbands. We had been inseparable for a few weeks, but that time had come to an end. I cared about them. I would worry about them. We would write, for a while, but it was likely I would never see either girl again.

I was grateful to find my home unchanged in the months I had been away and to find my aunt Charlotte as steady and strong as ever. She met me at the ferry terminal, and the two of us smiled at each other, awkwardly at first, then with our usual rapport. We loaded my things into the De Soto and shut the trunk with some difficulty. Before we got into the car, on an impulse, I threw my arms around her. "I've missed you!"

"Kiddo," she said, awkwardly patting my back, "I'm so glad you're home."

On the drive over the canal and up the peninsula to Port Townsend, I regaled her with tales of Peggy's pregnancy,

Sally's nerves, our shopping trips, the films we had seen. I told her what San Diego was like, bustling with soldiers and sailors. As I gazed into the restful vista of evergreens and the shimmering gray water of Puget Sound, I described the blandly persistent sunshine, the palm trees and bougainvillea that grew everywhere in Southern California.

"It sounds like a nice place to live," she said, as we passed over the canal.

"Too noisy," I said promptly. "And crowded."

"It won't be so crowded after the war, I expect."

"Maybe not. But I like interesting weather, and there it's always the same. Hot and clear every day." I settled back into my seat, smiling as we shot quickly by the familiar landmarks. An intermittent rain grizzled the windshield, and I sighed with appreciation. I hadn't seen a drop all the time we were in San Diego. "I missed the rain," I said.

"Did you?"

There was something serious in the way she asked the question. I turned to watch her profile as she drove. "Yes, of course I missed it," I said. "Does that surprise you?"

"Actually," she said, with an air I couldn't puzzle out, "it doesn't."

"What do you mean?"

She glanced at me, one quick, sidelong look. "How does it feel to you, to see the rain, to be back on the peninsula? Water all around?"

"I guess it just feels like home. Like I'm back where I belong. Why?"

She kept her eyes on the road, not even smoking as she

drove through the rain and growing darkness. She seemed to consider her answer for a long time.

I said again, "Why, Aunt Charlotte?"

She lifted one shoulder in a half-hearted shrug. "Oh, no reason, I guess," she said unconvincingly.

"Aunt Charlotte!"

She laughed. "Well, I did wonder. Our kind always seem to like living by the water. The ocean, a river, a lake...the talent responds to water."

I shook my head. In the past months, distracted by Will and by the disruption of my life, I had given no thought to Charlotte's knack. "I don't have it, Aunt Charlotte. I like the water; you know that. I love to swim. I liked walking by the ocean in San Diego, but I never had any premonitions."

She gave me a quick glance and a smile. "That's kind of a shame."

I shrugged, but her probing made me wonder, though. Had there been a flicker of something when Will was leaving? We were standing right by the water, our eyes dazzled by the sun on the ocean, and there had been that shiver of—premonition? Anxiety? If that was a Blythe feeling, it was little indeed. Subtle, elusive as a soap bubble floating up from a basin of dishwater, surfing the breeze from an open window. I didn't want to hide my feeling from my aunt, necessarily, but I had no idea how to describe it, and I wasn't at all sure it was real, in any case. I decided it was best to let it lie.

Charlotte broke into my thoughts. "Now, Barrie Anne Blythe."

I corrected her. "Sweet. It's Barrie Anne Sweet now."

"Oh, right. Habit."

"Me, too. It's hard to get used to."

"I'll start again," she said lightly, as we rolled through Sequim and started the last ten miles up to Port Townsend. "You've told me all about Peggy and Sally and their husbands. You haven't said a word about Will."

A nervous chuckle rose in my throat. "Golly," I said. "Some wife I am."

"Tell me about that."

I cast about for something to say and settled for, "He got his hospital corpsman's certification. He really wanted that. It's his first step toward being a doctor."

"Good for him."

"He's on the *San Diego*, did I tell you that?"

"In your letter, yes. He's happy about it, I suppose."

"Happy enough, I think. They're all scared."

"I can imagine. I would be."

We reached the edge of town, and Charlotte turned up the hill toward our house. She said, as we pulled up in front of it, "You like married life, Barrie Anne?"

I sat still for a moment, gazing with a rush of nostalgia at the neat, square house of my childhood. The rain had stopped, but the spruce tree in the front yard dripped with its aftermath, and the garden glistened wetly in the vague, foggy light of a half-obscured moon. I confessed, "I'm not sure I know if I like married life. I only saw Will once a week, sometimes two, all the time we were there."

"That can't have been easy."

"No. Frustrating."

"Well," she said, as she opened her door. "Let's hope he's home soon."

I let the remark go unanswered, and I felt her quizzical look as I got out and went around to the trunk to unload my suitcases and boxes. I said, "I want to do some kind of war work. I don't know what yet."

"Plane spotting," she said promptly. "They need daytime people out at Fort Worden. Aircraft Warning Service."

I paused, a suitcase in either hand, and grinned at her. "As usual, you have a plan."

She grinned back, and the uncomfortable moment evaporated. "You bet," she said. "I even have the telephone number for you."

The happiest years of my marriage to Will were while he was overseas. We exchanged letters. I dutifully sent packages for his birthday and for Christmas. Charlotte subscribed to two newspapers, the *Seattle Daily Times* and the *Tacoma Tribune*, and like other families with men at war, we scanned the casualty lists every morning, hoping not to see a name we recognized. While Charlotte went upstairs to paint, I rode my old bicycle out to the Tibbals Hill bunker to take up my observation post, where I spent the daylight hours watching the sky for enemy aircraft.

That little concrete building was, oddly enough, a place of respite. It was always cool, and it smelled of soil and the wild fennel that grew all around its walls. It was soothingly quiet, with hours going by when I didn't see or speak to a soul. I liked going there, and I savored a conviction that I was doing something vital. It was a daylight job, and I never actually spotted any suspicious aircraft, but I knew how important it was for me to be watching, just the same. I took care to remain alert, to not be distracted by the beauty of the scenery. Bald eagles wheeled above the Sound, their commanding silhouettes outlined by blue sky. Belted kingfishers, with their fluffy topknots, often left their perches in the trees along the beach to flutter their blue-and-white plumage past my bunker. They eyed me through the unglazed window with fearless curiosity. River otters scooched along the beach below me sometimes, and once in a while I saw an orca breach, carving an arc between sea and sky. Their sleek black-and-white beauty was no less majestic than that of the eagles, and I cheered softly when I caught sight of them.

In the evenings, after I had cycled home, Charlotte and I listened to the war news on KJR, as everyone did. Occasionally a friend would drop by. Once a week we went to the old Baptist church for a sewing circle. Neither of us could sew or knit, but we made tea and rolled bandages. We collected the socks and scarves and mittens the other women produced and packed them to be sent overseas.

We pored over the news of the battle for Guadalcanal, because there was a rumor that was where the *San Diego* was, and we knew there were many casualties. I hated hearing the bell of the Western Union boy's bicycle. If it came too close, Charlotte and I would pause what we were doing and stare at each other, willing the doorbell not to ring. Eventually we

gleaned enough from Will's letters to know his ship was on its
way somewhere else, but we still froze at the sound of that bell.

I didn't have a service banner to hang in our window, with
a blue star to indicate someone in our family was in the armed
forces. I saw others around town, proudly displayed in our
neighbors' houses. I rather thought I would like one. It might
be nice, I thought, having people see it in our window. They
would know we were just like other families, doing our part for
the war effort. I didn't know where to find one, though, and I
didn't ask. I worried Aunt Charlotte might not like it, since she
and Will didn't get along. As the war rolled on, other stars began
to appear on those flags, the gold ones that meant someone was
dead. I saw them sometimes as I rode past on my bicycle, and I
wondered how it felt to those bereaved families, and whether
adding the gold star to the flag gave them any comfort.

Once Will had R & R in Hawaii and sent a postcard with a
gaudy picture of a hula girl. I propped it in the window frame
over the sink, which Charlotte didn't seem to mind. Its corners curled in the steam of dish washing, and one morning we
found it at the bottom of the basin, a sodden square, the hula
girl dissolved into garish shadows. I supposed I should have
taken it up to my bedroom before that happened. Instead, I
scraped the sodden shreds and stuffed the ruined postcard into
the bin below the sink.

I wrote Will about my war work, but he never commented.
I gave him reports of the weather, and rationing, and the short-
ages of gasoline and sugar and soap, things we didn't make
for ourselves on the peninsula. He responded with complaints

about his food, about his superiors, who he said knew less about medicine than he did, and about having to take turns sleeping in a bunk, which meant it was never clean.

It wasn't much of a correspondence. There were no declarations of love, no protestations of loneliness. None of us had possessed a camera in San Diego, and I had only the fuzzy snapshot from our courthouse wedding to remind me of the charm of his smile or the enchanting blue of his eyes, things that had so appealed to me, that I had fallen in love with. I began to feel that Will was a stranger, someone briefly met, barely remembered. Only my changed surname reminded me that I was, in fact, his wife.

I heard from Peggy and Sally several times. Peggy sent a birth announcement, and then at Christmas a rather blurry snapshot of a plump, bald infant. Sally wrote tight little letters, as if she was afraid of wasting ink. Both of them spoke of their husbands as if they were on the point of coming home, though I knew that couldn't be true.

Then, after the USS *San Diego* had been at sea for eighteen months, Will stopped writing.

We didn't know where he was, of course. Even if he had told us, the censors would have blacked it out. Information was closely guarded by the War Department, and there was no one we could ask. A month went by, then two. Three months passed, in which I dutifully wrote Victory Mail every week but received no reply. His birthday came and went. We sent a small box of cookies and popcorn and paperback novels, carefully addressed to the FPO address in San Francisco, but it was never acknowledged.

Six months went by with no word at all. Will had shipped out of San Diego two years before. We scanned the news reports, and listened to the radio, and hurried to check the mailbox after the mailman came. I began to have the odd feeling that Will had never existed, that I had imagined him, that my time in San Diego had been a fitful dream.

Once I wrote to Peggy, just to prompt a response. She wrote back immediately, a long, chatty letter about Henry's reports from the ship and their plans for the end of the war. I was embarrassed to tell her Will had stopped writing, so I told her about plane spotting, and my solitary days in the cement bunker at Tibbals Hill.

One morning, when we still found no mention in either paper of the *San Diego*, I said, "I think I should write to Will's parents."

Charlotte refolded the *Tribune*. "You haven't met them, have you?"

"No. He said they couldn't make it to the wedding because it was harvest time."

"You have their address?"

"I have Will's papers. He gave them to me in San Diego. Their address is there somewhere. They don't have a telephone."

She reached into the pocket of her housecoat for her cigarette lighter. "It seems strange they haven't written to you, either when you were first married or since Will's been overseas. You've been their daughter-in-law for more than two years. Not a word?"

"Nothing. Will told me they're kind of old-fashioned, but...otherwise, he didn't tell me much about them. All I know really is that they grow apples. He couldn't wait to get away from the orchard business."

Charlotte laid the paper aside and leaned back, steepling her long fingers. They were stained with paint, as they usually were. "Do you want to talk about what went wrong between the two of you?"

"Why do you think—"

"Come on, kiddo," she said gently. "Who knows you better than I do?"

"Damn," I said. "I thought I was hiding it."

"Why hide it?"

"Because I should have listened to you," I blurted. "I made a terrible mistake, leaving school, rushing into marriage."

"You're hardly the first girl to do those things. War does strange things to all of us."

"I was—well, I thought *we* were—so much in love."

"I know. I confess, I've never been a great believer in romance."

I chewed on my lip, trying to maintain my dignity, but all at once it just didn't matter. I gave in to the urge to spill it all to the person I trusted most in the world. I'm afraid I sounded childish, whining about things that couldn't be changed, but I had kept those words back for so long, I couldn't help myself. They poured out in a flood of complaints.

"It was so one-sided, Aunt Charlotte!" I exclaimed. "It was all about him, all the time. I felt as if—I don't know, as if he'd *hired* me to be his wife, to do chores and manage things. He wasn't interested in anything I did, not in San Diego, not once I came back to the peninsula."

"I'm no marriage expert, obviously. But when he comes back, you'll have to stand up for yourself, kiddo. Set guidelines."

"I guess so." I scraped at the egg residue on my plate. It made an irritating noise, and I dropped the fork, letting it clatter against the china. I stared at it, fighting the urge to say the worst thing of all.

When I looked up, Charlotte was gazing at me, her chin on her fist. "What is it?"

I shivered with the horror of my thought. I spoke it in a low voice, as if whispering made it less offensive. "I keep thinking...if something has happened to Will...it would all go away. I don't really mean it. I don't really want him to—" I broke off, ashamed, and looked away from the wisdom in her dark eyes.

"You don't want him to die," Charlotte finished for me. "Give yourself a break, kiddo. Everyone thinks terrible things from time to time. I know you don't mean it." She put up an admonishing finger. "And if he does die, Barrie Anne, I don't want you to think it's your fault."

"The thing is, we were miserable in San Diego. I mean, sometimes we were happy enough. Sometimes it was okay—but a lot of the time it wasn't."

"I'm sorry about that. I imagine it was a hard time."

"Everyone else seemed so happy. Excited, even. It was like a giant party every day."

"Not for you?"

I made a sour face. "I was bored. I couldn't play tennis, or swim, or even go for a run by myself. I was cooped up in a tiny apartment except when we went for a walk or went out to the pictures. I spent the whole time taking care of Peggy and Sally—not that I minded! I like them both." I stacked the dishes and got up to take them to the sink, but I paused with the plates in my hands. "If Will had been killed, someone would tell me, wouldn't they?"

"I think that's how it works."

"Now the war is almost over, you'd think someone would tell me something."

"It does seem strange," Charlotte said. I appreciated her bland expression. I knew she suspected Will had deserted me, but she was too kind to say so. I suspected the same thing. Or maybe I hoped for it.

"I guess I'll try writing to his parents."

"Might as well. It could be interesting."

I wrote that night after I returned from the fort. After some thought, I addressed Will's mother and father as Mr. and Mrs. Sweet, which seemed best since I hadn't met them. I explained that I hadn't heard from Will in six months and wondered if they knew if he was all right. I signed it with my full name, Barrie Anne Blythe Sweet, and mailed it the next morning.

Mrs. Sweet's reply arrived just five days later. It was waiting for me on the kitchen table when I came in from work, a plain white envelope, the kind you buy at a drugstore. My address was written in a tight hand, with ink droplets trailing beneath it. Charlotte hurried down the stairs when she heard me come in. She watched, her arms folded tightly, as I picked up the envelope and slid my thumb under the flap.

There was no salutation. The letter began partway down the page, only three lines.

I don't know who you are or why you wrote to us. William never mentioned you. If you're after money, we don't have any. It's awful mean of you to come at us with this story when we don't know where our boy is.

Sincerely,

Mrs. Franklin Sweet

"What does it say?" Charlotte's voice was gruff with tension.

My hand had begun to shake so violently I couldn't focus on the letter. Wordlessly, I held it out to Charlotte. She crossed to me in two swift strides, took the sheet from my unsteady hand, and read it for herself.

"Bastard," she swore under her breath.

"I don't understand," I cried. "He never told them we were married?" The shaking spread up my arms to my shoulders, and I tottered on suddenly nerveless legs.

Charlotte threw the letter on the table, and wrapped her long arms around me, holding me up but also embracing me with all her steady strength. After a moment, she guided me to a chair and settled me into it. "Tea," she pronounced, and went to fill the kettle. "With brandy in it," she added over her shoulder.

I drank the tea, and my shuddering subsided. Charlotte had stuck the letter somewhere, so I didn't have to read it again or even see it. We sat together through the long winter evening, switching from spiked tea to Charlotte's signature gin rickeys.

Fortunately, we'd thrown together a pot of soup the night before, and I managed to get a bowl of that down to dilute the gin and brandy burning in my belly. I wasn't used to drinking. In fact, I wasn't used to a lot of things. It seemed I was going to have to work on that.

At the end of the evening, after we had studiously talked about everything but Will, Charlotte reached across the table for something, and the letter from Mrs. Sweet fell out of her sweater pocket.

I looked at it in blurry disgust and slurred, "Sh-she shouldn't say that. M-marriage license. Have that."

"Good."

"Sh-shouldn't have said I wanted money."

"No, of course not."

"We g-got married. I can p-p-prove it."

"That's good. You may need to."

"But th-they don't want to hear! No-nobody—" I threw out my hands and knocked over my bowl, spattering the table with the remains of my meager dinner. "Oopsh," I muttered, and giggled.

Charlotte got up and came to lift me from my chair and guide me toward the stairs. Her own steps were none too steady, and the two of us banged against the wall and then the banister. We started to laugh, helpless, belly-aching laughter. We leaned on each other, laughing so hard we could no longer climb. We had to sit down on the staircase and laugh it out.

Eventually, my laughter drowned in a burst of tears. Charlotte pulled herself together enough to help me up the rest of the stairs and into my room. As she had when I was small, she helped me wriggle out of my dress and pull a nightgown over my head. I cried throughout the whole process, then, hiccuping, was done. Charlotte more or less rolled me into the bed, patted my head as if I were ten instead of twenty-three, and staggered off to her own room. The next morning, we both woke with splitting heads and ashy mouths.

A month later, Will showed up.

10

August 6, 1947

On the second anniversary of the bombing of Hiroshima, nightmare photographs of the devastated city appeared in the newspapers Charlotte bought. After the first glance, I averted my gaze. Emma's presence had made me more than usually sensitive, and the descriptions were ghastly. Images of burned children haunted my dreams, and I woke from them gasping with horror. Only reaching out to touch my own baby, my own delightful, mysterious, amphibious foundling, calmed me enough that I could sleep again.

Charlotte moved a lot of her things from Port Townsend, including a full carload of art supplies. It was high season in the garden, and I spent hours weeding and watering, loading baskets with produce for the market, trimming vines and turning compost while Charlotte worked in her studio with Emma at her side in her basket-cum-bassinet. Willow was torn between following behind me as I gardened, as she was used to doing, and standing guard over the baby. She solved the problem by demanding to be let in and out of the house a dozen times a day, until Charlotte said she was ready to cut a hole in the door for the dog.

The visit from the government men—if they were government men—had us both on edge. If I saw a dust cloud when I was in the garden, I hurried to the fence to be certain it wasn't the black Buick returning. When Charlotte heard our ring on the telephone, she picked up, because she had given her publishers the number, but she answered warily, careful not to say any more than she needed to.

We had taken the baby out twice more, once to the market, another time to the goat farm. We introduced her to the dairyman, who was delighted and insisted on taking her into his own arms so he could show her the goats that provided her milk. She crowed at the sight of the black-and-white does with their floppy ears and wispy beards. They bleated, and nuzzled her bare feet, making her chortle with laughter. The dairyman planted an unabashed whiskery kiss on Emma's forehead, and I nearly wept with pride.

We kept the pink cap on her head, tied under her chin. I told myself I would get used to hiding my baby's difference until she was familiar enough to everyone that it no longer mattered. I didn't try to guess how long that might take.

I loved being treated as a young mother. It made me feel as if I belonged to the community, no longer an outcast. When Charlotte and I brought Emma to the market, Mrs. Miller smiled at me, evidently forgiving me for the months I had lived sinfully alone and unchaperoned. She promised she and her husband and all her church would pray for my adopted daughter. Mrs. Urquhardt, so many times a mother herself, planted a rubbery kiss on Emma's hand and joshed me gently about how tired I must be.

Even timid Mrs. Robbins, who never spoke above a whisper, crossed the market to congratulate me and to say in a nearly inaudible voice, "My three have grown so fast. I can pass along some hand-me-downs for your little one. Sweaters and such."

I thanked her and introduced her to Charlotte. When Mrs. Robbins had crept away with her rabbity little steps, Charlotte took charge of Emma so I could manage my sales of produce and eggs. She carried Emma around the stalls, letting her touch the stalks of Brussels sprouts and the purple leaves of kale. When we went home that afternoon, Charlotte and I were tired and sticky from the heat, but we were content with feeling we had made a success of presenting ourselves as a family, a protective aunt, an abandoned wife, an adopted baby. It was unconventional, but I felt my neighbors were accepting it. Accepting us.

The next morning, with Willow at my side, I began my ritual walking of the garden fence. I had to be vigilant to ensure the panels were intact and the posts steady. The fence was high, to keep out the deer, and the crimped wires extended four inches into the soil, to stop the rabbits and raccoons from digging under. Any hole meant critters getting in and savaging my crops or my hens. From the safety of the giant cedar tree beyond the far corner of the garden, a squirrel chittered at Willow. The dog lunged at the fence in a frenzy of barking.

"Wasting your breath, Willow," I said, laughing. "Unless you learn to climb a tree, that squirrel will always win."

She threw me a scornful glance and then raced to the side gate and stood with her nose pressed against the wire, her tail quivering, waiting for me to let her out. She hadn't been away from the house for days, so I thought I might as well let her have a run. I unlatched the gate and swung it open for her to go through. She dashed around the circumference of the garden, tongue and tail flying, making for the cedar.

I latched the gate and leaned on it for a moment, savoring the summer sun on my shoulders as I watched the mock battle between squirrel and dog. Eventually Willow gave up and wandered off toward the orchard as I turned to pinching back tomato plants.

I often lost track of time when I was working in the garden, sometimes costing myself a sunburned neck for my carelessness. That day was one of those times, as the sun rose higher in the sky and the urgency of needing to get water on my pumpkin vines began to nag at me. Charlotte rang the ship's bell at noon, which was the first time I realized I was hungry. I washed my hands and splashed my hot face at the hose bib, then strolled toward the house, watching the field for Willow to come at the call of the bell.

When she didn't come, I didn't worry at first. It was full daylight, so there was no real threat from coyotes or even the rare bobcat that wandered down from the mountains. I sat down at the kitchen table with Charlotte for a salad of greens and sliced tomatoes with hard-boiled eggs, with Emma peacefully cooing and kicking in her cradle beside us. After I ate, I lifted her onto my lap to give her a bottle, then changed her diaper and laid her back in the cradle with the bunny rattle. I went to the sink to wash the used bottle, and as I rinsed it, I peered out the kitchen window. "I wonder where Willow got to?"

Charlotte came to the sink to dry the bottle. "Do you want to go look for her?"

"I need to cut some of those sunflowers—but yes. She's been gone a long time."

Charlotte submerged her hand in the sink water and closed her eyes for a moment. "Ah. I'm sure she's fine."

I drew a relieved breath. "Are you? Good. But still..."

Charlotte made a shooing motion. "Go find her, so you'll feel better. I'll watch Emma."

Automatically, a habit now, I got the Winchester out of the closet and carried it in the crook of my elbow as I went out of the house and down the path to the gate. I called to Willow again, but if she was on the shore she wouldn't hear me, which was one reason I relied on the bell.

The tall grass in the field, burned brown by the sun, brushed my knees. Grasshoppers leaped around my boots at every step. I had rolled up the sleeves of my plaid shirt, and the sun was hot on my arms, making me eager for the coolness of the orchard. When I reached the shade of the trees, I called Willow again. I was relieved to hear an answering bark, though it was faint. It wasn't the bark she gave when she was galloping toward me or when she had something in her teeth and didn't want to put it down. This bark was short, and I thought it sounded anxious.

Hurrying, but taking care with the gun, I clambered down the bank to the strip of sand. The tide was out but just beginning to turn. The beach was littered with seaweed and driftwood, dotted by an occasional empty clamshell. The old dock looked more crooked than ever, as if the waves had loosened its supporting posts even more than the last time I had been here. I shaded my eyes to peer up and down the beach.

Willow barked again, and this time I recognized her alarm. I turned to my left, in the direction of the sound, and ran over the wet sand as fast as I dared. She might be tangled in seaweed or even stuck under a snag, and the tide could rise swiftly.

I didn't have far to go. I rounded the curve of the beach to a small cove where the bank had been eaten away by the waves. Sometimes I fished there. When the tide was high, the seawater rose to the top of the bank, bringing in the schools of fish. When the tide was out, withdrawing into the center of the canal, a crescent of wet, gravelly beach was exposed to the air. Trees and bushes growing too close to the water had drowned over time, and their roots hung over the bank like deformed limbs.

I found Willow there, struggling to tug something along the beach, to pull it out of reach of the water creeping farther up the sand with each wave. I reached down to help her.

The moment my hand touched the water a nasty sensation gripped me. It was a feeling as distinct as a blow, a clear, shocking expectation that something horrible was about to happen.

Willow was worrying at the thing she had found, growling and snarling as she tried to get hold of the sodden material. There was a lot of fabric, folds and swirls of it. Whatever color it had once been had been leached out of it by exposure. It was a dress, I thought, a long dress, cotton or perhaps linen, with a full skirt and a gathered waistband...but how had a dress washed up on the beach all by itself?

It hadn't. There was a body inside.

My mouth dried as I gazed down at it, and my stomach churned. The hem of the dress was rucked up, turned nearly inside out. It covered the body's face and head, but there was no doubt. There was a person inside. A dead person.

I didn't want to touch it. I wanted to seize a handful of Willow's fur and pull her away, leave the corpse to the water, let the tide wash it out into the peaceful depths of the Canal, where no one would find it. Where I didn't have to deal with it.

I couldn't do that, of course. It would be an abrogation of my honor. It would violate my commitment to Emma. It was only right to make myself look. To know.

I pulled Willow away from the sodden mess. She sat down on the damp sand, her eyes fixed on my face, clearly handing over the problem to me. I propped the gun on a blackened madrona root, then crouched beside the heap of ruined material. The skirt and bodice were askew, beginning to separate at the waistband, probably loosened by the movement of the water. A line of buttons ran down the back of the bodice. The hiked up skirt revealed a full cotton slip with lace edges, much deteriorated now. Algae had begun to grow at the seams of the dress, and it stained my fingers as I tried to fold the fabric back from the head.

The half-destroyed material ripped under the pressure of my fingers. I had to use both hands to tug away the shreds. My heart was thumping as if I had been running, and my lip burned where I had caught it between my teeth. I pressed my hand over my chest, preparing myself, then bent to see what lay hidden beneath the ruined dress.

The first thing I saw was hair, straight and fine, tangled now. It was several shades darker than Emma's, probably the color hers would be when she was grown. The body lay face-down in the sand, and I had to bend further to see the face. It was partly hidden by strands of wet hair, but I could see part of it, the skin as white as the belly of a dead fish. I could see only one eye, and it was open, milky and staring. Had it once been as green as Emma's? I couldn't tell. The face and neck and shoulders, all that I could see of them, were swollen but not disfigured. At the side of the head was a horrid, deep gash, but any blood there had been was long washed away.

"Oh, you poor thing," I said, half under my breath, as if the sound of my voice could disturb her sleep.

She wasn't asleep, obviously. There was no question that she was dead. Had been dead a long time. Her skin was waxy, and it looked as if it would dent, perhaps even break, if I touched it with a finger. I didn't.

I couldn't help wishing I didn't have to prove to myself who she was, but I knew better.

I needed to see only one thing to be certain. I clenched my teeth against the queasiness of my stomach, dropped to my knees in the wet sand, and gingerly lifted up the one earlobe I could see. The flesh was icy to the touch and slightly rubbery, like a fragment of the ropes of kelp lying on the beach.

It was there. A gill, damaged by water and time and trauma. It was bluish, puffy at the edges but perfectly recognizable.

In the event, having faced what I had to do and then doing it, my stomach settled and my heartbeat calmed. I wasn't revolted by the appearance and feel of death. I wasn't afraid of it, either.

What I felt as I gazed at what had to be the remains of Emma's mother was a soul-deep sorrow. This dead woman had surely loved her precious infant as much as I now did. As much as I had loved my own Scottie. She wouldn't have wanted to leave her baby. She wouldn't have done so on purpose.

Willow pressed her cold nose against my cheek and whined. I looked up and realized she was warning me. The tide was sliding up the beach, marking the dark sand with white foam, each wave a little closer than the last. There wasn't time for reflection. I had to do something to stop the body from being washed out into the canal.

It seemed best to use the dress as a sort of sled. I folded the disintegrating fabric back over the remains as best I could and tried to find a handful that wouldn't tear when I pulled. When I thought I had one, I came to my feet and began moving backward, tugging. It was a sort of primitive method, but I couldn't see another way. The rising tide gave me no time to devise something more efficient.

The corpse was more awkward than heavy, tangled in the ruined clothes. The material of my makeshift sled caught on stones and bits of driftwood, slowing my progress. More than once it gave way, tearing into ragged pieces, and I had to find new purchase for my hands in order to keep moving. I didn't dare try to lift the body itself. I was afraid the whole thing, in its deteriorated state, would come to pieces.

I struggled backward, bent at the waist. The small of my back burned with effort, and my hat fell off twice. I jammed it back on my head, heedless of grit in my hair. Willow followed as I worked my way around the curve of the beach to a point where I thought I could pull the body up over the lip of the bank. I tried not to think of the desecration that might cause. I may have muttered an apology. I know I thought of one.

Before I took that final step, I trotted back to the cove for the .30–30. Willow stayed beside the corpse, keeping watch in her uncanny way. When I returned, I climbed up the cut in the bank, set the gun on dry ground, and then lay on my stomach to reach for the burden. Inch by inch, I wriggled the whole thing up the cut. Twice I lost my hold and had to climb back down to refold what was left of the material before resuming my belly-down position. It seemed vital to accomplish this task, to get the body out of reach of the tide. I didn't look at her face again.

I guessed I had been gone from the house at least an hour by the time the shrouded body lay safely at the foot of one of the pines. Drooping branches half-hid it from view. I picked up the gun, said, "Willow, come on. Home," and set off at a trot toward the house.

Charlotte was waiting on the back porch, smoking and frowning. When Willow and I came up the path, she said, "Thank goodness! You were gone so long I got worried."

"It's okay," I panted. "We're okay, but—things have gotten complicated."

We talked about it for a long time, drinking tea at the dining room table. I had abandoned the rest of my garden chores for the day.

"Those government men would love this," Charlotte said.

"We can't tell them, Aunt Charlotte! They'll take Emma from me. I couldn't bear it."

"I couldn't, either," she said. "We won't tell them anything." She shook out a cigarette, stuck it between her lips, and put her lighter to it. She had been smoking nonstop since I got back from the canal. "They're coming back, though."

"Are you sure?"

"Oh, yes. Quite sure. We need to take care of this, before someone else sees the . . . the . . ."

"The body."

"The body." She waved her cigarette, sending a tendril of smoke wafting toward the open window. "If anyone finds it and calls this CIA or whatever they say they are, we'll have trouble on our hands."

"You mean they'll want Emma."

Her mouth twisted. "You need to understand she's the sort of thing they're looking for. Because of Roswell."

"What?"

"Roswell. There was a crash there."

"I thought it was Maury Island."

"Roswell was after. They recovered one of those airships, and apparently there were people—well, beings—inside."

"How do you know these things, Aunt Charlotte?"

She puffed on her cigarette. "Newspapers," she said. "I kept that one, because I was sure this was going to come up again."

"But why doesn't everyone—I mean, surely if that had happened, everyone would be talking about it!"

"The government covered it up, and quickly. That's why I kept the paper. These men will never admit to anything."

"Even so, that has nothing to do with Emma, does it?"

"No, it doesn't. But they won't see it that way, kiddo."

"She's just a baby!"

"They won't care that she's a baby. They'd take one look and have her in one of their labs in a heartbeat. Wherever they took those other poor creatures."

The idea struck me dumb with horror. When a truck rumbled by on the road below the lane, we froze, staring at each other and listening to the motor's roar grow closer and closer, slumping in relief as it faded. The telephone rang twice, but neither one was my ring. I fed Emma and rocked her in my lap as I worried over the problem, like Willow worrying a bone.

Finally, when Emma had fallen asleep again, I said, "We can't leave the body out there. The critters will get to her."

"Do you know for sure it's a female?"

"I know. I didn't look, but I know. The water..."

"The water told you. Good, Barrie Anne. That's good."

"I think she's... She was... Emma's mother. The hair, the—" I broke off. I still had trouble saying it.

"Gills, Barrie Anne. It's not a dirty word. Emma has gills. You're saying this woman does, too."

"Yes. She does."

It was something of a relief to speak it aloud. Emma's differences—her gills—weren't going to go away because I didn't like acknowledging them. Twice more I had watched her sink beneath the water, grinning up at me as bubbles rose around her face. It was mesmerizing, and confounding, to watch her. I had to fight the instinct to snatch her out of the water and into the safety of the air. Each time I let her stay underwater for a few more seconds, while my heart banged in my chest and I could barely breathe myself.

I rubbed my tired eyes. "Aunt Charlotte, we're dealing with something we can't understand; I know that. We just have to do what needs doing."

"You don't want to find the explanation? Solve the mystery?"

"I don't think I do."

"Because you're afraid."

I had to think about that for a time. "Yes, I guess I am. I'm afraid for both of us. I'm afraid I'll lose her. I'm afraid someone will take her away from me. I'm afraid some mad scientist will turn her into an experiment. I don't care where she came from or what she is. She's my child. The rest of it doesn't matter."

Softly, Charlotte said, "It might matter to her one day."

I rose, Emma in my arms, and nestled her into her cradle. I stood for a moment, looking down at her, my hands in the pockets of my overalls. I murmured, "She's safe for now. That's what I care about."

This time, trudging back through the field to the orchard, I carried a shovel instead of the gun, and I had a roll of canvas slung over my shoulder. I wore the work gloves I saved for fence repair and cleaning the chicken coop. Charlotte, with Emma in her arms, came after me, while Willow bounded ahead.

The afternoon was winding to its end, but the air was still close and hot. The sun slanted through the apple trees onto the brittle yellow grasses of the field and glinted on the water in the distance, inviting glimpses of cool blue. It would have been nice to go to the canal, to wade in the shallows, to splash salt water on Emma's toes, but I knew there was no time to waste.

We found the half-disintegrated mound of material where I had left it two hours before. I dropped my shovel and the roll of canvas. Wordlessly, Charlotte handed me the baby and then crouched down in the soft layer of pine needles to pull away the dress fabric and look beneath it. I kept my distance. Once had been enough.

"Funny that it doesn't smell," Charlotte said.

"Smells of salt water."

"Yes, that, but not—not rot. Decomposition."

"I think that's because of the water."

"Right." Charlotte gave the dead body the same examination I had, lifting an earlobe with one long finger. Afterward, she bowed her head for a moment above the remains of Emma's mother. As she covered the face and head again, I heard her murmur, "Rest in peace, sister."

I whispered, "What did you say, Aunt Charlotte?"

"Never mind." She got to her feet and reached for Emma. Her expression was drawn, but her voice was steady.

I wanted to press her about what she had said over the body, but I felt the pressure of time, and of the snooping of the government men. We had talked about this, and decided the only thing we could think of to do was to bury the body. If Woods and Harrison, or men like them, came poking around the farm again, we couldn't risk their finding it. We also knew if we didn't inter the remains deeply enough, the scavengers would have it out again all too soon.

I spread out the canvas, and Charlotte set Emma on the mat of leaves while she helped me gingerly lift the body onto it. It was such a relief to cover it up, to wrap the brown canvas around the remains so we didn't have to look at them anymore. It looked almost decent when I was done, very nearly respectable enough for a funeral, except for the bits of cord I had used to secure it.

"It looks as if we're going to bury it at sea," I said.

"I don't think she'll mind," Charlotte answered. She had picked up Emma again. The baby seemed to have caught our solemn mood, turning her green eyes from one to the other. Willow, too, lay with her head on her paws, her ears drooping.

Charlotte said quietly, "We might as well get started. Why don't you dig for a while? If you get tired, I'll take a turn."

The roots of the apple trees crisscrossed the orchard, leaving almost no space between. I soon learned they made the ground all but impenetrable. I tried, jamming the shovel between roots and leaning on the handle, trying for purchase. I struggled that way for an hour but achieved no more than a shallow trench. Emma had fallen asleep, but she began to stir and whimper for her bottle.

I stopped digging and leaned on the shovel. My back ached, and my arms trembled with the unaccustomed labor.

"It's not going to work," Charlotte said. "The ground's too hard."

"We need to get it—her—to the garden, where the soil is soft. I can dig there."

"How do we do that?"

I blew out a long breath. "It's hardly dignified, but I'm going to have to use the wheelbarrow."

"Kiddo, I think the poor thing is long past worrying about dignity."

"Hope so." I shouldered the shovel. "I'll go get it. Can you stay? Watch over her?"

"Yes. See if Willow will stay, too. I'd feel better."

That part was easy. Willow watched me as I walked away but made no move to follow. I trudged back to the house with perspiration trickling down my neck and my ribs. I rolled the wheelbarrow out of the shed and trundled it with difficulty across the field. Its iron wheels caught in the tall grass and juddered over rocks. By the time I reached Charlotte, with Emma now squirming in her arms, I was exhausted.

As Charlotte propped Emma against a tree root so she could assist me, the baby began to wail in earnest. Willow crept close to her, dragging her belly through the hard dirt. She laid her chin over Emma's feet and the baby's wails died away at once. It was one more strange event in a day full of strangeness, but there was no time to contemplate it.

Charlotte took one end of the shroud, and I took the other. She said, "One, two, three," and we hoisted it unceremoniously into the wheelbarrow. I could feel the contents shift inside. My bit of canvas was hardly a substitute for a proper coffin.

Charlotte picked up the baby as I took the handles of the wheelbarrow.

"Nothing you can do to help now," I said. "This will take me a few minutes. You can go ahead and feed Emma."

"You're too tired to finish this today," Charlotte said.

"True, but I'll have to get the wheelbarrow inside the shed, at least. Out of sight."

She pursed her lips, nodding in acknowledgment of the necessity and started off toward the house. Willow trotted after her, as if she didn't trust Charlotte with Emma. I smiled briefly over that, then gritted my teeth, lifted the handles of the wheelbarrow, and followed.

The remains had been unwieldy and slippery, but they weren't heavy. I bumped the wheelbarrow back across the field with no more difficulty than I had when it was empty. I had to stop myself from apologizing to its contents once or twice, when the wheels grated across a stone. My hens ran to meet me as I came in through the garden gate, and I shooed them back toward their coop. I managed to maneuver the wheelbarrow and its burden into the garden shed and closed the door with weary relief.

When I went into the house, Charlotte was just putting Emma's bottle into soapy water. Emma was drowsing in her cradle, Willow keeping watch beside her. Charlotte said, "That dog has decided she's responsible for the baby, I think."

"It does seem that way." I went to the sink to splash water on my face and neck and rub myself dry with a towel.

As I hung the towel on its hook, Charlotte said, "Looks like we'll be burying Emma's mother in your garden."

"Afraid so."

"Do you want a marker?"

I shook my head. "Better not. It might attract attention."

Charlotte gave a wheezy laugh and pulled out her cigarettes. "Life is getting weirder by the minute," she said, as she pulled one out of the pack with her fingernails. "Makes you wonder what's coming next."

"Too much to hope this is the end of it, I suppose."

She grinned through a cloud of smoke. "You can hope, Barrie Anne. Always good to hope. Just don't count on it."

11

May 1945

The papers were full of the news of victory in Europe. Charlotte already took the *Tribune* and the *Times*, and she bought copies of the *P-I* at the drugstore, eager not to miss any detail of the surrender. People gathered on street corners and clustered in stores, chattering with friends and strangers over Hitler's suicide and Germany's defeat.

The AWS had been decommissioned the year before, but I had stayed on as a volunteer to settle any details or answer any questions that came up from our service. I was glad of that, glad to still have something I could do, glad to have those quiet hours in my little cement bunker.

I arrived home from Tibbals Hill one warm spring evening to find Charlotte in the garden, lounging on the weathered bench with a stack of newspapers on her lap, a cigarette in one hand, a gin rickey in the other. Behind her the rhododendron was at its peak, blossoms shining like pink stars above her head. The air was sweet with the scent of new leaves, and as I came down the path, a rufous hummingbird flashed between the camellia bush and the old cedar tree, a tiny arrow of scarlet and green.

"You look happy," I told Charlotte. I settled beside her and accepted a sip of her drink.

"Feeling damned cheerful," she said, brandishing her glass. "The Germans are done. Truman says Japan will fall before the summer's over. Things will pick up then."

Her work had been slow since the war, with paper and other supplies rationed. She never said much about money, but I had seen her poring over bills, and once I heard her on the telephone with the utility company, arranging an extension on the electric bill.

"I should get another job," I said. "We'll need the money."

"Nope. You're going back to school." Charlotte gave me a fierce, Revlon Raven Red grin, and brandished her cigarette. "Then when you have your teaching degree, we'll fix up the house. And this disgrace of a garden!" She laughed, tossed off the rest of her gin rickey, and got to her feet. "Are you hungry?"

I was, but my appetite didn't last long. As we were about to go in through the kitchen door, a voice spoke from beyond the gate. A man's voice, a voice I knew, though it sounded different from the way I remembered it.

"Barrie? Are you there? Barrie, it's me."

Charlotte and I both stopped in our tracks. She was walking

ahead of me, and she whirled to fix me with a wide-eyed gaze. I felt the blood drain from my face. My hands and feet went cold.

He called again. "Barrie?"

I had to force myself to move. I stumbled past Charlotte, taking stiff, reluctant steps along the path through the garden. He was waiting just outside the gate. The red jalopy, caked with dust, was parked behind him. We hadn't heard the motor above our conversation.

I've never seen a man so changed, from that day to this. He had been lean, but now he was bone-thin, his face marked with the sort of lines that develop when there's no fat at all beneath the skin. The shock of fair hair I had admired, that Randolph Scott look, was limp, even greasy. His glasses were askew on his nose, and there was an ugly piece of tape holding them together at the left temple.

It was that tape that told me how bad things were. The Will I knew was proud and meticulous about his appearance. He would never—

"Barrie," he said. He was facing me from outside the gate, but his eyes were on my feet. His voice scraped, as if his throat was dry. "Are you going to let me in?"

I stared at him, shocked into silence. Charlotte had come up beside me. She was reaching for the latch, but when I suddenly found my voice she snatched her hand back. With the full force of two years of resentment and confusion, I shouted. "Where the *hell* have you been?"

Will—this Will who was so little like the man I had loved

and married that I barely recognized him—threw up a hand to protect his face, as if my cry had been a blow. He swayed and clutched at the gate. His body folded over itself, and he came to his knees in the dry grass beside the fence.

Charlotte said, "Oops," and yanked the gate open. She bent to pull Will to his feet. From where I stood, I saw the icy whiteness of his face and the helpless drooping of his eyelids.

Charlotte said, "Come along with you, then," as if he was a child who had fallen down. I suppose at that moment he seemed that way, vulnerable, helpless. Supporting him with her shoulder, an arm around his waist, she assisted him in through the gate and along the path. She gestured to me with her chin. "Kiddo, better dig up some sandwich makings. Looks to me like he needs food."

I ran ahead of them into the house, leaving the door open behind me. With shaking hands, I took bread from the bread box and uncovered the butter dish. I turned, pressing my back to the counter as Charlotte helped Will in through the door and helped him slide into the nook. He slumped over the table, his head in his hands. I gazed at him in frozen dismay.

Charlotte shook her head at me, and murmured, "Never mind. We'll talk in a bit." She crossed to the icebox and took out the milk bottle. "Let's start with this," she said.

Will drank the big glass of milk she poured for him, draining it in one long, convulsive swallow. I pulled myself together enough to make a cheese sandwich, which he ate in four giant bites, so quickly I thought he might choke. His color improved almost at once, and when Charlotte set a plate of butter cookies in front of him, he devoured them all.

Throughout his hasty, desperate meal, I stood by the sink, my arms folded, watching him. I felt nothing for this man whose name I carried. No tenderness. No affection. No gladness at his presence. I didn't even feel sympathy for his physical miseries.

What I felt was resentment at his having interrupted our evening. And fury, because his current dependent state was yet another way for him to manipulate me. To control me.

I wished he had never come back.

Will didn't say very much except to mutter, "Sorry. I've been sick," as we guided him upstairs to my bedroom, more or less poured him onto my bed, and covered him with a light blanket. He was sound asleep before we were out the door.

In the kitchen, Charlotte and I took our usual places in the nook and stared at each other. "What do you want to do?" she finally asked.

My mind skittered away from what it meant to have Will here, Will reappearing after two years of silence, sick, helpless, dependent. "I don't know." I twisted my fingers together and scowled out into the twilight gathering over the town. The happiness of the day, the relief we all felt at the end of the war, had drained away the moment I heard Will's voice outside the gate.

Charlotte said, "He looks terrible. I'm guessing he hasn't eaten in a while."

"He's dehydrated, too," I said. "I've seen runners who look like that. Gray skin, circles under the eyes, muscle weakness."

"I suppose we can't really decide anything until he wakes up."

"I suppose not, but..." I twisted my fingers the other way, so hard my knuckles hurt.

"What?"

I released my hands, and rested my chin on one fist, gazing ruefully at my aunt. "I'm supposed to be happy. My husband's home from the war. He's not injured, at least not that I can see. A normal wife—a good wife—would be thrilled."

"Even if he's not a good husband?"

"But...he's hardly had a chance to be a good husband. A few weeks was all we had, and maybe...maybe he's changed."

Her mouth twisted, but she said, "It could be. Sure. Men are often changed by war."

I thought but didn't say, *Not always for the best*. We understood each other. We didn't need to speak it aloud.

I spent the night on the couch in Charlotte's studio, though I didn't sleep much. I lay in the paint-scented darkness, remembering the odd dreams I had experienced in San Diego, when I felt as if I couldn't breathe. Will's presence in the next room made me anxious and restive. I felt as if a long-vanquished fear had been suddenly revived, destroying my hard-won peace of mind.

I was already awake when I heard Will stirring in my bedroom. I hurried to the bathroom, then went downstairs to start coffee. I had to be at work in two hours, but I hated leaving Charlotte to deal with Will. I had a half-formed idea, conceived in the wee hours, that he and I could talk, and I could settle things with him before I had to go.

The percolator was bubbling, and I had bread sliced and ready for the toaster by the time Will came down the stairs. He looked much better than he had the night before, though still gaunt and in need of a shave and a shower. He stood in the doorway to the kitchen, his head hanging, looking at me from beneath his brows. The taped glasses looked even more pitiful in the morning light.

"Did you sleep?" I asked, as I set mugs on the banquette table.

"I did, thanks," he said. His voice sounded more like the old Will now, that deep timbre that had once made my skin tingle. "First good night's sleep I've had in weeks."

The percolator gurgled to a stop, and I unplugged it to bring it to the table. I poured coffee in each of our mugs, set the bottle of cream between us, and slid into the nook. Will sidled in opposite me and picked up his cup with a nod of thanks. For a short time we both sipped, taking turns looking out the window into the sunlit greenery, avoiding each other's eyes.

At last I set my cup on the table with a decisive click and said, "Okay, Will. I have to go to work soon, so you'd better tell me now."

He pushed his glasses up on his nose, and his mouth worked beneath his ragged mustache. It seemed he couldn't find words to explain himself. He looked so pitiful that I made an effort to moderate my voice, to speak more gently. "You really don't look well."

"I know. I looked in the bathroom mirror." He set down his own cup and wrapped his long fingers around it. "I'm going to need a razor."

It was an odd moment. I can see now, looking back, how strange it was, how utterly presumptuous, but at the time it seemed almost natural, a husband telling his wife he needed a razor. I looked into my coffee cup, biting my lip in confusion. I didn't offer to get him the razor. I also didn't tell him he would have to get his own razor.

For the first time in months, I thought of Peggy and Sally. If George had disappeared for two years without a word, Sally would have collapsed. Henry would never have done such a thing, but if he had... What would Peggy have said to him? She loved him so much, I imagined she would have forgiven him anything.

I didn't feel that way. I stared into Will's hollow eyes for a hard moment. "Where have you been?"

His eyes widened, and he tucked his chin as if preparing for a fight. "Aren't you glad I'm home safe?"

I snapped, "Do you know how long ago your last letter was?"

He pushed at his glasses. "I do," he said. "I'm so sorry. I kept meaning to write you, but I was so ill."

"Ill?"

"I'll explain, but—see, I was going to write, but—then I

realized I just needed to come home. Speak to you in person. I drove from San Diego to Seattle, where my car was—then straight over on the ferry. I probably should have stopped somewhere. Rested. Especially since I've been sick."

"Do you know what your parents wrote to me?"

He blinked. "My parents?"

"Yes, Will! Your parents! Your mother and your father. They don't even know we're married!"

He took off his broken glasses and fiddled with the earpiece. "No."

"You told me they couldn't come to our wedding because of the harvest."

"That was true. I mean, I knew it would be true. I didn't want to put any pressure on them when they were so busy and start off with them resenting you. See, I thought it would all be easier once it was done, and they met you and loved you—the way I do." He laid his glasses on the table and pressed the heels of his hands to his eyes. "You don't understand—you couldn't know what it was like over there."

"Then tell me."

"Those of you who stayed home—you can't imagine how ghastly it was."

I saw how his fingers trembled. I heard the way his breath scraped in his throat. Whatever his story might be, whatever had happened to him, he was in rough shape. That was obvious. I folded my arms tightly against my belly. "I'm sorry," I said inadequately.

He dropped his hands and looked me full in the face for the

first time. "I'll tell you all about it, Barrie. Just—not right now, okay? I can't bear to think about it. I'm exhausted."

There it was again. There was the assumption that he could walk back into his life—our lives—as if the silence of the past two years meant nothing.

I made another mistake that morning. I didn't tell him he couldn't stay. I didn't demand to know why he hadn't told his parents about me. I didn't tell him our marriage was over. He looked as miserable and vulnerable as a lost child, and I didn't say anything.

I heard the scratch of a match and looked up to see Charlotte in the doorway to the kitchen, putting the flame to a cigarette. Her expression was as grim as I'm sure my own was.

I slid out of the nook, my arms still tight across my midriff. "I have to go to work," I said, to the room in general.

Will said, "Couldn't you take today off, at least?"

"We're still at war with Japan, Will. I have responsibilities." It was a bit of an exaggeration. My responsibilities could wait a day, or more, but I needed to get away to think. To be alone.

He looked as if he was about to say something more, but Charlotte intervened. "Go and shower, kiddo. I'll see to Will." Her lips twisted, as if the name tasted bitter in her mouth. I cast her a despairing glance as I left the room. Her answering gaze was as angry as I had ever seen it.

As it happened, I found no peace in my cozy concrete bunker that day. When I left the house, Charlotte was staring at Will with her hands on her hips, and he was eating toast, ignoring her. I didn't say goodbye to either of them, but made my escape. I had hoped I would gain some clarity on my ride to the fort. I liked riding my bicycle, enjoyed the exercise, loved listening to the gulls crying overhead and the occasional hoot of a ferry going through a fog bank. It was different that day. I felt heavy, weighed down by guilt and confusion. Clarity didn't come. I passed the hours in that little room dutifully organizing reports and clearing away the last details of our work, but I fretted endlessly over what I was going to do. What Charlotte and I were going to do.

It was late afternoon before I came to the conclusion that I would have to tell Will to leave. I rehearsed the conversation in my head, over and over. I would say, I decided, that the house wasn't mine but my aunt's. I would say that she had taken me in for almost three years but that we were barely scraping by. I would press him to tell me where he had been and why he hadn't told his family about me, and I would say he had to go.

I couldn't imagine what his response would be. In truth, I didn't think I knew him anymore. My thoughts spun like bees around a rosebush.

I hated the idea of being a divorcée at the age of twenty-four. It was fine for Hedy Lamarr, but Hollywood people had different standards from ordinary people. The people in my small town would whisper behind my back, or stop talking the moment I came into the Mercantile or the soda fountain. I would be an outsider once again. Different from them. Unconventional. Not normal.

I cycled home with these miserable thoughts whirling in my head. I was numb to the beauties of the spring evening, full of dread over the confrontation to come. A solitary raven followed me, dipping this way and that, and its glossy blackness against the fading blue sky felt like an omen.

Will's jalopy was still parked behind Charlotte's De Soto, but now it sparkled, and so did the De Soto. Warily, I opened the gate and walked up the path. The sight of freshly laundered clothes neatly pinned to the clothesline beside the house startled me. I went in through the kitchen door and found a vase of store-bought tulips on the kitchen counter. Charlotte came down the stairs as I was shrugging out of my coat.

She was wearing her best trousers and a linen blouse. Her lipstick was fresh, and her hair was pinned up. "It seems we're going out to dinner," she said.

I dropped my handbag onto a chair. "What's going on?"

Charlotte shrugged and opened the drawer where she kept her cigarettes. When her Pall Mall was alight, she said, "I think your husband is trying to make amends."

"Where is he?"

"Upstairs, in the shower. He washed the cars, did laundry, went to the barber and the Mercantile." She tilted her head toward the flowers. "He brought those."

"That doesn't sound like Will."

She made a wry mouth. "Maybe you were right. Maybe he's changed."

I spread my hands and shook my head, at a loss.

She said, "Yeah. Me, too. In any case, he announced to me

when he came back that he wanted to take us both out. It wasn't my place to say no, or to say anything else, for that matter."

"You didn't talk today?"

"Nope. You should go and change."

I hesitated at the bottom of the stairs, but before I could decide, Will came out of my bedroom and started down toward me.

He was still too thin, of course, but his hair looked as it had before he went into the navy, clean and shining and thick. He had managed a new pair of glasses, black frames that exaggerated the blueness of his eyes. He held himself soldier-straight, and as he gave me a brilliant smile, a twinge of the old feeling flickered in my heart. I began to doubt myself, and the uncertain ground on which my resolve had rested began to shift and soften, like the sand on the beach at Fort Worden.

"Barrie," he said, reaching out his hand to me. His expression was one of pure contrition. His blue eyes glistened with it, and his mouth looked bruised and sad. "I have so much to tell you and a lot to make up for. Will you let me try?"

There was something about that hand, so masculine, so confident, that shook me. The past two and a half years had been devoid of masculinity. We had been a house—a town, even—of women. The touch of a man felt unfamiliar. The smell of aftershave and Brylcreem seemed to belong to another age.

Will's fingers closed around mine, and he bent his head to kiss my cheek. "It's marvelous to be here again, Barrie," he whispered. He pressed his lips to my hair and murmured, "I hope you'll give me another chance."

My mind spun. My tongue wouldn't work. Had I been mistaken? Had I misunderstood him from the beginning?

It was a masterful performance. After I had changed into a skirt and sweater, Will escorted Charlotte and me out to the jalopy. He didn't say much, except that he wanted to thank us for taking him in the night before. We didn't say much, either. I was dizzy with confusion, and I saw suspicion in Charlotte's face.

He helped Aunt Charlotte squeeze into the tiny back seat and held the passenger door for me. He drove to the waterfront and parked the jalopy in front of the Belmont hotel, a place Charlotte and I had never set foot in. We took a white linen–covered table by the window, looking out over Port Townsend Bay.

"Gin rickey, isn't it, Miss Blythe?" Will said to Charlotte. "What about you, Barrie?"

I was shaking my head. "Will. How can we afford this?" I didn't realize until too late that I had said "we." I should have said "you." But that was the way it went.

He said, "I saved up all my back pay. I haven't spent a cent of it."

After a time, Charlotte began to relax, softened by two gin rickeys. She propped her elbow on the arm of her chair, smoking and watching Will performing at his very best. I was softened, too, both by the glass of white wine he ordered for me and by his attentiveness. He told me how fit I looked, how pretty my new shorter haircut was. He reminded me of places we'd gone together in San Diego, and I remembered why I had fallen in love. I didn't exactly feel that I was in love again, but I felt *something*. Any emotion seemed better than the numbness that had gripped me earlier in the day, even if it was an emotion I couldn't quite name.

The three of us made conversation the way normal people do. We talked about the weather, admired the beauty of the setting sun over Port Townsend Bay. We lamented the price of gasoline and sugar. We wondered when the Japanese would surrender. I drank more wine. Will nursed a single beer throughout the evening.

I glanced around the hotel's elegant dining room and couldn't help thinking that Will—who was still my husband, after all—was the best-looking man in the room. There weren't a lot of men there, of course. So many were still fighting. The men present were old, past their years of military service. Will looked young, fresh, dramatically virile in comparison.

I had made a terrible mistake, leaving school to marry Will. I had admitted that, to myself and to Charlotte. Sitting in the window of the Belmont, being served a dinner of steamed clams and seared filet, I allowed myself to hope I could put everything right.

When we reached home, Charlotte said good night, and climbed the stairs. I made a pot of coffee, at Will's request, and he and I sat opposite each other in the nook, coffee cups between us. I had turned off the overhead light. The kitchen was dim except for slender shafts of moonlight that illumined the coffeepot, the hanging pots and pans, and the lenses of Will's spectacles.

He gave me a sorrowful glance. "I need to explain to you, Barrie."

"Yes, you do."

"It's been bad."

The glow I had felt at the Belmont had faded. I felt headachy from the long, tense day and scratchy-eyed from not sleeping much the night before. I took a single sip of coffee and propped my chin on my hand as I gazed out into the starlit garden.

"I know I should have written. I meant to, and then I was so sick. I kept thinking I'd write as soon as I felt better, but... Barrie, it's hard to explain."

"You'll have to try," I said. "You were sick?"

"That was part of it. I caught some parasite when the ship was involved in the battle of Tarawa. It was horrible to get rid of."

I glanced at him without turning my head. "Are you over it now?"

"I think so." He tasted his coffee and gave me a rueful look. "This is marvelous. God, I've missed good coffee. That navy slop is terrible."

I was determined not to be sidetracked. "What's the other part, Will? You said being sick was one part of it."

"The other part is much worse." He slumped over his coffee cup and rubbed his forehead with his fingers. "I'm so ashamed of it." He drew a shaky breath and straightened as if it took effort to sit up. He gazed into the shining surface of the coffee as he said, "Oh, Barrie. I had battle fatigue."

"Battle fatigue?" It didn't sound right, a corpsman having battle fatigue, but I didn't know enough to ask the right questions. "Will, I don't understand. When were you in battle?"

"It wasn't me, not actually *in* the battle, but it was the ship. The men who were in the battle were brought to the ship, and—and I had to treat the casualties." He still stared into his coffee cup as he spoke, and his voice throbbed with emotion. "You can't imagine—I don't even want you to imagine it, Barrie. I don't want to put such unpleasant ideas in your head. Young men blown to bits. Head wounds. Gut wounds. The floor of the sick bay would be so slick with blood our shoes would slip in it."

"That's horrible. But you wanted that, didn't you? To be a medical corpsman? To be a doctor?"

He shook his head. "Not now. I can't." He looked up, his eyes looking very dark through the lenses of his spectacles. "I'm not proud of it, Barrie, believe me. I tell myself that if I hadn't been sick, I would have been stronger. Would have been able to face it." He took off his glasses and wiped his eyes with his sleeve. "I'm afraid I—I broke down."

"Broke down?"

"Collapsed." He replaced his glasses. "Right in the sick bay. I don't remember much about it, I'm afraid. They discharged me. Put me off in Pearl, in the hospital."

"Why didn't someone let me know you were in the hospital?"

A shrug. "I can't say. Wartime, I suppose. Records get misplaced, lost."

I slid out of the nook and crossed to the counter. We had stowed the letter from Mrs. Sweet in the drawer beneath the telephone. I hadn't answered it, of course. There was nothing I could say to her. I pulled it out, took the single sheet from the cheap envelope, and laid it in front of Will.

"This is what your mother wrote to me."

He squinted through the half light, lifting the sheet close to his eyes. He sighed and started to crumple up the sheet. I snatched it away from him. Part of it tore, and he watched the fragment flutter to the surface of the table.

"This is the way my mother is," he said grimly. "She's angry. That's why I couldn't tell my parents we were getting married. I knew they'd be critical, mean, say horrible mean things to you. I didn't want our marriage to start that way."

I retrieved the fragment, smoothed the pieces together, and slid them back into the envelope. As I put it back into the drawer, Will said, "Barrie, please. I know it's all hard to grasp. The war has made everything so crazy! But will you give me another chance?"

When I turned, he was standing close behind me, his lean form silhouetted by moonlight. I was shivering, more from fatigue than from cold. Will encircled me with his arms and pulled me close to him, cradling my head against his chest. "We can still do it," he murmured. "We can be the perfect couple. Make a home together. Build a life."

I wanted to resist him. I wanted time to think, to consider what it all meant, but he was right—the war had made everything crazy. I couldn't find my way through the maze of my feelings.

And I had so longed to be part of a perfect couple. Have my

own home. Fit into the community the way I thought other couples did, respectable couples. Normal ones.

I hadn't decided anything, but I allowed him to hold me. It seemed cruel to push him away. He murmured into my hair, "Thank you, Barrie. I'll make it up to you. I promise."

12

August 11, 1947

I left Emma with Charlotte and went out to the garden early in the morning, when the soil was still damp with dew and the sun was just rising over the peninsula. I took my shovel from the garden shed, taking care not to look too closely at the wheelbarrow and its tragic contents. I set to work as far from the house as I could, in the corner where the big cedar cast its shade. Not much could grow in that sunless spot. The hens didn't even bother looking there for the bugs and worms they loved.

Willow, having made certain Charlotte was watching over the baby, came outside with me. She gazed up into the cedar branches in hopes of rousing her eternal squirrel enemy as I got to work.

Digging in the tilled soil of the garden was much easier than it had been in the orchard. With the protection of the garden fence, I wasn't worried about coyotes or other predators digging up my unsavory cache. I thought a three-foot trench should be deep enough.

I dug for two hours, achieving a grave about three feet deep and six feet long. Charlotte came out with a cup of coffee in one hand, Emma braced on her opposite hip. I peered up at her through the glare of sunshine and realized Charlotte hadn't done her eyebrows or painted her lips. Days had gone by since she last used makeup, and the dearth of it made her face look softer. It was nice to appreciate the fine texture of her skin. Her clear complexion was lovely beneath the rich brown of her hair. I told her that, which made her laugh and make some self-deprecating remark about her age.

She had put Emma in one of the new rompers from the Mercantile. The baby looked like a Kewpie doll, a scarf around her head, her green eyes vivid in her pink and cream face.

Charlotte handed me the coffee cup and then stood in the shade with the sleepy baby in her arms. She gazed morosely into the gaping hole. "It doesn't seem right to just drop the ... the remains in there, does it?"

"No. Nothing we can do about a coffin, though."

"I know."

"We could at least put a blanket over the canvas. Once it's in."

"I'd feel better about it." Charlotte shifted the baby to her other hip, and Emma gurgled a small protest. "Do you want me to find one?"

"If you don't mind. There are some old blankets in the chest in my bedroom. I'll get the—the wheelbarrow."

Charlotte started off through the garden but then turned

back. "Know what, Barrie Anne? The woman is dead. We're giving her the best burial we can. I don't want you to feel squeamish about it."

"I don't want you to feel squeamish, either."

Her lips twisted. "I don't, usually. This is just bizarre."

"Isn't it, though?" I shook my head, laid down my shovel, and turned to the garden shed. I was doing my best to be practical. I knew well that death comes for all of us, eventually. As a farmer, I understood that better than most. My hens sometimes died. The fish I caught gave up their lives so we could eat. I didn't shoot game, but I didn't hesitate to cook it when someone gave me a bit of venison or a wild duck.

An insight came to me as I maneuvered the wheelbarrow with its sad burden out of the shed and around the edge of the garden to the hole I had dug. I realized that what troubled me so, aside from the obvious, was my awareness that the broken, lifeless woman, wrapped in her shroud of canvas, could have been Emma. My Emma, so sweet and so beloved. I hoped I could exorcise that demon thought by making the burial as respectful as possible.

I couldn't bring myself to just tip the wheelbarrow over and let the remains plop into the grave. I wrestled with the bundle once again, trying to be gentle as I slid it out of the wheelbarrow and onto the mound of dirt next to the trench. I wriggled one end and then the other toward the grave and climbed in to lift the whole down to the bottom. It felt strange in my arms, cold and heavy, clearly lifeless yet heartbreakingly fragile.

Charlotte returned with the blanket, and I smoothed it over the tied canvas, tucking in the sides and the ends as if I were making a bed. My hands were gentle, though I knew that effort was for me, and not for the woman being laid to rest.

Charlotte gave me a hand to help me climb out, and the two of us stood for several moments without speaking as we contemplated the final resting place of a person we would never know and could never understand. The silence was broken when Emma gave an excited cry and kicked her feet against Charlotte's arm. We looked up to see what had attracted her.

A flock of crows was circling above us, a dozen or more of the black birds, their spread wings shining in the midday sun.

We saw lots of crows on the peninsula. They were clever, frequently irritating birds that seemed to know our habits and loved to turn them to their own advantage. When I was picking berries, I had to shoo them away or they would help themselves to my baskets. When we put things on the trash pile to be burned later, they would scatter the garbage in search of edible bits. If we scolded them, they scolded back and seemed to laugh at our efforts.

This performance was uncanny, though. They squawked and cawed, settling onto the branches of the cedar, lifting into the air, circling, settling again in some pattern that made sense only to them. Their cries made goose bumps rise on my neck. They carried on that way for five minutes or more, as if they knew what we were doing and wanted to bless it. Or curse it. Who knew with crows?

They didn't leave until I took up the shovel to complete the burial, and then they lifted from the tree in one black, gleaming cloud. They flew away into the clear sky, all of them together, with only one or two cries drifting in their wake.

When the hole was filled, and I had smoothed the dirt so it was even with the surrounding ground, Charlotte said, "It's too obvious."

"What do you mean?"

"I think if anyone came looking, they would see right away what this is. That it's a grave."

I gazed down at the oblong of freshly turned dirt. "You think someone's going to come looking?"

"They'll be looking for something. I don't think they know what."

"A premonition?"

"Dishwater this morning."

"More water magic."

"It didn't take much."

She turned Emma in her arms. Emma waved her fists and kicked with exuberance when she caught sight of me. Despite everything, I found myself smiling. After so many months of misery, the joy the baby gave me had a special intensity. It warmed my heart and my spirit so that I felt I walked in sunshine every day.

I moved around the grave to drop a kiss on Emma's forehead, and she cooed a response. I said, "I guess I could move some plants to disguise the spot. I have a lot of thyme. It spreads, and it would survive transplanting."

"Good idea."

"It's awfully sad, isn't it, Aunt Charlotte?" I didn't really feel sad, but I felt as if I *should* feel sad, should feel some sort of regret.

"You mean, this poor woman we've just buried?"

"Yes. Because her loss is my miracle. My baby. It doesn't seem fair."

"Life is rarely fair. But think about that later, Barrie Anne. You need to get that thyme planted right away."

I didn't like the note of urgency in her voice, but I was glad to think about something other than the poor dead woman now resting below the tilled earth of my garden.

I forgot all about Charlotte calling her "sister."

The black Buick reappeared that afternoon just as I was finishing my transplanting chore. Willow gave a single warning bark and bounded toward the house. I propped my shovel against the garden fence and hurried after the dog. The dust cloud was still swirling when I reached the front room. Charlotte was at my elbow.

"Emma's in your room," she said. "Sound asleep."

"Okay."

"Do you want me to stay down here?"

"Unless she starts to cry." Willow was on the front porch, barking furiously at the two men, who gazed warily from the car windows. I let her bark as they peered through the dust, eyeing her.

Charlotte said, with satisfaction, "I don't think Willow likes these fellows."

"She made that clear the last time." I let the barking go on a moment longer. When it subsided to an angry rumble, I opened the door and said quietly, "Willow, come." She did, but slowly, backing toward me while keeping her eyes fixed on the two men. Woods and Harrison waited until I put my hand on her ruff before they left the safety of their car and started up through the dry yard.

Charlotte muttered, "G-men again. As I thought."

"G-men?"

"You know, government men. Like they say in the movies."

"Oh."

"How odd they look. They match, like a set."

"I know. It's peculiar." I pulled Willow aside as the two men approached the door. "Mr. Woods. Mr. Harrison. Did you forget something?"

"No," said the shorter man. I wasn't sure I recalled which of the men was which. He helped me by taking off his hat and nodding to Charlotte. "We weren't introduced before, ma'am. I'm Mr. Harrison. That's Mr. Woods."

She returned his nod but didn't say her name.

I said, "Do you want to come in out of the heat?"

"Thank you, Mrs. Sweet." I stepped back, with Willow stiff-legged beside me. The men came in, and Charlotte shut the door after them. I gestured to the kitchen table, and they moved ahead of us. Charlotte gave me a sidelong glance, and I waggled my eyebrows at her.

Woods and Harrison waited for us to sit down before they took chairs. As before, they set their hats on the table, but this time it appeared Harrison wasn't worried that my table might be dirty. He didn't check it. Woods put his briefcase on the floor beside his chair, and Harrison took his notebook out of an inside pocket. It seemed to be their routine, as if it were rehearsed, a set of predetermined actions. The two men looked at the two of us for at least thirty seconds without speaking.

In the silence, I sensed Charlotte's temper rising, and I resisted an urge to kick her under the table.

Instead I said, with what I hoped was a decisive tone, "Gentlemen, I have work to do. This is a farm."

"Yes," Harrison said.

Woods said, "We have work to do also, Mrs. Sweet. We're under a lot of pressure."

"Pressure for what?"

Harrison said, "Answers."

Charlotte leaned forward and put her paint-stained fingertips on the table. "Mr. Woods, Mr. Harrison. I'd appreciate it if you would speak bluntly. You're following the saucers, aren't you? But we haven't seen them. Any of them."

"How do you know we're following the saucers?"

Her fingers tapped an irritated rhythm. "Why else would you be here? We read the newspapers. We know there have been incidents in the Pacific Northwest. What I don't know is why you're troubling my niece about them. Again."

"We're troubling lots of people," Woods said, then colored with embarrassment at the admission.

Harrison cast him a sour glance, then turned back to us. "My associate means we're asking lots of people what they've seen. We're only trying to keep America safe."

"From what?" I asked.

"That's the question."

Charlotte said, "Because of Roswell?"

The two men turned their heads to her in one queerly synchronized movement. A beat passed before Harrison said, "What do you know about Roswell, Mrs...."

"Miss. Miss Blythe." Charlotte lifted her hand from the table and folded her arms. With no cosmetics and her hair pulled back into a bun at the nape of her neck, she looked splendid, with a kind of salt-of-the-earth nobility. My chest warmed with pride in her.

She said, "What I know about Roswell is what the *Tacoma Tribune* printed. Now, as long as you've come, why don't you tell us what you know about it?"

Woods started to speak, but Harrison put up a hand to silence him. He said, "That's restricted, Miss Blythe."

"What does that mean?"

"It means I can't tell you."

Woods said, despite Harrison's warning hand, "Not that there's anything to tell."

The look on Charlotte's face could only be described as a smirk. "It's in black and white, gentlemen. You can't deny it. There was a flying-saucer crash there a few weeks ago."

Harrison said, "It wasn't a saucer."

"The air force reported they found a flying disk."

"The initial reports were wrong."

"Indeed," Charlotte said. "In that case, why are you here?"

"We're following up on calls from citizens." Harrison riffled the pages of his notebook, but he didn't open it. "There have been a lot of... events in this area."

"Not here," I said.

The two heads turned to me this time. Woods said, "You're the closest resident to Hood Canal in this neighborhood."

"Yes?"

"We have multiple reports of something in—that is, something that may have been—in the water."

"I thought that happened at Maury Island."

Woods said, "Have you seen odd lights?"

My mouth dried. I said, "Lights?" but my voice cracked on the word.

Charlotte said, "What kind of lights?"

"Well, lights under the water," Woods said, shifting uneasily in his chair.

Harrison scowled at his companion, and then at Charlotte and me. "Just tell us if you've seen anything out of the ordinary."

Charlotte said, "Don't you think if we had seen something, we would have called the authorities?"

"Maybe. Maybe not."

"Why not, for heaven's sake?" she demanded.

Harrison shrugged. Woods said, "Those Maury Island fellows—they're trying to make money on it."

"How do you make money on something crashing into Puget Sound?" I asked.

"Artifacts," Woods said glumly.

"Oh," Charlotte said, with a sly air of triumph. "Artifacts, like the ones found in Roswell. Which you're now denying."

"That was a weather balloon."

"Baloney." Charlotte stood up and went to the front room

to collect the *Tribune* from the couch where she had been reading. She brought it back and smacked it on the center of the table. I hadn't seen it yet. I leaned forward to read the headline, one copied from a New Mexico paper. The newspaper was the *Roswell Daily Record*, and the headline read: "RAAF Captures Flying Saucer on Ranch in Roswell Region."

"What's the RAAF?" I asked.

"Roswell Army Airfield," Woods said.

I settled back in my chair, and as Charlotte had done, I folded my arms. I was aware of the edge in my voice, but I didn't try to moderate it. My anxiety was making me angry. "Mr. Harrison. Mr. Woods. You're saying that report is false. But you're here trying to get me—or my neighbors—to say we've seen something similar? You do see how ridiculous that is?"

"Now, now, Mrs. Sweet," Harrison said. He put up a hand, like a traffic policeman. "Now, just calm down. There's no need to be hysterical."

"Hysterical?" I demanded. "Because I pointed out that you're contradicting yourself?"

"Be reasonable, ladies," Woods said. "We're just doing our jobs."

"We're just minding our business," Charlotte snapped. "And you're keeping us from it."

Harrison steepled his fingers, and his lips pursed before he said, with exaggerated gravity, "It would be wise for you to tell us if you've seen anything in the water. Or in the sky," he added, seemingly as an afterthought.

"Wise?" I said, ignoring his amendment. "Mr. Harrison, are you threatening us?"

"No, no, no," Woods put in. "No, Mrs. Sweet. No one is threatening you."

Harrison said, "We want to have a look around your farm. Go out to the canal, see if we find anything unusual."

My belly tightened. I avoided looking at Charlotte. "You can go through that empty field to the little apple orchard and on to the shore from there. That's not my land." I stopped myself from telling them to stay out of the garden. Emma began to whimper just then, and Charlotte started for the stairs.

"That must be your baby," Woods said. "How is she?"

"She's fine, thanks. Probably hungry."

Harrison said, "You still have our card, with the number?"

"Sure." I stood up, and they did, too, though they each looked down to be certain Willow was still lying under the table. They picked up their hats, and I led them to the front door. I had no intention of letting them go out the back and into my garden with its newly planted bed of thyme.

At the door we said stiff goodbyes. I watched them walk down the short path to the lane, turn right, and then circle out into the field. I moved to the kitchen window so I could watch them fording the tall yellow grass toward the orchard and the canal. I tried to remember if I had left anything behind when I brought the body back from the shore. I went over and over the details of the day and our makeshift funeral, hoping against hope we had left no clues of our activities.

Charlotte came back downstairs with Emma in her arms. I took the baby, bouncing her against me as Charlotte filled a bottle and set it to warm. The two men in their black suits looked out of place, incongruous, silhouetted against the yellow grass and then the pale greenery of the apple trees. In a few moments they disappeared, but I kept watching, cuddling Emma.

"Did we clean it up enough?" I worried. "What if they can tell where it was lying?"

"The tide will have cleaned up the first spot," Charlotte said.

"Yes, I think so," I said. "But where I had to pull the whole thing up the bank—and then it was under that tree—"

"Hysterical," Charlotte muttered. "I wanted to slap him when he said that."

"I felt the same. Are men ever hysterical, or is it just women?"

"When I was young, women could be put away for being hysterical. Could be shut up in an asylum. It was considered a mental illness."

"Who made the decision to put a woman away?"

"Oh, Barrie Anne, I think you can guess that. A husband. A father. A male doctor." She took the bottle from the saucepan and sprinkled a little milk on her wrist before handing it to me. "It was something that worried my mother, that some man would accuse us of that, just because of our little talent."

"Someone else saw the light," I said. "They were trying to get something out of us about that."

"I know."

I held the warm bottle in my hand for a moment, gazing at Charlotte. "You said something about seeing a light in the water before. You said it the day Emma came, but I forgot about it until this moment."

"What did I say?" She didn't look up from rinsing the saucepan.

"You said you saw something like it a long, long time ago. That you would tell me another time."

"Did I?" She took up a dish towel to dry the pan.

"You did. I think now is a good time."

She put the pan away, then stood folding the dish towel against her shirt, creasing its edges over and over. "I was young," she said. "We all went on the train to New York to meet the *Mauretania*. Our cousins from Kinloss were on it."

I gave Emma the bottle, careful to make no sound to interrupt.

Charlotte twisted her head to gaze at the window, but blindly, as if she were seeing a completely different place from the farm. "We were on the dock, my parents and Grandmother Fiona and I, waiting for our cousins to disembark. Behind the ship there was this glow, like phosphorescence, but brighter, as if someone had turned on a lamp underwater. I pointed at it, all excited, and my mother slapped my hand down."

I watched her profile, her chin lifted, her eyelids heavy with memory. "She rarely slapped me," she said softly. "It hurt. I cried, I think. She wouldn't explain, wouldn't answer my questions. Then the cousins came down the gangway and there was a lot of chatter and excitement. I didn't understand for a long time what had happened."

I waited, hoping she would go on. When she didn't, I prompted her, "What was it, Aunt Charlotte? Did your mother explain?"

She blinked and gave a bitter little laugh. "Mother, oh, no.

Never. It was Grandmother Fiona. She said the light was part of the magic. That it follows us. And she said my mother hated it, wanted it all to go away."

She glanced down at Emma, her eyes bright with affection. "And it did go away. Until now, I guess."

"I don't know what it all means," I breathed. Emma was peacefully suckling in my arms, my little mysterious babe. I thought, in a way, I could understand why my grandmother wanted it to go away. Had wanted to escape it. I could imagine—and understand—that she craved a normal life. That she wanted Charlotte to be a normal daughter. With Emma cuddled against my heart, I could understand why the grandmother I had never met had felt threatened.

Charlotte lifted down a glass from the cupboard. She turned on the tap, but before she filled the glass, she let her fingers trail through the flow of water. "You know, Barrie Anne, that Maury Island thing?" she mused, as much to herself as to me. "That was a fake."

"It was?"

"Those men saw something all right, something that fell into the water. That part was true. But the artifacts aren't real. They faked those, just as Woods and Harrison suspect."

"And the Roswell things?"

She shook the water from her fingertips and wiped her hands on her trousers. "Absolutely real. That's why the government's so nervous. They're trying to hide that, and they want to track down any other incidents before the public finds out about them."

I moved closer to the window, peering through the tangle

of the rosebush, watching for the men to return. "It's odd,"
I mused. "These stories—weird events—all coming at once."

Charlotte was at my shoulder, glass of water in hand.

"It's the bomb," she said in a matter-of-fact tone.

"What? The bomb?"

"Yep. All this started with the first tests of the A-bomb.
In—guess where?—New Mexico. Where Roswell is."

The logic of it, the sheer rationality of it, stunned me. I
moved my hand, making Emma lose her hold on the nipple
of the bottle. Her whimper of complaint brought me back to
myself, and I moved the bottle into its proper position with a
whispered apology to the baby.

"Do you think all of this—I mean, the saucers, Emma, the
woman—is it about the bomb?"

"Maybe not about the bomb, but connected to it." She
put her glass on the counter, took out a cigarette and rolled
it between her fingers. "The bomb changed everything. It
dropped on Japan and was tested in New Mexico and other
places, but its existence affects the whole world. The potential
for destruction is literally unlimited. It threatens every form of
life, in the air, on the ground, under the sea. I don't know why
everyone doesn't see that. We're all having to adjust to it, to the
awareness of it. We're all..." She hesitated, waving her unlit
cigarette in the air as she searched for the right word. "We're all
adapting," she finished. "Adapting to a world that is profoundly
changed. That terrifies some people—like those men out there,
searching for something that will answer their questions."

I pondered that for a long time as we waited for Woods and
Harrison to reappear.

They were gone for more than an hour. Eventually Charlotte and I moved into the front room, where Emma fell asleep under the blue baby blanket with its pattern of white bears. I couldn't see the orchard from there, but I spotted the two dark figures finally coming back through the field. They were shading their eyes despite their hats and seemed to be gazing toward the garden.

Charlotte and I hurried back to the kitchen window and stood watching, shoulder to shoulder. "You could send Willow out into the garden," she muttered. "They're afraid of her."

"What if they have guns?"

"I suppose G-men might carry guns."

"I'm not even sure they're really government men. I've never heard of this CIA before."

"I haven't either. But if not government, then who?"

There was no answer for that. We watched as they waded back through the long grass, their path arcing toward the garden fence. "I could get the .30-30 out, but I'm not sure I could fire it at a human being."

"No, of course not. You planted the thyme, didn't you?"

"I finished it just as they drove up."

"I'm guessing they're not farmers. Or gardeners. They won't notice it's a new planting."

"I hope you're right about that."

Woods and Harrison walked into the trampled area outside my garden gate. They stood there for a moment, peering through the crimped wire and gesturing to each other. I didn't draw a decent breath for five full minutes.

They finally stepped back from the fence and walked along

it in the direction of their car. Charlotte went into the front room to watch them climb into the Buick. "They're gone," she called a moment later. I sagged against the counter, weak-kneed with relief.

Charlotte came into the kitchen and reached for the teakettle. "Aunt Charlotte," I said, "was this what your feeling was about? Your premonition?"

She gave me a bleak look and shook her head. "Part of it. Not all."

"You still have it, then."

"Yeah. Like a bad case of the flu, it just won't go away."

13

June 1945

When Will reappeared, we settled into a pattern that was deceptively domestic. I went to work each morning. Charlotte shut herself into her studio. Will busied himself working in the garden, or repairing a loose step, or resetting a post in the fence. When I came home from Tibbals Hill, he had usually shopped for dinner and was cooking when I came in the door. Charlotte never commented on any of this beyond a raised eyebrow. I didn't know what to say, and I had no idea what to do beyond carrying on as I had done for the past three years.

The garden had never looked better. Will cut the grass, trimmed the hedge, and pruned the sprawling camellia bush. He spread gravel under the bench and cut back the shrubs that blocked the sunshine from it. He raked the gravel in front of the house and tidied the flower beds, which had always more or less grown at random.

I said once, "I had no idea you were a gardener."

"My father's an orchardist," he said. "My mother always kept a huge vegetable garden. I know a few things."

His parents were still a sore point for me. He promised, in the first few days of his return, that he would write to them and explain, but I hadn't seen a letter go out, or one come in, either. It was nice, though, to have someone buy groceries, and he seemed to have plenty of money. He told me his back pay had accrued lots of interest. I knew nothing about money, since Charlotte and I had never had much, so it seemed logical enough.

"He's courting you," Charlotte said one afternoon. It was one of my days off, and Will had driven away somewhere in the jalopy, saying he had a line on a job. When I asked what it was, he winked at me, and said he would tell me all about it when he landed it.

"Courting me? Is that what you think?" We were lounging in the newly tidied garden, with glasses of lemonade and the morning paper beside us.

"I do, kiddo. I think he's trying to win you back. I don't know if it's working."

"It's kind of sweet." I picked up my glass and traced a pattern in the condensation. "I don't know if I trust it. It was all such a shock."

"That it was." Charlotte smoothed the newspaper over her knees, but she gazed off into the summer sky, her lips pursing. "How do you feel about him now?"

I knew the answer to that one. "I feel sorry for him," I said promptly. "He thought war was going to be glory and medals. Instead, it broke him."

"Not sure pity is a good basis for a marriage."

The lemonade was cool and tangy, and I savored a mouthful of it. After I swallowed, I said, "You're not exactly the 'You made your bed, now lie in it' sort of person, are you, Aunt Charlotte?"

She laughed and reached underneath the paper for her cigarette pack. "To be honest, Barrie Anne, what I know about marriage could be written on the back of a postage stamp."

"I don't think I know much more than you do." I was wearing shorts, and I stretched my legs out into the sun. My knees were freckled. I hadn't noticed that since my Phys Ed courses in college. "But I keep thinking that I did get married, wisely or not. I made all the promises."

"Even the love, honor, and obey ones?"

"I must have. I said whatever the judge told me to. It all went by in a blur."

"Just you remember, Barrie Anne," she said, as she flicked her lighter, "Will made promises, too. Seems to me you've kept yours better than he has."

I said ruefully, "So far."

"Has he found a job?"

"Not yet, I guess. He said the lead didn't work out, but that he had other possibilities."

"What kind of work?"

"I'm not sure. I suggested working as a gardener—he's obviously good at that—but he just said he would have to see."

We weren't sharing a bed. Obviously, Charlotte knew that. Will didn't mention it, but he had taken to kissing me each night as we went to our own bedrooms. One day he left a nosegay of flowers beside my bed. One night after dinner he took us out for ice cream, insisting that Charlotte come along. He teased the soda jerk who put our sundaes together and smiled dazzlingly at the other customers, who smiled back and gave me envious glances.

It was a strange time, but there's something persuasive about going through the motions, carrying on as if everything is normal. I guess Will understood that.

He came home one day with a grin on his face. He had gained weight and had taken to wearing a porkpie hat he had bought at the Mercantile, jamming it onto the back of his head in a way that made him look boyish. Carefree. That day his eyes were very blue in the summer sunshine, and his skin had bronzed as he worked in the garden. It was that Randolph Scott look again, the one that had first enchanted me.

He took my hand and pressed it to his chest. "Come for a drive, Barrie," he said. "I have a surprise for you." I made an uncertain movement, and he hastened to say, with his most charming grin, "Aunt Charlotte can come, too."

"No, thanks," Charlotte said dryly. "I'm going to work on the beast this afternoon." The beast was her latest giant canvas, the one I fell asleep looking at every night, since I was sleeping in her studio. I savored seeing the shapes and colors emerge, bit by bit, geometric swirls and spirals in vivid tones. They seemed to leap out into the room, even at night. I thought the painting perfectly expressed the growing relief from the grimness of the war years, the easing of the darkness and sorrow that had weighed on the whole world and was now being replaced with lightness and energy.

I said, "I love the painting, Aunt Charlotte. One of my favorites ever. Will, you should go in and look at it."

"I'd love to. I'll do it this evening." Will squeezed my hand. "For now, get your scarf," he said. "And a pair of sunglasses. We're going down to Brinnon."

"There isn't much to see in Brinnon," Charlotte said doubtfully.

His laugh was as innocent and enthusiastic as that of a boy who had acquired a new toy. "I know. It reminds me of home!"

It was one of those heady, blue-crystal days we knew well on the peninsula, days that made it seem as if summer could last forever. The bay glittered as if dusted with diamonds. In the distance, the Olympics glittered, too, their highest peaks frosted with snow, vivid against the sky. Heads turned as we drove through town, and I felt almost as glamorous as I had three years before, riding in the open car with my handsome fellow, my scarf rippling in the breeze and the sun glinting off my dark glasses.

I couldn't help it. I had felt sad for so long, used up, tossed away like something broken and of no further use. Now I was Hedy Lamarr again, young, pretty, and full of hope.

Will turned his head to assess me. "You look wonderful, Barrie."

I answered, in all honesty, "So do you, Will."

The road running south of Quilcene and through the low for-
ested hills was twisty and narrow. Old trees leaned this way
and that, and banks of blackberry bushes tumbled alongside the
highway. Sometimes the road curved near Hood Canal, sometimes off through the woods. On my left I caught glimpses of
narrow beaches, occasionally a rowboat tied to a private dock.
I was captivated by the richness of the evergreens, the spiciness
of the air, even the down-at-the-heel charm of the few homes
that teetered on the banks, looking as if they might slide into
the water at any moment. The closer we got to the banks of
Hood Canal, the happier and more carefree I felt, almost like
the prewar, pre-Will, Barrie Anne Blythe.

We hadn't yet reached the town of Brinnon when Will
turned off the highway into a dirt lane. There were three
mailboxes beside the turn, mounted on weathered gray posts.
The jalopy's wheels bumped along sun-dried ruts as we drove
through thinning woods and past a few open fields. We passed
a farm with a tidy house, a barn, and several outbuildings.
We passed an abandoned shack, its porch hanging half off the
front, its yard a mass of weeds and a bit of broken furniture.
At the very end of the lane, we came upon an old farmhouse,
a faded white frame structure with a shingled roof and dirty
windows.

Will pulled the jalopy up in front of its dry-grass yard and
grinned at me. "Ready?"

"Ready for what?"

He jumped out of the car and came around to my side to

open the door. He gave me his hand, and when I was on my feet, he tucked my hand under his elbow. "It's ours, Barrie." He made a grand gesture, to include the house, the two out-buildings, and the enormous neglected garden behind it.

"What? I don't know what you mean." I gazed at the farm-house without understanding.

He laughed and pressed my hand against his side as if this were the most delicious surprise he could have invented. "It's ours! I bought it yesterday."

I suddenly had trouble finding my voice. "Will...you did...what? How? How could you have bought it?"

"I told you." He bent and kissed my cheek. "I saved my back pay."

"But...this house?"

"It's a farm, Barrie. You'll quit that stupid job, and we'll move out of Charlotte's house and down here."

"I thought you were looking for work up in Port Townsend."

"This will be even better! We'll have our own house. We'll learn to run the farm. It's going to be wonderful."

"Wait. Will, wait. You *bought* it?"

"I did." He beamed at me.

"But how could you buy it without asking me? I'm sup-posed to live on a farm?"

"We, Barrie. *We* are going to live on a farm." His smile faded, and his eyes glinted in a way I remembered, a way I hadn't seen since he returned. There was no charm in that look. "I did what I thought was best for my family."

My heart began to thud, and my cheeks felt cold despite the generous sunshine. "Are we a family?" My throat was so tight

I sounded as if I were choking. "You're assuming we can go back to what we were."

"What we were? What does that mean? I never changed, Barrie. Of course I've made mistakes, but..."

"Mistakes." I didn't have words for what I was feeling or thinking. The reality of the past three years blurred, as if a fog had fallen over it, and I couldn't seem to peer through it to discern the truth. Will stood before me, so sure of himself, so confident he could turn the world the way he wanted it to go. Could turn *me*.

His face changed again. The anger disappeared, and his eyes grew shiny as his mouth drooped. Even his voice dropped, vibrating with disappointment. "You're not happy. I thought you would be. I was sure you'd be excited, and I wanted to surprise you. To make up for—for hurting you by being gone so long. For not—" His voice cracked, and he swallowed. "For not writing. I know I should have."

I stood there, irresolute. I didn't like seeing him unhappy, despite everything. I thought of the sick bay on the *San Diego* and his shoes soaked with blood. I thought of him being ill and alone in the hospital. I thought of him, collapsing beside our gate, starving and dehydrated, and my mind spun in confusion. "Will, wait—"

He seized my hand. "Let me show you, Barrie. You'll see! Don't say anything until you have a look."

He pulled me after him as he crossed the yard to the house. He said he didn't have keys yet, but we peered in through the front room window and tramped along the front porch, our steps echoing on the boards. He led the way off the porch and down a short path into the garden, pointing out the crimped wire fence, the shed with its doors wide to show an empty interior, and the other outbuilding, which he called the garage. "We'll keep a tractor. Make it easy to till the garden."

I said faintly, "But, Will, I wouldn't know what to do with a tractor. Or—" I pulled my hand free and stood by the side gate, bewildered, gazing around at the tangled overgrowth in the garden, at the yellow grass of the yard, at the cramped, splintery back porch and the uncurtained kitchen window.

"Oh, come on, Barrie," he cried. He was suddenly manic in his enthusiasm. "Come and look into the kitchen! You're going to fall in love with this place!"

Not knowing what else to do, I followed him onto the back porch. He stood by the door, beckoning to me. Beside him, I peered in through the little window in the back door. I saw a battered range and a woodstove set between the kitchen and the front room. I could just see the foot of a set of narrow stairs and near the back door a row of pegs for jackets and a tall pottery jar with a dusty umbrella sticking out.

"Don't you love it?" Will exclaimed, his arm encircling my shoulders.

The odd thing, perhaps the strangest thing in those weeks full of strangeness, was that I thought I might. The summer sun glowed on the white clapboards, which were in desperate need of a coat of paint. The air was sweet with the scents of salt water and a jumble of untended rosebushes in riotous bloom along one side of the house. The garden was vivid with greenery, though it seemed all the plants had grown into a tangled mass. Rich, well-dug black soil showed here and there.

I looked over my shoulder and saw an aging apple orchard at the end of an empty field and beyond it an enticing glimpse of sapphire water.

"Is that Hood Canal?"

Will followed my gaze. "Yes!" He jumped down from the porch and started back to the garden gate. "Let's go see it."

My sandals weren't the best shoes for tramping through the long grass of the field or for navigating the root-choked earth beneath the apple trees. I had to slip-slide my way down the cut in the bank to the gravelly beach beside the canal. There was no wind, and the smooth water glistened like satin. As I pulled off my sandals, a raven flapped out of one of the tallest evergreen trees. It alighted on an ancient, disintegrating dock, finding a foothold on a tilting bollard. It looked at me in silence, its big, curving beak closed, its head tipped to one side. I gazed at it, openmouthed. They were brave, ravens, but I hadn't been this close to one before. Its eyes, even in the glare of the sunlight, were fiercely bright, and it shifted from one foot to the other as it stared at me, its wings lifting, ruffling in the light breeze, settling again.

Cool water foamed over my toes, distracting me from the bird. For a moment I closed my eyes at the ecstasy of salt water on skin, at the persuasive music of the waves. The feeling was magic. Pure, powerful, irresistible magic.

When I opened my eyes, the raven was gone.

A moment later Will joined me, taking my hand, drawing me out farther into the water, until it reached our knees. Will turned me to him. His eyes were the same sapphire as the water, glowing with excitement through the sun-glazed lenses of his glasses. His hair flopped in glossy locks over his fore-head, and his smile was eager and earnest. "Tell me," he said. "Tell me you love it as much as I do."

I felt off-balance in my spirit, just the way my body felt with wet sand shifting beneath my bare feet. I couldn't find my center, the core of me that knew the last three years couldn't be explained away. The water, the feel and the sound and the smell of it, distracted me. I couldn't resist the picture of myself living at the farm, learning to drive a tractor, figuring out how to tame that wild garden. I was eager to move out of my aunt's house, to have my own home to organize and decorate. The waves seemed to call to me, assuring me that this was my true home.

I yearned, in my innocence, to believe once again in true love. I longed to trust that my husband was what he said he was and that we could move past the disappointment and deceit of the past. With the cool water splashing at our knees, I let him pull me close and kiss me. I let him lead me back to the farm-house, though I felt a powerful reluctance to leave the water. The waves swirled and pulled at my ankles, as if the water didn't want to let me go, either.

At the house, we shaded our eyes to peer in every window. We imagined how it would look after we had painted and cleaned and repaired and added amenities. I admitted to him that I did, indeed, love the place. Had fallen in love with it, in fact, as swiftly as I had once fallen in love with him.

When we were back at Aunt Charlotte's house, sunburned and hungry, giddy with our news, I tried not to see the doubt in Charlotte's eyes, because it reflected the doubt I had buried in my own heart, covered over with fragile hopes.

Only once did she ask me, "Are you sure, Barrie Anne?"

I tried to sound unafraid. "I'm sure, Aunt Charlotte. We're going to be a normal couple, with a house and land and... well, all of it. I want that. I really do."

She didn't answer. I know now that I hadn't convinced her. It wasn't too long before I knew I hadn't convinced myself, either.

14

August 20, 1947

When I was expecting Scottie, I studied Dr. Spock until I knew the book by heart. I absorbed his advice about feedings and baths and fevers and teething. During the months of my pregnancy Dr. Spock had reassured me that I could find my own way through the myriad details of caring for an infant. But now, helpful though Dr. Spock was, his book fell short of preparing me for the wonder that was Emma.

We talked to her all the time, Charlotte and I. Mostly it was baby talk, the silly, loving things adults say to the infants they care for. Charlotte always referred to me as "Mama" around Emma, and I called Charlotte "Auntie." When Willow nosed Emma and licked at her bare feet, we said corny things like, "Oh, look, Emma! The dog loves you. The dog loves the baby."

When we were in the garden we named things for her, with no expectation that she would understand.

Charlotte would say, "Roses, baby. Those are roses."

Or I would say, "Look, Emma, the punkins are getting so big! Would you like a punkin of your own? Pretty soon we'll carve a jack-o'-lantern, Emma's own jack-o'-lantern."

Once I heard Charlotte, sitting with Emma on the porch, saying, "That's your mama, Emma. Can you say 'Mama'?"

Of course we knew she couldn't say "Mama" yet. She couldn't say anything. We were pretty sure she couldn't be more than three months old. Dr. Spock said not to expect distinct words before nine or ten months and not to worry if they came a long time after that.

She was getting bigger by the day. Neither Charlotte nor I knew how fast an infant should grow, and we marveled at her swiftly lengthening legs and arms, her broadening shoulders, the delicate tapering of her fingers. She loved the bunny rattle we had bought at the Mercantile and held it before her for long minutes at a time, examining the celluloid ears, touching the mouth and eyes of the face, shaking it to hear the beads rattle inside, then holding it still, her pink lips parted, wondering at the silence that followed.

On a day when we woke to an unseasonal rain, I carried Dr. Spock's book downstairs in one arm, Emma propped on the opposite shoulder. Charlotte was already in the kitchen, her first cigarette of the day burning in the ashtray and the percolator chuckling cheerfully beside her. "Reading that again?" she said, pointing at the book.

"I was just checking some things. Spock says babies will grasp toys around three or four months." As I spoke, Emma had the bunny rattle firmly in her little fist and was bumping my shoulder with it, kicking with delight at each hollow thump.

"I guess she's right on schedule," Charlotte said. "That's comforting, isn't it?" She poured two cups of coffee and carried them to the table. "I have her bottle ready." She nodded toward the range, where the bottle waited in a steamy saucepan.

"Oh, thanks." I maneuvered the bottle and the baby, tested the temperature, and then settled at the table across from Charlotte. "This rain is nice. Breaks the heat, and it's good for the garden." As Emma began to suckle, the rattle still clutched firmly in her hand, I took a sip of coffee, careful to keep the hot cup well away from the baby's feet.

The rain dripped down the windows and peppered the shingled roof in a steady rhythm. The dry field beside our place would be green by tomorrow, and there would no doubt be deer feeding there. I drank more coffee, settled Emma's warm little body closer to me, and sighed with contentment. It was nice to have a day of enforced idleness. I might sweep or wash some baby clothes, but with rain falling, I could take a day off from the garden. Weeds would be leaping out of the ground by tomorrow, but I would deal with them then.

I asked, "How's the project coming?" Charlotte's work had picked up, and she was busy with drawings for a surgical manual.

"It's fine. A bit tricky, different colors to delineate tendons from muscles. These are the illustrations that most often come back for correction."

"And the beast?"

Charlotte grinned and drew on her cigarette, blowing the smoke away from me and Emma. "As ever," she said cheerfully, "beastly."

"This one is different. I've never seen you do anything realistic."

"You saw it?"

"I always like looking at your big canvases. I didn't think you'd mind."

"I don't mind at all. What do you think of it?"

"I hardly know what to think, Aunt Charlotte." She raised her eyebrows. "Oh, that doesn't mean I don't like it; it's just . . . it hardly looks like your work."

"It doesn't feel like my usual work, either."

"What's the inspiration?"

Charlotte shrugged as she crushed out her cigarette. "The image was in my mind, the bridge, the canal, the water. Somehow I had to put it on canvas. It's only half-finished."

"What's left to put in?"

She didn't answer directly. Her gaze fell on Emma, peacefully drinking her goat's milk, and a look of wistfulness curved her lips. "I'm not sure," she said. "I've been remembering something my grandmother used to say, when I was a girl."

"Grandmother Fiona."

"I wish you had known her."

"I do, too. What did she say?"

"She told me once that there is a universe beneath the sea."

When she didn't go on, I prompted her. "What did she mean by it?"

She gave me an enigmatic smile. "Oh, Grandmother Fiona meant it literally."

"Really?"

"Really."

I pondered that for a moment, staring out through the rain-streaked front window. "Is that your thought, in this painting, Aunt Charlotte? A universe under the sea?"

"It's an idea that's been growing since I started it." She gave a faint chuckle. "I have a lot of time to think when I'm painting! I've been imagining a world beneath the sea, perhaps once well-known but forgotten in this modern age. We know there's a universe beyond the sky, but the sea is vast, too."

"Aunt Charlotte!" I said. "Surely we would know if there was a world under the ocean. Our scientists would have found it!"

She shrugged. "Perhaps. The planet is two-thirds water, after all. Very little of the ocean floor has been mapped." She brought out her cigarette pack and tapped it thoughtfully on the tabletop. "Or maybe they have found it, and they're not telling us."

The idea made my heart give a little flutter. "You're thinking of Roswell."

"Yes. Roswell, all the other sightings—they deny them because they're afraid of what they mean. Because they can't imagine other worlds."

"But surely we would have some evidence of a world beneath the sea..." She gave me an arch look, her eyebrow curving high, and I let the thought trail off. Her smile grew smug as she saw I had gotten her message. She didn't need to say it aloud. We *did* have evidence, two significant bits of it. One was buried in my garden. The other was cuddled at that moment in my arms.

Charlotte shook out a fresh cigarette. "We live in a world of mysteries, kiddo. Women like us—our kind—we don't mind not understanding. We trust our intuitions. We're comfortable with questions we can't answer. The men I've known feel just the opposite."

"Why is that, do you think?"

"I can't speak for all men, of course, but most of them like things to be measurable. Provable. Predictable. Women are more connected to the mysteries, as if it's in our blood to be aware, to be sensitive..." She dropped her hands and wrapped her arms around herself. "I think it's what Grandmother Fiona knew and what my mother tried to deny."

"Why would she deny it?"

"Purely out of fear. It wasn't safe for a woman to be different. To have a reputation for strange behavior." She made a gesture with her chin, and her mouth tightened. "It's still not safe, Barrie Anne. Remember that."

"You mean, like my neighbors thinking I'm strange for living out here alone." I sighed. "I guess things haven't changed all that much for women."

"I thought they had, during the war. Women were so much freer to make their own choices, work wherever they wanted to, because they were needed, of course. But now the men—and a lot of women, to be fair—want things to go back to the way they thought they were. Happy housewives, packs of children, husbands devoted to their families. Of course, most of that was an illusion, even when I was young."

"So you don't think we'll be going back to those days."

She shook her head, and declared firmly, "Nope."

In my arms, Emma gave a kick and let the nipple slip from

her mouth. She repeated, in a voice an octave higher than Charlotte's, "Nope."

I jumped and gazed down at her, openmouthed. She gave me a milky grin and cried again, "Nope. Nope. Nope."

I didn't realize my fingers had gone limp until my coffee cup slipped from them and fell to the floor. It didn't break, but I had drunk only half the coffee. Charlotte jumped from her chair, tossed her still-burning cigarette into the sink, and grabbed a towel to mop up the spill. When she straightened, we stared at each other.

Charlotte said, "Did she just—"

I could only nod.

"What does the book say about words?"

"Nine months, ten . . . or a lot later."

"Hmm." Charlotte carried the sodden towel to the sink and wrung the coffee out of it. She draped it over the faucet and turned to face me. "I think, Barrie Anne," my aunt said, "you should give up on Dr. Spock, or on any of the other so-called experts. The manual doesn't exist that will help you raise this particular child."

Emma delighted in her first word. All that day, whenever one of us picked her up, whenever Willow came to sniff her neck or lick her bare toes, she exulted, "Nope! Nope! Nope!" at the top of her lungs. When we laughed, she said it again, and again, flailing her chubby arms and grinning like a fair-haired, pink-cheeked monkey.

The drizzle lasted until late in the afternoon, when the sun broke through the clouds to glisten on the wet grass and dripping leaves. I lifted Emma from her basket and put her pink hat on her head. "Come on, baby," I said. "Let's go check on the garden."

"Nope!" she crowed, pumping her feet with delight.

I said to Charlotte, "She loves the garden."

Charlotte said, "She loves everything. I've never seen so much joie de vivre."

"I know. It's adorable." I kissed one of Emma's hands and snuggled her close as I pulled on my own straw hat. Willow waited for us at the back door, her tail waving, her own doggy smile full of the joy of life.

Charlotte followed to manage the door for us, but as I started through, I caught the look on her face. "Aunt Charlotte? What's wrong?"

"I don't know exactly," she said. She had pulled her hair back in a careless twist, exposing hints of silver at her temples. She was holding a cup of cold coffee, and she had dipped her fingers into it. It looked as if she was stirring it, but I knew that wasn't what she was doing. She was trying to see what was coming.

She said, "I feel worried."

"You don't know why?"

She shook her head. "I can't get it." She turned her gaze through the open back door. The wet garden steamed gently after the rain, fairy clouds rising above the greenery into the slanting sunshine. "Everything looks washed clean," she murmured. She pulled her dripping fingers from the cold coffee and licked them dry. "But I feel as if another storm is coming. A bad one."

"You're not talking about weather."

The look she bent on me was bleak. "No. Not the weather. And that's all I can tell you."

I squeezed Emma closer. She squirmed in protest, saying again, "Nope! Nope!" Charlotte and I both laughed ruefully.

"We'll have to teach her another word," I said.

Charlotte stroked the baby's cheek with her forefinger. "How about 'Mama'?"

That brought a misty smile to my lips. I pressed a kiss on Emma's head. "Yes," I said. "How about that, Emma? Can you say 'Mama'?"

She squealed, "Nope!" and Charlotte and I both laughed.

The worrisome moment receded as I carried Emma out into the garden and strolled down the rows of string beans. The vines drooped under the weight of ripe vegetables. I picked one and let Emma suck on it while I walked past the tomato plants, lifted a cucumber leaf with my foot to see that there were three more cukes ready to be harvested, and peered over the fence to the jumble of blackberry bushes that grew wild there. Picking them was hard, sticky work, but they were popular at the market. They would be ripe, I thought, in another ten days or so. After that, I could start on the apples. They weren't technically mine, any more than the blackberries were, but no one else seemed to want them. It was nice for a small farmer like me to have an autumn crop.

We should do well this winter, I congratulated myself, as I turned with Emma back toward the house. Charlotte was getting more work. I had a lot of produce to sell and some to put up. I pictured the pantry filled with jewel-like jars of red jam, yellow applesauce, green beans. In the root cellar beneath the house I would keep potatoes and pumpkins.

A sense of well-being lifted my heart. I strolled around the fence, relishing the sunshine after the cleansing rain. Willow trotted beside me, and Emma made slurping noises as she gummed the now-slimy string bean.

The peace was shattered by the clanging of the ship's bell from the back porch. I started, and Willow gave me a look before she ran ahead in answer to the summons. I followed as quickly as I could, trying not to jostle the baby.

"What is it?" I panted, when I reached the porch.

Charlotte's face looked grim, and she waved me inside. "I walked down to get the mail," she said. "It's been a couple of days. The electric bill came, and *Life* magazine. And this." She pointed to an envelope waiting on the kitchen table.

I handed Emma to her, and Charlotte set about untying her cap and relieving her of the sticky string bean. She went to the sink to wash Emma's hands, but I felt her eyes on me as I picked up the envelope, slit it with a ragged thumbnail, and took out a handwritten sheet. It rattled in my suddenly shaking fingers.

It had been four years, but I recognized the handwriting. This time, Will's mother knew my name.

Dear Barrie Anne:

I am sorry I did not write before this. We are all real sorry you and Will lost your baby. It would have been real nice to have a grandbaby.

I think you and Will could have another baby. Your still young. We are good Catholics, and we don't believe in divorce. I

hope when he comes to see you, you will be a good wife, a purl,
as the Good Book says, and give him another chance.

Sincerely,

Mrs. Franklin Sweet

I handed the letter to Charlotte, and she read it with her eyebrows raised high. I said, "When he comes..." and shivered.

"That's the oddest family," Charlotte said. "Did you know he went home?"

"I don't know anything. Haven't heard a word, just like before."

"He must think he's coming back."

"I guess they got your letter about Scottie." It was a measure of how much I had healed that I could speak my baby's name without my voice breaking.

"I suppose. No one answered it."

"I don't want Will here. Ever again."

"I know, Barrie Anne. He probably knows that, too. Made his poor mother write this."

I said sourly, "He should have checked her spelling."

Charlotte's chuckle was just as sour. "Yes. I suppose—unfortunately—there's the property issue."

"I hoped he had just walked away from it. Left it as—I don't know—maybe an apology."

"Not to dash your hopes, kiddo, but I don't think Will is capable of apologizing."

"No." I creased the letter between my fingers and shoved it back into the envelope. "I thought I was safe, Aunt Charlotte. I thought he couldn't risk showing his face."

"Me, too." She shifted Emma to one side so she could put a full bottle into the saucepan.

I stood gazing down at the issue of *Life* that rested on the table with the electric bill. The cover was a photograph of England's Princess Elizabeth in an elaborate gown and a double string of pearls around her neck. I didn't care at all about the dress she was wearing, or even the jewels, but I wondered what it must be like to be a princess, to have everything you could possibly want or need. To have nothing to worry about.

I turned the magazine over so I didn't have to see it. I took Emma back from Charlotte and carried her into the front room to change her diaper. When that was done, I gave her the bunny rattle and sat with her comforting weight on my lap as I gazed blindly out the front window. Anxiety fluttered under my breastbone. I couldn't have him here. I couldn't see him, not ever again. But could I stop him from coming?

"Barrie Anne?" Charlotte called from the kitchen. "The bottle's ready."

I got up, Emma in my arms. She wriggled against me, kicking her little feet, and exclaimed, "Ba! Ba!"

Charlotte said, "Good God. Bottle? Or Barrie?"

15

September 1945

It turned out that Will had paid cash for the farm, a detail that made Charlotte's eyebrows flare, but that thrilled me. Even before we took the keys and moved in what few things we had, I adored the place. Everything about it delighted me: the trees in the orchard studded with red apples ready to be picked, the tangle of the garden begging for me to tame it, the ramshackle charm of the house, and especially the propinquity of the canal.

Charlotte, at least outwardly, had accepted the change in my circumstances. When I boasted that we didn't need a mortgage, she said, "A woman of means. Impressive." When I asked her to shop with me for a percolator and a toaster, she insisted on making those things a belated wedding gift. She found the snapshot the justice of the peace had taken on the day Will and I were married, and she put it in an old but very pretty Bakelite frame she had in one of her drawers.

When she gave it to me, the two of us standing in my new-old kitchen, I gazed at it for several moments with tears stinging my eyelids. "It seems like that was another life," I said. "A different girl."

"It was, in a way, kiddo," she said mildly. "An old philosopher said you can never step in the same river twice."

"River? Goodness. Water again."

"Yes. Why does that strike you?"

I set the frame on the kitchen counter. "I don't know, Aunt Charlotte. It's just that when we looked at this place—I wasn't sure about it until we went to the canal. It was a warm day, and we waded into the water. I felt—"

"Felt what?"

I looked up at her, surprised by the eagerness in her voice. She raised her eyebrows, waiting for my answer. "I felt as if I'd come home."

"Ah."

"It wasn't about Will, either. It was—I know it sounds odd, but it was about the water."

"But no premonition."

"No. It just felt good. Wonderful, really."

"Well," she said, beginning to unpack the toaster from its box, "It seems you may have the Blythe affinity after all."

"I don't know, Aunt Charlotte. Maybe I'm just an ordinary person. I'm not sure I want the talent."

"In that case, don't worry about it." She patted my shoulder. "You either will have it, or you won't. Now, let's concentrate on setting this house to rights."

I didn't want to talk about premonitions. I was excited about having my own house, my own things. I was thrilled about the apple orchard and the garden. The last thing I wanted was one of Charlotte's little feelings reviving my doubts, spoiling the moment. I said, "I can hardly believe I'm here, that this place is mine. Ours, I mean," I amended.

"But here you are, kiddo. I hope you'll be happy."

"I'll do my best."

She arranged the toaster beside the sink and then pulled out her cigarettes. "You always do your best, Barrie Anne. I have no doubts about that."

I found an ashtray in one of the boxes I was unpacking and handed it to her. "Aunt Charlotte, you're such a help. I appreciate it."

"Anything I can do."

We smiled at each other and plunged into the task of emptying boxes.

Those first two weeks on the farm were full of newness and discovery. Will delivered the promised tractor, and it turned out I had a knack for driving it, having learned to manage my aunt's cranky De Soto. We picked what seemed like a thousand apples, and I made two dozen jars of applesauce. Will nailed up loose boards on the two porches and fixed three cracked window frames.

I didn't ask any more questions about his time in the hospital or how he had made his way back to the peninsula. He was so happy, and looked so well, that it seemed a shame to spoil his good mood. Or mine, for that matter. He asked my opinion about everything, from the position of the kitchen table we would buy to the curtains I would want on the windows.

We shopped for furniture at a secondhand place in Brinnon. The proprietor of the store was a thin, gray sort of woman, past middle age, with a wrinkled face and dusty-looking hair. Her store suited her. It was crammed with furniture past its prime, and its shelves bristled with mystifying knickknacks, things I couldn't believe anyone had ever wanted when they were new. The smell of mold and dust in the air made me wrinkle my nose, but Will complimented the woman on the abundance of her inventory and flattered her with questions about quality and provenance.

By the time we left, having bought a scratched but solid kitchen table and four sturdy, mismatched chairs, she was all over smiles, beaming at Will and tossing in extras, a standing ashtray, a match holder to hang on the wall. She promised she would have the things delivered the next day.

As we left, she patted my arm and leaned close to whisper, "I hope you know how lucky you are, young lady. Such a handsome husband! So charming and thoughtful!"

I pondered those words on our drive home. They seemed like an omen to me, in my entranced state. It was true enough that Will had been charming to her, and to me as well, in her presence. In fact, he was always at his best with such an audience. He tended to hold my hand at such times or to tuck it under his elbow. He opened doors for me and circled my shoulders with his arm. He even occasionally kissed my cheek or pushed back an errant strand of my hair in paternal fashion.

I turned to appreciate Will's clear profile and to smile at the jaunty way he rested his elbow in the open window of the jalopy. I told myself the shopkeeper was right; he was handsome, and he was charming. If he was also unpredictable, perhaps I should see that as part of his appeal.

It happened again when we bought a bed. Will saw a notice on the bulletin board at the market, and he and I went to one of the outlying farms to have a look at a decades-old four-poster bed. The turned mahogany posts had been oiled and oiled again, and they glowed a lovely reddish brown. Will asked the widow who was selling it a dozen questions, drawing her out about her long marriage, her old home in Montana, her husband, who had passed away only months before. We drove away with a paper bag full of oatmeal cookies, another of ripe plums, and the promise that she would include the mattress when we sent the delivery truck to pick up the bed.

"How do you do that?" I asked, as we wheeled away in the jalopy. I had to tie a scarf over my hair against the dust, and we both wore dark glasses.

"Do what?" Will said.

"Charm old ladies. I think this one would have given you anything in her house you admired."

He cast me a sidelong, self-satisfied glance. When he smiled, his white teeth caught the sun, and he looked very much like Randolph Scott in a publicity still. "Just showing my interest," he told me.

"That's nice. She really liked you."

"Oh, sure," he said in an offhand way. "Lonely women are the easiest."

There was something about that answer that bothered me, but I couldn't think what it was. I told myself the two women we had met had enjoyed the encounters and that their pleasure

in Will's flattery and interest was real. We hadn't caused them
any harm.

Still, it troubled me, the way a tiny piece of gravel under
your heel irritates you, but not enough to make you stop and
take off your shoe. I tried to put it out of my mind.

When Charlotte showed up with a Mercantile bag, Will's
charm wasn't in evidence. He was polite enough but cool.
Charlotte's lopsided smile told me she understood, but when
I said I would speak to him, she said, "Don't, Barrie Anne. It
won't do any good."

"How do you know that?"

"There will always be people with an automatic ... let's call
it antipathy for people like me. They sense our difference, I'm
afraid. They can't get past it."

"I hate that!"

She shrugged. "You're not one of those people." She passed
me the Mercantile bag. "Sheets and pillowcases. I thought
you'd need them."

"Oh, this is perfect, Aunt Charlotte! Thank you."

"Your old quilt won't be big enough, either, but I didn't
want to choose a new one without you. I wasn't sure what colors you might like."

"You shouldn't have to buy that as well."

"There's one up in the attic, you know. It belonged to your
parents. It should be the right size, if you like the pattern. I'll
need to air it out, though. Mothballs."

"I'd love to have it. I'll come get it, and we can hang it on
the clothesline here."

"Does Will let you drive the jalopy?"

"Well..." We gazed at each other and both laughed. "I don't really know," I finally said. "I haven't asked him."

"I'll bring it, kiddo. You're busy enough. When do you get your telephone?"

I loved those days of making the farm our own. It was satisfying to scrub the floors clean, to make the windows sparkle, to see worn but decent furniture fill the old rooms with their uneven floors and homely woodwork. I wished I knew the history of the house. I was certain it had been built by hand, perhaps by the first people to farm here, when Brinnon was little more than a logging town.

I was even happier when I started on the garden. I knew very little about what it needed, but I discovered there was something instinctual about the work. With just a spade and a bucket, I began a voyage of discovery. Will wanted to bring in the tractor and till everything under, but I stopped him. I found carrots and potatoes growing under the thicket of weeds and blackberry vines. There were summer squashes and pumpkins struggling toward the sun, and lettuces that had reseeded and were drooping against the earth for lack of water. I found a basket propped against the back wall of one of the outbuildings. It was gray with cobwebs, but I washed it clean and started the job of salvaging surviving plants. I created towering piles of weeds, planning to haul them into the empty field with the tractor.

One evening I came in through the back door, sunburned and grimy but content with my day's work. My basket held four lumpy but usable carrots, a straggling head of lettuce, and three plump striped tomatoes. Will stood grinning as he watched me dump my haul on the counter. "You're covered in dirt," he said. "And you have a dozen new freckles on your nose."

"I know."

"They're adorable."

I looked up at him in surprise. Although we had both been working on the place, sometimes side by side, sometimes not seeing each other for hours, we hadn't really talked since the first day he showed me the farm. We also hadn't resumed our relationship in any meaningful way beyond casual conversation. We didn't kiss or embrace. We hadn't spoken of his long silence, or his illness, or—still a circumstance that niggled at me—his parents.

He crossed the kitchen to the range. "Go have a bath, why don't you? I'll see if we can put together a dinner out of this stuff. Scrambled eggs okay? I can toss a salad."

Bemused, I climbed the stairs to run a bath. I hadn't known, when we were in San Diego, that Will knew how to cook. It had been a surprise, in our weeks in Port Townsend. He didn't do laundry, or iron, or any other housework. I took for granted that all those chores were my responsibility. I didn't know any other men who could cook—but then, I didn't really know any other men.

It was lovely to indulge myself for a few minutes. I soaked in a tub, washed my hair, did my best to dig the garden dirt out from under my nails. I was tired, but in that good way, as when I had played a game of tennis or had a good long swim. When Will called from downstairs that dinner was ready, my hair was still damp, but I felt relaxed and happier than I had felt in a very long time.

The autumn evenings were closing in earlier and earlier. Will and I sat across from each other in our mismatched chairs, at our scratched but sturdy kitchen table. We ate fresh eggs from the market and a salad of our very own lettuce and tomatoes, with boiled carrots and a glass of root beer. The windows were dark, reflecting the light of a candle he had produced from somewhere and stuck in a mason jar. In the candlelight, we toasted each other with root beer.

The confusing and anxious years of Will's absence seemed to recede, to bubble away like the tide going out. The tide left marks on the sand, and Will's strangeness had left marks on my heart, but both, I thought, would fade. We had our own home, in a perfect spot. Life brimmed with possibilities on that lovely night, and I felt like the bride I had once expected to be.

When we climbed the stairs, side by side, I knew what was going to happen. I told myself I was ready. It was time to put the past behind us. To remember the romantic dreams that had brought us together. We could still recover that sense of hope and optimism. We could still become the perfect couple, Randolph and Hedy, happy together. Our marriage could begin again.

I went to bed with my husband in a mahogany four-poster rich with the scent of furniture wax. The new sheets were crisp and clean. The inherited quilt smelled of sunshine and salt breezes. After three years of abstinence, my body tingled with desire, just as it should. Though the night was dark, the world seemed bright with hope.

16

December 1945

I don't know why you don't have a telephone yet," Charlotte complained.

We were at the kitchen table. She had a cup of coffee in front of her, but I was drinking warm water with grated ginger in it. My stomach had been roiling for days. "I keep bringing it up," I told her. "Will says he'll see to it, but he hasn't done it yet."

"Where is he this morning?"

"He drove off early. He said he was going to the bank in Bremerton."

"Bank?"

"To get some cash." I sipped my water and chewed on a fragment of ginger, hoping I wasn't going to be sick again.

"I don't understand where this money is coming from. He still doesn't have a job, does he?"

"No. I'm pretty sure he stopped looking when he bought the farm." I swallowed nausea and my voice went thin with the effort. "I can't explain it, Aunt Charlotte. Maybe we've run out of money. Maybe that's why he hasn't had the telephone installed."

"But he said he was going to the bank?"

"Yes." I stared into my cup of yellowish water and added, a little ashamed, "He says that a lot, to tell you the truth."

We sat in silence for a moment, and I pressed my hand to my belly. It felt as if I had eaten something bad.

"Tummy upset again?" Charlotte said, frowning across the table.

"Constantly." I fished another piece of ginger out of my cup and chewed it.

"Nerves, you think?"

"Probably." Charlotte knew how difficult Will had been the past few weeks.

The work of the farm had kept us busy all autumn. There had been a hundred things to do before winter set in. I threw myself into the chores, learning as I went, overcoming my customary shyness in order to consult neighbors at the market for advice and suggestions. At first Will joined me, and I liked watching the reserved farm wives glowing under his attention. I felt as if their approval of him reflected on me. Their husbands, upon learning he had been a navy corpsman in the war, treated him with respect and offered their help with cutting firewood for the winter or building the chicken coop we were planning. Sometimes they asked him for medical advice, which he delivered with assurance and which they accepted with solemn nods.

Will figured out that I could drive the jalopy as well as he could. That seemed fine at first, but soon enough I found it meant that I was making most of the trips to the market alone. I wasn't as good at casual conversation as Will was, so market days weren't as pleasant as when he was there. I realized before long that he had lost interest in our projects. When Mr. Miller or Mrs. Urquhardt asked after him, on my solitary market days, I found myself making excuses for his absence, not wanting to admit that he just hadn't wanted to come.

I remembered all their advice, though, which was good, because I needed it. I built the chicken coop by myself. Will seemed to be busy with something else every time I brought it up, so I did it on my own. I had seen pictures of beautiful hens in an old farm catalog, and I couldn't wait to have some of my own.

I bought a roll of wire and talked the store into delivering it. There was a stack of boards behind the garden shed, most of them usable. I had to learn how to bury posts, how to hammer nails, how to match bits of lumber, how to sand and caulk and fit on a roof, but I did it. I bruised my thumbs and got splinters in my palms, but in the end, I had a usable coop with shelves for the nesting hens.

I was surprised by how much I enjoyed the whole process, and I was as proud of my results as if I had built a palace. The fact that one wall was crooked didn't bother me in the least, and when Will pointed it out, I told him if he wanted it straightened, he was welcome to fix it. He scowled at me and walked away. I stuck out my tongue at his retreating back.

I used the tractor to skid some fallen applewood up to the house so we could chop it into stove lengths. Will wielded the ax for a while, but he soon tired of that, too. I got used to him disappearing in the jalopy every day, coming back with a few groceries but never really explaining where he had been or how he had spent his time. I was busy planning and building and even beginning to dig out the garden when the weather wasn't too cold. I tried not to notice that I was more at peace when my husband wasn't home. When he wasn't there to question me about it, I often walked through the empty field and on to the shore of the canal.

As the water grew chilly with the fall weather, I didn't wade, but I strolled our little stretch of beach, picking up shells and colored stones and bits of sea glass for my collection.

I sighed, thinking of those days. It was too cold now, the days too short, for me to wander on the beach.

Now, as I chewed more ginger, Charlotte said, "I'm worried about you, Barrie Anne."

"My stomach, you mean?"

"Yes. But not just that. You and Will…"

My stomach churned again. I pushed away from the table, and started toward the stairs, but before I had taken three steps I knew the bathroom was too far away. I swerved to the back porch and vomited in the muddy ground below the steps.

When my stomach was empty but still cramping with sickness, I straightened to find my aunt beside me, a warm washcloth at the ready. I mopped my face and my mouth and leaned on her as we went back into the house.

"Well, Barrie Anne." Charlotte settled me at the table with more warm water and another spoonful of ginger. I felt shaky and uncertain, but I noticed her fingers were wet, and I understood when she said, "I think it's time we get you to Dr. Masters."

I said, "It's probably just the flu, don't you think?"

"Doesn't look like the flu to me. You're pregnant, kiddo. They can do a rabbit test to make sure, if you doubt me."

"I don't want to do that. They kill the rabbit."

"Okay, softie, no rabbit. But you should see Dr. Masters anyway."

"I'll have to get some money from Will."

Charlotte gave me her fiercest grin. "I believe that's what husbands are for."

"I don't know when he'll be back."

"Never mind. I'll get this one."

Without a telephone, we couldn't make an appointment with Dr. Masters. We decided to drive up to Port Townsend and take the chance he wouldn't be out on a call. I put on my winter coat. Charlotte said, wrapping a woolen scarf around her throat, "The heater's out again. Better get your gloves and a hat."

"You need a new car."

She laughed. "This *is* my new car!"

The De Soto had coughed and died in the middle of Water Street right after Will and I moved to the farm, stranding Charlotte and leaving her without any transportation. We found out when we came to town to pick up the last of my belongings. Will, in one of his most charming phases, when he could be sweet even to my aunt, took Charlotte to look at cars.

The Studebaker was used—experienced, as Charlotte joked—but significantly less tired than the poor old De Soto. It was the color of a fresh bruise, something between black and purple, but the interior was pristine, and it had—so Will said—good wheels. Its heater was the only unreliable thing about it. It had already stopped working twice since Charlotte bought the car, but she was proud of her B sticker for gas rationing and insisted the good mileage made it worthwhile.

Both of us bundled up as if we were going for a hay ride before we set off for Port Townsend at Charlotte's usual brisk pace. She was driving so fast, in fact, that I almost missed seeing Will in his jalopy on the highway. He was driving south, while we drove north.

"That's odd," I muttered.

"What?" Charlotte kept her eyes trained on the road. It was one of the advantages of her fast driving, that she didn't allow herself to be distracted.

"We just passed Will. Headed home, I guess."

"I thought he went to Bremerton?" Still with her eyes on the road, she fumbled a cigarette out of her breast pocket and punched in the lighter.

"He said he was going to Bremerton."

"Hmm." She didn't have to point out that Bremerton lay in the opposite direction.

"Maybe he changed his mind?" I said faintly, my empty stomach quivering.

"Does he use a different bank?"

I had to spread my hands in a gesture of helpless ignorance. "He doesn't tell me, Aunt Charlotte. Things started out all

right, when we first moved to the farm, but then..." I pressed
the back of my hand to my mouth and gazed in nauseated misery at the mist-drowned fields of Beaver Valley.

"Yes?" Charlotte's prompt was gentle.

I dropped my hand, and a rush of anger gave me a respite
from my churning stomach. "He's so moody," I snapped. "I'm
tired of trying to keep him cheerful. I do things the way he likes
so he won't criticize. I stay out of his way when he's in a bad
mood. It's impossible, really. On his bad days, nothing makes
him happy. On his good days—well, there haven't been many
of those lately. I guess I'm just lousy at this marriage thing."

"Maybe," Charlotte said lightly, as she flicked her cigarette
out the window and then rolled up the glass. "Or maybe it's a
lousy marriage."

I contemplated that as we drove through Chimacum and up
toward Port Townsend. The fog cleared as we left the valley,
and wintry sunshine shimmered on the choppy waters of Port
Townsend Bay. As we turned up toward Morgan Hill, I said,
"Will was right about one thing, Aunt Charlotte."

"Was he?"

"He told me I would love the farm. And I do."

"That's something, at least." She parked the Studebaker in
front of Dr. Masters's pretty white house. His office was at
the side, marked with his name on a little sign beside a bright
green door.

My nausea returned in full force, and I groaned. "Hope I
don't throw up in there."

"He'll have a remedy for that. Come on. Let's have Dr. Masters
confirm you're in the family way."

Watery sunshine gleamed on the wet landscape as Charlotte drove us back through town and south toward the canal. Wordless and miserable, I slumped in my seat.

When we reached Chimacum, my aunt touched my arm. "Shall we stop for a bite?"

I shook my head. "I couldn't."

"But Dr. Masters said you should eat several times a day. That will help with the nausea."

"It won't help if it comes right back up." I shook my head, disgusted with myself. "Sorry, Aunt Charlotte. This has turned me all whiney."

"Dr. Masters said you'll feel better after the first few months."

"At least my stomach will feel better." I made myself chuckle, but it was a grim sort of effort. "Sorry. Doing it again."

"That's okay. But let's talk about it."

"I suppose we should. It's not really your problem, though."

She clicked her tongue. "I hope you don't mean that."

I reached across the seat to touch her elbow. "I meant I got myself into this situation. You tried to stop me."

"No point worrying about what's done." She put out her hand to signal the turn toward Brinnon. "But everything that happens with you is my 'problem,' as you put it. Nothing will ever change that."

"Thanks, Aunt Charlotte." I swallowed and thought my stomach felt a little bit better. Dr. Masters had given me a green concoction in a glass bottle, something he made himself, and fed me a tablespoon while I was still in his examining room.

We hadn't killed the rabbit. After examining me, Dr. Masters said there was no point in sacrificing a bunny, because he could assure me I was pregnant. He guessed three months, and when I looked at a calendar and remembered those first days at the farm in September, I knew he was right. He congratulated me, and when tears of anxiety filled my eyes, he patted my shoulder and told me it was natural to have mixed feelings.

I didn't say so to Dr. Masters, but my feelings weren't mixed in the least. They were painfully clear.

"I don't know what Will's going to say," I told Charlotte.

"You don't think he'll be happy?"

"He's rarely happy."

"That's bleak."

"I know." I sighed and pushed myself into a straighter position. I was grateful for the bottle that now rested in my handbag. Which Charlotte had paid for. "He might be glad of it, actually," I mused. "Because now I can't leave."

"Why can't you leave?"

"I'm trapped," I said. It was a blunt statement, and it was the first time I had admitted the truth, even to myself. "The marriage was the first step, although I have doubts now about the romance. I think the farm was Will's way of persuading me to give the marriage a second chance. A baby will tie me to him for good."

"Do you think it's possible, Barrie Anne, that he really cares about you?"

I didn't answer for a time. I gazed through the trees, catching glimpses of the winter-gray salt water. As we turned off the highway into our lane, I said, "I don't know what Will cares about, Aunt Charlotte. I suspect he cares about something for a time and then gets tired of it and goes on to the next thing. I might be one of those things."

"And sometimes he comes back," she said, with a sour twist of her lips.

"Yes," I answered. And under my breath, "And sometimes I wish he hadn't."

It was almost dinnertime when I walked up to the house, my handbag over my arm. I hadn't been able to persuade Charlotte to stay. She said an announcement like mine should be made in private, and once I was out of the car, she backed and turned and scooted off down the muddy lane. Will's jalopy, with a canvas cover over it, was parked beside the fence. The farm was quiet.

I trudged up the short stair to the porch and let myself into the front room. I found Will in the kitchen, peeling carrots. A glass of beer was at his elbow. He looked up, frowning. "I don't like you to leave without telling me, Barrie."

"Sorry," I said.

He put down the peeler and picked up his beer glass. "So?" he said. "Where were you?"

"Charlotte took me to the doctor."

"Why? What's the matter with you?"

I dropped my handbag on the table and pulled out the bottle of green medicine. It was thick and syrupy and tasted of peppermint, but I guessed I was going to learn to like it. "You know my stomach's been bothering me," I said. "I told you."

"Everyone gets an upset tummy once in a while. Charlotte should quit fussing over you. How much did the doctor cost?"

"How much did that beer cost, Will?"

He banged the glass down. "That's my business. I handle the money around here."

"Do you? Well, then, you can repay Charlotte for Dr. Masters's fee."

"Why? Her choice to haul you off to the doctor for a little tummy upset."

"It's been going on for weeks, Will."

"You should have told me. I would have taken you to the doctor if you thought you needed it."

"Would you? Where did you go today?"

"I told you I had to go to the bank."

"In Bremerton."

He picked up his beer glass and turned back to the sink. "Yes. As I said."

"Then why did I see you coming from the other direction?"

Over his shoulder, he snapped at me, "I'm not having this third degree, Barrie. I have business to take care of, business that bought this house, that pays for groceries. Steaks tonight, because I bought them."

I took a spoon from a drawer and uncapped the medicine. "What business is it, Will?" I asked, as casually as I could.

He gave an irritated snort. "I've explained this to you before, Barrie. I invested my back pay. Maybe a woman just can't understand how money is made."

I poured a spoonful of the green stuff and swallowed it. It definitely tasted better now that I knew it was helping. I crossed to the sink to drop the spoon in the strainer. "You didn't ask what Dr. Masters said."

He shook water droplets from the lettuce and set it on a dish towel. "I don't think my mother ever went to the doctor for a little upset stomach."

"Even when she was pregnant?" I bit out the words. He spun to face me, and it occurred to me that this was the first time I had claimed his whole attention in weeks.

His voice turned to gravel. "What did you say?"

"I said—"

"Never mind! I heard you. What did you mean?"

I gazed at his blue eyes, the line of his jaw, the forelock of fair hair that I had once thought so charming, and felt as if I were talking to a stranger. An ugly, angry stranger. "What do you think I meant? I'm expecting," I said. "I'm...that is, *we're*...going to have a baby."

"Are you sure?"

"Of course I'm sure. Because Dr. Masters is sure. And because I'm sick morning, noon, and night. I gather you haven't noticed."

"Did you do a test?"

I turned my back on him and reached for the kettle. As I filled it, my heart pounded with a simmering anger that banished my nausea. I set the kettle on the stove, but before I lit the gas, I faced my husband and tried to speak in a level tone.

"We don't need a test, Will. I'm more than three months along, maybe four, which you could probably figure out for yourself if you were paying attention."

"Paying attention? You mean, to your women's issues?"

I spit out, "Your *wife's* issues."

He drained his glass and reached for the bottle to fill it again. When he had picked it up, he took a foamy swallow, wiped his mouth on the dish towel hanging over his shoulder, and then tossed the towel toward the rack. It missed, but he didn't bend to pick it up. "You're impossible to make happy, Barrie," he said. "I've tried to do everything I can. I bought you this farm. Provided you a home."

"I had my own home."

"You mean the house you were sharing with that dyke?"

I choked. "What?"

"Dyke. Homo. Your aunt. You know how that looks to people, you two living in that house together?"

I'm ashamed to say it took me a full minute to understand what he meant. I gaped at him, so deeply offended I couldn't speak, then so angry I didn't dare move for fear I would hit him with something.

Finally, when I could draw a decent breath, I leaned forward and hissed, "Don't you *ever*—ever again in your life—speak of my aunt Charlotte that way. If you ever, ever use such a word again, I—I will *kill* you."

He laughed in my face.

I burst into tears, whirled away from him, and ran for the solace of my garden.

The rain clouds had cleared away. The air was frigid, but white stars littered the black sky above the peninsula. I hugged myself against the cold and gazed up into their icy brilliance. I tried to understand what was happening. I felt alone, despite the life growing inside me. I was burning with anger, but I was afraid, too—of pregnancy, of childbirth, of the responsibilities of motherhood.

And what would I do about Will?

I picked up a shovel I had left waiting against the fence. I had meant to turn over a pile of compost that morning. Now I banged the shovel against the ground in a welter of frustration.

I wanted to flee from all of it—the pregnancy, Will, even the farm—but everything had spun out of my control. I had no car of my own. The tractor wouldn't get me past the end of the lane. I couldn't walk off in the dark with no coat, no money, not even a flashlight.

I sobbed, and swore, and crushed a clod of dirt into a hundred pieces.

I didn't realize Will had come outside until he spoke.

"Barrie, Barrie, come on now. Put down the shovel."

I started, which made me drop the shovel into the dirt. Will came up beside me and settled his own wool coat around my shoulders. "Come inside," he said, in a tone so mild I didn't recognize it. "It's freezing out here." He pulled a handkerchief from his pocket and handed it to me. "There's no need to cry. Come into the kitchen. You'll feel better after you've eaten."

He bent to pick up the shovel and lodged it safely against a post. I was shivering now, my teeth chattering and my cheeks slimy with tears. I wiped my face dry with the hanky as I started for the house. Will followed.

He had set the table with knives and forks and had fried the steaks in our biggest pan. There was a glass of milk already poured beside my place, and he had set out the butter dish and a plate of sliced bread. I shuddered with the aftermath of tears, but I was hungry, too.

Will served me and sat down opposite with his own meal. We ate in a tense silence. When we had finished, I got up to carry the plates to the sink, but Will jumped up, saying, "I'll do that. You're probably worn out. Not every day you find out you're going to have a baby."

I sank slowly back into my chair, not knowing what to think. It hardly seemed possible that this solicitous man was the same person who had called my aunt a filthy name, had laughed at my anger, and had made no remark on the news of my pregnancy. I watched him at the sink, the lock of hair falling boyishly over his forehead, his glasses fogging from the hot dishwater. I was at a complete loss to understand the twists and turns of being married to Will Sweet.

He stacked the last bowl and ran soaking water into the saucepan. As he was draping the dish towel over the rack, he threw me a guileless grin. "My mother is going to be so happy about this!"

17

August 27, 1947

Emma added new words to her repertoire every day. "But-ton," which came out as "bup-m." "Dog," which sounded like "dod" and which we thought was adorable. "Bird." "Milk," though the "l" was missing. Charlotte and I both started saying "mik" and grinning indulgently. Even "crow," since we saw crows whenever we went out into the garden. That one sounded like "ko," but we knew what she meant.

She had sprouted six tiny teeth, perfect as pearls against the abalone pink of her mouth, and she had decided that her favorite food in the world was toast. It should have been too soon for that kind of food, but we knew, from the first time she seized a piece of toast from my plate and began to lick the butter from it, that it was a decision she had made for herself. It was funny to see her little face shiny with butter, and it was irresistible to watch her employing all six of her teeth to rend the crust from the bread and gnaw the rest of the slice until it disappeared, bit by bit. She learned that word, too, and began demanding "Toast! Toast!" every morning.

"She must be older than we thought," Charlotte murmured one afternoon, as we watched her sleeping in her cradle.

"But she's so tiny, Aunt Charlotte!"

"I know." Charlotte braced her elbows on the sofa as she pondered Emma's rosy face.

"So much we don't know about her, isn't there? Did you get any idea how tall the—her—"

Like me, she couldn't bring herself to refer to the dead woman buried in our garden as Emma's mother. Still, that's what she was, or had been. I knew it must be true, even if I didn't want to talk about it.

I straightened Emma's blanket. "She was sort of small, I guess," I said. "But I didn't take a good look. Maybe I should have, for Emma's sake, but..." I shuddered, remembering the feel of the shroud and the shifting and sliding of the disintegrating corpse it held.

"Makes you wonder what other surprises this little cupcake has in store."

I gave a rueful laugh. "How will we keep up?"

Charlotte straightened, smiling at me. "No idea, kiddo. No idea at all. We'll just have to deal with them one at a time."

We had taken to giving Emma her bath upstairs, in the enormous clawfoot tub that was original to the house. It was a hideous thing, made of painted cast iron that was chipping in a dozen places, but Emma loved it.

Neither Charlotte nor I had yet gotten used to watching Emma in the water. I wondered if we ever would. More than once I found myself holding my breath so long I had spots before my eyes. Charlotte clasped her hands as she watched, smiling as if a baby underwater was something she had waited her whole life to see. Just the same, she stayed with me, close by the tub, both of us ready to snatch the baby out at the first sign she was in trouble.

Such a sign never came. The moment we lowered Emma into the water, she settled to the bottom as if she had been waiting for the opportunity. She grinned up at us through the clear water, her pale hair frothing around her head, a cloud of shining bubbles rising to evaporate on the surface. She stayed in the water—*underwater*—for a long minute, agonizing for Charlotte and me, clearly delightful for her. When I couldn't bear it anymore, I snatched her up, my hands under her slippery armpits and my own breathing ragged. She crowed with pleasure and blinked water drops from her spidery eyelashes.

"Like a frog," Charlotte said. "You can imagine what people thought of such a thing in the nineteenth century."

"You mean Morag."

"Yes, Morag Stuart. Not, it seems, the only one of her kind."

I clutched Emma close to me, thinking how marvelous it was, and how heartbreaking. I had begun to think of her as my very own, the child of my heart, but these moments reminded me that my Emma was in many ways as mysterious as the watery light I had seen the night before Willow found her on the beach. I thought about that a hundred times, and I thought about my great-grandmother's universe under the water. I knew it might have brought Emma to us. I feared it would want her back.

I wrestled with all these thoughts, but I never spoke them aloud. I felt as if anything I put into words would be irreversible, would declare a new reality—and I didn't want to face it.

Charlotte had gone through all her medical texts, looking for explanations for Emma's difference. She found none. Perhaps someone in the government, someone who knew who or what had appeared in our skies, or in our waters, would have an idea, but I was never going to ask. I couldn't risk it. I didn't care how many Harrisons or Woodses or other men showed up in their black suits and ties. I intended to tell no one about Emma. Or about the body we had buried at the far end of the garden beneath the shelter of the giant cedar.

I considered myself a patriot. I had done my share of war work. I was the wife of a veteran, though he had vanished. I loved my country, and I respected my government.

But they couldn't have my daughter.

In any case, as Charlotte and I had assured each other a dozen times, what good would it do? It wasn't as if a tiny baby could tell them anything. Let them figure it out for themselves, if they could. Let them follow their false leads and write their uninformed reports. Let them deny evidence and seek evidence, all at the same time, foolish as that was. We wouldn't help them.

Charlotte came to me one morning at breakfast with a heavy medical book in her hands. "I have an idea about the gills," she said.

The word still gave me shivers, but I shifted the baby to my left arm so I could lean over the page she was pointing at. It was an ink drawing of an ear.

"This is the pinna," she said, tracing the scrolls of the outer ear. "Also called auricle. Just behind it is the mastoid, which is part of the temporal bone. Emma's gills are below the mastoid, and it seems to me—maybe—that they're close enough to the vertebral arteries and the interior carotid artery to allow oxygen exchange to take place." She straightened and touched Emma's hair with her sensitive artist's fingers. "That's my best guess. A lot of science starts that way, with guesses."

"I'm not sure I understand it."

"Well, it may not be scientific at all."

I couldn't resist a shiver of worry. "Not to be like your mother," I said, "but I would much prefer a scientific explanation."

"That would only work if we posit she has other anatomical differences, but I don't see how we're going to find that out."

"Probably the government men would find a way. Just what I'm afraid of."

Charlotte's hand lifted to squeeze my shoulder. Her hand was strong, and the pressure comforted me. "Don't worry about it, kiddo. I will happily take that rifle of yours and shoot one of them if they try to take her."

That made me laugh. "You've gotten awfully fond of that gun."

"Never too old to change."

"I should teach you how to use it."

"That might be a good idea." She gave my shoulder another squeeze, patted it, and then released me. She crossed the kitchen to pour herself a cup of coffee. She stood in a flood of summer sunshine as she lit her first cigarette of the day. "What's on your chore list today?"

"Digging potatoes. It's been such a hot summer, and the vines are starting to go."

"Shall I help?"

"Oh, thanks, but no. It's too hot out there for Emma, I think. I'll find my spading fork in the shed and get a good start before the sun gets too high. Maybe rest after lunch."

"Good. I'll make sandwiches."

With the plan in place, and with Emma fed and dressed, I tugged on my gardening boots and took down my straw hat. Willow followed me out through the screen door and stayed at my heels as I lugged an empty basket to the potato patch.

For an hour I dug with the spading fork, loosening the potato plants and separating the plump tubers from their parent plants. I took pride in every single one, their weight and length and bright brown skin. The day promised to be one of the broiling sort, with neither clouds nor breeze. I hurried, hoping to fill the basket before the heat drove me indoors.

When a dust cloud appeared in the lane, I was on my way to the root cellar beneath the house, my arms straining with the pleasant weight of a nearly full basket. I didn't recognize the car and didn't think too much about it at first. Occasionally cars came too far up the lane and had to turn around in front of my house, but this one rolled gently to a stop beside our patch of yellowing grass. The driver waited for the dust to settle before opening the door and climbing out. He was a plump, smallish man with a worn bowler and a medical bag.

I set down my basket and dashed toward the back porch, kicking off my boots and stepping inside the door.

"Charlotte!" I called, in a rough whisper. "Charlotte, where's Emma? It's Dr. Masters!"

She appeared at the head of the stairs. "She's with me. I'm painting."

"Do you know why he's here?"

She shook her head. "I'll stay up here with her. Maybe it's just a social call."

We both knew that wasn't likely. Port Townsend was more than an hour's drive away.

A year and more had passed since Scottie's death, which was the last time we had seen the doctor. With Will gone, I couldn't pay Dr. Masters's bill right away. For six months, I had sent a few dollars to his office, whatever I could manage. When I got halfway to the total, he sent me a receipt that read "Paid in Full." I didn't think for a minute he had come to collect the balance.

I hung my hat on its hook and brushed soil from my overalls before I went into the front room to open the door for him. He looked hot and uncomfortable in his suit and vest. His upper lip was beaded with sweat.

"Mrs. Sweet," he said, as he removed his bowler. "I've caught you working, I see."

"Hello, Dr. Masters." I held the door wide. "Yes, I was in the garden. Sorry about my clothes. Won't you come in? What brings you all this way?"

"I had a house call at one of your neighbors'. Mrs. Urquhardt."

"I hope she's well?"

"She is. No doubt she'll tell you herself, but she's expecting again."

"Oh, my goodness. Her house is bursting with children already."

"That it is. They seem happy enough, though."

"She's going to need her crib back!"

"Yes, probably. In time." He stamped dust from his shoes and shook more from his hat before he stepped inside. He smiled up at me. I had forgotten I was taller than he was. "You look well," he said. "I'm glad to see that."

"I am. Thank you. A glass of lemonade?"

"That would be most welcome." He followed me toward the kitchen. Willow paced beside him, giving him curious looks, and when he set his medical bag on the table, she nosed it.

"Willow, no," I said mildly, and she stepped back and sat down, still watching the visitor.

"Seems like a nice dog," Dr. Masters said.

"Best dog in the world." I took the pitcher of lemonade from the icebox and set a glass on the counter. "Please sit down, Dr. Masters."

He did, and when I set the glass before him, he took a deep draft of it. "This is excellent," he said. "I didn't realize how thirsty I was."

I poured myself some lemonade, and settled into a chair opposite him, taking a sip myself. The taste of lemons reminded me of my days in San Diego, sunshine and still air, palm trees and gasoline, and the pervading sense that enormous events were on the horizon. I hoped this was not one of them.

Dr. Masters set down his glass. "Mrs. Urquhardt told me the wonderful news about your new baby daughter," he said. Our eyes met, and the memory of Scottie hung in the air between us. I remembered how kind he had been, how gentle his hands, when he finally took my baby's cold body from my arms. I looked away, shy about the quick tears that burned my eyes.

He said, in his calm way, "I thought I would stop in, since I was so close. Such a fine thing, that you have a baby again."

"Yes," I whispered, and cleared my throat. "Yes," I said again. "She's sleeping."

"Ah. Nap time." He smiled again. "I'd love to peek in on her, though."

His intent was kindness itself, but it terrified me. He wanted to examine her, to reassure me—and himself—that my adopted daughter was healthy, after the tragedy of Scottie. I couldn't think of how to stop him. Charlotte and I had hoped to postpone this moment as long as possible. Forever, if we could.

A step on the stair told me Charlotte had been listening. She came into the kitchen with Emma on her shoulder. Dr. Masters rose. "Miss Blythe, how nice to see you again. And is this the newest member of the family?"

"Yes," Charlotte said. "This is Emma."

Emma craned her neck to see the newcomer. She was wearing her pink cap, tied under her chin. She gave the doctor her rosy, pearl-dotted smile, and waved one starfish hand. "Nope!" she crowed. Charlotte's eyes widened, and I sensed the wave of anxiety that came from her. Emma waved her hand again, this time toward Willow. "Dod!" Her enunciation was hardly perfect. The consonants were mushy, and the vowels were distorted, but her intent was unmistakable.

"Goodness," Dr. Masters said, surprise in his voice. "I understood your baby came to you almost as a newborn."

"N-not quite," I stammered.

Charlotte said, "She's precocious, isn't she? I didn't think babies talked until much later."

"I think 'precocious' is an understatement," Dr. Masters said. He walked around the table and reached for Emma. The baby kicked with delight at meeting a new person and went willingly into his hands. Charlotte and I stood helplessly by, avoiding each other's eyes. My stomach clenched with anxiety, and Charlotte groped automatically for her cigarettes.

"Goodness," Dr. Masters said again, holding Emma up in his hands and smiling into her face. "Aren't you a beauty, little Emma?"

She gave her high-pitched gurgle. Dr. Masters returned to his chair and settled the baby into the crook of his arm. "Tell me about her," he said, his eyes still on the baby.

"She came from a little town in eastern Washington. Her mother died in childbirth, or just after, and wasn't...that is, there was no father."

"Isn't it a miracle that she found her way to you?" he said warmly. He reached into his pocket and drew out a stethoscope. Emma immediately reached for it. Dr. Masters pressed the smooth metal against her palm, and her little mouth stretched wide with delight at the new sensation.

"What's the date of birth?" Dr. Masters asked as he fixed the earpieces of his stethoscope into his ears.

I said hesitantly, "The birth certificate says May twentieth, but..."

Now he looked up at me. "That doesn't seem quite right, does it?"

I shook my head. "I thought maybe there was a mistake. Since she's so—precocious."

"She's very small," he mused, turning back to Emma. "You don't know anything about her parents, I suppose."

"Nothing."

"Lots of such stories since the war," he mused. "She looks fine, though, Mrs. Sweet, nothing to worry about. Just small. Rationing could account for that, or even poverty, if the birth mother wasn't well-nourished during her pregnancy. I have to say, though, I've never known a baby so young to say words. Even if she's six months old and not three."

I clenched my hands together in my lap as he listened to Emma's heart and lungs and ran his fingers down her chubby legs. He tweaked her toes, making her gurgle with laughter. He wriggled her arms and legs, flexing the joints. He put his palm on her forehead and looked into her eyes. "Look at those emerald eyes!" He chuckled. "You're going to break some hearts, aren't you, little lady?" She chortled.

Dr. Masters smiled above her head. "I'll just have a quick peek into her ears." He started to untie the strings of Emma's cap.

Charlotte, standing by the sink, drew a sharp breath, which made her cough. I couldn't move. I felt as if ice had slipped into my veins, freezing my hands and feet and face. I watched Dr. Masters take his brass otoscope out of his bag and then bend forward to look into Emma's ears, first one and then the other. She squirmed, but when he crooned to her, she was still. He pressed the auricle flat on each ear to look inside. When he was done, he straightened and tucked the otoscope back in his bag.

He snuggled the baby into the crook of his elbow and began to replace the crocheted cap. "I'm glad to say, Mrs. Sweet, that your Emma is perfectly healthy. And obviously bright." He set the cap on her head, and began to pull down the sides.

I reached for her, saying, "I can do that, Dr. Masters." I was too late.

As he pulled down one side of the cap, his fingers caught in the web of pink yarn. He had to lift the cap again, untangle his fingers, and start over. He stopped cold, hissed a breath, and peered at Emma's left ear. I dropped my hands and hugged myself anxiously as Dr. Masters lifted the auricle with one finger.

I had the oddest thought at that moment, a complete irrelevance, that Dr. Masters's hands were the cleanest I had ever seen. My brain, avoiding the collision that was to come, spun after the idea, wondering how he washed them, how he kept his nails so trim, if he wore gloves...

He said, "What on earth—" as he stared at the peculiarity behind my baby's delicate ear.

Charlotte crushed out her cigarette and stalked toward the table. "It's a birth defect, isn't it?" she said.

I stared at her in surprise. She had been very, very clear that she didn't consider Emma's gills to be a defect. For a moment I couldn't breathe, wondering how this would go, whether she could make her suggestion seem reasonable...what the doctor would say. Or do.

Dr. Masters turned his face up to her. He had gone pale except for two spots on his cheeks that were so red they looked painful. Hoarsely, he said, "Birth defect?"

In the midst of my anxiety, I felt a stab of pity for him, this benevolent physician who knew what it was to lose a child. Who only meant to be helpful.

Charlotte pressed on, saying, "We heard there are a lot of those since the war. Since the bomb."

"Beg pardon?"

"Yes," she said, managing such a pragmatic tone I had to look away from her or else stare in amazement. She waved one negligent hand. "I read a lot of medical news, Dr. Masters. I'm a medical illustrator—can't remember if you knew that. In any case, I don't remember where I saw it—something in one of the journals about the rate of birth defects rising since the A-bomb."

"But that would be in Japan..." the doctor said, faltering.

"They tested the bomb stateside," she said easily. "Before they used it overseas."

"I haven't seen those reports. What journal was it?"

"Gosh, I've forgotten. I'll see if I can dig it up."

I reached for Emma, lifting her from the doctor's grasp. His hands were trembling slightly. Charlotte said, "We're so glad Emma's little difference isn't obvious. Some of the ones I've read about are terrifying, aren't they, Barrie Anne?"

"Yes," I said in a rush, "so upsetting. We've been lucky."

Dr. Masters stared up at me, biting at his lower lip. He started to say something further, but his voice cracked, and he stopped, swallowing as if his mouth had gone dry.

Charlotte said, with stunning aplomb, "Doctor, it's so hot today. Maybe more lemonade? Or a glass of water?"

He passed a hand over his forehead. "Yes, please. I'd appreciate that. I'm just...you must forgive me..."

"Oh, I understand," Charlotte said. "We were startled at first, too." She filled a glass at the sink and carried it back. "I've seen illustrations of vestigial tails on infants, but never these—whatever they are."

He accepted the glass and took a long drink. As he set it down, he said, almost as if speaking only to himself, "It's strange, you know. So strange, and . . . well, I was at a medical conference not long ago, and there was a rumor going around about a baby with—with an anomaly behind the ears."

"Gills," Charlotte said. "Like a frog."

He glanced up at her. "Well, yes. You could call them that, I suppose. But it was just a rumor. No one would admit to being the physician who had seen the baby. Most of us dismissed it as one of those odd stories that get started, but—" He picked up the glass again, and drank. "I should probably take a photograph. If these—uh, abnormalities—are going to start appearing, a medical journal—"

"Oh, please don't publish about it," Charlotte interrupted. "It's hard enough on the poor little tyke, no father, losing her mother. We're hoping she can just have a normal life."

Dr. Masters didn't answer right away, instead continuing to gaze at Emma with an expression of utter bemusement.

For long moments, the only sounds were from the baby, giggling as Willow licked her bare toes, and from a pair of house finches chittering in the rosebushes. Dr. Masters drained his water glass, set it on the table, and then pinched the bridge of his nose as if his head ached or as if he was trying to think. I couldn't think of anything else to say to him, and when I looked up at Charlotte, she shrugged.

We waited. There was nothing else we could do. Emma was warm and soft in my lap, and I pulled her close to my heart, knowing I would do anything—anything—to protect her. There would be no photograph. I would see to it there was no article in a medical journal. It didn't matter how much I liked Dr. Masters, how much I appreciated his kindness. I wouldn't— couldn't—allow it.

I forced my mind to stop there. Not to go to a place from which I couldn't return. Not unless it proved to be necessary.

At last, Dr. Masters dropped his hand and spoke again. "Where did you say Emma came from, Mrs. Sweet?"

"Malden."

"And you have the birth certificate."

"We do. Do you want to see it?"

"No, that's not necessary, but—no doctor's notes or any comment on her...on her condition?"

"Nothing. A nun brought her, and the sister didn't say a word."

This was the story we had decided on, Charlotte and I. We had heard that nuns often took in unwed mothers and found homes for their infants. The explanation seemed to satisfy Dr. Masters. Gradually, the spots receded from his cheeks, and the shaking of his hands ceased.

Charlotte and I avoided each other's eyes as another silence stretched in the sunny kitchen. I kissed Emma's head. Dr. Masters scratched one eyebrow. "Well," he said. He drew a deep breath and released it slowly. I suspected it was a technique he used whenever he faced a medical predicament he couldn't solve. He stroked Emma's bare foot with a finger. She grinned up at him, and his own face softened.

He smiled back, tenderly, a little sadly. I wondered if he was remembering Herbert as a baby. His only child, gone too young, one of far too many. I knew how painful that loss must be. My own had been different, of course, one small death in the midst of many great ones, but it hurt just as deeply.

"Well," he repeated, still caressing the baby's foot. "This is a truly strange thing, isn't it, little Emma?"

"Don't you think, Dr. Masters," I said, "that as long as it doesn't bother her..."

"Right," he said. "That's right. Just...just a rare condition." He squeezed Emma's toes and released her foot. "Let me know if the...the condition troubles her at all. Call me if it...causes any problems."

"We will," I said.

Charlotte said, "No problems so far."

"Good. Good." He reached for his medical bag and began reordering its contents. "You two are doing all right, then, living out here?"

"We love it," I said, glad to be able to speak honestly.

Charlotte nodded. "It's peaceful."

Dr. Masters reached for his hat, and as he pushed himself up from his chair, he said, "Just keep an eye out, won't you? I'm told there are some men going around, dropping in on people's houses and asking a lot of questions."

"Oh, we know," Charlotte said.

I said, "They've been here twice."

Dr. Masters frowned. "They've been to the Urquhardts', too. They say they're from the government, but I've never heard of people from the government acting that way."

He snapped his bag shut and reached for his hat. "Well, I hope you ladies will take care. Two women alone, with no close neighbors—I'll have a word with the sheriff about you."

"That's kind," I said. "There's no need, though, truly. We have Willow, and they're afraid of her." The dog thumped her tail in acknowledgment. "I also have a gun, and I know how to use it."

That made him chuckle. "You're full of surprises, Mrs. Sweet." He settled his bowler on his head. "Let me know if you need anything for your little one."

I stood, balancing Emma on my hip. "Thank you for examining her."

"It's good to see you doing well."

Emma wriggled against my hip and crowed, "Nope! Dod!"

"She's awfully proud of those words, isn't she?" he said with a smile.

"Very," I said, with rueful sincerity.

"Interesting. I've had a couple of patients who formed words at six months and spoke sentences at twelve months. I've heard of babies saying 'Mama' and 'Papa' really early, but no other words. Babies have their own schedules, of course." He turned toward the front room, adding, "Still, as she grows, her speaking won't be so remarkable. By the time the little ones start school, all of them seem to speak at about the same level."

Emma squealed, "Nope! Nope!" as I followed him to the door.

Dr. Masters laughed. "That's often a baby's favorite word."

I laughed, too, giddy with relief now that our moment of danger had passed. "You'll send me a bill," I said. "For the house call."

"No, not this time," Dr. Masters said. "No charge today."

"If you're sure. Thank you for coming."

"She's a lucky little girl. I'm delighted you found each other."

He said his goodbyes, went out the door, and walked through the yard to his car. Charlotte came to stand at my shoulder, and we watched as he backed and turned and drove away in obscuring billows of dust.

"Of course it's not just luck you found each other," Charlotte murmured.

"What?"

She gave me a sidelong glance. "It wasn't an accident. I mean, there was an accident, the one that took Emma's first mother's life, but the rest—the magic brought her, Barrie Anne. A little water magic, as Grandmother Fiona used to say."

"Not so little, I think."

"No." She smiled and touched Emma's head with her palm. "No, in this case, a very great water magic. Grandmother Fiona would be proud."

The dust cloud Dr. Masters's car had raised began to settle, and we turned back toward the kitchen. "I think we convinced the doctor," Charlotte said.

"You were amazing. When did you think of all that?"

"On the spot." She tapped her forehead. "Pretty good tale, don't you think?"

"Pretty good doesn't begin to describe it. You almost convinced me!"

She laughed and pulled her cigarettes out of her pocket. "The best stories are the ones that could be true."

"It's going to be hard sometimes," I said, feeling a wave of fatigue over the challenges to come.

Emma made an odd little sound, a tiny little hum, as if in agreement. I looked down at her and found her small face drawn in an intent expression, like that of an old woman, her mouth pulled down, her eyelids heavy. I hadn't seen it before. It chilled me. "What is it, Emma?" I found myself whispering, as if she could understand my question.

She gazed up at me, her emerald eyes dark as jade beneath their fair lashes. She breathed a tiny sigh, then said, solemnly, softly, her sweet high voice fragile as a crystal bell. "Dod. Ko. Mik." They weren't the right words, but they were the words she could speak. All she had with which to express herself. I understood her perfectly.

With another wistful sigh, she laid her head against my shoulder, and I felt her little spirit reaching out to mine, heart to heart, daughter to mother. It was both infinitely sad and sweet beyond bearing. Through a tight throat I said, "It's all right, little one. We'll face it all together."

Charlotte stared at us, her cigarette hanging unlit from her lower lip. "How could she know?" she breathed.

I managed a tiny smile above the baby's head. "Because she's one of us. Our kind."

Charlotte nodded gravely. "I see I'm not the only one who knows things, Barrie Anne."

"I don't know if I know it, or just feel it, Aunt Charlotte."

"One and the same, kiddo. One and the same."

18

April 1946

My garden that first year was an act of faith. A year before, I wouldn't have known a mound of potatoes from a row of pea vines. I didn't know a thing about irrigation or fertilizer. I couldn't have said what mulch was, much less how to make it or what to do with it.

Will pointed that out one day in March when he found me building a compost bin out of the last of the salvaged boards. "What are you going to put in it?"

"Potato peels, coffee grounds, eggshells, anything that makes compost."

"It's going to stink."

"Probably. It's good for the crops."

"Come on, Barrie. Admit you don't really know what you're doing."

"You're the one who bought the farm," I snapped. "Did you know what you were doing?"

"Apples," he said, pointing at the orchard beside the canal. "I know about apples."

"Good. The orchard is all yours." I was six months pregnant, busy getting ready for a baby and learning to be a farmer. I was beginning to fatigue easily, and I was short on patience and not interested in arguing.

I sometimes reflected that it might not be fair to expect Will to converse with me in the same way I conversed with my aunt. I didn't know if such things were different for men than for women because I had no experience with such relationships. Charlotte and I had always had lively discussions, tossing up ideas, debating them, sometimes coming to an agreement, sometimes not, but content enough with the argument.

That didn't work with Will. He didn't discuss or debate or even argue. He issued pronouncements, as if he were my commanding officer. If I disagreed, he would say something dismissive and walk away before I could respond. Once in a while he went too far, and I lost my temper, as when he called my aunt that unforgivable name. When that happened, he would ignore me for a while. A day would pass, sometimes two, and then he would do something sweet, something kind, and behave as if nothing had ever happened.

At least he never said that about Charlotte again. Of course, I didn't tell her about it, but I understood from her—more by inference than directly—that women like her were accustomed to being insulted. I vowed, in the secrecy of my own heart, that I would never allow Will to insult her again, not to her face, and not behind her back, either. I didn't think I would actually *kill* him, though I had to admit it had felt good—felt cathartic—to blurt the threat, empty though it was.

I had to admit, also, that by this point there was no affection left between us.

I had no experience of marriages, of course, with my parents gone when I was so young, but I wondered. How many marriages plodded along like ours? Why did they continue? It seemed that habit and circumstance, perhaps just inertia, held them together. The only thing I knew for sure was that marriage—at least, *my* marriage—wasn't the romantic state the movies showed. It wasn't romantic in the least. At best, it was functional. At worst—well, the worst was yet to come.

One evening in early April, when it grew too dark to work in the garden, I settled myself on the steps of the back porch with a cup of tea. I could feel spring in the softening air, see it in the busyness of the juncos and finches as they foraged for nesting materials. Buds were setting on the rosebushes, and from my seat on the steps, I could smell the rich fragrance of newly turned earth. I gazed up into the deepening twilight, watching the stars flicker to life, one by one.

Will opened the back door and said, "Barrie? What are you doing?"

"Just taking a rest." I held up my teacup so he could see it.

I was startled when he came to sit beside me, stretching his long legs down to the bottom step. He said, "Nice evening, isn't it?"

Wary of his unpredictable moods, I said hesitantly, "Yes, it's beautiful. Do you want some tea?"

"I'll get it if I do," he said. "You must be tired."

"A bit." I sipped tea, watching him above the rim of my cup. He was leaning back on his hands, his chin tipped up, looking up into the early stars. His fair hair glowed in the light from the kitchen behind us, and his profile was clean and strong, nearly movie-star handsome.

He said, still gazing into the smattering of stars, "Once you have the baby, Barrie, you should meet my parents."

"Oh!" I couldn't think what else to say. The idea made me both nervous and curious. I suspected Mr. and Mrs. Sweet weren't the sort of parents my friends had, the sort who had often invited me into their homes, fed me cookies, asked polite questions about school. I had only one unpleasant letter to judge them by, and that had hardly been encouraging.

"Don't you want to?" Will asked, and for once, there was no challenge in his voice, just the question. "They're going to be the baby's grandparents, after all."

"Of course I want to," I made myself say. "It's just—well, we've never talked about this. I wasn't sure if you—"

"My mother is going to be thrilled." A note of something crept into his voice. I didn't know what it was—not anger, exactly, but a sort of resentment mixed with satisfaction.

"That's good, isn't it? That she'll be happy?"

"I can't wait to tell her. It's one thing David hasn't been able to do, give her a grandchild."

"David?"

"My brother. I told you."

I frowned, trying to remember what he had said, but it

had been four years, and not a word since then. "David—he's younger than you?"

"No, two years older. You've forgotten."

"I guess I have."

"That's okay."

This wasn't like Will, either, and though I wanted to know more—a lot more—I took care with my next question. "I guess...you and David...you're not close?"

He gave a single bark of sour laughter. "No, we're definitely not close."

"What is he like?"

Will dropped his chin and gazed into the gathering darkness. Starlight sparkled on the lenses of his glasses, hiding his eyes from me. "David," he said, biting off the name as if it tasted bitter in his mouth, "is the easy one. The smart one, the popular one. The favorite son."

"Oh, Will," I said. "*You're* smart. Surely your family knows that."

"I'm not a doctor."

"David is a doctor? Is that why you wanted to be a corpsman, because—" I broke off the sentence. I didn't need to ask. He had wanted to go into medicine to compete with his brother.

He pulled up his feet to a higher step so he could rest his elbows on his knees. "It was a mistake. It didn't suit me."

I set my teacup to one side and linked my hands around my swollen belly. Despite the coolness there had been between us, I felt sorry for him. It seemed pitiful that his principal reason for being glad about the baby was because it would please his mother. I hoped when the baby actually arrived, he would love it for its own sake, but even then, I couldn't begin to predict what this most unpredictable of men might do.

I said carefully, "We'll go and meet them, Will, when the baby comes. I promise."

His voice was choked when he answered. "Thanks, Barrie. Thank you."

I put my hand on his arm and felt the shudder of his muscles beneath my fingers. How long had it been since we touched each other? "Come on, Will, it's getting cold. Let's go in and make dinner."

He surprised me one more time by standing and extending his hand to help me to my feet, and even opening the door for me to pass through. I reflected, as I preceded him out of the dark and into the brightness of the kitchen, that this might have been the first honest conversation, the first real sharing of history and feelings, that we had ever had.

It was, unfortunately, also the last.

The last week of April was cool but sunny, with breezes that smelled richly of sweet box and more faintly, but distinctly, of apple blossoms. My body had reached the ungainly stage, and bending over the tilled rows in the garden was all but impossible. I concocted a kneeling pad by stitching flour sacks together with yarn. It was soon stained dark with garden soil, but it served well enough.

I had spent the dark winter months studying the Burpee

catalog, memorizing instructions. I was delighted with the results of my compost bin. Impatient, I began turning the mulch too early, but I could hardly wait to spread it on the soil I had hoed and raked in anticipation of the growing season.

One sunny morning I was so eager to begin my planting that I left the breakfast dishes soaking in Lux Super Suds. I knew the sink full of water would be cold and greasy by the time I came back, but I couldn't wait. I pulled on the garment I thought of as my gardening sweater. It was nearly as stained as my kneeling pad, and it was also missing two buttons, but those didn't matter. It would no longer close around my bulk in any case. I dropped a bag of seeds into one of the pockets and carried my kneeling pad outside, where I set it beside a well-turned row.

Grunting, I worked my way down to my knees and began pressing wrinkled, dried-up-looking pea seeds into the dirt with my bare fingers. I could have worn gloves, but I relished the sensation of the cool, dark soil against my skin. I thrilled at every industrious worm I turned up and freed it carefully to go back to its work. I crumbled soil into my palm, trying to judge how fertile it would be, how much water it would need, how firmly to pat it down over my seeds.

I worked happily most of the morning, until, thirsty and needing the bathroom, I struggled to my feet, balancing my belly as best I could. I decided I could put in my tomato stakes later that afternoon. Charlotte was due any moment, coming to have lunch and to help me fill out the layette I had begun. The Sears Roebuck and Montgomery Ward catalogs were laid ready on the table. I planned to make bologna sandwiches and green salad for our lunch, but first I needed to get those dishes washed.

Charlotte was enjoying the baby preparations as much as I was. She had taken me to the Mercantile in Port Townsend to buy maternity smocks and skirts with elastic waistbands. She showed up unexpectedly one day a few weeks later, laden with brushes and cans of paint, all of which she carried up the stairs and into the nursery. "Don't ask," she told me, with a flap of her hand. "It's a surprise." She closed the door and stayed up there for hours. When she finally called down the stairs to invite me in, I hurried to see what she had been up to.

When I stepped through the door, I clapped my hands in delight. She had painted the ceiling to look like a summer sky, a clear pale blue with puffs of white cloud. Three seagulls tilted their silvery wings over the imaginary horizon. It was lovely. I could just imagine a child growing up under that summer sky, going to sleep with those seagulls keeping their watch over-head, knowing this charming little room as a refuge, a safe place. A home.

I loved the baby already. I had no preference for a boy or a girl. I kept a list of names on the kitchen table that I played with every day over breakfast, adding a name, crossing out others. I was getting close, I thought. My father's name had been Scott, and I thought that sounded nice. Scott Blythe Sweet. It had resonance. My mother had been Thelma, which I didn't care for so much. I was considering Suzanne. Or Sarah.

I suspected Charlotte already knew whether we would have

a boy or a girl, but she only smiled at my list and didn't offer to tell me. I didn't ask. It seemed part of the wonder of it all, not knowing until the baby arrived.

Will barely glanced at my list, though I left it where he could see it. He also barely glanced into the nursery, although once I saw him squinting up through his glasses at the sky ceiling. A crib had arrived, donated by Mrs. Urquhardt and delivered by her silent husband in their much-dented Ford truck. Charlotte discovered a small bureau in the secondhand store, and together we stripped it of several coats of paint and repainted it to match the ceiling, sky-blue all over with puffs of cloud emerging from the drawers. We were almost ready.

Very soon now, I would be a mother. As I trudged up from the garden to the house, I caressed the swell of my abdomen, but there was no response. In the early months, when the baby started to move, I felt as if I had swallowed a fish that wriggled this way and that in my belly. Now it moved less. I thought the poor little thing must be running out of room.

When I reached the kitchen, I found Will standing beside the table, looking down at an envelope in his hand. The mail we received consisted mostly of bills or catalogs, so it was an event to receive an actual letter. Sometimes I heard from Peggy or Sally or one of my college friends, but not often. I peered at the envelope from across the table. Even upside down, I recognized the handwriting. It was Will's mother's.

I watched him open the envelope and draw out two sheets of that same drugstore paper she had used when she wrote to me. He stood beside the table, reading it, then rereading it.

When he didn't say anything, I prompted him. "What does she say, Will?"

He looked up, and I gasped.

He was transformed, a stranger, a person I had never seen before. His face had gone ashy, and his eyes were narrow and angry behind his glasses. White marks framed his mouth like scars. He said in a bitter tone, "Oh, she's happy about the baby. Nice of her to mention it."

"But that's—that's good, isn't it?"

"Yes."

"When did you tell her?"

"I wrote to her last week."

"I didn't realize that. She hasn't written before, or called, so . . ."

"No telephone. And she's not much of a writer."

I stretched my hand across the table. "Can I read it?"

He snatched the letter out of my reach. "It's addressed to me."

"Of course, but—Will, she's my mother-in-law! She's going to be the baby's grandmother! I'd like to get to know her, at least through a letter. Your father, too."

"You don't know what they're like."

"But you said she's happy about . . ." My remark withered before the tension in his face. He wouldn't look at me, and I saw that his hand, holding the envelope, had begun to tremble violently. I pressed a hand to my throat. "Will, tell me what's the matter."

"One line," he said, biting off the words. "She wrote one

line about the baby. She wrote another line about the farm. Everything else is David."

"Oh, surely not," I said, without thinking. "Let me see it."

He said, "No! I told you, it's addressed to me!" He stuffed the letter roughly back into the envelope, folded the whole thing in half, and shoved it into his pants pocket. "David has a new clinic. David was in the paper. David is going to marry the daughter of a congressman. That's all she cares about."

"I'm sure that's not true. You must be exaggera—"

"Don't talk about it!"

"But, Will, this is crazy. I—"

"Don't use that word!" he snapped. I shrank back as he bent toward me, his face suffused with fury. "Don't ever call me that!"

"I didn't—"

"They always said that to me, and I hate it! It's not fair!" He kicked at the chair beside him, and it banged to the floor, making me jump. Even the baby jumped at the noise, quivering in my belly like a startled bird. Will was shouting now. "You hear me, I *hate* it!"

"You mean the word?" I quavered. "Who said that? David?"

"Not David!"

"Will, calm down! I didn't mean—"

"It wasn't David. It was my father! And my mother, who damn well knows a thing or two about crazy!" The china in the cupboards rattled under the force of his voice. He slapped the table with the flat of his hand, then swept the catalogs and my list of baby names to the floor. He stood with his arms raised, the fingers open wide. His whole body shook so hard it didn't seem possible he could stay on his feet. He took a step toward me, and despite his trembling, he appeared to swell with anger, to grow taller, wider, his eyes glittering and his mouth opening as if he wanted to bite something.

Crazy. "Crazy" was the right word, the perfect word to describe a man who looked like a snake poised to strike, his fist in the air and a thread of spittle dripping from his lower lip.

I felt horribly small and vulnerable. Hastily, awkwardly, I slid out of my chair and made a futile attempt to hide behind it. The chair's back pressed against my pregnant belly, a reminder that the danger was not just for me.

I had never felt so alone in my life. I couldn't reach the telephone, and even if I could, who would come? There was a sheriff in Brinnon, but he was half an hour away. There were the Urquhardts, but they—or any of our neighbors—would consider a family dispute none of their business. Who hadn't seen a wife or a child with bruises everyone pretended not to notice?

I took two steps backward, my eyes on Will. "I don't know anything about this," I protested. Fear thinned my voice and shortened my breath.

He staggered around the table, drunk with fury. "You just had to write to my parents! You couldn't use a bit of judgment, a bit of patience. You made me look bad, when I hadn't had a chance to explain that I'd been sick, or—"

"Will, I didn't know!" I took another step, and my back hit the counter. I was trapped.

"How dare you?" he shouted. "Just like my mother, criticizing, comparing—" He grabbed my arm, and when I tried to pull free, he threw his other arm around my neck, catching me in a grip that bent my head at an impossible angle. His elbow tightened around my throat.

For one ghastly moment, I couldn't breathe, and in my panic, I couldn't see. I forgot everything in the need for air. I scrabbled at his arm with my fingers, but it was like trying to scratch a rock. As my need grew desperate, I kicked at him. He swore, and his elbow loosened a fraction, admitting one quick breath into my lungs before it tightened again. It was a vicious grip, an intentional one. I had no doubt it was possible he might choke the life out of me, and my baby with me. He was completely out of control.

I squirmed in his grip, trying to break free. One hand was trapped by his body. The other thrashed about, seeking something to hold on to, a weapon, anything to loosen his arm. My hand splashed into the cold dishwater standing in the sink. I scooped a handful of soapy water and threw it upward.

"Goddammit!" Will thundered, so close to my ear that it hurt.

He released me all at once, and I stumbled away from him. I felt a ripple in my stomach, as if the baby was trying to get away, too. Will was pawing at his eyes. His spectacles spun away to the floor as he blindly reached for the towel rack.

A car door slammed from the road. I left Will scrubbing at his stinging eyes as I hurried toward the front room, moving as quickly as I could with my unbalanced body.

Charlotte was on her way up the path. She wore her usual trousers, with a scarf tied over her hair and her handbag on her arm. I banged through the front door and stumbled down the path to meet her. I lost my balance just as we met, and my swollen belly collided with her flat one as she put out her arms to catch me.

"Barrie Anne! What on earth...?"

"Aunt Charlotte, can we just get out of here? Drive somewhere?"

She cast one grim glance at the house, turned me with her arm, and hustled me back to the car. She saw me into the passenger seat, tossed her handbag at my feet, and trotted to the driver's side. She hit the ignition, shifted into reverse, and backed and turned. She gunned the Studebaker's motor as she reached the lane, stirring a tremendous cloud of dust behind us. "You okay, kiddo?" she barked.

I stared down at my hands, still wet from the soapy water. "Yes," I said. "I think so. Yes, I'm okay."

"You want to tell me?"

"I thought he was going to kill me!"

"Should we go to the police?"

"They won't believe me. They'll just say—" A wild laugh bubbled in my throat. "They'll say I'm hysterical! Just another hysterical woman!"

"But you're not hurt? You or the baby?"

I tried to take a deep breath, to calm myself. "No, I'm not—I'm not hurt. Not really. Just shaken up." I held my hand before my face and saw it was trembling. "He was out of control. Tried to choke me. I couldn't breathe, but I was right by the sink. It was full of soapy water. I scooped up a handful and threw it in his eyes."

"Water. Good." She drove on, steadily and fast, as we both tried to catch our breaths. As my panic began to subside, I imagined the baby's terror receding, too. It was strange, feeling like two people in one body, both of us shocked by our experience.

Charlotte said, "Do you want to tell me what happened?"

"Absolutely, but first—Aunt Charlotte—Oh, God. I think I've had a premonition."

Charlotte told me to put my head back and close my eyes as she drove the rest of the way to Port Townsend. By the time we reached the town, I was feeling better. My trembling had stopped, and the baby was quiescent. Charlotte pulled the Studebaker to a stop in front of the soda fountain. "We need a Green River," she said.

I managed a weak smile at her. "Good idea. But first, I really, really need the ladies' room."

I went to the restroom behind the soda fountain, and as I washed my hands I gazed at my reflection in the little oval mirror above the sink. My neck was red where Will had gripped it. My sweater and overalls were stained with garden dirt. My hair was shoved under a worn bandana, and my face was pale under its scattering of freckles.

I shrugged, and turned my back on the mirror. Nothing seemed to matter less than my appearance at that moment. I waddled off to the soda fountain, where Charlotte was perched on one of the high stools at the counter, and I wriggled myself onto the one next to her.

We ordered two Green Rivers, and sat in silence until they came. Except for the swell of my pregnant belly, it was a lot like the old days, me sipping green bubbles, Charlotte smoking and fiddling with her glass. I emptied half my glass, then leaned on my elbows and stared into the depths of what was left. Delicate bubbles swirled in it, popping as they reached the surface. I said glumly, "I can see why you don't like these feelings, Aunt Charlotte."

She clicked her tongue in sympathy. "You kind of get used to it. That first one is a blow, though. I remember."

"My hands were wet."

"Of course." She drew a lungful of smoke and tipped up her chin to direct it at the ceiling.

"I don't think my premonition is going to help anything."

"They're like that sometimes."

"Then what good are they?"

"I'm not always sure. I guess it helps to be prepared."

I was beginning to have my doubts about the whole thing, actually. The familiar bright light of the café, with its shining zinc counter and rows of colorful glass bottles, the customers who laughed as they came in, called greetings to one another, passed menus back and forth—it was all so ordinary. Normal. Feelings, water witches, premonitions—such things belonged in books. In films, like *I Married a Witch* or *The Wizard of Oz*. They didn't suit a modern soda fountain.

"So it's a bad feeling." Charlotte prompted. She propped her chin on her hand, looking directly at me.

"I thought so, but now...Really, Aunt Charlotte, I'm not even sure—"

She waggled the fingers under her chin. "Don't hide from it, Barrie Anne. Never works."

"What does work, then? What does it all mean?"

She looked down into her glass, then out through the window with its litter of advertising posters as her fingers groped automatically to pick up her cigarette from the ashtray. "I think," she mused in an undertone, "that the talent needs to be nurtured. I remember Grandmother Fiona making light of her 'little feelings.' She used to say, 'Oh, that's just the way we are,' like saying red hair ran in the family, or weak eyes. But she only spoke of it that way to stop my mother from being angry with her, or my father from making fun, or even threatening to turn her out if she didn't act like a respectable woman."

"Didn't she act like a respectable woman?"

"She usually did. But when she knew something—when she had a feeling—she could be insistent. And when she was right about something, it made my father nervous, and that made him angry."

"Right about what?"

She turned from the window, taking a long drag on her cigarette. "It was mostly trivial things, the weather, a telegram." She smiled in memory. "The last straw, the thing that frightened the housemaid off, was the milk delivery."

"What? The milk?"

Her smile grew. "Silly, isn't it? She was swishing her hand through the maid's mop bucket, and she said, 'Oh, dear, no milk today.' Turned out the milkman's wagon had a broken axle. When we heard that, that poor housemaid turned white as a sheet, her little red freckles standing out all over her face like flyspecks. I wanted to fetch the swatter and have at her, but I didn't get the chance. She left that same day."

"That seems odd. I wonder what she was really afraid of?"

Charlotte put out her cigarette and shook her head. "She was afraid of the big things, the ones Fiona should have kept to herself. She often knew when there was going to be a death, for example."

My heart began to flutter, and in my belly, the baby gave a feeble kick. "A death?" I repeated faintly. I felt suddenly a bit dizzy.

Charlotte didn't notice. "My brother was a sweet man, but he thought all this talk of premonitions, Grandmother's talent, the family legends, was just women's foolishness. I'm afraid I thought that myself until the war. It seems moments of intense emotion can trigger the talent. And water, of course. Like dishwater." She fell silent, smoking and gazing absently at the mirror beyond the soda fountain. "Especially when there's water involved. A river. A lake. The ocean, a rainstorm. Dishwater." She was quiet for a moment, while I finished my drink. Then, in a deceptively offhand manner, Charlotte said, "Now will you tell me?"

The words wouldn't come at first. Her mention of death made my half-felt premonition seem more ominous than I had thought. I feared putting it into words, making it real. I cleared my throat, and my fingers strayed absently to the sore place on my neck. "The thing is," I said finally, tentatively, "it

wasn't as if I had a clear picture or anything. I just had this..."
I couldn't find the word.

"Feeling?" she finished for me.

The baby wriggled suddenly, and I covered the swell of my belly with anxious fingers. "There is no good word, I guess."

"Nope." She sipped at her soda.

Mine was finished, but the soda jerk, seeing, set another full one in front of me. He smiled and tapped the counter with his finger. "This one's for the baby. On the house."

That forced me to muster a smile, despite the pain of my throat and the grimness of my premonition. "Thank you." I took the fresh glass and held my palm against its surface. I ran my finger through the smears of condensation, and the conviction of what I had experienced returned to me as I rubbed my wet fingers together.

"Are you going to tell me about it?" Charlotte said.

I took a first sip from my new glass and swallowed. The baby stopped its movement, settling itself just above my bladder. "I don't know how to describe it," I said.

Some things lend themselves to words, like the blazing feeling of being in love, or the crushing sense of sorrow when someone dies. Others—like the one I was struggling to explain—are too subtle to be easily articulated. Words don't reach the essence of them. Words can't express their elusive, shifting reality.

I said at last, "I just had this—it was like an impression, or even a belief—that Will is going to die. Not right away, but soon. While he's still young. It felt like—like it was just around the corner or maybe just down the street.

"It was like when you look at a plant—a tomato plant, maybe—and even though it has leaves and it's getting sunshine and water, you know instinctively that it's not going to survive. That there's something wrong, something you can't see and you can't fix."

"Well, as you know, I'm no good with plants, but—kiddo, that's a tough one."

"I'm not explaining it very well."

"You were pretty clear. I mean, death is fairly definitive."

"Do you think it's because he hurt me?"

Her eyes narrowed. "If he made those marks on your neck, I may kill him myself." She took a long, bubbling drink of her soda, as if anger had made her thirsty. "Yes, Barrie Anne," she said tightly. "I think the stress of being attacked by the bastard could definitely cause you to have a premonition."

"I don't trust it."

"You haven't had any practice."

"You had a premonition about Will, Aunt Charlotte. What was that like?"

"I knew he was going to break your heart. We all experience these feelings differently. Mine come like waves, the kind that drench you when you're not looking." She sighed and reached for her smoke. "It hit me all at once, and then it was like it had already happened. But I've had a lot of practice."

"I'm not sure I want this talent."

"Wish I could tell you you're going to have a choice."

"I don't know what to do now."

She raised her eyebrows as she drew on her cigarette. "I know what you're going to do, and there won't be any argument about it. You're coming home."

"My garden—" I began.

She threw up her hand, nearly tossing her burning cigarette across the counter. She said in a fierce whisper, "I mean it. You have a baby coming. You can't stay with someone who's violent. Who's probably going to get himself killed." She added, as if I was twelve again, "I forbid it."

I said, "I've made a mess of everything."

"No. Will made a mess of everything. I'm not going to allow you to blame yourself for things that aren't your fault." She crushed out her cigarette, dropped three quarters on the counter, and pushed off the soda fountain stool.

I followed her out to the car, hoping I wouldn't see anyone I knew. My dirty overalls strained over my belly even though I had let out the straps as far as they would go. My buttonless sweater hung around me like something picked out of a ragbag. I felt bloated and ugly, a woman no one could want. A woman whose husband had turned on her.

Charlotte drove me home to our foursquare house and parked in front of the garden fence. She said, "Your room is always ready. Why not go and have a lie-down?"

"I don't have anything with me. No clothes, no money. Not even a toothbrush."

"Your old housecoat is hanging in your closet. I have extra toothbrushes. Enough money to get us by for a bit." She opened the door, and I stepped into the quiet, cool foyer with a sense of relief that almost brought on my tears again. "We'll run down for your clothes when things have cooled off. Better yet, we'll buy new ones."

I knew there was something wrong with this plan, but I couldn't think what it was. I didn't want to feel like a child again, powerless and dependent, but there was no help for it. My neck had begun to ache, a reminder of the ugly scene at the farmhouse. I rubbed it as I lumbered up the stairs and into my old room, which was ready and waiting, just as promised.

I suffered a fresh flood of guilt, thinking of Charlotte dusting that room, mopping the floor, keeping the linens and the curtains clean. I wondered, as I struggled out of my overalls and the dusty flannel shirt I wore under them, if she did all that because of her old premonition. That would be, I supposed, the point of having it. Being prepared. Ready for what was coming.

I found an ancient nightgown in the bottom drawer of my bureau, just loose enough to accommodate my belly. I put it on, wondering if there was anything I should be doing about my own little feeling—which wasn't little at all, of course. It was enormous, a crushing conviction, and I wanted with all my being to deny it. I longed not to have had the premonition at all.

I was so tired I couldn't think anymore. I slid beneath the coverlet of the bed and nestled my sore neck on the pillow. Charlotte was right, as usual. I needed to rest both my body and my mind. I needed to escape what my life had become, at least for a little while. I told myself I would think what to do later.

I slept for a solid, dreamless hour and woke reluctantly. There was no sound except the brushing of tree branches against the window. Charlotte was probably painting, always a silent endeavor. I lay for a moment appreciating the peace before I rolled to my side and pushed myself up and out of the bed. I found the housecoat in my closet and put it on.

I walked downstairs quietly, so as not to disturb Charlotte at work. I went into the kitchen, which was redolent with achingly familiar scents—the morning's coffee, the lingering whiff of Pall Malls, the bunch of bananas ripening in a Depression glass tray. As I ran water into a glass at the sink, I glanced out through the white lace curtain that covered the little kitchen window. I caught a flash of red beyond the rhododendron bushes.

I leaned forward as far as my stomach would allow and lifted the edge of the curtain. My hands began to shake even before I confirmed my fear. My overfull glass jittered against the counter as I set it down, spilling water across the edge of the sink.

Will's jalopy was parked behind the Studebaker. He had wasted no time. It was clever, but I knew by now how clever he could be. I knew his tricks, and I understood why he was here.

He had lost control. Now he would try to regain it, and the first step was to give me no time to think.

I let the curtain fall and backed away from the sink. Charlotte's studio was on the opposite side of the house from the street. She wouldn't see his car. She wouldn't see him walk up the path.

The front door opened and closed with a small click. Will had lived in this house, and he knew we never locked doors. A moment later he stood in the arched doorway to the kitchen, his hat in his hand. His shoulders slumped, and his eyes behind his spectacles were red from the dust of his drive. He emanated dejection.

"Barrie," he said, in a voice that throbbed with sincerity. "I'm glad I found you. You just—you can't know what it's been like."

I said sourly, "I'm sure you're going to tell me."

"There's no need to be nasty," he said. He took a step toward me, and I took a step back, which made him slouch even more and look for all the world as if he might weep.

"You're telling *me* not to be nasty?" I snapped. "My neck still hurts, Will."

"I didn't mean to hurt you. It was an accident. You must know that." He heaved a sigh full of sincerity.

"An accident?" The hubris of his claim stunned me. "You choked me!"

"I did not. I would never do that."

"Am I imagining how much my neck hurts, then?"

"I told you, I didn't mean to—I was upset. I wasn't thinking."

I leaned against the counter, weary of his dramatics. Was I supposed to try to understand? To forgive—again?

I thought of Ingrid Bergman in *Gaslight*, struggling to understand what was true and what was not, doubting her own sanity as her husband manipulated her. Will was very, very good at that manipulation, every bit as good as Charles Boyer. Was I as gullible as Ingrid Bergman? As easily persuaded?

Will pulled off his glasses and made a half-hearted attempt to clear dust from the lenses. His voice trembled, but just slightly, as if he were trying with all his might to control it. "It was my mother's letter, Barrie. It reminded me of such hard times. And then—you have to admit—you said horrible things to me."

"What are you talking about? I didn't say anything horrible to you!"

He replaced his glasses and regarded me with a nearly convincing expression of hurt. "You said I was crazy. It's the one word that sets me off."

"I didn't say you were crazy." I shook my head, wishing I could clear my thoughts. He was doing it again, confusing me, making me doubt myself. The baby in my belly kicked, but weakly, one tired little foot. It was just enough to make me feel off-balance. "That's not fair, Will. What I said was that the letter—that is, the whole thing with your mother—"

"Okay, okay." He gave me a tremulous smile. "It doesn't matter now, Barrie. I'm not angry anymore."

"*You're* not angry."

He missed the emphasis. "Right. That's why I came to get you. It's all over, and you'll know next time not to say that, right?" He gestured to my housecoat, which didn't quite close over my stomach. "Come on, go get your clothes on. Do you have anything nice here? I'll take you out to dinner. Charlotte, too, if she'd like to come." He pushed back that boyish lock of hair and tilted his head expectantly.

Reality seemed to blur around me. It was as if Will were a magician, an evil sorcerer who could call up a fog, distort my vision, confuse the whole world. I mistrusted my memory of the day, my understanding of what had happened. I mistrusted my own feelings.

I found myself blurting, foolishly, "I don't want to go to dinner."

He started toward me, his arms out. "That's okay, then," he said, in a tone meant to be soothing. "We'll have dinner at home. You're tired. You were in the garden for hours this morning."

I moved, backing away from him, until I felt the cold edge of the kitchen sink through the thin fabric of my housecoat. I put my hands behind me for balance, and felt the spilled water droplets on my fingers. My confusion dropped away in the instant. I looked at Will, taking in his sorrowful expression, his guileless blue gaze, his boyish lock of hair, and I knew. My vision was clear at last, and my understanding with it.

Anything that had existed between us was done. Ruined. Irretrievably broken. And I understood that if I let him persuade me again, deceive me again, it would be my own fault.

The clarity of my understanding gave me energy, and it reverberated in my voice. "Don't touch me, Will. Don't ever touch me again."

For an instant, a flash of fury penetrated his facade of charm. "Barrie! You're my wife. I know women in your condition are emotional..." The effort required to restore the smile to his lips was obvious, but it was a heartbeat too late. Indeed, it was a lifetime too late.

I had already drawn breath. "Never again, Will. Never again. We are *finished*."

I could see that he understood the conviction in my words,

and he must have seen the determination on my face. His facade of regret and warmth shivered into pieces, dropping from him like the false front of a building on a film set. He wasn't quite as pale, quite as angry, as he had been before, but he was every bit as dangerous. He reached for me, and I put up my hands to defend myself.

He seized my wrists with both of his big hands, then held them with one. He raised his right hand, flexing the fingers, preparing his fist to strike.

I closed my eyes, readying for the blow. I could *feel* that blow. I knew how much it would hurt, how my skin would bruise, how a bone might crack. There would be a terrible small sound, a violent sound I would never forget, and I would fall—

"Get away from her." It was Charlotte. Her voice was low, clear, and as sharp as a knife blade. I had never heard that voice before.

My eyes flew open. Will dropped my wrists and spun to face the doorway. He threw up his hands, his palms facing outward, crying, "Hey, hey, there's no need for that—"

"I said," Charlotte said, in that unfamiliar tone, "get away from her." She was holding a long black object. I stared at it, and her, in openmouthed amazement.

Will's voice was shrill, and this time the tremor in it was real. "Don't point that at me!"

I said, breathless with shock, "Aunt Charlotte! Is that a gun? Where did you get a gun?"

"It is a gun, in fact," she said with satisfaction. "To be specific, it's a Winchester. A .30-30, I believe it's called. Get away from Barrie Anne, Will. Get away from both of us. I'd rather not make a mess in my kitchen."

He backed away from me, his hands still lifted, his eyes wide with alarm. Watching Charlotte point a gun—a gun!—at Will didn't seem real. It was like being in a gangster film. The thought prompted an inappropriate giggle in my throat, the beginnings of hysterics. I suppressed it by pressing both hands over my mouth.

Neither Charlotte nor Will noticed. He was moving sideways toward the door, which meant he would have to pass her. She swiveled as he moved, keeping the ugly black barrel aimed in the direction of his midsection. Her jaw was set, and her face was smudged with paint. She looked like a Hollywood Indian on the warpath.

Will's shoulders no longer slumped. There was no remnant of a smile on his mouth. He said tensely, "Come on, Charlotte. You wouldn't shoot me." But he kept moving toward the door.

She took one sidestep, to give him room to get by, but she didn't relent. I saw, to my consternation, that her finger was looped over the trigger. I dropped my hands to cross them over my belly. "Aunt Charlotte," I whispered.

She said, "Shhhh."

Will had reached the doorway and was backing away, his hands still extended in a futile sort of protection. "I can't believe you're doing this," he growled.

I couldn't, either. I couldn't think of a person in the world less likely to use violence than Charlotte Blythe, nor could I forget my awful premonition.

She said, "Out, Will."

He was within reach of the door now. He turned the handle and moved into the doorway, where apparently he felt a bit bolder. He said, with a trace of a whine in his voice, "Barrie's my wife. This is none of your business."

"Out."

"You have to be kidding. You wouldn't shoot me!"

"Shall we find out?" With an awkward movement, an action I felt certain she had never performed before, she brought the gun up to her right shoulder.

The entire situation was bizarre. Ridiculous. Another nervous giggle bubbled up in my throat, even as Will took a long step backward, out onto our tiny porch, and slammed the door behind him.

I whirled to the window to see Will cover the distance to the gate in four long strides. In a flash he was in his car, revving the engine, then gone in a storm of scattered gravel and a spume of exhaust.

I turned back to my aunt, my inadequate garment falling open as I spread my hands. Half laughing, half crying, I said, "Aunt Charlotte! Where did you get that thing?"

She lowered the gun and gave me a paint-spattered, lip-sticked grin. Or tried to. It was more of a grimace. She spoke in her own voice this time, and it cracked with tension. "This was your father's."

"My father had a gun?"

"Bought it from the Montgomery Ward catalog."

"Why?"

"He used to hunt ducks, I think. Or maybe it was geese."

"But how did you know how to use it?"

She laid the gun gingerly on the floor, and once it was out of her hands, her smile steadied, and so did her voice. "Kiddo, I haven't the least idea how to use a gun. I've seen them in movies. That's it."

"You mean it's not loaded?"

"Good God, I hope not." She pushed it with her toe. "Not that I would know."

"Don't touch it!" I cried. "What if it went off?"

She gazed down at it, her lips pursed. "I don't even know if it works anymore. I've never touched it. I hate guns."

"Why did you keep it all this time?"

She arched her eyebrow at me, and I understood. She had had a feeling. My water witch of an aunt had known she was going to need it.

She said offhandedly, "The thing was still in the box. Haven't seen it in years."

I crossed the kitchen and stood with her, looking down at the ugly gun with its wooden stock and long, single barrel. I said in an undertone, "Would you have shot him, Aunt Charlotte?"

She gave me a hard look as she reached into her trousers pocket for her cigarettes. "You're damned right I would have." As she shook out a smoke, she added, "If I could have figured out how."

19

September 1947

It had been an unusually hot summer, and the apples in the little orchard reddened early. One clear morning, when we were just sitting down with our coffee, and Emma, who was sitting on my lap, was chewing on a piece of toast, I said, "I think some of the apples are ready to be picked."

"Isn't it early for that?" Charlotte was unwrapping a fresh pack of cigarettes, but I noticed with satisfaction that she had been smoking less and less. I thought the fresh air and exercise of farm life were affecting her, all to the good.

"It's a bit early, I think, but I don't want to lose any. We can have lots of applesauce, and maybe some apple butter to sell."

"I have no idea how you make apple butter."

I laughed. "I don't either, but there's a recipe in the *Woman's Home Companion*. Don't I learn everything from books or catalogs?"

"You do. It's a useful attribute."

"Isn't it, though?" I used my napkin to wipe butter from Emma's cheeks, and planted a kiss on her forehead.

She waved her toast at me, and crowed, "Toast! Toast!"

"Yes, Emma. Toast. Can you say 'Mama'?"

"Nope!" We laughed, and she did, too, kicking her feet and dribbling half-chewed toast down the front of her romper.

Charlotte put her unlit cigarette down. "Why don't you give me the baby, and you go pick the apples before it gets too hot?"

"That's a good idea. Thank you." I wiped the rest of the butter from Emma's hands and face and tried to lift her to hand her to Charlotte. Her little hands seized hold of the straps of my overalls and clung. "Nope!" she said. "Nope!"

This was new. Ruefully, I wriggled her fingers free, and set her on Charlotte's lap. "Emma, I won't be gone long. You can stay with Aunt Charlotte."

Charlotte circled the baby with her arm. "Mama will be right back, Emma."

"Nope!" she exclaimed, and then, as Willow rose to follow me out of the kitchen, she cried, "Dod! Dod!"

I watched in amazement as Willow stopped in midstride, one forefoot still lifted. She gazed at me, her ears drooping, and I could have sworn she was apologizing. I said, half in jest, "It's okay, Willow. You can stay with Emma if you'd rather."

Willow set her forefoot down. She paused for another moment, looking between me and the baby, clearly torn. A moment later she gave in, and turned back. When she reached Charlotte's chair, she nosed Emma's bare leg before she sat down.

Charlotte said, "Emma, don't you think Mama would like to have the dog with her?"

Emma piped, with emphasis, "Nope!" Willow, with a long sigh, slid to her belly and lay stretched on the floor, her chin on her paws.

Laughing, I left them to it, and headed out with my basket to the apple orchard.

It was lovely to be among the apple trees, with the morning breeze riffling their leaves. The apples were warm from the sun, and at least half were already red, splashed with threads of gold. The trees were old ones, Mr. Miller had told me, a heritage variety. The apples were Baldwins, introduced to the Northwest in the early part of the century. I already knew them to be sweet and crisp, and once my basket was full, I picked one more to eat on the spot.

I finished it, and tossed the core into the field for the birds. I was about to head back to the house, but as it so often did, the canal called to me. I thought a few more minutes of my absence could cause no harm. I left my basket in the shade and made my way to the shore.

The water glistened like rumpled blue satin in the early sun. I couldn't resist it. I worked out of my garden boots, rolled up the legs of my overalls, and waded in.

Cool saltwater splashed over my hot skin, and I closed my eyes at the deliciousness of it. I waded in farther, and stood with my face lifted into the sun, feeling both connected to the whole of the wide world and yet wonderfully isolated. When a low-cresting wave soaked the thighs of my overalls, I opened my eyes, laughing. There would be water dripping into my boots as I walked home, but it didn't matter. They would dry out quickly in this heat.

I bent low, gathered up water in my hands, and sprinkled it over my neck and shoulders. I bent again, just to let the water run between my fingers. It made me think of Grandmother Fiona—my great-grandmother—dipping her fingers into the mop bucket to see what was coming.

I didn't try to see what was coming. I wasn't even sure I wanted to. I was happy enough with what was happening right at that moment.

I lost track of time, communing with the water. When a crow squawked at me from a half-submerged tree, I started, a little ashamed of my self-indulgence. I squinted up at the sun. "You're right, crow," I told it. "It's time I got back."

I waded out of the water, rolled down my trouser legs, and scrambled up the bank to the orchard. I retrieved my basket of apples and set out through the field. As I had expected, water dripped from my overalls into my boots, and my toes made squishing noises as I walked.

As I lifted the door to the root cellar to stow my basket, the house above me seemed strangely quiet. I didn't feel any particular alarm, but it was too early for Emma's nap, and usually Willow managed to get Charlotte to let her out so she could meet me at the gate. I set the basket of apples on the nearest shelf in the shadowy cellar and hurried back up the steps. I closed the door against the heat, then trotted up to the porch and in through the back door.

Charlotte stood with her back against the kitchen counter, a bemused expression on her face. On the floor, on a blanket, Willow sat next to Emma, who was also sitting. Sitting up by herself, for the very first time.

She squealed with delight when she saw me and waved her arms to be picked up.

As I lifted her in my arms I said, "Aunt Charlotte! Did she do that on her own? You didn't help her?"

"No, I didn't. And yes, she did," Charlotte said. A half-smoked cigarette hung from her lip. She grinned and took it between her fingers. "But that's not the most interesting thing that happened just now."

Emma wriggled in my arms and crowed, "Nope! Nope!"

"Good lord, I'm afraid to ask," I said.

"I was washing dishes, and I laid her on the blanket there on the floor because it's cooler. Willow lay down beside her, and the two of them were playing a little. Emma was practicing saying 'Dod,' as she does—"

I hugged Emma tighter. "I know."

"And every time she did, Willow laughed. I mean, dogs don't laugh, I guess, but—it sounded like laughter to me."

"I think she does laugh, when she's feeling playful."

"I was just draining the sink—about ten minutes ago—when these two got awfully quiet. I turned around in a hurry, and I found Willow sitting up, staring at the door, and Emma sitting up, too. And staring at the door."

I frowned. "Staring at the door?"

"As if they were frozen, the two of them."

"But—but why would they do that?"

"It was a little eerie until I figured it out. Willow always knows when you start for home. This time Emma did, too." Charlotte waved her cigarette in a grand gesture. "She *knows* things, Barrie Anne! The little rascal knows things. And not a drop of water anywhere near her."

It took me a moment to grasp what Charlotte was saying, and another to remember where I had been ten minutes before. "But I was in the water," I said. "The canal was beautiful this morning, and I went in, just for a few minutes. Rolled up my trouser legs and waded into the water up to my knees. You can see, my overalls are still wet." I shook my head, wondering. "She knew. She knew when I started for home."

Charlotte drew on her cigarette and blew her puff of smoke toward the open window above the sink. She smiled and pointed her cigarette at me. "You see? It's all connected."

Emma, in my arms, kicked her bare feet and cried, "Nope! Nope!"

"Emma, darling," I said, kissing her soft hair, "you can use your other words."

"Dod!" she said. "Dod!" Willow came to us and licked Emma's toes, grinning up at me. Laughing.

A few days later, Charlotte sold one of her big canvases to a buyer from Seattle who spotted it in the window of a Port Townsend gallery. A nice sale in years past had always meant a celebratory dinner out. We debated over going out this time, because of Emma, but we finally decided it would be good to be seen with her. We also thought it would be fun to dress her up in something frilly. Even Charlotte, who didn't possess a single dress, was enthusiastic about the idea.

In preparation, I bathed Emma in the big tub. I knelt, my elbows on the cool cast iron, and watched with bemusement as she sank peacefully and happily beneath the water. I was still wary about it. I felt like one of the grebes on the shoreline, keeping a fierce maternal eye on her chicks as they tested the water.

Charlotte had said to Dr. Masters that Emma was like a frog, and in the tub, that's what she seemed to be—a plump, pink, energetic frog. I knew the analogy wasn't perfect, but I didn't think there was going to be a perfect analogy. Emma was unique. She kicked and bubbled and grinned as I watched for the slightest sign of distress. No such sign ever appeared, but still, I was relieved when it was time to lift her up so I could soap her hair and wash her bottom.

When that was done, I lifted her slippery body out and wrapped her in a towel. I held her close for a moment, my cheek on her wet head, her rebellious feet kicking at my midsection. "Did you like that, Emma? You like your bath?"

"Baf! Baf!" she crowed.

"Yes, bath. I know you love your bath." Laughing, I rubbed her dry and carried her into the nursery. I took one of Mrs. Urquhardt's hand-me-downs from a drawer, a much-worn but still serviceable pink seersucker dress, with a lace collar and a smocked bodice. A few faint stains marred the smocking, reminders of baby girls who had come before and who had now no doubt gone on to Mary Janes and pleated skirts. I wondered if Mrs. Urquhardt felt nostalgic about the memories these faded marks represented. I certainly did.

Leaning over the crib, I diapered Emma and pulled the dress over her head. She glowed from the warm water and sat in the crib like a tiny, lacy-collared buddha, banging the side of the crib with her bunny rattle.

"Aunt Charlotte, you should see," I called. "She looks precious."

Charlotte came to the nursery and lounged in the doorway. She had put on a pair of pleated trousers, which she wore with a blouse and cardigan and a string of blue beads around her neck. She said, "I love the dress. I wonder how many babies have worn that?"

I brushed Emma's fluff of pale hair so it lay smoothly across her scalp. "Mrs. Urquhardt had four girls, didn't she? I wouldn't be surprised if they all wore it."

"Nice of her to pass it on."

"I thought so, too. I gave her a dozen eggs."

"Good."

I smiled up at my aunt. "You look nice."

"Thanks. Let me take the baby while you dress." She bent over the crib and lifted Emma in her arms. Emma seized the necklace and tugged on it, and Charlotte gently freed her fingers. "No, no, baby," she said. "I don't want that to break."

"It's so pretty," I said. "I haven't seen you wear it in a while."

"Farm life," Charlotte said. "Not much point in dressing up."

"That's the truth. Where did you get it?"

"In Taos. They called them donkey beads, but I don't remember why."

Later, at the Olympic Inn, over a plate of freshly shucked oysters, Charlotte said, "Oh! I just remembered about the necklace."

I was feeding Emma tidbits of fresh bread and chuckling as she gummed them into paste. I said, "You mean why they're called donkey beads?"

"Yes. They come from the Middle East, and they used to put them around donkeys' necks to ward off evil spirits."

"Odd thing to have acquired in New Mexico, then."

"There are donkeys in New Mexico," she said, chuckling. "But the necklace was a gift."

I didn't press her to tell me from whom, but I saw her touch the beads with her fingers, and a look of reminiscence softened her face.

It was a lovely night. We were seated at a window table overlooking the canal. Waning sunshine glistened on the mirror-smooth water, and a few sailboats lingered, drifting in the calm. The oysters were salty and sweet, and Charlotte had a gin rickey by her right hand. The waitress cooed over Emma and admired her pink cap.

It was marvelous to be out, to be showing off my little girl, to be wearing nice clothes. I couldn't remember the last time I had changed my overalls for a dress, but it felt good. I was startled to remember how much I enjoyed putting on lipstick. I had a bit of a struggle with my hair. It had gotten too long and too ragged, and it wasn't helped by my efforts to shorten it with a pair of sewing scissors. I had settled for gathering up the strands and pinning them into something resembling a chignon, but I knew, making a face at myself in the mirror, that the effort wasn't entirely successful.

I was pushing the last oyster toward Charlotte when she said, "It was Georgia who gave me the necklace. It's supposed to be good luck." She scooped out the oyster and ate it, then added, "I'd like to go back to Taos one day. I'd like to visit her grave."

"Do you still have friends there?"

"I think so. People tend to stay in Taos once they find it—if they're the Taos kind of people, that is." She patted her lips with the cloth napkin, leaving a Raven Red lip print on it.

I said, "Taos is in New Mexico, isn't it? Like that place the men mentioned, where there was a"—I lowered my voice and glanced around to be certain no one was paying attention to us—"a weather balloon. Remember?"

"Roswell," Charlotte said promptly.

"Do you know where that is?"

"Way out in the middle of nowhere."

"We're kind of in the middle of nowhere, too, aren't we?"

"You might say that." She picked up her drink and regarded me over the rim of the glass. "You mean you see a similarity. Their weather balloon. Our—hmm—discovery."

We gazed at each other for a few meaningful seconds before, in perfect agreement, we let the subject drop.

Over grilled salmon, fresh from the Sound, we chatted about trivial things. We smiled indulgently as we watched Emma taste ice cream for the first time. Her green eyes went wide with pleasure, and even the waitress giggled as she smacked her lips and waved her arms in a demand for more.

On our way home, a replete and ice-cream-sticky Emma fell sound asleep in my arms. I yawned, too. "That was fun, Aunt Charlotte. Thanks."

"The salmon was good."

"And the oysters." I was struggling to keep my eyes open. "I love that place, even if it is a bit far."

"It's nice to be able to drive somewhere without feeling guilty about it," Charlotte said. "I hated rationing."

"Maybe you should take the sticker off," I said, pointing with my chin at her prized B gas rationing marker, still affixed to the Studebaker's windshield.

"Never! It's an artifact!" She laughed.

"That's one way to look at it," I said. My head dropped back against the upholstered seat, and my heavy eyelids drooped.

Charlotte said, "You can nod off, kiddo. I'm fine. We'll be home in ten minutes."

I couldn't resist. For once, the Studebaker's heater was working, and I drowsed through the drive with a delicious sense of well-being at having a full stomach, a comfortable seat, and the sweet weight of a baby in my arms. When Charlotte parked the car in front of the house, I blinked several times to wake myself. Emma stirred on my lap as Charlotte pulled on the brake.

She didn't put her hand on the door, though, or turn off the engine.

An uneasy feeling brought me fully alert. I lifted my head.

Charlotte was making no move to get out of the car. "What is it?" I whispered.

"Someone's in the house."

I sat up abruptly, waking Emma. She began to whimper as I stared in alarm at the lighted window of the front room. "You didn't leave the light on?" I asked Charlotte.

"I remember checking that all the lights were off when we left."

"I don't see a car."

"No." Charlotte's voice was tight. "Stay here. I'll go and check."

"Not alone, you won't," I said firmly. "We'll go together. It's probably—we probably missed a light."

"That's the front room lamp, Barrie Anne."

"I know." We both knew perfectly well we hadn't left the lamp on. We also knew we had locked the door, a habit we had acquired after the government men started showing up.

I lifted Emma to my shoulder and patted her back. Her whimpers eased, and she tucked her head into the crook of my neck. Charlotte turned off the motor, and she and I opened our doors at the same time. We climbed out, but we left the doors ajar.

Willow appeared, coming around the house at a dead run. She charged up to the car with her ears back and her hackles up. She skidded to a stop beside me and wound around my legs, whining.

Charlotte said, "You didn't leave the dog out."

"No. She was in the kitchen, on her blanket."

We hesitated just long enough to cast each other a glance

and then started up the path, side by side. Willow walked close enough to me that I felt her tension through my own muscles. I put my hand protectively over the back of Emma's head. I tried to breathe evenly as we stepped up on the front porch, but I was poised to run.

Charlotte had her keys in her hand, but she tried the door-knob first. It turned, and the door opened. She muttered, "Should have changed the locks."

"Yeah, I guess I should have."

I started forward, but Charlotte put out her arm to stop me. She moved ahead, stepping through the doorway and into the brightly lit front room.

I couldn't see past her, but I knew immediately who was in the house when she snapped, "What the hell are *you* doing here?"

I sidled past her so I could see him for myself. Willow came with me, and a low growl emanated from her throat. Emma stiffened in my arms and whispered, "Dod. Dod," into my shoulder. Goose bumps rose on my arms and the back of my neck.

Will was in the doorway to the kitchen. Behind him I could see he had made himself at home. A plate with the remains of a sandwich still rested on the table alongside an empty glass. A cigarette was burning in an ashtray, which was unusual. I had never known Will to smoke.

He leaned against the doorway, the lamplight flashing from the lenses of his glasses. "Who's this?" he said lightly, as if we had said goodbye an hour earlier instead of more than a year.

I knew he meant Emma, but I said, "Answer Charlotte's question. What the hell *are* you doing here?"

He pressed a hand to his chest, and said, "Barrie, Barrie. Is that any way to talk to your husband? Whose baby is that?"

"How did you get here without a car?" Charlotte asked.

"Shank's mare," he answered, as if it were a casual question. His shoes were scuffed, and one sole had come loose. For all his cavalier attitude, he looked as if he'd been sleeping rough, his hair overlong and none too clean, his shirt stained, his wrinkled trousers muddy at the cuffs.

I said, "You can't stay, Will. I don't know why you're here, but you can't—"

His face tightened. "I need to talk to you, Barrie."

"I don't need to talk to you."

"We're still married."

"I used to think that mattered. I no longer do."

Charlotte set her handbag on the sofa, but I noticed she kept her keys in her hand, and when she moved, it was to be closer to the telephone where it rested on the counter. "What is it you want, Will?" she said.

He spoke without looking at her. "Not that it's any of your business, but I want to talk to my wife."

Charlotte said, "She doesn't want to talk to you. You might as well go."

I saw the spasm of fury that shook him, making him clench his fist and then thrust it into his pocket to hide it. I remembered my own fury, and my humiliation, all because of him.

Everything came rushing back, every detail, every hurt, every loss. I thought I was over it, but now resentment and anger erupted anew, and I shook with tension. My arms tightened around Emma, and she squirmed in protest.

I had tried to put it behind me. I had tried to forget. Now it swept me in a heart-pounding flood, and I hated Will for making that happen.

20

May 1946

I had been with Charlotte in Port Townsend two weeks when the Shore Patrol arrived.

Those were strange weeks. I rose each day thinking not about my ruined marriage but wondering how my garden was faring in my absence. I worried that my tomato starts weren't getting enough water, and I feared my lettuces were in danger of bolting due to the stretch of warm weather. If I did think about Will, it was with a sense of relief. His scowls and silences, his outbursts of criticism, had been exhausting, and I was glad to be free of them. Once my sore neck stopped aching, I didn't think about him at all. I even forgot the nasty premonition that had so troubled me on the day I left my husband.

Charlotte and I fell easily into old rhythms. Except for the impending birth of my baby, now so close, life in our little square house was much as it had been during the war.

I didn't go out to Tibbals Hill, of course, because there

was nothing left to do there. Instead, while Charlotte worked in her studio, I tackled her neglected garden with my newly acquired knowledge of plants and fertilizer and soil. I went to see Dr. Masters once. He advised me to eat more, saying he would like to see me gain more weight. He didn't ask why I was in town. I didn't tell him I was going to have a baby with no father.

There had been no word from Will, but I assumed he was at the farm. I made no effort to call him. He didn't try to telephone me, and if he had, I would have refused to speak to him.

Despite the drama of running away from Will and Charlotte threatening him with a gun she had no idea how to use, those two weeks were pleasant enough, sunny days, cool nights, good food, and best of all, no arguments to shatter the quiet. It was a time for resting, recovering. A time of welcome peace.

The peace ended the instant the Shore Patrol arrived.

A Navy jeep roared up to our garden gate and came to a dust-swirling, gravel-scattering stop. Two big men in dark blue uniforms and white leggings climbed out and started toward the house.

In San Diego, all of us learned to recognize naval uniforms. I knew what the SP armbands meant and the batons slung from wide white belts. I understood, without being told, that the appearance of these sailors at our house meant trouble.

Charlotte was painting. I was trying to wrestle some order into the haphazard flower beds that flanked the house. I couldn't imagine my belly could get much bigger, despite what Dr. Masters had said. I couldn't see my feet without bending very far over, and if I tried it, I risked losing my balance.

Just the same, I was on my knees on a couple of old towels, a cracked and ragged straw hat on my head, weeding a patch of petunias just beginning to set buds.

I struggled to my feet and leaned against the railing of our tiny stoop to catch my breath as the two burly men let themselves in through the gate. My heart beat a painful rhythm in my chest as I watched them come up the path, their helmets under their arms, their eyes narrowed against the spring sunshine. This could only be bad news. I felt a rush of resentment at this new intrusion, along with a flicker of panic over what it could mean.

They both seemed impossibly young, though they couldn't have been much younger than my own twenty-five. They looked enormous, looming before me, stiff-necked and straight-backed. One was dark-haired and dark-eyed, with a thin mustache over full lips. The other was Nordic, fair and light-skinned, with an arching nose and blunt chin. He spoke first.

"Ma'am," he said. He tucked his chin and looked down the blade of his nose at me. "We're Navy Shore Patrol. We're looking for William Sweet. Hospital Corpsman William Sweet."

Still breathless, and with my heartbeat thrumming in my ears, I blurted, "Why?" My voice cracked on the word, and I had to blink against dark spots clouding my vision. I think I may have wavered a little on my feet. I found I was clinging to the railing with both hands.

The dark one took a step toward me. "Are you all right, ma'am?"

The fair one spoke over him. "Are you Mrs. Sweet?"

I forced my lungs to open for one good breath and said, "Yes. Yes, that's me."

"Corpsman Sweet's parents gave us this address." It was the Nordic one, speaking in a tone as stiff as his posture. "And another one in some place called Brinnon."

The dark-haired sailor said, "Mrs. Sweet, perhaps you should sit down. Is there a chair—a bench, maybe?"

I drew another deep breath, an easier one this time. I wasn't sure what to call them. Mr.? Sailor? I left out any title. I said, "My husband and I have separated. He's not here."

The tag over the blond man's pocket read BERGSEN. "You must know where he is."

"I don't."

"You think he might be in this Brinnon place? It's a rural route, his mother said. Not a real street address."

"I left him there. I don't know where he is now." Bergsen scowled at me as if he suspected me of lying.

The other man's pocket label read SANTANGELO. "When was the last time you saw your husband, Mrs. Sweet?" He kept his gaze on my face, away from my swollen figure, but they could hardly have missed my advanced pregnancy.

"Why are you looking for him?" My voice sounded tinny. I swallowed, trying to loosen the constriction of my throat.

"I don't think—" Santangelo began, but Bergsen interrupted.

"Corpsman Sweet jumped ship," he said. "In Honolulu."

"Honolulu?" An ache began in the center of my head. I pulled off my hat and pressed my palm to my forehead. It was a pointless exercise. This new pain wasn't going to give way so easily. I said, mumbling a bit, "But that was...He's been out of the service for..."

"Ma'am," Santangelo said, stepping closer to me with a worried look. "I really think you should sit down."

"Yes," I admitted, my voice still thin. "I think...Perhaps we could..."

He put a strong hand under my elbow. "Some water, too, I think, Mrs. Sweet. May we go inside, out of the sun? You look a little faint."

I didn't argue. My knees felt weak, and the ache in my head sharpened. I left my hat where it lay and leaned on Santangelo's arm as we walked through the front door and turned to the kitchen with Bergsen just behind us. Everything seemed blurry with sunshine, the pots and pans on their hooks, the glass fronts of the cupboards, the aluminum of the teakettle. The nook was too cramped for me now, swollen as I was. Charlotte had brought a straight chair in from the dining room for me to use. I sank onto that, blinking my eyes against the glitter of the light and the pain in my head.

Santangelo opened three cupboard doors until he found the row of drinking glasses. Bergsen stood by, impatiently tapping his fingers against his baton. It took a few moments, and several sips from the glass of water Santangelo ran for me, before I could think clearly again.

Charlotte heard the noise of the faucet, and she hurried down the stairs. "Barrie Anne? You okay?" She stopped in the arched doorway, staring in surprise at the two tall sailors.

I set down my glass with exaggerated care. My hand felt limp, and my vision refused to clear. "Aunt Charlotte, these men—they're the Shore Patrol. The navy."

"I can see that." She crossed to me with a strong step and gripped my shoulder as she faced the men. "What do you want with my niece?"

"Nothing," Santangelo said.

At the same moment Bergsen said, "We need her to tell us where her husband is."

"Why?" Charlotte's smoky voice was rough with anxiety.

My voice was no better. "Something about Honolulu, Aunt Charlotte. They're saying—I don't know what they're saying. I told them I don't know where Will is."

Charlotte snapped, "What about Honolulu? What does it have to do with Barrie Anne?"

"Ma'am," Santangelo said, lifting one calming hand, his palm turned out. "Ma'am, I'm sorry. Let me explain. Mrs. Sweet's husband—Corpsman Sweet, that is—went UA in Honolulu."

"UA?"

"Unauthorized absence."

"What?" My voice was little more than a thread of sound. I don't think they heard me.

Charlotte's hand tightened on my shoulder. "You mean Will jumped ship."

"Yes, ma'am. Sorry to say so."

"That was a while ago, wasn't it? It had to be. Why show up here now?"

"Did you know, ma'am?" Bergsen tapped and tapped at his baton. The two sailors seemed to crowd our small kitchen, to make the ceiling seem lower, the walls closer together. I peered at them past Charlotte's paint-stained smock. Bergsen's rocky features made him look like the villain from a Disney cartoon. Even Santangelo looked as if he should be cast in some war movie about fierce sailors.

Charlotte said, "I didn't know, and nor did Mrs. Sweet. Her husband was—what did you call it? UA?—from his marriage, too. She didn't hear a word from him for three years."

"I'm sorry about that," Santangelo said. "Can you tell us when he came back?"

I swiveled in my chair so I could face the sailors. My headache had receded to a dull throb. "Will came back a year ago," I said. "He told us he'd been sick in Honolulu. He had an infection, and he was hospitalized with battle fatigue."

The two men exchanged a glance, and a wave of shame washed over me. "It wasn't true, then."

It wasn't true. It was another lie. Another deception. The cruelty of it stunned me, the cruelty to me, to Charlotte, to the baby getting ready to come into the world.

Bergsen said, "Corpsman Sweet was never in the navy hospital."

I was glad I no longer cared about saving my marriage. Glad I no longer loved my husband. It would have been even more painful if I had, and it was bad enough as it was. I bore his name. I was about to give birth to his child. I trembled, even safely seated, as I tried to comprehend the enormity of the news these men had brought.

"Why are you here now?" Charlotte demanded. "Surely that was years ago."

The sailors exchanged another glance, and Bergsen gestured

with his wide chin to Santangelo, handing over the explanation. Santangelo blew out a breath and came to crouch beside me, to look into my face.

"Mrs. Sweet," he said quietly, "I'm not glad to have to tell you this. Especially as you're—It seems you're about to—"

"Yes," I said. "Very soon."

"Just get to it," Bergsen gritted.

Santiago ignored him. "We hate to upset you—"

"I'm not upset," I lied. In truth, I was feeling as if I were about to be sick, but I had no intention of revealing that to these men. I was fighting a war of my own in that moment, a war with shame and confusion and fear. I had no idea what responsibility I might bear for Will's misdeeds. I set my jaw and gritted, "Go on."

"Well. The navy believes Corpsman Sweet was stealing ration stickers from the government and selling them on the black market."

Charlotte exclaimed, "Ration stickers!"

Santangelo, still squatting beside me, looked up at her. "Like the one in the window of that Studebaker in front of your house."

She snapped, "I know what they are. He certainly didn't sell me that one. But how does anyone steal them?"

Bergsen said, "There was a warehouse at the base in Honolulu. Corpsman Sweet is accused of stealing cartons of X stickers, the ones for people who needed to do lots of driving during the war. Government people, doctors, that sort of thing."

"Are they—were they—worth that much?"

"Yes," Santangelo said regretfully. "And also, Corpsman Sweet is suspected—"

"Come on, he's guilty," Bergsen muttered.

Santangelo gave a small, embarrassed cough. "I'm afraid it seems that way, yeah."

"Guilty of what?" I asked. My head swam again under the force of these revelations, but it seemed best to get it all out. To face all the hard truths at once.

Bergsen said, "Stealing from pharmacy stores and selling what he stole."

"Pharmacy?"

"Yes, ma'am. Drugs. There were a hell of a lot of 'em stored on the base. 'Scuse my French. Morphine, heroin, amphetamines."

"But...how could he..." This evidence of my naïveté made my cheeks burn. "Will surely wasn't that sort of man... He wouldn't have anything to do with drugs!"

"Hospital corpsman," Bergsen growled. "He knew all about 'em."

Santangelo patted my knee with a big, gentle hand before he got to his feet. "I'm sorry, Mrs. Sweet. There are mobs— organized crime gangs—with the know-how and the means to sell all that stuff. Your husband got mixed up with them."

"Are you sure about all this?" Charlotte demanded.

"Oh, we're sure, ma'am," Bergsen said. "That's why we're here."

"Even though the war is over?" I said miserably. "You're still looking for him?"

"The navy doesn't forget such things. They might overlook the UA, now that the war's done, but not the criminal activity."

All that money, and I just took his word for where it came from. I had been so gullible. So foolish. I hadn't asked questions, hadn't demanded to know why there was so much money, enough to buy a whole farm. I couldn't think how I was going to live with the humiliation.

Santangelo said, "Mrs. Sweet, we're going to need to find him. Maybe at this Brinnon address?"

I drew a long, slow breath, accepting what had to be accepted. Without conscious thought, driven by instinct, I picked up my water glass and thrust three fingers into it. The water was clear and cool, and I felt it vibrate through my fingers, up into my arm, a delicate flow of energy that cleared my vision and dissipated my headache as if it had never been. And I knew.

"He's not there," I said to Santangelo.

"How can you be sure of that, ma'am?"

"I just am. I'm quite sure."

Charlotte's gaze met mine in an intense moment of recognition. I saw her eyes drop to my hand, the fingers still submerged in the water glass, before she turned her face away to hide a growing smile.

Bergsen said, "Sorry, Mrs. Sweet, but we're going to have to check that."

"Of course. I'll show you where the farm is. It's tricky to find."

Charlotte turned back to me. "Barrie Anne, you don't need to go down there."

"I don't mind. I think it's best to settle it. So these gentlemen will be satisfied." I looked down at my dirt-stained overalls. "Let me just change."

"We appreciate this, Mrs. Sweet," Bergsen said.

Santangelo said, "I'm not sure you should go in your—" He blushed and shuffled his feet. "Your delicate condition," he managed to mumble, not looking at me. "Is it far?"

"A bit more than an hour's drive, now that we don't have the war speed limit."

Charlotte tried again. "Barrie Anne—"

"I want to do this, Aunt Charlotte. I need to do something. Try to set things right."

She repeated, "None of this is your fault, kiddo."

"My husband is a traitor." I bit out the words as I crossed the kitchen to the stairs. "I'll never forgive him for that."

The Jeep had only two real seats, but the sailors gave me one of them. Bergsen settled behind the wheel, and Santangelo squeezed himself into the jump seat, which was no small achievement. They put on their helmets, buckling them against the wind, and we set off. Charlotte leaned against the porch railing, smoking, frowning as we spun away.

I had changed into a fresh maternity smock and tied a scarf over my hair. Bergsen drove fast, so the wind tugged at the ends of my scarf and dried my face. The Jeep had no top, and between the wind and the rattling engine, it was too noisy for conversation. When it was time for a turn, I pointed. Bergsen shifted and followed my pointing finger. As he drove, I huddled in the passenger seat, half-nauseated, as much by the spinning of my mind as by the rough ride.

My husband. The father of my baby. A liar. A thief. How had he deceived me? How could I have thought I was in love with him? How could I have allowed him to twist my life into these knots of misery and confusion and guilt? How could I have been so utterly, irredeemably blind?

In forty-five minutes, we reached the turnoff into our lane, with its three lonely mailboxes on their weathered posts. As Bergsen braked and swerved into the lane, he shouted, "Not on the map! I would have driven right past."

"I know."

I could see now that this was one thing Will had liked about the farm. It could be terribly hard to find.

We drove past the Urquhardts' place, with its rusty pickup and dusty sedan, and then the abandoned cabin with its boarded-up windows and broken porch slanting into the untrimmed grass. The ruts and bumps of the lane jarred me, and the weight of the baby seemed to bounce directly on my bladder. I was glad to get out of the Jeep when we finally reached the end, and our farmhouse.

Bergsen shut off the engine and climbed out while Santangelo extricated himself from the jump seat. The three of us stood listening to the ticking of the engine as it cooled and gazing at the farm. I saw my house—more than a little ramshackle, with its rickety porch and peeling paint—through their eyes and felt a rush of embarrassment.

"No car," Bergsen said.

"No." I didn't repeat my statement that Will was gone. I wasn't going to try to explain. They wouldn't have believed me.

My poor house looked abandoned. Weeds were growing in the path to the front porch, and the grass had gone yellow for lack of water. The curtains in the upstairs bedroom were drawn. The few flowers I had put in the front window—daffodils and hyacinths that had unexpectedly sprung up in the garden—drooped in their vase, brown, dead. They seemed to symbolize something, but my mind skittered away from deciding what that might be.

I had fled, after Will attacked me, without a house key. I led the sailors up onto the porch and tried the front door knob. It was locked. I stretched on tiptoe to recover the spare key from above the lintel, and I felt like an intruder in my own house as I inserted it into the door.

I started inside, but Santangelo stepped in front of me. "Better let me go in first, Mrs. Sweet," he muttered. Bergsen sidled past me to follow his partner. I walked in behind them and looked around at the home I hadn't seen for two weeks.

The house *smelled* empty. There was no sign of Will. There was nothing on the range but the empty teakettle. China and flatware waited on the table where I had set it two weeks before in anticipation of Charlotte's visit, and the sink was sticky with old dishwater, gone scummy as it dried. The catalogs I had stacked on the table lay scattered on the floor where Will had thrown them. The list of baby names, with Scott at the top of the boy's column and Sarah and Suzanne underlined in the girl's, had skidded halfway to the front room. Bracing myself with a hand on the wall, I picked it up, and laid it on the table. I stood and stared at it all, the disordered remnants of the life I had thought I was living.

Santangelo said, "Mrs. Sweet? Okay if I check upstairs?"

I nodded. Bergsen went through the kitchen and stepped out onto the back porch. I followed him and gazed at my garden drying in the heat. Weeds had popped up between my carefully tilled rows. The rows of pea seeds had begun to sprout, their slender stalks rising bravely above my enriched soil, a tiny army of seedlings eager to do their duty. My crooked henhouse still sat vacant, waiting for occupants.

I rested against the post at the top of the porch stairs while the men looked around.

"Anything in that shed over there?" Bergsen asked, pointing. "Or that barn?"

"A tractor," I said with a pang of memory. I had enjoyed learning to drive that old tractor. "Gardening tools. This is—was—going to be a farm."

He cast me a measuring glance, the first real interest he had shown in me. "Yeah? You own it?"

"Yes."

"Family money?"

"No. Will paid for it. He said—" I stopped speaking when I saw the suspicion in his eyes. I didn't blame him.

"Said what?" he prompted.

I told him the truth. "He said he saved his back pay, while he was sick."

"Back pay? That wouldn't have covered a down payment on this place."

"I didn't know that."

There was scorn in the quirk of his lips, and I didn't blame him for that, either. I felt the same scorn for my naïveté. It was humiliating.

Bergsen said, "Come on, Mrs. Sweet. Everything will be easier if you just tell us what you know."

I turned away from him to look out past the empty field to the apple grove. I fixed my eyes on the blue gleam of the canal and wished I could go there, slip through the shady orchard, slide down the cut in the bank. I longed to feel soothing salt water swirling around my ankles, yearned to have no sound in my ears but the rush of the water and the seagulls' raucous fragmentary songs.

I blew out a breath. "Mr. Bergsen, I've told you everything I know. He's my husband. He convinced me. He bought the farm without telling me, a surprise. I guess I didn't ask enough questions."

"Sweet was going to be a farmer?"

"The farmer is me. That is, it was going to be." I felt the baby give that half-hearted kick, as if it were stretching its toes. I pressed a hand over my belly. "Now I don't know what's going to happen."

"You can't live out here all by yourself, with a baby to take care of." He spoke the words as if there could be no argument.

"I suppose not."

"Sure looks like Sweet's gone, but I'm going to make sure." He went down the two steps, saying over his shoulder, "You wait there, ma'am."

I watched as he crossed to my garden shed, opened the door,

and took a long look at my tidy array of spades and forks and hoes. He closed the shed and then went to the barn and did the same. I could just see the blunt nose of the tractor past his broad figure, and I felt a powerful urge to tell him—to tell them both—to just go, to leave me there to tend my garden in peace.

Despite everything, even understanding the deceit Will had used to get me into this place, this was my home now. I wanted to air out my house. I wanted to irrigate my drooping garden. I wanted to pull those weeds defiling my carefully raked rows. The Burpee catalog said it was almost time to plant tomatoes and corn, and—

I wanted to have my baby here. I wanted to start my life over, here on my own farm.

We gathered in the kitchen, the two big sailors and me. Santangelo said, speaking to Bergsen, "No sign of Sweet."

"No. Not outside, either."

I refrained from pointing out that I had already told them this and that they hadn't listened. I had no doubt that if I had been a man, they would have paid attention. I left the thought unspoken. There was no point.

Santangelo said, with the courtesy that seemed to be natural to him, "Mrs. Sweet, do you have any idea where Corpsman Sweet might have gone?"

I shook my head. "None. He goes—he used to go—to Bremerton a lot. He said that's where he was going, anyway, whenever we needed money. Something about a bank, but I don't know which one."

Bergsen said, "Probably not a bank. The black market is all cash."

"But the war's over. No one needs stickers now, do they?"

"No. It would be the drugs."

Santangelo said, "He probably had a storage place of some kind, someplace he kept the cash. You're right, though. The market for stickers has dried up. And maybe his inventory of drugs is gone."

"We'll find him," Bergsen said.

"I don't see how," I said. "You've been to see his parents. I don't know of anyone else."

"No friends? Siblings? Other family?"

"He has a brother, a doctor. I haven't met him, and I gather they don't get along. I don't know of any friends other than the ones we made during the war in San Diego." I shrugged. "They were more my friends than Will's. I guess you could say he's a bit of a loner."

"We heard that," Bergsen said.

Santangelo said, "Did you part amicably, Mrs. Sweet?"

I couldn't help a sour chuckle. "No, Mr. Santangelo. No, we did not part on good terms." I meant to stop then, but the whole situation was so surreal, these two clean-cut sailors, my sad little farmhouse, that I blurted, "He came to Port Townsend a couple of weeks ago to try to get me to come home, and my aunt Charlotte pulled a gun on him."

For the first time, Bergsen's stiff face relaxed into a reluctant smile. Santangelo laughed aloud. "Your aunt—that lady we met—did an Annie Oakley on him?"

"She didn't actually shoot him." I didn't feel a need to tell them she had no idea how to use the gun.

I didn't know how to use it, either. But I meant to learn.

Bergsen said, "Well. Might as well start back."

"Yeah," Santangelo said. "We'll get you back to your aunt's house, Mrs. Sweet. Thanks for showing us how to get here. Too bad about this place." He waved a hand that included everything, the house, the garden, the outbuildings. "Nice location, so close to the water. Looks like it has a lot of potential."

He started for the front door, and Bergsen followed. I walked with them into the front room, but when Santangelo held the door for me, I shook my head. He raised his eyebrows and cocked his head at me in question.

I said, "I'm going to stay here."

Bergsen, already through the door, looked back at us. "What? You can't do that."

"Of course I can. This is my farm."

"We can't leave you here alone," Santangelo said, frowning. "You might—" His gaze grazed my stomach before he turned his head away, looking to his partner for help.

"He's right," Bergsen said. "We're not leaving you here. What if Sweet comes back?"

"I doubt very much he's coming," I said. "But if he does, I'll call you."

"We're headed to California," Santangelo said. "It could take us a long time to get back."

I was beginning to feel unbearably weary, from the heat, from lugging my pregnant body around, and from trying to grasp the events of this disturbing day. I leaned against the doorjamb and looked at my two escorts. "Mr. Santangelo, Mr. Bergsen. I appreciate your concern, but I can take care of myself."

"Your aunt—" Santangelo began.

"I'll call her." If the telephone was still working.

Bergsen scowled at me. "No," he said, with a decisive air. "We're taking you back where you belong."

After the humiliation of the news they had brought me, this was too much. I wanted to collapse on the divan and have a good cry. Or kick my heels and throw a tantrum.

I pointed to their Jeep, waiting in the lane. "Go, gentlemen. You're not the ones to decide where I belong or don't belong. I understand that you mean well, but I don't take orders from you. In fact, I'm not taking orders from anyone, ever again. If I want to stay in my own house, I'll do it."

Santangelo said, "Mrs. Sweet, please think—"

"I'm sorry, Mr. Santangelo. Under the circumstances, you've been very kind, and I thank you for bringing me here. Now, if you don't mind, I need to rest."

"You're waiting here for your husband," Bergsen said, making Santangelo give him a sidelong look.

"No. I told you he won't be coming."

"He spent a lot of money on this place."

"Really? I don't know much about that."

He scowled at me. "If you're covering for your husband, ma'am, you're going to be in a lot of trouble."

Santangelo said, "Come on, Bergsen. Leave the lady alone."

Bergsen shot him a look, then turned his hawk-nosed face back to me. "Last chance, Mrs. Sweet. I'm warning you. Tell us what you know."

"I would," I said wearily, "if I knew anything at all. I would be happy to. Relieved to be able to do something to help you.

There's nothing. Now, you men should head for California. You've done all you can, and I need to lie down."

For a tense moment, I thought the two of them might actually force me to go with them. Bergsen even took a step in my direction, as if that thought had occurred to him, but Santangelo shouldered him to one side, saying, "Come on, Bergsen. Nothing more for us to do here."

A beat passed, and I watched Bergsen's stiff posture relax into acceptance. "Yeah, okay. We'd better try the neighbors, though."

"We'll do that."

That meant my neighbors would know all about Will and his desertion—of me and of the navy. The entire town would have the story by evening, and that would be the death blow to my dreams of being accepted as part of the community.

The two sailors stepped out onto the porch, and the front room immediately felt more spacious, as if they had given me back my breathing room. Santangelo said, "Do you have some food, Mrs. Sweet?"

"I'll manage. Thanks."

Bergsen said, "If your husband comes back, call the police."

"Okay."

"I mean it. You don't want to be an accessory."

"No, I don't. You're quite right."

Santangelo lingered as Bergsen went down the steps and walked toward the Jeep. "Are you absolutely sure, Mrs. Sweet? Are you sure you wouldn't like us to take you somewhere else? To a neighbor, maybe?"

"Thank you. No."

I closed the door as he stepped off the porch. I leaned my forehead against the warm wood for a moment, listening to the receding roar of the Jeep, glad I didn't have to suffer that jolting drive again. When I straightened, I glanced out the front window to be certain they were gone before I moved to the divan and settled my bulk on its worn cushions. I put my head back and closed my eyes as I tried to sort out my feelings. The silence of the house, broken only by intermittent fragments of birdsong and the whisper of tree branches, eased my soul and slowed my restless heartbeat. Before I realized I was going to do it, I fell asleep.

I slept a long time without moving, without dreaming, the kind of heavy, intractable sleep that is hard to rouse from. When the telephone jangled with my own three short rings, I opened sticky eyelids and saw that it was twilight. The telephone rang again, which answered one question at least. We still had telephone service.

It rang again and again before I could lever myself off the divan and reach the kitchen. I took up the receiver in the midst of the fifth ring and said hoarsely, "Hello?"

"Barrie Anne, thank God!" Charlotte said. "I've been worried about you."

"Sorry, Aunt Charlotte. I was going to call you, but after the sailors left, I fell asleep."

"They left? They wouldn't bring you back here?"

"They wanted to. I'm staying."

She was silent for so long I was afraid we'd been cut off. At last she said, "I had a feeling you would."

"Will's gone." I heard a telltale click somewhere on the line, but it didn't matter. Everyone surely knew by now. They knew my husband had abandoned me. They understood my husband was a traitor. He was a thief. A con man. The shame of it filled me, threatened to drown me. No matter where he was now or what he was doing, I had to live with that shame, and I didn't know how I was going to manage it.

Charlotte said, "Are you sure he's gone?"

"Oh, yes," I said tiredly.

"They checked upstairs?"

"Yes, and the shed and the barn. I don't think he could hide in the henhouse. Besides—"

"Besides, you knew, didn't you? You knew he wouldn't be there."

"Knew it as surely as if it had already happened."

She managed a small chuckle in acknowledgment of the little Blythe talent. "Still, kiddo. Why didn't you come home?"

The wistful warmth in her voice filled me with compunction, but I was as certain of this step as I had been that Will was gone. "Aunt Charlotte, you've been wonderful, but this is my home now. It feels right to be here."

"I don't think you should be alone, Barrie Anne. You could go into labor at any time."

"I know, but if I need help, I can call you."

"What if I'm not here?"

"Dr. Masters says first babies take a long time to come."

Another silence stretched down the telephone line. I listened to the faint buzz of the wires and glanced around the house, already thinking of what I should do first to set it to rights. While I waited for Charlotte to speak again, I ran a glassful of water at the tap. I drank some of it. I dipped my forefinger into what was left.

She said at last, "Well. You're a grown woman now, Barrie Anne. I suppose you can decide where you want to live."

"Thanks, Aunt Charlotte."

"I'm coming down, of course."

I laughed. Of course she was coming! I didn't need a feeling to know that.

"I'd better stop and buy some things. What do you need?"

"Everything, I'm afraid. The icebox is empty."

"Okay. I'll see you in a couple of hours. I'll run by the store."

"Thank you so much, Aunt Charlotte."

"You bet, kiddo."

"Oh, and, Aunt Charlotte—?" I lifted my finger out of the water glass.

"Yes?"

"Bring the gun."

21

September 18, 1947

Will was striving for nonchalance but failing at it. He and I faced each other, both of us simmering, both shaking with fury. For me, being openly angry with him was new. For him, showing his anger was revealing his weakness.

Charlotte said, "I'll take Emma upstairs and put her to bed." I handed her the baby, and as she took her, she murmured, "Shout if you need me."

"Okay."

As she started for the stairs, Emma began to wail. I had to grit my teeth not to run after the two of them.

I stood my ground, Willow stayed close at my side. Her hackles were up, and her tail was straight out behind her, her ears laid back. I had never seen her look at a human quite the way she was glaring at Will.

He saw it, too. "What's wrong with your dog?"

"Nothing's wrong with her."

"I don't like dogs, Barrie."

"So what?"

It felt good to speak my mind. To speak my truth. It felt better than I could have dreamed. How many women ever reach that point? How many wives endure forever in silence, like poor, cowed Mrs. Robbins, who never spoke above a whisper?

"'So what'?" Will snapped, then made a visible effort to regain his offhand manner. "Do I have to remind you that this is my house, too? I found it. I paid for it. I—"

"You paid for it with stolen money."

His eyes narrowed, and I thought this was the moment he would lose his control, begin to shout at me. Maybe even attack me, as he had done before. He stiffened and took a step forward.

Willow growled louder, a wonderfully terrifying sound. She, too, took a step forward, and that stopped Will where he was, as surely as if he had run into a wall.

I said with satisfaction, "You're afraid of her."

"When did you get a dog? She looks mean."

My anger had cooled enough for me to think clear, hard thoughts. To be as cagey as Will himself. I felt as if I had lived multiple lifetimes since I had last seen Will, and I was stronger, tougher, wiser for my experiences. I said in as chilly a tone as I could produce, "This is Willow. She *is* mean. You want to be careful around her. She'll bite you if you do something she doesn't like, and she never likes anything I don't like."

Willow had never bitten a person in her life, but I had told the truth. She wouldn't let Will or anyone else hurt me if she could possibly help it. Her stiff tail vibrated with tension, and no wonder. The strain in the room was as thick and hot as a summer thundercloud.

Will stepped back, drawing a hissing breath through his nostrils. There were new lines in his face, around his mouth, fanning from his eyes. He had aged more than a year's absence could account for. I wondered, briefly and without much real interest, where he had been and what had happened to him, but I wasn't going to give him the satisfaction of asking.

He reached for his cigarette, now burned almost to nothing. He took a final drag and then crushed it out in the ashtray. "I can see you're still angry," he said.

"You can see—? Good lord, Will. After everything you've done, you're going to try to turn this around on me?"

I was gratified—no, triumphant—to see the flicker of doubt that crossed his face. He had gotten away with so much, deceived me so thoroughly. He probably assumed he could do it again. I felt a vague curiosity about what story he meant to try on me, but I didn't really care. I was finished with him. And I didn't want him in my house.

He said, "Come on, Barrie," and tried a tentative smile.

I said, "Go away, Will."

"You wouldn't send me out on foot in the middle of the night?"

"Damn right I would."

He raised his eyebrows and tried again to affect a breezy attitude. "Barrie! Swearing? I have to say, you've changed. I'm not sure I like it."

"It doesn't matter, Will." I passed him to go to the sink and fill the teakettle. I set it on the range and lit the burner. "You don't need to like it or not like it. I'm managing on my own here just fine. You can't stay. You're welcome for the sandwich, but that's it."

"You can't exactly force me to go."

A slow grin began on my face, and I turned from the stove so he could see it. "I can, actually," I said. "I'm sure if I call the Shore Patrol, they'll be happy to come and get you."

He snorted a disbelieving laugh. "You wouldn't do that!"

"Why not?"

"You'd put me in jail?"

I leaned my back against the counter, the same position I had been in when he had assaulted me more than a year before. This time, I wasn't clumsy with pregnancy. This time, I was lean and muscled from garden work and strengthened by having no doubts about who Will was. Or who I was, for that matter. I doubted he could hurt me now. Besides, I had a strong young dog beside me, a dog who would do anything I asked of her.

I said, "You belong in jail, Will. Black-market stickers, for God's sake? Drugs?"

"I didn't do those things. They're lying about me."

"Really? Then where did all the money come from? Don't tell me the old story about back pay. I know you jumped ship, and I know you were never in the hospital. What I don't know is where you were for three years."

It was interesting for my new, wiser self to watch him try to deceive me again. His face crumpled, and his lips actually trembled, seemed to loosen and swell as if with incipient tears. He said, in a pale imitation of a penitent, "Oh, Barrie. I'm so sorry. I should have just told you the truth."

I knew better than to let him try another line with me, but the words came out just the same, automatic, reflexive words, as if he were a man like any other. "You should have, yes. You could do it now."

He took off his glasses and wiped them on his shirttail. Without the glasses, the lines around his eyes were more distinct. He put the glasses back on and drew a shaky breath. "The thing is, Barrie, I—I really was ill. I wasn't in the navy hospital, it's true, but—I was in the hospital. I sort of lost my mind for a while, the blood and the injuries and everything—"

I gazed at this man who had diverted the course of my life. So many feelings had been centered on him: love, desire, hurt, loss, resentment, anger, and finally, now, a pure absence of emotion that left my mind and heart as clean as a windswept sky. I knew his features—the straight nose, the fair hair falling over his forehead, the blue eyes behind his glasses—but I understood, at last, that I didn't know *him* at all. He was a stranger. An unwelcome, manipulative, deceitful stranger.

"I don't believe a word of it," I said.

"You can't imagine what it's like, Barrie, not being able to forget, to shut out all the—"

"You were on the run, weren't you? When you showed up in Port Townsend again. You were running from your mob gang, or whoever it was you were dealing with. Are you running now?"

He didn't answer for a moment. I saw the muscle flex and release along his jaw, and I knew he was angry, furious, but didn't dare show it. "I'm in trouble," he admitted. "Money trouble. I'm not sure what I'm going to do."

Willow lay at my feet, her chin on her paws but her eyes and ears following Will's every move, responding to his every word. She sensed everything I felt, I was sure. I saw Will's gaze slide to her now and again, wary and fearful.

"I can't help you, Will. You have to go. You don't belong here."

He sagged into the nearest chair, pulled off his glasses again, and buried his head in his hands. "Barrie, I have nowhere else to go."

"Go to your parents."

"I can't. They told me—" His sentence broke on a sob, and his shoulders hunched.

I steeled myself against a tiny spurt of pity. "Told you what, Will? That you burned that bridge, too?"

He drew a shuddering breath and lifted his head. Actual tears glimmered in his eyes, and he left his glasses lying where they were. "I never meant for any of this to happen. I never meant to jump ship, or to get sick, or to cause you any unhappiness. I thought it was all behind me, and then—when we lost the baby—"

It was too much. I snapped at him, "When *we* lost the baby? *I* lost Scottie, you bastard. You never laid eyes on him. You weren't even here!"

"Your aunt pulled a gun on me!" he cried. "You threw me out, both of you."

"Because you assaulted me, Will. My aunt thought I was in danger. So did I."

"I would never have really hurt you—"

"You did hurt me."

"I told you, it was an accident."

"That's nonsense. You lost control, and you hurt me, but you're not going to do it again. You're going to leave, and for good."

Slowly, with trembling hands, Will picked up his glasses and put them on. He pushed himself up and stood slack-shouldered beside the table. "At least let me sleep here," he muttered. "I don't have any money, and I'm on foot. I don't know where I'm going to go, but I'll head out in the morning."

It was my third big mistake with Will Sweet, and it was the worst mistake of all. It was the fatal mistake, but I didn't know that. No premonition rose to warn me.

I sighed. "Okay. You can sleep on the divan, but just until morning. Then you're gone."

He said, with a reasonable simulation of humility, "Thanks, Barrie. You'll hardly know I'm here."

"I'd better not. Willow won't like it, either."

He stiffened at that, with a spark of anger in his eyes. If I had any doubts, that spark told me the humility, the repentance, all of it was false. He said, "I'll need to use the bathroom."

I nodded. He turned up the stairs, and with Willow on my heels, I went around putting out lights and locking the doors. By the time Willow and I made our way upstairs, he had left the bathroom and was standing outside the closed nursery door. He said, "You haven't told me whose baby that is."

"She's my baby." He raised his eyebrows. "I adopted her."

"From where?"

"What does it matter? She's my daughter. She's nothing to do with you."

"She has my name."

"You don't know that. Go to bed, Will. This is none of your business."

For one frozen instant, I thought he might go into the nursery. The fingers on his right hand twitched as if they longed to turn the doorknob. I said hastily, "She's sleeping. Go get some blankets from the linen closet. There's an extra pillow there, too."

"I know where the blankets are, Barrie. My house, too, remember?"

I put my hands on my hips and regarded him wearily. "Not anymore, Will. I'm glad you bought it, because I love it here, but it's not yours anymore."

"My name is on the deed."

"Do you want to challenge me? That means legal action. I don't think you can risk appearing in court."

We were whispering, but I knew Charlotte would be listening, though her light was out. Will cast a glance at the nursery door, a speculative look on his face. There was no sign now of the fake tears, the pretend sorrow. "I'm surprised anyone would let you adopt a baby, with no husband in the house."

"A lot of things would surprise you," I said. I pointed to the stairs. "Go and sleep. We don't have anything else to talk about."

In the low light, his eyes glinted a glacial blue, and his mouth curved in something like amusement. He said, "We'll see about that, Barrie." He turned to the linen closet, opened the door, and took a blanket and pillow from the shelf. I opened my own door to let Willow go in, then closed it again to watch Will descend the stairs. As he started down, he touched his forehead with one hand, the sort of salute he had once used as a charming farewell.

It was nearly midnight, a late hour for a farmer, and I was exhausted, emotionally and physically. I was uncomfortably aware of Will downstairs, and I couldn't help replaying the scene between us in my mind, wondering if I had said too much, said too little, made threats I couldn't back up. My heart fluttered with anxiety, and my mind roiled with ideas of going to the police, of going to a lawyer, of writing to Will's parents. I hoped I wouldn't need to do any of those things. I didn't want him to go to prison. I only wanted him to go away, off to whatever future he could devise for himself.

I went into the bathroom and ran water into the sink to wash my face. I was looking at my tired face in the mirror, dipping my hands into the water, when it hit me. It wasn't a premonition so much as it was a compulsion, but it was undeniable just the same. It gripped my solar plexus with an ache of need.

I shook the water from my hands without doing anything about my face and hurried out of the bathroom.

I stood at the top of the stairs, listening. There was a rustle and creak as Will settled himself on the divan. I could just see the circle of light thrown off by the lamp in the front room, its edge stretching into the dining room and reflecting off the surface of the range and the chrome handle of the icebox. As I put one tentative foot on the top stair, the light went out.

My pulse thrummed in my throat as I crept down the stairs as quietly as I could, trying to avoid the creaks in the middle. I moved on tiptoe to the coat closet and eased the door open. The .30-30 waited behind its shelter of coats and sweaters. I slid it out without making a sound and then retraced my steps with exaggerated care. The ache of compulsion didn't ease until I was back in my bedroom and had laid the .30-30 on top of my bureau, where I could snatch it up in a moment.

I put on my pajamas and got into bed. I lay there for a while, but tired as I was, I couldn't force myself into sleep. I got up again and settled into the armchair next to the window with an afghan around me. I gazed out into the star field glittering above the canal. A meteorite flashed across the black sky as I watched, but it was a distant one, small, there and gone almost before I realized it. It was nothing like the one I had seen the night before Willow found Emma on the shore. Emma, child of the sea. Brought to me, it would seem, by the ocean.

Thinking of that made my heart flutter with wonder at the marvel of it all. I resisted an urge to go into the nursery, to bring her into my own bed. She was sleeping better since she started spending the night in her crib. If I went in, she would wake, and I would have to go down to warm a bottle, which would wake Will. I couldn't face him again. Not tonight.

With luck, he would be gone when I got up. If not, I would send him off with some food and with what little money I had. That was just kindness. It wouldn't help anything for me to be cruel to him. I just wanted him to go away. To disappear from my life, and Charlotte's, and Emma's, forever.

I sat staring up at the stars, listening to the creaks of the old house around me, hearing the occasional chittering of a night bird. I watched an owl, silhouetted by starlight, arrow over the empty field, and I felt a twinge of sympathy for the little field creature that would fall prey to those hungry claws.

My eyelids grew heavy at last. I was just thinking I should get back into bed when I drifted off.

I've always disliked staying awake too late. It invariably means a hard sleep in the early hours of the morning, the kind that weighs down the eyelids and muddies the brain. It happened to me that night. Even in the armchair, with my head at an awkward angle against the arched back, I slept thickly, dreamlessly, body and mind worn out.

Until Charlotte burst into the bedroom, shocking Willow and me into sudden, alarmed wakefulness. "Do you have Emma?"

22

May 1946

I went into labor two weeks early.

I should have known it was coming, I suppose. I was paying attention to the calendar, placing all my faith in Dr. Masters's prediction of a date. I should have realized my body was the real authority, and its demands wouldn't be denied. I was caught by surprise in the midst of staking tomato plants.

I felt a rush of warmth between my thighs, warmer even than the high spring sun that burned my shoulders and made the air glitter with dust motes. There was no pain, not then, but my overalls were drenched from groin to knee. The tilled soil beneath my boots soaked up the waters, but I knew what had happened. It made me a little shaky, but I put down the cedar stake in my hand and started toward the house, walking wide-legged like some sort of giant duck. My overalls cooled quickly, and the material stuck to the insides of my thighs as if I had sat myself down in a mud puddle.

I was alone at the farm. Charlotte had been there the day before to stock the icebox and the cupboards, frowning over my isolation. I pointed to the calendar, assuring her I still had time, and urging her to go home until the day drew nearer. I had baby things—diapers, a layette, the cradle—but I hadn't done anything to prepare for a home birth. I kept thinking I had time. The needs of my garden consumed me, planting, watering, weeding, fertilizing, trying to bring it back from its two weeks of neglect.

I wouldn't admit to myself that part of the allure of the garden chores was that they kept me from thinking about Will and his failings, worrying about a future as a mother alone, fussing about how I would give this baby a good life.

I waddled my way up the three steps to the kitchen door. Just inside, I stripped off my sticky overalls and left them in a pile. I kept towels there to rub off the garden mud, so I grabbed one and tried to wipe off the worst of the mess. I started upstairs to run a bath, but halfway up the staircase, the first contraction gripped my body with a hard hand. It didn't last long, but it made me sag onto the tread to wait for it to pass. Despite the towel, I was leaving dribbles on the wood of the stairs, and my legs began to shake in earnest. I clung to the banister and tried to decide what to do first.

When the contraction eased, I inched my way back down the stairs and worked my way into the kitchen, leaving a trail of greasy-looking droplets behind me. I took down the telephone receiver and settled onto a chair while I gave the operator Charlotte's number. Fortunately, she was home.

"Aunt Charlotte?" I thought my voice sounded small and

high, like a little girl's. I took a deep breath, feeling its resonance deep in my swollen belly, and tried again. "Aunt Charlotte, I think I'm—that is, I think my water broke—" Another contraction rippled through my belly, making me grunt and grip the edge of the table with my free hand.

"Barrie Anne? You're in labor? But you have two weeks still!"

My aunt had also placed her trust in the calendar. We had planned for her to come to stay three days before my due date, to be sure I wouldn't be alone when the baby came. All I could say, when I caught my breath again, was a hoarse "I know. I know. But it's started."

She said, in a voice tight with anxiety, "Is it bad?"

"No. Not bad. But steady."

I had read books about childbirth. Dr. Masters had given me a pamphlet and told me not to listen to the neighbors' tales of horrible labors. I knew quick labors were rare. I knew it got harder as it went on. I believed what the pamphlet told me, that this was a hard job to do but not torture.

Dr. Masters had been right about the neighbors. When I went to the Mercantile in Port Townsend or to the Brinnon market, some woman was sure to regale me with dramatic tales of how she had suffered giving birth. I did my best to be polite and to forget it all the moment I was alone.

Over the last week, since the two sailors had left me here, I had been alone a lot. I enjoyed it. I liked being alone with my garden and my quiet house and the cries of the gulls and the cheeping of the finches. It was a time to contemplate and heal. I had expected it to last a bit longer.

Charlotte roared down to the farm in just over an hour, the Studebaker rattling and coughing up the lane. By that time I was lying on my side on the divan, my legs curled up, my head on a pillow. It was true that the contractions weren't terrible, but they were powerful, and they left me breathless and dry-mouthed. Charlotte came in, dropped a half-filled valise by the door, and hurried to kneel beside me.

I said, "Don't look so worried! It's perfectly natural, remember?"

"It's too early," she said.

"I guess so." I felt the contortion of my face as another contraction began.

She waited until it had passed, and I lay back on my pillow, panting. "I'll call Dr. Masters."

Oddly, that hadn't occurred to me. "Okay. I need to clean up the floor, though." I started to push myself up, but I didn't get far. I sank back, shaking my head. "Aunt Charlotte—I don't think I can do it. I don't even think I can get upstairs to my bed."

"I'll clean the floor. I'll get some towels, and—and other things. Don't worry!"

I laughed a little. My aunt was more worried than I was.

Dr. Masters didn't come right away. Charlotte cleaned the mess I had made on the floor and set my overalls to soak. She made tea, and I drank a little. My contractions continued, getting stronger and stronger as the daylight waned. A waxing gibbous moon rose in the east, the color of old pewter. I could just see it through the front room window. As I labored, I watched it rise out of my sight, leaving a faded field of stars. A coyote yipped from the field next to the farm. I got up to use a bucket Charlotte brought in from the porch, though it was embarrassing.

By the time Dr. Masters arrived, around ten o'clock, Charlotte had managed to get me into a nightgown and bathrobe and to cover the divan beneath me with a sheet. As the night cooled, she also brought the wool blanket from my bed. When Dr. Masters came, he sent her up to get some sleep. "Nothing will happen for a while yet," he said. "He's early, our baby, but I doubt we'll meet him before morning."

Charlotte did as she was asked, although I knew she didn't want to leave me. I felt a rush of love for Dr. Masters, so calm and assured. He held my hand through my contractions and mopped my wet forehead when they were done. As the night wore on, the pains came faster and faster, and as the light began to rise, the final stage began.

Dr. Masters assured me, afterward, that there was nothing I could have done differently. My baby's weakness wasn't due to the stress I had been under, or to what I ate, or to the bending and digging I had done. Scottie just wasn't strong enough to stay in the world.

He was born at nine in the morning, without incident. Dr. Masters laid him in my arms for a few minutes before he took him to wash and then to examine. I waited eagerly for him to bring my baby back to me, but when he did, I saw the truth on his face.

I put Scottie to my breast, though he couldn't manage to suckle. I cradled him in my arms, stroking his soft, furry scalp, memorizing his little pinched face with my fingers. Charlotte wept, the only time I had ever seen her openly cry. I didn't. I could cry later, I thought. I could cry afterward. For now, I didn't want to waste a single precious moment of my doomed motherhood.

Dr. Masters stayed with us until the end. He offered to call the funeral home, but I said no. Charlotte patted my head and let her fingers linger on Scottie's blanketed form for a moment. In a voice still thick with tears, she said, "Dr. Masters, I'll stay with Barrie Anne and the—and Scottie." I had insisted we call him by his name. It was the only time I had spoken all day.

"All right," the doctor said. His face was drawn, and his eyes were red from lack of sleep. He said again, as he had said before, "I'm terribly sorry, Mrs. Sweet. It's not uncommon, but I know that's no comfort." I gazed at him, exhausted, wordless, numb with misery.

Charlotte spoke for me. "We'll deal with the undertaker in the morning." She was standing beside the divan, and she placed a hand on my shoulder. "Barrie Anne's parents are buried in the cemetery in Port Townsend. She'll want Scottie to lie beside them." Her voice broke, and her fingers trembled on my skin.

I held my baby all night, sleeping sometimes, laying him down occasionally to limp up the stairs to the bathroom and then down again. He grew cold. His eyes were closed as if he were sleeping, and his tiny, wizened face seared itself into my memory.

The vastness of the pain I felt was too much to take in all at once. I think I understood even then that it would always be part of me. I would, I supposed, one day get used to it. I knew I would never get over it.

In the morning Charlotte called the undertaker to make arrangements for Scottie's burial. We dressed him in the gown we had chosen for his christening and wrapped him in one of the receiving blankets we had bought. Mrs. Urquhardt had heard the news on the party line and showed up with a tiny pillow she had crocheted as a baby gift. I laid my baby's head on the pillow, covered his face with a corner of the blanket, and held his tiny, still form against my heart as we drove to Port Townsend.

Not until the solemn-faced undertaker took Scottie's body from me did it occur to me that Will knew nothing of what had happened. Standing outside the funeral home, dry-eyed, sore in body and heart, I said, "Aunt Charlotte, I don't know how to let Will know."

She put her arm around me to lead me to the car. Her eyes were swollen, but her voice was steady. "I don't give a damn if he knows or not, but I'll write to his parents for you."

We went to the foursquare house, and Charlotte insisted I lie down and try to sleep. I obeyed, too listless to resist, allowing her to fold me into my girlhood bed once again. I stared at the ceiling, and contemplated the idea that my life, at the age of twenty-four, had come to nothing.

My neighbors, Mrs. Urquhardt and Mrs. Miller and even Mrs. Robbins, surprised me by showing up at the cemetery for Scottie's burial. They had driven up together in Mrs. Urquhardt's ancient Ford, wearing black dresses with long, drooping hemlines and flat black hats with bits of veil that hung below their eyebrows. Mrs. Miller took my hand in her gloved one and whispered that my baby was with God now. Mrs. Robbins didn't speak, but she patted my shoulder, and I knew that for her it was an expression of heartfelt sympathy. Mrs. Urquhardt enveloped me in a soft-bosomed hug and said, "We're all real sorry, Mrs. Sweet. I went over and watered your garden last night, so don't worry."

I thanked her, and she drew back to give me a look full of maternal sympathy. "Where's that handsome husband of yours? Too brokenhearted to be here? I could understand. So sad."

I felt Charlotte stiffen at my side, but none of that mattered to me now. I said, bluntly, "My husband is gone, Mrs. Urquhardt. He won't be coming back."

Her eyes widened, but I didn't think she was really surprised. I suspected she already knew Will was gone, and that all my neighbors did. We didn't have a Brinnon newspaper, but we had a party line, and that was better than any newspaper could ever be.

She hugged me again. "Well. Mr. Urquhardt will keep an eye on your farm. Give your garden a once-over, anything you need."

A man in clerical robes appeared beside the freshly dug grave, a Bible in his hands. The undertaker was there, too, the expression on his face just as grim as it had been the day before. I suddenly felt, as the tiny coffin was lowered into the earth, that I was outside my body, watching the scene from a distance. The people in their black clothes, the minister in his white robe, Aunt Charlotte, unlipsticked, wearing a long black sweater over her trousers and a beret on her head, and me still in a maternity smock, no gloves, no hat, only a scarf tied over my hair, the edge pulled down over my forehead to shade my eyes. Dr. Masters showed up at the last moment, a small, plump figure in a dark overcoat, carrying his hat in his hands.

The minister read something, but I couldn't hear it. I was too far away, watching the sad little knot of people, seeing them sniffle into their handkerchiefs. I looked up and saw eagles swirling far above the cemetery, first two, then four, their white heads gleaming in the sunshine, their great jagged wings barely moving as they rode the currents of air. I longed with all my soul to fly with them, to leave this behind. To go where Scottie had gone.

When the gravedigger began to shovel clods of earth on top of the coffin, I was jarred back into myself. Dr. Masters was pressing my hand. Charlotte's arm was around my waist, and we were soon making our unsteady way to the car. Mrs. Miller, Mrs. Robbins, and Mrs. Urquhardt followed at a respectful distance. The undertaker and the minister stayed behind, their heads bent together as they conferred.

Charlotte opened the Studebaker's door for me. My neighbors assured me of their help and support on the farm. Mrs. Miller murmured, "Is that your folks' grave, there beside your baby's? Such a comfort that must be."

It was no comfort to me at all, but there was no point in saying so. I managed to say, "So kind of you all to come. Thank you."

Then it was over. Charlotte took me to her house, prepared a cup of tea for each of us with as much brandy as tea in it, and settled me on the bench in the sunshine.

"I know the whole thing is godawful," she said, sitting beside me with her cigarette pack and a lighter. "But darkness won't help. A little sun is good for you. Drink up, and then maybe you can eat something."

I did everything she asked of me. It was easier than thinking for myself. The brandy loosened my tears, and I cried on and off the whole afternoon, but I did eat some salmon and salad at dinner, and I took a sleeping powder Dr. Masters dropped off. I went straight to bed after dinner, but I was awake again at two in the morning. I got up, went to the bathroom, and then padded down to the kitchen and out to the garden.

The moon was full by then, and the night was unusually warm for May. I sat on the back step in the moonlight, listening to the rustle of critters in the shrubs and the faint ringing of the buoy out in the strait. I cried for a while, hot tears that cooled on my cheeks. I wrapped my arms around myself, remembering the feel of a baby in my arms, first so warm and alive, then so cold and still. Dr. Masters had said there would be other babies for me, but of course I had no husband. It wasn't likely.

I propped my shoulders against the railing of the steps and dozed again, fitfully, knowing I should go back to bed, feeling as if even getting to my feet was too much trouble. I woke to the sound of Charlotte's percolator and the smell of her first morning cigarette, all familiar things, the sounds and scents of my girlhood.

But I was no longer a girl. This was no longer my house. As the sun rose above the Cascades to the east and glinted on the surface of the lagoon, I knew what I needed to do. I wanted my garden, my apple orchard, my little crumbling farmhouse. I wanted to be in my own home. I had to face my future, do what I could to build a life, expend my grief in hard work. I had failed at being a wife. I had lost my chance of being a mother. All that was left, it seemed, was to discover if I could do one thing well. I could at least become a good farmer.

I gathered myself together, pushed myself to my feet, and went in to explain to Charlotte.

23

June 12, 1946

I had been alone in the days preceding Scottie's birth, but once Charlotte had returned me to the farm and left me there on my own, I was alone in a way I had never been. When I was pregnant, I never felt solitary. My baby was there, always. I talked to him often and crooned to him as the two of us fell asleep at night. Now it was different. Charlotte had wanted to stay, but I insisted she go back to her own home. I wanted—and needed—to begin my life anew.

My body recovered quickly from the aftereffects of childbirth. My heart was another matter. I slogged through the early days of that summer. When self-pity began to overwhelm me, I redoubled my efforts in the garden. When I felt as if I couldn't face another morning or another empty evening, I set my hand to some task I had been putting off, like painting the porch railings or scouring the windows until they glittered blindingly in the sunshine. I often forgot to eat, but my body reminded me of that when I went too long with no sustenance, and I was forced to fry an egg and toast some bread. Most of the time, I was too miserable even to cry.

The one room I neglected, never cleaned, never entered, was the one intended to be Scottie's nursery. I shut the door on everything inside—the tiny sky-blue dresser with its sweet little clouds emerging from the drawers, the cradle with its plaid quilt, the diapers and bottles and baby clothes. I built a fire at the far side of the garden and burned the catalogs we had meant to pore over. I looked at the list of baby names and felt as if it had been written by a stranger. Even my handwriting looked different to me, an artifact of another time. I threw it on the fire with the catalogs.

When I walked past my tidy henhouse, still waiting for its occupants, it seemed like a metaphor for my efforts of the entire winter. It had been a well-intentioned project, a hopeful endeavor, but in the end, a failure.

On a cloudy day in June, with rain threatening, I used the last of my coffee to make myself a cup. I brought my coffee cup and the tea caddy to the bare kitchen table. The tea caddy held the last of the housekeeping money Will had given to me. I turned it upside down and counted the bills and change that fell out onto the scarred wood. With a feeling of mounting dismay, I counted it a second time, just to be sure. It held forty-three dollars and sixty-two cents. Out of that I would have to pay the telephone bill and the electric company, and I needed some food. The icebox was empty. I could ask Charlotte for help, of course, but I didn't want to give her any argument for persuading me to come back to Port Townsend.

I shoved the money back into the tea caddy, picked up my coffee cup, and held it in my two hands as I gazed past the front room to the empty lane. The darkest of all dark thoughts hovered at the edge of my mind, the abandonment of hope, the admission of final defeat. Weakly, I tried to thrust that thought away, but as the rain began to spatter the dust and rattle against the windows, my strength nearly failed me.

When a strange truck rattled into the space before my front yard, I set down my cup. It was a pickup that had once been brown but was now spotted red with rust. There were cartons of something piled in the back, and a man at the wheel. I didn't think it was Will. I didn't care enough even to dip my fingers into my cold coffee to find out.

The driver opened his door, settled a flat-brimmed hat on his head against the sprinkle of rain, and swung his feet onto the running board. As he stepped down, I remembered who he was. I had seen him once or twice at the Brinnon market, though it was his wife I knew, his wife who had kindly come to Scottie's funeral.

It was Mr. Miller. He and his wife were members of a small church, one that held its services in someone's barn. I couldn't remember the name of it. Mrs. Miller was the kind of woman who brought God into every conversation, but I didn't mind. She had promised to pray for me, and I knew she was sincere about her intention.

Mr. Miller stood for a moment, surveying my place. He had never been to the farm that I knew of, not since Will and I had moved in. He pulled out an enormous red handkerchief, wiped his nose with it, and then started up the path to the front door.

I set down my coffee cup and pushed to my feet. I felt as heavy and slow as an elderly person, moving stiffly as I came around the table and crossed to the front room. I didn't really want to talk to anyone, but except for the Urquhardts, who shared my lane, the Millers were my closest neighbors. It made no sense to be rude to them.

He knocked, and I opened the door. "Mr. Miller," I said. My voice creaked, and I cleared my throat. "Please come in out of the rain."

"It's just a sprinkle, Mrs. Sweet." As he stepped through the door, he seemed to belatedly remember his hat, and he snatched it off in such haste it nearly sailed across the room. He said, "I'm sorry Mrs. Miller couldn't come to call, but she's got her Bible study today."

"That's all right," I said. I stepped back and indicated that he should go ahead of me to the kitchen. "I'm sorry, but I just ran out of coffee, so I can't—"

"No, no," he said. "No, I've had my coffee, thanks. I came to bring you some hens. From our church family."

He had a strong Southern accent. I hadn't known that. I couldn't remember if we had ever actually spoken. I said, "You brought—what did you say?"

He turned his hat in his hands, looking everywhere but at my face. "Hens," he said, creating a two-syllable word out of it in his broad dialect. "Our church family been praying for you, you see, Mrs. Sweet? My Matilda said you built yourself a henhouse but didn't have no chickens for it, so we went around and every family contributed one."

"Hens?"

Now he managed to meet my eyes, briefly. I saw with surprise that his were a clear brown, with thick lashes. A fleeting smile brightened his face, and I thought he must have been a handsome man when he was young. Now he was wrinkled and weathered and grizzled as if he shaved only every few days. "Yes, ma'am," he said, the smile vanishing as quickly as it had come. "I have some hens for you. Is the coop out in the garden? Next to that shed?"

"It is, but—Mr. Miller, I don't have feed yet, or scratch, or even straw—"

"Now, ma'am, you don't got to worry about none of that. Our church family put everything together to get you started."

I didn't know what he meant by "church family," but I was so stunned I didn't ask. I didn't know what to say or what to think. A gift of chickens? It didn't seem possible.

When I heard the cackle and chatter of chickens from the back of his truck, I peered curiously through the front window, saying, a little foolishly, "Chickens."

"Yes, ma'am." He gestured with his hat toward the back of the house. "I'll just have a look at your henhouse. Make sure the ladies have what they need."

"Ladies?"

His quicksilver smile flashed again. "Hens," he said. "You ain't never kept chickens?"

"No." I knew I was doing a terrible job of accepting this kindness. I was embarrassed at the sluggishness of my body and brain. I put out a hand and gripped the doorjamb to steady myself. "I'm so sorry, Mr. Miller. This is—I've read all about keeping chickens, and I will—I'll do it right, I promise. I just—" I made a futile little gesture with my free hand and bit my lip to stop its trembling.

He cleared his throat in an embarrassed way. "Now, now, Mrs. Sweet. Now, now, don't take on."

I made myself breathe and straightened my spine. "I'm sorry," I said again. "I'm fine, Mr. Miller. I'm more grateful than I know how to say."

"No need," he said roughly. "Just being neighborly."

"I'll take you to the coop. You'll see I put everything in there the way I was supposed to—at least I tried. I found the instructions in a magazine."

He didn't speak again until we reached my chicken coop. The rain had eased, and a watery shaft of sunlight fell on my homely little henhouse. I felt suddenly defensive about it. I hadn't painted it yet, and one wall was crooked. It smelled nice, though, with the spicy fragrance of sawn wood. The floor was solid, and I had built a perch for roosting and six nesting boxes. I forgot my awkwardness as I watched Mr. Miller eye my construction. "I didn't think they needed a run, because they'll have the garden."

He scanned the expanse of my garden and nodded in apparent approval of the fence. "Best shut them in at night," he said.

"I know. Coyotes."

"And raccoons." He scratched his chin, then said, "Poop boards?"

Startled, I said, "Sorry?"

"Easier to clean if you put poop boards under the perch."

"Oh."

"I'll give you a hand."

Mr. Miller did much more than give me a hand. He installed the poop boards so I could rake out the chicken manure beneath them. He found two squares of mesh in the cluttered bed of his truck and nailed them neatly into the unglazed windows. He added supports under my construction to straighten the crooked wall. He used three of my discarded boards to make a ramp and then stood back and admired the whole.

With every improvement he made, my mood brightened. By the time he was done I felt almost cheerful. I said, a little shyly, "I thought I would paint it one of these days."

"The ladies won't care much about paint," he said, but he favored me with one of his quick smiles as he said it.

He backed his truck up to my garden gate, and one by one he set the hens free inside the safety of the fence. The sky had cleared as if to welcome them, and they were beautiful in the sunshine. I had studied chicken breeds in the catalogs, and now I surveyed my new family with satisfaction. I counted four Rhode Island Reds, three white Leghorns, two speckled Hollands, and one beautiful golden bird whose name I couldn't remember. Mr. Miller said, as he released her, "Orpington. Best all-around chicken in the world."

Finally, he hefted a fifty-pound bag of Peck's Feed for Poultry out of the truck. I shut and latched the garden gate as Mr. Miller carried the bag across to the henhouse. He rummaged through the pockets of his baggy overalls for a knife and slit the top of the sack. "Wanta keep this from the ladies," he warned. "Garbage can with a lid is good storage." He took a handful of feed from the brimming sack, and scattered it on the ground, calling, "Chk-chk-chk. Here, chk-chk-chk."

It must have been a language all chickens understood, despite these hens coming from different homes. They came running, a gay rainbow flock, glossy feathers ruffling, sturdy yellow claws digging into the dark earth of the garden.

I didn't know whether to laugh with pleasure at the hens' beauty or weep with sheer gratitude at the gift of them. "Mr. Miller—I don't know how to thank you, or how to thank your—your church family."

"Naw," he said gruffly. "Christian charity."

I didn't know anything about Christian charity, either, but this exercise of it, from neighbors I didn't know well, lightened the weight of my heavy heart. With a bucket, I filled the metal water trough I had set along the fence, and then Mr. Miller and I stood together for a little while, watching the ladies settle in. A little spark of hope—the first I had felt since Scottie's death—was born in my soul. I wondered if I dared nurture it.

I apologized again for not having coffee to offer. Mr. Miller said, "No, that's all right, but I wouldn't say no to a glass of water before I head back."

I led him up onto the little back porch and in through the kitchen door. I felt his gaze taking in my old kitchen table, my slightly uneven floor, and my secondhand furniture. He didn't comment, but I saw him look at the floor more than once.

"If I spill something," I said wryly, as I handed him a glass of water from the tap, "it runs right out of the kitchen and races toward the front room."

His sweet, brief smile flashed once more. I was bemused by the way it transformed his weathered face. He said, "Old houses have their quirks. I kinda like 'em that way."

He drank his water, picked up his hat from where he had hooked it over the back of a chair, and started toward the front room. I followed and nearly bumped into him when he stopped abruptly two steps from the door. He pointed to the wooden box, clearly marked WINCHESTER, lying beneath the window where Charlotte had deposited it three weeks ago, before I went into labor.

Mr. Miller said, "That yours?"

"It is now. It was my father's."

He gave me a sharp-eyed glance. "You shoot?"

I gave a shrug. "I haven't had it out of the box yet." Charlotte had, of course, but she had put it back after threatening Will with it, claiming it terrified her.

"Well," he said, again turning one syllable into two. "Well, I'd feel a sight better about you being all the way out here by yourself if you knew how to use that Winchester. A .30-30, is it?"

"I'm sorry, Mr. Miller, but I have no idea. I've never touched it."

He looked at the box and looked at me again. "Got any ammo?"

I didn't know that, either. I went to the box and knelt beside it to pry up the lid. Inside the wooden slats was another box, one made of heavy cardboard, printed with the Winchester logo and some words that meant nothing to me, but which I assumed described the kind of gun it was. I lifted that out, surprised by its lightness. Underneath it was a box of ammunition and an old sales receipt. I picked it up and saw my father's name written in fading script: *Mr. Scott Blythe, Port Townsend, Washington State. COD.*

Wordless, I lifted the gun in one hand, the ammunition box in the other. I came to my feet and held both out to Mr. Miller.

He accepted them with something like reverence. "Been in that box how long?"

"My parents died in 1928."

"Oh, my goodness gracious." He set the box of bullets on the divan and caressed the gun with his fingers, turning it this way and that, trying the lever, peering in the barrel.

"Is it still good?" I asked. "Usable?"

His grizzled eyebrows rose. "Usable? Oh, yes, ma'am. This is a wonderful old piece. Doesn't look like it's been used much at all."

"Can you show me how to fire it?"

"Yes, ma'am. Yes, I surely can do that."

Mr. Miller was as meticulous about the Winchester as he was about the hen house. First, he insisted on making sure it was clean. He used a bit of an old towel to wipe imaginary specks of dust from the barrel and the lever and the trigger guard. When he was satisfied with that, he led me outside, around to the giant cedar tree. He reached into one of his endless pockets for a creased piece of paper and tacked it to a skinny spruce on the far side. "In case we miss," he said, with one of his lightning smiles.

He spent a moment or two showing me how the lever worked, where to insert the bullets—which he called "rounds"—and warning me there would be a kick when the gun fired. He showed me how to sight along the barrel and how to nestle the stock against my shoulder. Then he walked me back about forty paces and stood aside to watch me take my first tries.

We spent twenty minutes in the shade of the cedar. When we were done, I had missed the target completely six times, but I had hit the piece of paper ten. My instructor grunted satisfaction each time the bullet thwacked into the tree. The hens cackled fiercely at the first two or three shots but then subsided.

Mr. Miller took the gun from me when there were still four cartridges left in the box. "Keep those," he advised. "You don't wanta be without ammo. I'll bring you more for target practice."

I relinquished the rifle with reluctance. My right shoulder ached, and my ears rang from the shots, but I had no intention of admitting any of that. It was satisfying to aim, to squeeze the trigger that fit my finger so well, and then to hear the rewarding sound as my bullet struck. I couldn't picture myself shooting anything that was alive, but having the gun in the house would indeed make me feel safer, and now there were the chickens to protect. My chickens.

"I don't see a car," Mr. Miller said, as I saw him out to the porch.

"No. I don't have one."

"I thought there was a red jalopy."

"It was—that is, Will took that. When he... when he left."

He shook his head and made tsk-tsk noises. "I don't hold with what your husband did, Mrs. Sweet. Leavin' a young woman all on her own." He settled his hat on his head, but he stood for a moment, squinting into the fresh rain clouds gathering above the peninsula. "Got any money at all?"

"I have forty-three dollars," I said. "And sixty-two cents."

"Uh-huh. Not a lot, then."

"I'm afraid not."

"Can you drive?"

"Yes. I can drive a car, and I drive the tractor."

"Well, that's good, then. The church has an old pickup they been meaning to sell. International, 1938. What say I tell them you'll pay—let's see—twenty-five dollars for it? Wouldn't leave you much, but you need a way to get to the market. Sell those eggs the ladies are going to lay for you."

"Oh, my goodness. That would be wonderful, Mr. Miller! How kind of you."

"Good, good. All settled, then."

"I don't think I can ever repay you or your—your church family, but I'm more grateful than I can say. I hope you will tell them for me."

"You bet." The smile lit his face, come and gone so quickly it was easy to miss it. "What are neighbors for?" he said, and left me shaking my head, stunned by the change in my fortunes.

When my benefactor departed in his wheezy old truck, the empty cages rattling in the bed, I stood on the front porch, leaning against a supporting post, tracking the dust cloud as he rattled and banged his way back toward the highway. When the dust subsided, I straightened and went to make room in the coat closet under the stairs, a space where the gun—my gun, as I thought of it now—would be accessible but well hidden.

From the kitchen, I could hear the chickens chortling away in the garden, and my awareness of them—living beings who would need my care—altered my perceptions of the farm and

of the life I would be living there. I felt, though I was so solitary, more alive for their cheerful presence.

Later that same day, my aunt arrived with a big-eyed puppy
in her arms, and my transformation was complete. I was
wounded, but I was not destroyed. I was alone, but I was no
longer lonely.

I thought, at the time, that it was enough.

24

September 19, 1947

I was out of my bed and into the nursery before I was fully awake. Charlotte stood back to let me fly past her. Her hands were pressed to her mouth, and her eyes were wide with terror. I had never, ever seen Charlotte so afraid before.

The crib was empty. Emma's blanket was gone, too, but not her pink hat. It lay on the bureau, on top of the lacy dress she had worn to dinner, just as we had left it.

I spun, searching the corners, my own fear thrilling through my bones. "Oh, God," I moaned. "Where is she?"

"Where's Will?" Charlotte hissed.

"He slept on the divan—" I didn't finish the explanation. Still in my pajamas, barefoot, I dashed back into my bedroom for the .30-30 and then raced down the stairs, skidding on the lowest tread so that I almost fell. Willow leaped the final three steps to stay beside me. I reached the front room at a dead run.

Will wasn't there. The brown cotton blanket I had given

him had been tossed over the arm of the divan. His shoes with the separated sole were gone, as were his jacket and hat. I whirled and ran to the back door and threw it open.

"Willow!" I shouted, as I thrust my bare feet into my gardening boots. "Find Emma!"

It wasn't a command the dog had ever heard, but Willow was no ordinary dog. Willow was a gift dog, a dog perfectly designed for the Blythe talent. She knew what I needed, and she knew how to follow her instincts. She had brought the baby home in the first place, and she would do all she could to bring her back.

I stumbled out to the porch, my left foot not yet all the way into my boot, in time to see Willow gather herself to leap over the garden gate and race across the field of drying grass. Her ears were back, her body low to the ground. She ran faster than I had ever seen her, a blur of legs and fur and flying tail. Under different circumstances, I would have appreciated the beauty of it. Now I was nearly rigid with terror.

This was no coincidence. Will, for his own reasons, had taken Emma out of her crib and out of the house. It was hard to believe he would harm her, but there were many things about Will that were hard—no, impossible—to believe.

I looked back to see Charlotte in the doorway. She was dressed in trousers and a loose shirt and shoes on her feet. She had powdered her face, done her eyebrows, applied her lipstick.

She pointed to the Winchester. "When did you get that out?"

"Last night. I had to have it. It was a—oh, damn it, it was a feeling."

She nodded. "Go."

I whirled and ran after Willow.

I trusted the dog to choose the right direction. I couldn't keep up with her, but I ran as fast as I was able to in the clumsy rubber boots. I saw Willow disappear among the apple trees, dotted now with ripening apples. The soil beneath them was littered with windfalls, and treacherous. I picked my way among them at an awkward trot, the gun carefully pointed toward the earth. Mr. Miller had said never to run with the rifle in my hands, but my sense of urgency overrode his advice.

I broke out of the orchard onto the bank. The sun was just up, the water shading from dawn gray to morning blue. Willow had stopped on the gravelly strip of the shore. The tide was out, leaving the beach littered with sea wrack and driftwood. Willow, for once, paid no attention to the wealth of junk served up by the tide.

Her gaze was fixed on the ancient dock. At its end a battered boat, unpainted, uncanopied, hardly more than a rowboat, was tied to one of the pilings.

I had never before seen a boat there. I knew the dock wasn't safe. Its sun-bleached boards were rotted all the way through in places, and it was often completely submerged. Now it was laid bare by the receding water, but that wouldn't last.

Will was bending over the rowboat, attempting to undo the mooring rope with one hand. In the grip of his other arm was my daughter. He held her around the middle as if she were a rag doll, forcing her little body to bend with him. She was wrapped in her teddy bear blanket, the little white bears gleaming with incongruous cheer in the early sunshine. One end of the blanket trailed in the water. Her head was just visible below Will's shoulder, her puff of pale hair vivid as sea foam against the backdrop of blue water.

I heard Charlotte's wheezing breath behind me as she clambered down the bank, but I kept my eyes on Will and my grip on the .30-30. I propped the rifle against my hip, praying it had rounds in it. I didn't know if I'd have a shot without risking the baby. I didn't know, either, if I had it in me to fire at a human being. The idea of it curdled my belly at the same moment my muscles sang with adrenaline, demanding action.

Willow stopped a dozen steps ahead of me. I saw how she trembled. She, too, longed for action. I whispered, "Wait, Willow." Then, louder, I called, "Stop, Will! Please! You can't mean to do this!"

He jerked upright, so swiftly I saw Emma's little head bob on her slender neck. She clutched at his shoulder as his grip shifted. I shouted, "Don't drop her, for God's sake!"

He spun toward me. Emma was at his side, under his elbow, but when he saw the gun, he lifted her, putting her back to his chest, her face toward me. Her short arms flailed at the rough movement, spreading like angel wings. Her eyelids fluttered in alarm. Even at a distance her eyes were very, very green.

Behind me, Charlotte drew a noisy, horrified breath.

"Will!" I cried. "What are you doing?" At the sound of my voice Emma's face crumpled. She began to cry, her pearl-studded mouth wide. Her tiny fingers opened and closed, reaching for me in a futile gesture that wrung my soul.

Will renewed his grip around her middle. Her blue blanket unwound from her little body and fell to the boards of the dock, tangling around his feet. He kicked it away, and as it fell into the water, he barked a laugh. "Come on, Barrie," he said. He didn't raise his voice, but it was deep and strong, and it carried through the hiss and swish of the moving water. "You're not stupid. You know what you have here!" His arm tightened on Emma, giving her a little shake. She wept harder, her gasping sobs echoed by the frenetic cries of seagulls circling over our heads.

I said, "I don't know what you mean." I took two cautious steps. Willow stayed ahead of me, angling her body between me and Will.

"You could have told me," Will went on, in a conversational way that mocked my tension. "You hid it from me, just when I really needed a break."

"What are you talking about?" I dared one step more. Willow moved with me, her eyes fixed on Will.

Will didn't seem to notice the dog. He said, as gleefully as if he had just opened a treasure chest, "You have the evidence right here! And now I have it."

"What evidence?"

"Aliens!" he cried. "Like the ones they got in Roswell."

"It didn't happen," I said desperately. "That was a weather balloon—there weren't any aliens, Will—"

"Oh, yes, there were, but the government won't admit it." He gave Emma another shake, as if she were no more than a stuffed toy. Her sobs became wails, and he had to raise his voice above the sounds of her cries. "There are people looking for something just like this kid, and they'll pay good money."

"No one's looking for her, Will. She's mine!"

"Oh, they're looking, all right! Everybody knows that. Where'd you find her? Pull her out of that crashed disk?"

"What crashed disk?"

"The one on Maury Island, of course."

"No! No, that's not—How would I do that? I've never been there. She has nothing to do with any of that! Will, please—"

His face tightened. "I'm not stupid, Barrie. I see what she's got behind her ears. What else did you hide from me?"

"Will, you can't do this. Surely not even you would—"

"Not even me?" he snarled. "Nice way to talk about your husband!" He shifted Emma to his hip again and bent to reach for the mooring rope.

"Will, please! She's all I have—"

"All *you* have?" he shouted. The rope came free, and he straightened, holding it up as if it were a flag of victory. "You have the farm, the house, your life! I've got nothing. Nothing!"

My heart fluttered like a trapped butterfly beneath the thin fabric of my pajama top. I sucked in a breath, desperate to control my fear. I kept a tight grip on the .30-30, but I didn't think, even in that awful moment, that I could bring myself to use it.

Will crouched, and with Emma nearly upside down in his precarious grip, he extended one foot into the boat as he steadied himself on the dock with his free hand.

I moaned, "No!"

That seemed to be the signal Willow was waiting for. She broke, bounding away from me, racing down the dock. As she lunged forward, she emitted a sound I had never heard from her, that I had never heard from any dog. It wasn't a bark, or a snarl, or a growl. It was more like the roar of a lion than any sound a dog should make, and it cut through Emma's cries, the gulls' shrieks, the rush of the waves.

It shocked all of us. Charlotte gave a guttural exclamation. Will froze, his mouth open, his grip on Emma loosening. I began to run after Willow, struggling to avoid the rotted boards, awkward in my boots, desperate to get to my baby before she was beyond my reach.

Time slowed sharply, as if someone had applied brakes to the world. Everything seemed to happen at once, but the events moved forward without momentum, as if giving each of the actors in the scene time to reflect on what they were doing. Willow leaped at Will, seeming to float across the distance between them, clearing the end of the dock without effort. Will gasped and stumbled backward into the boat in a vain effort to get away from her.

In his panic, he dropped Emma. She tumbled over the side of the boat, her little arms flailing. Her crying stopped abruptly as she fell headfirst into the clear, cold water, and my heart seemed to stop midbeat.

All of it unfolded in slow motion, the frames of a film grinding forward one by one. I heard Will's panting breaths. I saw the sun shimmer on the drops of water thrown up by Emma's plunge. I saw Willow's fur flutter in the breeze her leap created. My next breath seemed to freeze in my lungs, refusing to move either in or out.

Willow landed hard in the boat, skidding on a layer of scum in the bottom. She gathered herself in a heartbeat and jumped at Will, seizing his wrist in her teeth. She shook his arm with all the force of her strong jaws, growling now with ferocity, her ears flying from side to side.

If Will had been a rat, he would have been dead. As it was I wondered if his forearm would break. Blood sprayed the dog's muzzle, and Will screamed in pain. The color drained from his face, and I felt a fierce gratitude that the blood was his and not hers.

I suppose all of that took only seconds, but I couldn't tell. Time had become a fractured thing, shards and pieces and chunks of it scattering in random patterns, too disparate for me to follow. I know I was still moving, that Willow still had Will's arm in her jaws, that my baby was in the water, but the order of events, the speed of them, was impossible to comprehend.

In fact, time didn't resume its normal flow until the moment I racked the lever action of the .30–30 and raised the stock to my shoulder. Then it seemed to move almost too fast, the tension building at an unbearable rate.

"Call off the dog!" Will shrieked. "She's biting me!"

I didn't need to call her. Willow gave his arm one last vicious shake, sending spatters of blood into the bright air, before she released him. Immediately, in a blur of silky fur and feathery tail, she dove after Emma. She hit the water with a terrific splash and drove herself toward the spot where the baby had gone down, her tail streaming in her wake.

Will clutched his bloody arm as he stared after her. His voice was thin, panicky. "The baby's going to drown! Barrie, do something!"

"No," I said grimly. "She's not going to drown."

I prayed I was right. It was the deepest water she had ever

been submerged in, to say nothing of the coldest. I wasn't there to pull her out, but I couldn't afford any doubts now. If I went after her myself, if I dove into that water, I would have to drop the gun, and I didn't dare. It was our only defense.

I kept the .30-30 pointed at Will and put my trust in Willow.

For agonizing moments there was no sign of Emma. The frantic dog paddled this way and that, dipping her muzzle below the water, coming up with her head streaming and her sodden ears drooping. I looked for the telltale bubbles of Emma's breathing, but I couldn't see them through the roiling water.

The gun shook in my hands as Willow, who usually kept her head high above the water, gathered herself to dive straight down below the surface. It was like watching one of the river otters immerse itself, swiftly and smoothly. I hadn't known Willow could do it. I was certain she had never done it before. I had always understood she was no ordinary dog, but this— this was magnificent.

She came up again a moment later. She had Emma's nightgown in her jaws, but no baby. Emma had slipped free.

Will panted, openmouthed, as he gaped at the spot where the baby had disappeared. Blood dripped down his arm, and the rowboat rocked beneath his unsteady legs. I heard Charlotte sobbing helpless breaths from the shore, Charlotte, who couldn't swim. Willow paddled in frenzied circles and then, releasing the nightgown, she dove again. The nightgown floated away, a scrap of pale cotton on the rippled surface of the water. A second later Emma's diaper appeared, swirled on the surface, and sank out of sight.

I suspect my water baby only gave up her first chance at a

free swim out of pity for Willow. When the dog surfaced again, a shining, naked Emma was gripping her ruff with her small hands. All six of her teeth showed in a joyous grin, her earlier tears forgotten in her customary ecstasy of being in the water.

Willow began to paddle toward the shore, and Charlotte waded in to meet her. Emma squealed with joy as the dog pulled her steadily forward. Water streamed across her head and shoulders and splashed in her open mouth. Relief flooded me, and I saw it in every line of Willow's body as well.

Will exclaimed hoarsely, "Damn it, Barrie! What a find! She's worth a fortune!"

I focused on him again, the gun steady now. "She's not a commodity, Will. She's a baby."

He pressed his hand over the dog bite, which bled steady drops that ran over his hand and dripped onto his pants. "That baby's not human!"

"Of course she is."

"For God's sake, Barrie, I have eyes!"

"Go away, Will. Row away in your pathetic little boat, and don't come back."

I knew him well by that point in our ragged relationship. I understood how his mind worked, at least as well as anyone can understand a man like Will. When his face changed, his expression smoothing, even a winsome smile beginning to curve his mouth, I was not impressed.

Neither was Charlotte. From the shore, where she was knee-deep in the water, lifting Emma from Willow's back, she called, "Don't trust him, Barrie Anne." Despite the slap of the waves against the derelict dock, I heard her clearly. I knew what she meant. She, too, understood the tangle of cruelty and perversion and deception that was Will Sweet.

And now we knew what her premonition had been about, the one that wouldn't fade. I should have had it myself.

Will steadied himself in the boat, but he didn't sit on the bench to take up the oars. They remained shipped in their locks while he made an attempt at his old insouciant charm.

"Come on, Barrie," he said. "I know we've had our problems, but... This is a great opportunity for both of us. She'll still be your baby. You'll take care of her, but listen, I know how to make the most of this. We can—"

"No, Will. We can't, and we won't." He blinked and staggered a little with the rocking of the boat. I kept the gun at the ready.

I could see Will wasn't convinced I would fire at him. He probably didn't believe I *could* fire at him. I wasn't sure myself.

I didn't want to shoot him, despite everything. I just wanted him to go away.

He forced a grin and seized the piling so he could climb out of the boat. He stood at the end of the dock, folding his cuff over his bleeding arm and pressing it with his hand. "Look, I'm sorry, Barrie, for—for this morning, for everything... I only wanted to have a look at this baby that means so much to you. Then when I realized—"

I waved the gun in the direction of the boat. "Get back in, Will. None of this has anything to do with you."

"You don't want to raise a child alone, do you?"

"I'm not alone."

His tenuous hold on his temper vanished in an instant. His

eyes narrowed in a way that chilled my heart, and the grin twisted into a sneer. "Not alone? You mean, because your dyke of an aunt is here? What kind of influence is that for a child?"

For answer, I lifted the stock of the gun to my cheek. "Get away from here, Will, or I swear I *will* shoot you."

He choked a mirthless laugh. "You won't. You might think you hate me, but you wouldn't pull the trigger. You couldn't live with that."

"Oh, I think I could." I spoke firmly, but it was as much a ruse as his pretended humor. I wasn't at all sure I could live with it.

I didn't want to shoot at a human being in the heat of anger. Will had betrayed me. He had used me. He was a liar and a cheat. He was a traitor. But who would I be if I allowed that to make me into a killer? I felt repugnance for the act, in my gut, in my heart, in my soul.

It was a good, clean feeling, inarguable, even comforting. It told me I was still myself—or perhaps it was that I was myself again. I felt strong, as I had the day of my first plunge from the high diving board. I wasn't angry. I didn't hate him. But I had Emma to protect. I had a duty that overrode any other emotion.

As the untethered boat floated away from the dock, bobbing on the receding tide, I had an image of that diving board in my mind. It had seemed as daunting as the sheer rock face of a mountain until the moment I gritted my teeth, bounced on my toes, and arrowed into the water twenty feet below. As Will came toward me, his face hard and determined and, even now, handsome, I remembered the giddy sensation of triumph

I felt when I had done it. I had made the dive. I had conquered my fear, and I had never been more myself than I was in that moment.

He said, "You can't get away with hiding her, Barrie. I'm making this call. I know who will pay for this story. Don't worry, I'll make sure you get your share." He strode past me as if the gun weren't there. Out of habit, I averted the barrel as he passed me, instinctively not wanting a person in my line of fire, then wishing I had shoved him with it, pushed him right off the dock into the water.

Will paced down the splintered boards toward the beach. Charlotte stood at the edge of the foaming water, Emma clutched tight against her, Willow bristling angrily at her knee.

Even when the tide is going out, as it was at that moment, there are waves. Waves on the canal tend to be mild, as a rule. The wind raises whitecaps, but the tide changes aren't particularly dramatic. We don't have rogue waves. We occasionally see a modest tide rip, where two currents strike each other, causing turbulence, but it's unusual.

That day was different. A single wave rose to sweep the rickety dock where I was standing. It wasn't forceful. It didn't throw me off balance. It did, however, drench my legs and splash into my garden boots. My feet were wet, and I knew. I knew what I had to do, because the water told me.

Will would reach Charlotte in another moment and wrest Emma from her arms. I couldn't trust that even Willow would be able stop him. He would risk another dog bite in order to get his hands on the baby, and I would lose my chance.

I had to shoot him.

25

September 19, 1947

There was no time to think it through. No time to consider the consequences. No time to judge the best action.

I aimed as Mr. Miller had taught me. I sighted right between Will's shoulder blades. I drew one swift deep breath, and then I squeezed the trigger.

It wasn't the way it is in the movies. My ears were buzzing with adrenaline, and I didn't hear the gunshot. If it hadn't been for the kick against my right shoulder, I might not have been sure I had actually pulled the trigger. I smelled the gunpowder, though. And I tasted it, as if I had breathed it in, a metallic tang on my palate.

I wasn't even sure I had hit him. Will didn't cry out or fall all at once. He didn't sprawl dramatically, instantly dead, the way actors did in the Westerns.

He took another step toward Charlotte and Emma. I gritted my teeth as I prepared to pump the rifle again.

That first step was normal, his momentum unbroken. The second wasn't.

He staggered and tried, his leg moving, his foot reaching. It never found purchase. His foot missed the ground somehow, like missing a tread on the stairs, and slowly, slowly, he began to crumple. His knees gave way. His torso tilted, first back and then to one side. His neck bent as if he were trying to look behind him. To look at me.

When he fell, it was in a sort of pile, his arms beneath him, his knees askew, his head at an awkward angle. His face sank into the damp sand.

Charlotte groaned and blocked Emma's eyes with her hand. Will made a choking sound, something between a cough and a gasp. His shoulders shook with a spasm, then slumped and went still. He didn't make another noise.

I pumped the rifle again and stood with my legs braced, the stock buried against my shoulder, Will's tumbled form still in my sights. The Winchester's barrel was as steady as a rock. I took fierce pride in that as I waited. My belly was tense, my mouth dry as dust, but the only emotion I felt was relief that Emma was safe in Charlotte's arms.

I didn't move. Charlotte didn't, either. Willow took a tentative step toward Will's twisted body, but I hissed, "Willow, no!" and she stopped.

The water swished and burbled as the tide drew back from the shore. The warm autumn breeze tugged at my unbrushed hair. A gull screamed, high in the sunshine, and another answered as Charlotte and Willow and I stood, frozen. I was in pajamas and rubber garden boots. Charlotte's shirt was wet where she held Emma close against her chest, and her shoes were soaked with salt water. Willow stood dripping, her lopsided ears pricked forward, waiting for guidance. Our three figures made a bizarre tableau, with Will's broken, unmoving body at its center.

I lowered the rifle at last. "I'm going to check," I said. My voice was thin, the words lifting into the breeze. I wasn't sure Charlotte had heard me.

But she had. "Be careful."

"Yes." Her voice was thin, too, the horror of what had just happened—what I had just done—sapping it of its vibrancy.

With the .30-30 at the ready, I walked the rest of the short distance to the end of the dock and plodded across the sand, my bare toes slipping sideways inside my rubber boots. Willow trotted toward me, circling Will's tumbled form to take up her customary position at my knee. I took the last steps gingerly, my muscles tensed, ready to—what? I didn't know.

I stopped within arm's length of Will. It was clear that the crisis—at least this part of it—was over. I could see part of his face, one blue eye open, staring at nothing. His forehead was half buried by sand. One hand was turned palm up, the other palm down.

There was surprisingly little blood. I surmised the bullet—my bullet, I made myself admit—had not gone all the way through his chest. He had coughed blood onto his mouth and chin, and there was a dark spot in the sand beneath his head where blood had soaked in. I saw the round's entry in his back, a small, nearly inconspicuous hole torn through his shirt, squarely between his shoulder blades.

Charlotte said, "He's dead, I gather."

"Yes."

"Are you all right?"

I took a step back, away from the lifeless form. "I think so."

"You had no choice, Barrie Anne."

"I know."

"Emma—"

"Oh, I know, Aunt Charlotte. I did it for Emma. I'd do it again."

"Good girl."

I flashed her a glance. "The thing is, what do I do now?"

She chewed on her lip for a moment, and I knew she was craving a cigarette. Emma was squirming against her, trying to lift her head toward me. "First," Charlotte said, "it's what do *we* do now. We're in this together."

"Okay." My voice sounded flat and dull against the harmony of sea and wind. I felt empty, as if all feeling had been shocked out of me. I couldn't quite grasp the import of what had just happened. Of what I had done.

It was a bit like watching some film noir, where terrible things happen, shocking things, but when you walk out of the dark theater and into the sunshine, you know they're not real. What had just happened didn't seem real, either. I stared at Will's body and tried to comprehend the fact of his death. Of his being dead.

"Secondly," Charlotte said, now in a tone she might have used for dictating a grocery list, "Emma needs breakfast and clothes. She's sopping wet and completely naked."

I lifted my gaze to Emma. Her hair clung to her scalp in

nearly transparent strands. Charlotte had wrapped her arms around her to keep her warm, and her sleeves were soaked. Willow pressed her wet head against my wrist. It was cold. The day's heat hadn't yet reached our little beach.

"Take Emma home, will you?" I said. "I'll try to—I don't know—maybe get Will into the boat? Push it out into the water?" The little rowboat bobbed, empty, a few yards from the end of the dock.

"Not a good idea," Charlotte said. "Eventually, he'd be found. There would be questions."

"Police?"

"More questions."

Emma kicked in her arms and crowed, "Toast! Toast!"

I looked down at the lifeless bundle at my feet. It no longer seemed like Will at all. It bore less significance than the coyote I had once shot at. Less significance than a fish I caught for dinner. It seemed—

"Irrelevant" was the word that came to mind, but I knew that wasn't right. Will had been a human being. Flawed, selfish, cruel, but a man. He couldn't be discarded, just thrown into the water the way I might a dead crab I found among the kelp and seaweed.

"We'll have to bury him," I said. "Next to—" I broke off.

The full impact of what I had just done suddenly engulfed me, like a rogue wave on a calm day. Will was dead. Shot. With my gun. By me. It was impossible, but it had happened.

My throat clenched against a rush of bile, but I couldn't stop it. I turned away and bent to vomit into the sand, my hands braced on my knees, my belly convulsing again and again.

Willow whined and tried to lick my face. I clung to her damp fur as I spat bile and waited for the bout of sickness to end.

When it was over, leaving me queasy but steady enough, I laid the Winchester on the sand and leaned on Willow for support as I straightened. Charlotte had come up beside us, and she pressed Emma into my arms.

"You take her," she said. "Feed her, get both of you dressed. I'll—" She paused and looked past me to the grotesquerie that had once been a living being. "I'll see if I can get him into the trees, at least. So no one will see him from the water."

Emma threw her sea-chilled arms around my neck and kicked her bare feet. "Toast! Toast!"

Charlotte said, with a pale attempt at a grin, "Pretty sure she thinks the word is 'toast-toast.'"

I swallowed the nasty taste in my mouth. I couldn't answer Charlotte's grin, but I didn't think I'd be sick again. "Toast-toast it is," I said. My voice sounded a bit stronger, and holding Emma helped to quell my trembling. "Come on, rascal, let's get you dried and into some proper clothes." I leaned down to pick up the gun, but Charlotte stopped me with her hand on my arm.

"I'll keep it here. Just in case."

"He's dead, Aunt Charlotte."

"I know, kiddo. Leave it anyway, will you?"

"Okay. There's another round all ready. You know how to pump it?"

"I saw you do it."

"Do you want Willow to stay?"

My aunt shook her head. "No, I'll feel better if she goes with you."

I touched her arm with my hand and was surprised that, like I had been, she was shaking. Guilt filled me at having brought her into such ugliness. I said in a voice that cracked, "You're my rock, Aunt Charlotte."

Her eyes reddened, and she shook her head, uncharacteristically wordless. I knew she didn't trust herself to speak.

I told myself, as I hurried away with the baby in my arms, that Charlotte's tears were of shock, a symptom just like me losing my dinner into the sand, but they disturbed me. She sniffled over romantic movies, sometimes. She had cried at Scottie's funeral, but that was the only time I had seen her weep. She had always been strong, unflappable, steady no matter what happened.

If I had only listened to her, back when Will talked me into leaving school! Guilt again. I told myself I would worry about that later. Apologize later. We had challenges still to face.

I ducked through the orchard, avoiding the ripe apples that dangled near my head. I crunched through the dry field, my feet sweating now inside my boots, the sun burning my shoulders through my flimsy pajama top. Willow preceded me through the gate, and Emma kicked and crowed as we went in through the back door.

Surely a lifetime had passed since I flew through that door, desperate to find my baby. Everything had changed. The Barrie Anne Sweet who ran frantically from the house that morning was a different woman from the one who returned. I had learned something vital about myself, something I might never have known if Will hadn't tried to take Emma from me.

I knew now that I could kill, if the stakes were high enough. I could shoot a human being and then walk right up to him, stand over him to be certain he was dead. If he hadn't been dead, I would have shot him again. I could do it, if I had to. I would do it, for my child. I would kill.

All the soldiers who had gone to fight the war must have learned that same thing. As I dressed Emma and made the toast-toast, I allowed myself to wonder if they ever got over that realization. I wondered how they learned to live with it.

With Emma hastily dressed in a romper and her pink hat, and having pulled on my overalls and sturdier shoes, I hurried back toward the beach. I hadn't eaten anything myself, but I had drunk a glass of milk while the baby had her toast-toast. I didn't think my still-aching stomach would tolerate anything more.

I dreaded seeing Will's body in that hideous position again, but Charlotte had spared me that. She had managed to drag him off the beach and up the cut to the cover of the apple orchard. I found her perched on a piece of fallen applewood, the rifle across her lap. Will lay on his belly, his legs splayed. His shirt had come loose as she pulled him over the edge of the bank. It was bunched up over the back of his head, exposing his back.

It had been an excellent shot. There was a tidy-looking hole showing that the round had pierced his spine. I wouldn't turn him over to look for an exit wound, but I was convinced the lack of blood around him suggested there was none. I already knew there was blood on his face, smeared on his chin. I had no urge to look at it again. In fact, I didn't think I could bear to look at his face again, and I didn't see a need to do it.

Charlotte and I gazed at each other across the lifeless form. "Garden, I guess," she said.

"Again."

She seemed to have regained her composure. Her gaze was clear, her voice level. "I hate that you have to go through this, kiddo."

"I hate making *you* go through it."

She shrugged. "Will did this to himself. He betrayed everyone—you, his family, the navy, the country. I suppose we could call someone to help us. Your Mr. Miller? We could try to explain—but that could be messy."

"He's been so nice to me. I hate to drag him into it. And there are people around here who already think I shouldn't be on my own, people like Mr. Robbins. They could use this as a reason to drive me out. Crazy woman who goes around shooting people. Who shot her own husband."

"Yeah." Charlotte pushed herself up and braced the gun against an apple tree. "But they'll never know, because we're not going to tell them." She reached for Emma, who cooed at her and patted at her cheek with an open hand. Charlotte pressed her lips against the baby's fingers before she asked, "Are you going to get the wheelbarrow?"

"I guess I'd better." I blew out a breath and pulled on my gloves. "Looks like we've developed a system for this."

There was no mirth in her chuckle. "Let's not get used to it."

It was easier wrestling Will's remains into the wheelbarrow than it had been with the previous occupant. He was a lot heavier, but his parts didn't threaten to disintegrate at the slightest touch. I managed to avoid looking at his face as I wriggled the dead weight of his corpse into the wheelbarrow and began the chore of trundling it back through the field.

His weight made that part much harder. In places it was all but impossible. I had to thump and bump the wheelbarrow through the grass, pushing with all my might, sometimes having to go to the front of it and pull. Every clod of dirt became a mountain to climb, every rut a canyon that threatened to overset the whole thing. Weeds and opportunistic blackberry vines caught on the wheels, impeding my progress. It was one of those jobs you can't think about, but simply take one frustrating step at a time, and when that one is past, face the next. I was panting and hot, and my muscles burned with effort by the time we reached the gate.

We chose a different spot in the garden, so that Will wouldn't lie close to Emma's mother. We selected a site near the fence on the opposite side, where the cedar tree's branches overhung the garden. Nothing but moss grew in that shade. We thought it was best to keep his grave inside the fence, so the critters wouldn't get to it.

The body had begun to stiffen by the time I had dug a

deep-enough hole. Charlotte set Emma on a patch of grass with her bunny rattle, and between us we rolled Will's remains up in the blanket he had slept in the night before. Grunting and sweating, we hoisted him to the edge of the grave. It was unceremonious, to say the least, but it was the best we could do. We tipped his blanket-wrapped body up onto the mound of dirt, then let it slide over the edge.

I stood for a moment, looking down at it. "I can't tell his mother and father."

"Nope."

From her patch of grass, Emma piped, "Nope! Nope!"

I smiled at her, but I was still thinking about what was to come next. "I can't tell the navy, either. They'll have to go on looking for him."

"No help for it." Charlotte took up the shovel and began refilling the grave, starting at the foot and working her way up. Her face was red from the heat, with great beads of perspiration rolling from her forehead to streak her powdered cheeks. "You and I are the only ones who will ever know about this."

"It would be nice if I could forget it," I said. The shock of the actual event had begun to subside into a dragging misery, and I wondered if I could ever feel truly happy again.

Charlotte paused, a shovelful of dirt in her hands. "What you need to remember, Barrie Anne, is that you saved Emma. Memory is a two-edged sword."

Emma, hearing her name, flopped to her hands and knees and began to crawl toward us, her diapered bottom waggling like a puppy's tail. Willow tried to stop her, but she cried, "Nope! Nope, dod!"

Despite ourselves, Charlotte and I both laughed, nervous, near-hysterical guffaws that echoed around the garden. They made me feel like a ghoul, someone who would laugh at a funeral when everyone else was weeping. I was glad when our laughter subsided, and I could assume a properly solemn demeanor.

Charlotte emptied her shovel of dirt into the grave and dug the blade into the mound for another. I picked up Emma and watched Charlotte dig. An odd stillness settled over the garden. No birds sang. Even the hens were quiet.

Willow tilted her head up, her mouth closed, her ears turned forward, and I followed her gaze up into the branches of the cedar tree.

The crows were back. This time they perched in silence, at least a dozen of them, shiny black sentinels looking down at us as if waiting for us to finish our grisly chore. They shifted their feet, sidling this way and that, but though one or two opened their beaks, none of them made a sound.

"That's creepy," Charlotte murmured. She was leaning on her shovel, gazing up at the flock of birds.

"Will hated the crows."

"Did he? They probably knew that." She bent to her task again. "Weird birds, crows."

"Bird!" Emma cried, kicking her feet against my hip. "Dod! Bird!"

"Yes, sweetie," I said, adjusting her weight in my arms. "Dog and bird."

She grinned, her tiny teeth gleaming white against the shell pink of her mouth. "Mama!"

I caught my breath and squeezed her to me. "Yes, Emma, that's right! Mama! I'm your mama! Charlotte, did you hear?"

"I heard," Charlotte said with a chuckle. "Good girl, Emma. Next you learn to say 'auntie.'" She scraped the last of the mound of dirt into the grave and smoothed it with the back of the shovel so it was level with the ground around it. She stood back with a satisfied look. "There. Transplant some moss over it, and no one will notice a thing."

I was about to answer when there was a rustle and flap above our heads. All of us, Charlotte and Emma, Willow and I, looked up.

The crows were leaving, flying up and away, an odd funeral cortege disbanding, scattering into the wind. I watched them go, mesmerized by the unity of their action and by the silence.

"Creepy," Charlotte repeated.

"Maybe," I answered, lifting Emma to my shoulder. "Or maybe it's perfect."

26

October 15, 1947

At the last market of the season I still had produce to sell. My pumpkin vines had flourished, so I could lay out eighteen small, golden sugar pumpkins, perfect for pies. I also had potatoes and carrots and a dozen jars of blackberry preserves. Charlotte and I were especially proud of those. The glass jars with their felt-topped lids glowed like garnets in the autumn sun. Charlotte had devised pretty labels for them, with a drawing of a generic flower and the words "The Blythe Farm," which we had decided to be.

I wasn't Mrs. Sweet anymore. I had gone to the Jefferson County Courthouse to resume my maiden name. We had talked it over at length and decided, with Will's history, it would be harder for any of his connections to find me if I resumed my maiden name. It took some effort to make sure my neighbors understood. I didn't explain my reason, but clearly they assumed it was because of Will's desertion.

Mrs. Robbins colored when I told her, as if I had revealed something embarrassing. Mrs. Miller patted my shoulder in sympathy. Mrs. Urquhardt said, "Are you sure? What if he comes back?"

I said, "I'm quite sure he's not coming back. He's gone."

She said, in her blunt way, "Does this mean divorce? I don't really hold with divorce."

"I don't either, Mrs. Urquhardt." I looked down at my feet, as if humiliated by the whole thing. "It wasn't my choice, I'm afraid. It just—happened."

"So you're Miss Blythe now, I guess. Or is it Mrs.? I don't know how that works."

"I don't, either. Maybe everyone can just call me Barrie."

On that final market day of the year, it seemed everyone was out, knowing they might not see their neighbors again for weeks. A sharp breeze made the air crisp, but it didn't affect the festive air. Mrs. Urquhardt's oldest daughter had become adept at knitting, and she was selling scarves and hats for Christmas gifts. Charlotte made me promise not to watch as she bought several things from her. Mrs. Miller came to my table with a little packet wrapped up in a sheet of the funny papers from the *Trib*. She held it out in her gloved hand, saying, "For your little one. And don't she look purty?"

Like my other neighbors, Mrs. Miller didn't call me Barrie. She also didn't call me Miss Blythe. She avoided the whole issue by not calling me anything.

Emma did indeed look pretty. Charlotte had dressed her in a pinafore over a plaid dress, with thick cotton stockings beneath to keep her warm and a boiled wool hat of bright green that tied under her chin and made her eyes glow like emeralds. The two of them perched together on a chair behind my table, Charlotte in her usual trousers and a double-breasted jacket, with Emma on her lap. Emma looked up at Mrs. Miller and gave her a toothy grin. "Nope!" she cried.

I had never seen Mrs. Miller smile, much less laugh. When she emitted a high-pitched, girlish giggle, Charlotte's eyebrows rose, and I had to bite my lip before I said, "Sorry about that. It's one of her words. She uses it for everything."

"Ain't you the smart one?" Mrs. Miller said, gazing indulgently at my daughter. "So little, and talking already."

"Thank you so much for the gift, Mrs. Miller. Shall I open it now?"

Mrs. Miller nodded shyly, and I unfolded the newsprint. Inside it was a small stuffed bear, handmade of yellow chenille, with black button eyes and a smiling mouth formed of black cross stitches. "Oh, this is beautiful!" I exclaimed, with complete sincerity. "You made this for my Emma? My goodness. How kind. You're so clever."

I turned and handed the bear to Emma. She kicked her feet with delight, took the bear in both hands, and hugged its soft body to her chest. Her emerald eyes seemed even greener against the butter yellow of the bear's fabric. Mrs. Miller beamed at her.

Charlotte, grinning, said, "Say thank you, Emma."

I held my breath, afraid our little rascal might do just that. Luckily for us, she squealed, "Nope! Nope!" Mrs. Miller laughed, and I could breathe again.

"What a beautiful evening it is," Charlotte said, blowing a ribbon of smoke into the dusk.

"Isn't it?" I said lazily, stretching out my legs and gazing up into the moonless sky.

We had loaded the garden bench from the Port Townsend house into the International and hauled it down to the farm. It fit perfectly against the back porch, and Charlotte had done a planting around it. Her plants were more or less dormant now, but in the spring we would have fragrant lavender and lilac—although I warned her the lilac might get too big—and patches of moss to rest our feet on. The three of us sat there after supper, Emma nodding sleepily against my shoulder while Charlotte smoked and I watched the stars come to life, like candles being lit here and there in the darkness. It was getting too cold to sit outside for long, but we had bundled up in sweaters and scarves, loath to give up our evening chats. Willow lay in front of us, our faithful guardian against the night creatures.

I said, "How's the beast coming?"

"It's finished," Charlotte said.

"Finished! Really?"

"Yes, you should go in and see it."

"I will, before you sell it."

"Oh, I'm not going to sell that one."

"You're not? What are you going to do with it?"

"I don't know for sure."

I pondered that for a moment before I said, "I'd love to hang it in the front room."

She took a long, thoughtful drag on her cigarette. "You know, I think I like that idea. There's something special about that particular canvas—something..."

"Magical," I finished for her, and she laughed.

After a few minutes of silence, she said, "I've been thinking of something."

"What are you thinking this time?" We had been trying to imagine what the future held for us. Charlotte was spending half the week in Port Townsend and half at the farm. She said she worked better in the town house, but she didn't want me to get too tired juggling Emma and the garden and the hens.

"I should say," Charlotte said, "that I've been remembering." She tipped her head back and blew a narrow ribbon of smoke that fluttered up and away into the darkness.

I yawned. "Remembering...?"

"When I first came to Port Townsend, when Scott and Thelma were so ill."

"You don't talk about that much," I said. I blinked to wake myself up. Charlotte spoke too little of the past, and I didn't want to miss a word. "It must have been awful."

"You don't talk about it, either, Barrie Anne."

"I don't remember it very well."

"You remember me coming?"

"Sort of."

"You didn't like me much at first."

"Didn't I? I think I was confused by everything that was happening."

I had never told her—and I never would—that my seven-year-old self thought it was her fault my mother and father died.

I figured out the truth by the time I was eight, but that first year we spent together I was about as miserable as a child can be.

Charlotte spoke softly, with a wistful tone that wasn't like her. "It was hard for me to understand you. I didn't know much about children. I hardly knew anything about you beyond pictures of you at Christmas and on birthdays." She took the last puff of her cigarette and ground it out beneath the toe of her shoe. "I don't know quite how to put this into words, but what I've been thinking—why I'm remembering how lost I felt with you at first—is that all children are mysteries. Enigmas."

"Now you're talking about Emma."

Charlotte pulled her sweater up to her chin and curled her legs beneath her. "Yes."

"There are things we'll never know about her," I admitted. "And she's going to have questions."

"You had questions, that's for sure. You asked where your parents had gone."

"Did I ask that? I don't remember what you told me."

"I told you the truth. That I didn't know." She blew another stream of smoke and added, "I was never any good at that heaven stuff."

"Do you think Emma will be satisfied if I say I don't know? Was I content with that answer?"

"In time you were. I had to repeat it, though."

We sat in silence for a bit, while bats began to dart from the big cedar tree, sailing this way and that in search of insects.

I said softly, "Do you think we'll ever know, Aunt Charlotte? That is, know for sure?"

"You mean, where Emma came from?"

"Yes."

"Well, Barrie Anne." She uncurled her legs and set her feet on the ground. She gazed up into the starlight as she said, speaking more slowly than usual, "The thing is, kiddo—I know a little bit. I've known since that first bath time. I didn't have enough information yet, but when I dipped my hands into that water, I knew. Not where she came from exactly, but why."

I felt my eyes stretch wide. "You've never told me that!"

She looked back at me, her face dim and pale in the faint light of the stars. "No."

"Why not?"

Her smile was as faint as the starlight. "I'm not sure. At first it was just vague, a—"

"A feeling."

"Yes. A feeling. Then, when we found the—the other one, and buried her, I understood."

"Yes," I breathed.

She arched one eyebrow. "You had the same feeling."

"I think so. I thought I might have been imagining it."

"You know, Barrie Anne, it's important to trust yourself. To trust the talent. Try it now. Tell me what you thought."

I gazed at her, my lips parted in uncertainty. Her suggestion—her command—hung in the air between us like a puff of cigarette smoke. I could wave it away, or I could breathe it in, or I could leave it to dissipate in the night air as if I had never noticed it at all.

Finally, I said in a small, dry voice, "I thought—or I felt—that Emma's mother was trying to hide her from something. Or someone."

Charlotte breathed a long sigh. "Yes. I felt the same. We'll never know exactly what she was fleeing, but it seems she thought it was worth her life to protect her daughter."

As I nodded acknowledgment of this judgment, I remembered something I had let slip away in the rush of events. "Aunt Charlotte, when we found—when we found her, Emma's mother, and you were kneeling beside her, you said something curious. I meant to ask you about it, but so much has happened, I forgot until this moment."

"Yes?"

"You said, 'Rest in peace, sister.' You said it so naturally."

"Oh, that. Yes, I did say that, didn't I?" She smiled into the darkness. "It was instinct, I suppose, but I meant it. We are sisters, aren't we? Emma's first mother, Emma herself, you and I. Grandmother Fiona, even my mother, though she tried to deny it. We share the water magic. We share a heritage, though Emma and her first mother—and perhaps those babies Dr. Masters mentioned—they have something we all thought was lost forever."

I turned that idea over in my mind. I decided I liked the idea of a sisterhood. I who had so wanted to be normal, to be like other people, had now found my joy, my life's purpose, in something that was very, very far outside the norms of convention.

I rubbed Emma's warm back and felt the sweet puffs of her breath against my neck. She was sound asleep. I said softly, "I'll think of the woman resting in the garden as my sister, then. And do all I can to take care of our child."

"I know you will."

"There's been so much sadness. Is it selfish to just want to be as happy as I can, for as long as I can?"

"Of course not."

She pushed herself up from the bench. "You should take pride in what you've accomplished." She waved her hand around at the farm, at the neat henhouse with its sleeping hens, at the tidy garden—at the two well-disguised graves with their different secrets. "Look at what you've done, and all by yourself. Come on now, it's time to put that child in her bed."

She started for the house, and I followed, cuddling the sleeping baby against my shoulder. Willow came after us, and once we were all inside, I said, "Aunt Charlotte, I had my hands in that same bath water, that first time. Why didn't I know right then, as you did?"

She paused, one foot on the bottom stair, facing me. "The talent has always been an unpredictable thing. Sometimes I worry that we're losing it. Grandmother Fiona was better at it than I am. My mother hardly had the knack at all, and what she did have, she suppressed. It could still fade, if we're not careful."

She started up the stairs then, and I followed, with Willow behind me. I went into the nursery to settle Emma for the night, and when I came out, I found Charlotte, now in her housecoat, leaning against the doorjamb of her bedroom.

"I want you to practice it, Barrie Anne. Deliberately. We're only given so many talents, and even an odd one like this, this bit of water magic, is worth preserving."

"Even though it's unpredictable?"

"It's often useful. It has served you well already, and you may need it again one day."

"Do you think—if I had used it, I might have prevented Will—" I had trouble saying his name. Speaking it made my stomach clench with remembered shock, a horror that would never completely fade.

"It wouldn't have mattered, Barrie Anne. You have to let that go. He would have kept coming back, trying to—" She waved a hand. "Trying to make you into what he wanted you to be, I guess."

"I think that was it, Aunt Charlotte. He wanted to make me into the perfect wife."

"He could have started by being a perfect husband," she said sourly.

"I know."

"The thing is, eventually he would have figured out how special Emma is, and then you'd have had the same problem."

"I guess you're right. It wouldn't have changed anything."

"Just the same, you should do your best to preserve the talent. You're going to need to teach it to your daughter."

"I've thought of that. But you'll help, too."

"Maybe. We'll see."

"You're not going to leave!"

A slow smile grew on her face. "I wonder," she said, with obvious relish. "Maybe you should put your hands in water and see if you can figure out what I'm going to do."

"Aunt Charlotte!"

"Just promise you'll try it now and again."

"I will, but—"

"It will all turn out the way it's supposed to," she said. "I teach you. You teach Emma. The Blythe gift continues, and that's magic in itself." She turned to go into her bedroom, saying over her shoulder, "Don't worry. There will still be surprises."

That made me give a sleepy chuckle. "Good night, Aunt Charlotte."

"Good night, Barrie Anne."

With Charlotte and Emma asleep in their beds, I found myself wakeful. I kept thinking about what Charlotte had said and wondering what surprises—good and bad—lay ahead for me. For Emma. Even for Charlotte, who had given up so much for a child she barely knew.

I was in my pajamas. I put my long woolen bathrobe over them and went downstairs to warm some milk to make me sleepy. When it was ready, I carried the mug outside, drawn by the peace of the starry night. I leaned against the porch post and gazed across my drowsing farm. Willow sat quietly by my side.

There were things to do to put the garden to bed for the winter—mulch to spread, plants to cover, a final weeding. I wanted to put up some insulation in the henhouse, and I was thinking of getting a rooster to keep my ladies happy, perhaps have a few chicks to expand the flock.

I stood sipping hot milk and listening to the faint chuckling of my hens at roost in their cozy coop. I was just beginning to yawn when a shadow moved beneath the old cedar tree. I stiffened. It was poised above Will's secret grave, and my throat closed with a sudden feeling of panic. Without realizing I was doing it, I dipped my fingers into the cooling milk in my cup. My panic receded, and I began to laugh.

It was a raccoon, of course. An innocent animal, an innocent feeling. I sucked the milk from my finger as I watched the raccoon scamper away, flashing a barred tail and two small black eyes that glittered with starlight. Willow emitted a soft grumble, but the critter was already gone. I said, "Shush, Willow. It's okay."

Wide awake again, I set down my nearly empty mug, drew on my garden boots, and made my way through the dark rows to the cedar tree. I made Willow stay behind me, in case the raccoon was still there, but when we reached the fence, it had vanished. I released her, and she snuffled along the base of the fence, following the varmint's scent.

I found myself standing at the foot of Will's grave. There was nothing to mark it. No lingering outline disturbed the blanket of moss that grew from the edge of the fence to the head of a row of pea vines. Those vines were dry now, ready to be cut and added to the compost pile.

I knew where the grave was, though. I remembered with painful clarity exactly where Will lay, his head toward the fence, his feet more or less toward the house. It was as if I could see him below the ground, wrapped in my old blanket, his blue eyes sightless, his shock of hair full of dirt, his lean body pierced by a bullet I had fired. I would never forget, no matter how fervently I wished I could.

I had gone back to the beach once to be certain there were no traces of blood and to make sure the old rowboat had floated off into the canal. I found that the dock had given in to the waves at last, its rotting boards broken free to sink beneath the water. The bollard was completely submerged. All that was left were the tilting pilings, and I guessed they wouldn't last the winter.

This night was not the first time I had lingered here. More than once, in the month since the disaster, I found myself leaving whatever chore I was doing to stand beside the hidden grave, gazing down at the concealing moss while I struggled to sort out my feelings. I thought about Will, about what he had done, and about what, finally, I myself had done to put an end to all of it.

I couldn't regret my action, really. He had left me no choice. I could have regretted meeting him, and I certainly could have wished I had never married him, but if I hadn't, he would never have bought Blythe Farm, and Willow and I would not have been here to save Emma. That thought made me shiver with horror.

"I guess I have to thank you for that," I whispered to Will, dead in his makeshift grave. "But I keep wondering. Were you ever happy, ever in your life?" Willow gave me a questioning glance, and I shook my head. "Never mind, Willow." She went back to sniffing the ground.

I heard a foghorn sound its lonesome bass warning from beyond Hood Canal. I glanced up past the tree line to see that a bank of clouds had rolled in from the east, obscuring the mountain peaks. Soon the stars would be obliterated, too, and Blythe Farm would be in total darkness.

"Come on, Willow," I murmured. "We'd better get inside."

The two of us made our way back through the sleeping garden and up the steps to the kitchen door. I paused in the very spot where I had first laid eyes on my surprising daughter. I looked back over my beloved little farm and breathed a sigh over the many questions that would never be answered and the many that would still arise. That, I supposed, was life, and not only for our kind. For all kinds.

Willow whined and scratched at the door. "Okay, Willow. We're going."

I opened the door, and when we were through, I turned the lock against the darkness, closing my little family safely inside.

Acknowledgments

The path of this novel was a strange one, with many twists and turns. It began with emailed input from the members of my first writers' group, was guided by the insights and vision of another quite wonderful first reader, my own son, and ended with an exacting editing process that made it a much better book than it might have been.

My heartfelt thanks go to Brian Bek, Jeralee Chapman, Niven Marquis, and Catherine Whitehead, all of the Tahuya Writers Group; to Zack Marley; and to my editors, Sarah Guan of Orbit and Redhook in the US, and Anna Jackson of Orbit UK.

The teacher and students of Julie Christine's writing class at the Writer's Workshoppe at Imprint Books in Port Townsend, WA, patiently listened to early chapters, and gave me the encouragement I needed to move forward with the book.

I owe a great deal to Dean Crosgrove, PAC, US Army Ranger, Ret. He is a man of many talents! He created Emma's physiology for the novel and taught me how to write about shooting a .30–30. Any errors are, of course, mine, but thank you so much, Dean.

Thanks, too, to Jake Marley for his support and for the field trips we took together to research historical details. I hope they were as much fun for him as they were for me.

My gratitude goes to my terrific agent, Peter Rubie of Fine-Print Literary Management, for his guidance, wisdom, energy, and humor. When the path gets bumpy—and sometimes it does—he's wonderful at making the rough places plain.

Finally, I will always be grateful for the example and inspiration of my grandmother, the dedicatee of this book. She encouraged all her grandchildren to create without fear and urged us to become our true selves, as she had done. She didn't have much, but she gave what she had with a generous hand. She was a rebel, a bohemian, an intellectual, a musician, and an artist to the end of her days. I remember her with much love.

extras

www.orbitbooks.net

about the author

Louisa Morgan is a pseudonym for award-winning author Louise Marley. Louise lives in the Pacific Northwest where she and her Border Terrier, Oscar, ramble the beaches and paths of Washington State.

Find out more about Louisa Morgan and other Orbit authors by registering for the free monthly newsletter at www.orbitbooks.net.

if you enjoyed
THE WITCH'S KIND

look out for

THE SISTERS OF THE WINTER WOOD

by

Rena Rossner

Every family has a secret . . . and every secret tells a story.

In a remote village surrounded by forests on the border of Moldova and Ukraine, sisters Liba and Laya have been raised on the honeyed scent of their Mami's babka and the low rumble of their Tati's prayers. But when a troupe of mysterious men arrives, Laya falls under their spell – despite their mother's warning to be wary of strangers. And this is not the only danger lurking in the woods.

As dark forces close in on their small village, Liba and Laya discover a family secret passed down through generations. Faced with a magical heritage they never knew existed, the sisters realise the old fairy tales are true . . . and could save them all.

1

Liba

If you want to know the history of a town, read the gravestones in its cemetery. That's what my Tati always says. Instead of praying in the synagogue like all the other men of our town, my father goes to the cemetery to pray. I like to go there with him every morning.

The oldest gravestone in our cemetery dates back to 1666. It's the grave I like to visit most. The names on the stone have long since been eroded by time. It is said in our *shtetl* that it marks the final resting place of a bride and a groom who died together on their wedding day. We don't know anything else about them, but we know that they were buried, arms embracing, in one grave. I like to put a stone on their grave when I go there, to make sure their souls stay down where they belong, and when I do, I say a prayer that I too will someday find a love like that.

That grave is the reason we know that there were Jews in Dubossary as far back as 1666. Mami always said that this town was founded in love and that's why my parents chose to live here. I think it means something else—that our town was founded in tragedy. The death of those young lovers has been a pall hanging over Dubossary since its inception. Death lives here. Death will always live here.

2

Laya

I see Liba going
to the cemetery with Tati.
I don't know
what she sees
in all those cold stones.
But I watch,
and wonder,
why he never takes me.

When we were little,
Liba and I went to
the Talmud Torah.
For Liba, the black letters
were like something
only she could decipher.
I never understood
what she searched for,
in those black
scratches of ink.
I would watch

the window,
study the forest
and the sky.

When we walked home,
Liba would watch the boys
come out of the *cheder*
down the road.
I know that when she looked
at Dovid, Lazer and Nachman,
she wondered
what was taught
behind the walls
the girls were not
allowed to enter.

After her Bat Mitzvah,
Tati taught her Torah.
He tried to teach me too,
when my turn came,
but all I felt was
distraction,
disinterest.
Chanoch l'naar al pi darko,
Tati would say,
*teach every child
in his own way*,
and sigh,
and get up
and open the door.
Gey, gezinte heit—
I accept that you're different, go.

And while I was grateful,
I always wondered
why he gave up
without a fight.

3

Liba

As I follow the large steps my father's boots make in the snow, I revel in the solitude. This is why I cherish our morning walks. They give me time to talk to Tati, but also time to think. "In silence you can hear God," Tati says to me as we walk. But I don't hear God in the silence—I hear myself. I come here to get away from the noises of the town and the chatter of the townsfolk. It's where I can be fully me.

"What does God sound like?" I ask him. When I walk with Tati, I feel like I'm supposed to think about important things, like prayer and faith.

"Sometimes the voice of God is referred to as a *bat kol*," he says.

I translate the Hebrew out loud: "The daughter of a voice? That doesn't make any sense."

He chuckles. "Some say that *bat kol* means an echo, but others say it means a hum or a reverberation, something you sense in the air that's caused by the motion of the universe—part of the human voice, but also part of every other sound in the world, even the sounds that our ears can't hear. It means that sometimes even the smallest voice can have a big opinion." He grins, and I know that he means me, his daughter; that my opinion matters. I wish it were true. Not everybody in our town sees things the way my father does. Most women and girls do not study Torah; they don't learn or ask questions like I do. For the most part, our voices don't matter. I know I'm lucky that Tati is my father.

Although I love Tati's stories and his answers, I wonder why a small voice is a daughter's voice. Sometimes I wish my voice could be loud—like a roar. But that is not a modest way to think. The older I get, the more immodest my thoughts become.

I feel my cheeks flush as my mind wanders to all the things I shouldn't be thinking about—what it would feel like to hold the hand of a man, what it might feel like to kiss someone, what it's like when you finally find the man you're meant to marry and you get to be alone together, in bed . . . I swallow and shake my head to clear my thoughts.

If I shared the fact that this is all I think about lately, Mami and Tati would say it means it's time for me to get married. But I'm not sure I want to get married yet. I want to marry for love, not convenience. These thoughts feel like sacrilege. I know that I will marry a man my father chooses. That's the way it's done in our town and among Tati's people. Mami and Tati married for love, and it has not been an easy path for them.

I take a deep breath and shake my head from all my thoughts. This morning, everything looks clean from the snow that fell last night and I imagine the icy frost coating the insides of my lungs and mind, making my thoughts white and pure. I love being outside in our forest more than anything at times like these, because the white feels like it hides all our flaws.

Perhaps that's why I often see Tati in the dark forest that surrounds our home praying to God or—as he would say—the *Ribbono Shel Oylam*, the Master of the Universe, by himself, eyes shut, arms outstretched to the sky. Maybe he comes out here to feel new again too.

Tati comes from the town of Kupel, a few days' walk from here. He came here and joined a small group of Chassidim in the town—the followers of the late Reb Mendele, who was a disciple of the great and holy Ba'al Shem Tov. There is a small *shtiebl* where the men pray, in what used to be the home of Urka the Coachman. It is said that the Ba'al Shem Tov himself used to sit under the tree in Urka's courtyard. The Chassidim here accepted my father with open arms, but nobody accepted my mother.

Sometimes I wonder if Reb Mendele and the Ba'al Shem Tov (*zichrono livracha*) were still with us, would the community treat Mami differently? Would they see how hard she tries to be a good Jew, and how wrong the other Jews in town are for not treating her with love and respect. It makes me angry how quickly rumors spread, that Mami's kitchen isn't kosher (it is!) just because she doesn't cover her hair like the other married Jewish women in our town.

That's why Tati built our home, sturdy and warm like he is, outside our town in the forest. It's what Mami wanted: not to be under constant scrutiny, and to have plenty of room to plant fruit trees and make honey and keep chickens and goats. We have a small barn with a cow and a goat, and a bee glade out back and an orchard that leads all the way down to the river. Tati works in town as a builder and a laborer in the fields. But he is also a scholar, worthy of the title Rebbe, though none of the men in town call him that.

Sometimes I think my father knows more than the other Chassidim in our town, even more than Rabbi Borowitz who leads our tiny *kehilla*, and the bare bones prayer *minyan* of ten men that Tati sometimes helps complete. There are many things my father likes to keep secret, like his morning dips in the Dniester River that I never see, but know about, his prayer at the graveside of Reb Mendele, and our library. Our walls are covered in holy books—his *sforim*, and I often fall asleep to the sound of him reading from the Talmud, the Midrash, and the many mystical books of the Chassidim. The stories he reads sound like fairy tales to me, about magical places like Babel and Jerusalem.

In these places, there are scholarly men. Father would be respected there, a king among men. And there are learned boys of marriageable age—the kind of boys Tati would like me to marry someday. In my daydreams, they line up at the door, waiting to get a glimpse of me—the learned, pious daughter of the Rebbe. And my Tati would only pick the wisest and kindest for me.

I shake my head. In my heart of hearts, that's not really what I want. When Laya and I sleep in our loft, I look out the skylight above our heads and pretend that someone will someday find his way to our cabin, climb up onto the roof, and look in from above. He will see me and fall instantly in love.

Because lately I feel like time is running out. The older I get, the harder it will be to find someone. And when I think about that, I wonder why Tati insists that Laya and I wait until we are at least eighteen.

I would ask Mami, but she isn't a scholar like Tati, and she doesn't like to talk about these things. She worries about what people say and how they see us. It makes her angry, but she wrings dough instead of her hands. Tati says her hands are baker's hands, that she makes magic with dough. Mami can make something out of nothing. She makes cheese and gathers honey; she mixes bits of bark and roots and leaves for tea. She bakes the tastiest *challahs* and cakes, *rugelach* and *mandelbrot*, but it's her *babka* she's famous for. She sells her baked goods in town.

When she's not in the kitchen, Mami likes to go out through the skylight above our bed and onto the little deck on our roof to soak up the sun. Laya likes to sit up there with her. From the roof, you can see down to the village and the forest all around. I wonder if it's not just the sun that Mami seeks up there. While Tati's head is always in a book, Mami's eyes are always looking at the sky. Laya says she dreams of somewhere other than here. Somewhere far away, like America.

4

Laya

I always thought
that if I worshipped God,
dressed modestly,
and walked in His path,
that nothing bad
would happen
to my family.
We would find
our path to Zion,
our own piece of heaven
on the banks
of the Dniester River.

But now that I'm fifteen
I see what a life
of pious devotion
has brought Mami,
who converted
to our faith—
disapproval.
The life we lead
out here is a life apart.

I wish I could go to Onyshkivtsi.
Mami always tells me stories
about her town
and Saint Anna of the Swans
who lived there.

Saint Anna
didn't walk with God—
she knew she wasn't made
for perfection;
she never tried
to fit a pattern
that didn't fit her.
She didn't waste her time
trying to smooth herself
into something
she wasn't.
She was powerful
because she forged
her own path.

The Christians
in Onyshkivtsi
built a shrine
to honor her.
The shrine marks a spring
whose temperature
is forty-three degrees
all year,
rain or shine.
Even in the snow.

It is said
that it was once home
to hundreds of swans.
Righteous Anna used to
feed and care for them.
But Mami says the swans
don't go there anymore.

There is rot
in the old growth—
the Kodari forest
senses these things.
I sense things too.
The rot in our community.
Sometimes it's not enough
to be good,
if you treat others
with disdain.
Sometimes there's nothing
you can do
but fly away,
like Anna did.

5

Liba

When we get back from our morning walk, Mami is in the kitchen making breakfast and starting the doughs for the day. Tati shakes the snow off his boots as he walks in. "*Gut morgen*," he says gruffly as he pecks a kiss on Mami's cheek. She pins her white-gold hair up and says, "*Dubroho ranku*. Liba, close the door quickly—you're letting all the cold in."

I let the hood of my coat drop down. "Where's Laya?"

"Getting some eggs from the coop," Mami sings. She and Laya love mornings, not like me, but I'd wake up early every morning if it meant I got time alone with Tati.

I shrug my coat off and hang it on a hook by the door as Mami pours tea at the table. "*Nu?* Come in, warm up," she says to me.

I shake the chill off and start braiding my hair, which is the color of river rocks. Long and thick. I can't pin it up at all. "Your hair is beautiful like moonstone, *dochka*," Mami says. "Leave it down."

"More like oil on fur," I say, because it's sleek and shiny and I never feel like I can tame it. It will never be white and light like hers and Laya's.

"Do you want me to braid it for you?" Mami asks.

I shake my head.

"Come here, my *zaftig* one," Tati says. "Your hair is fine; leave it be."

I cringe: I don't like it when he calls me plump, even though it's a term of endearment, and anyway, I know what comes next. Laya walks in and he says, "Oh, the *shayna meidel* has decided to join us." The pretty one. I concentrate on braiding my hair.

Laya grins. "*Gut morgen.* How was your walk?" She looks at me.

I shrug my shoulders and finish braiding my hair, then sit at the table and lift a cup of tea to my mouth. "*Baruch atah Adonai eloheinu melech haolam, shehakol nih'ye bidvaro—Blessed are you, Lord our God, king of the universe, by whose word all things came to be.*" I make sure to say every word of the blessing with meaning.

"*Oymen!*" Tati says with a smile.

Instead of trying to be something I will never be, I do everything I can to be a good Jew.

6

Laya

When I was outside
gathering eggs,
I searched the sky,
hoping to see something—
anything.
One night I heard
feathers rustling
and turned around
and looked up—
a swan had landed
on our rooftop.
It was watching me.
I didn't breathe
the whole time
it was there.
Until it spread
its wings
and took off
into the sky.

Every night I pray
that it will happen again
because if I ever see
another swan,
I won't hold my breath—
I will open the window
and go outside.

That's why I rake my gaze
over every flake of bark
and every teardrop leaf,
hoping. I see that
every finger-branch
is reaching for something.
I am reaching too.
Up up up.

At night I feel
the weight
of the house
upon my chest.
It's warm
and safe inside,
but the wooden planks
above my head
are nothing like
the dark boughs
of the forest.
Sometimes I wish
I could sleep outside.
The Kodari is
the only place
I feel truly at home.

But this morning
I'm restless
and that usually means
something is about to change.
That's what the forest
teaches you—
change can come
in the blink of an eye—
the fall of one spark
can mean total destruction.

There is a fever
that burns in me.
It prickles every pore.
I'm not happy with
the simple life we lead.
A life ruled
by prayer and holy days,
times for dusk and dawn,
the sacred and the profane.
A life of devotion,
Tati would say.
*The glory
of a king's daughter
is within*.

But I long for what is
just outside my window.
Far beyond
the reaches of the Dniester,
and the boundaries
of our small *shtetl*.

It hurts,
this thing I feel,
how unsettled
I've become.
I want to fit
in this home,
in this town.
To be the daughter
that Tati wants me to be.
To be more
like Liba.
Prayer comes
so easily to her.

Mami understands
what I feel
but I also think
it scares her.
She is always sending me
outside, and I'm grateful
but I also wonder
why she doesn't
teach me how to bake,
or how to pray.
It's almost like she knows
that one day
I will leave her.

Sometimes I wish
she'd teach me
how to stay.

I close my eyes
and take deep breaths.
It helps me
resist the urge
to scratch my back.
I want to crawl out
of this skin I wear
when these thoughts come
and threaten to overwhelm
the little peace I have,
staring at the sky,
praying in my own way
for something else.

Something is definitely
inside me.
It is not glory,
or devotion.
It is something
that wants to burst free.

7

Liba

Night falls and Tati comes home from work. It's well past eleven. Laya is already asleep beside me. She was restless all day, I could sense that—and I wanted to ask her what was wrong, but I never got the chance. Suddenly, there's a knock at the door.

And another.

The knocks are so loud, they feel as if they could wake the dead. I can't imagine how Laya sleeps through it. I creep to the top rung of the ladder to our loft, where I can just barely see the door. Tati goes to open it. Mami baked all day and into the night—*babka* for matters of the heart—and I wonder if she knew that this was coming.

Is it the Tsar's army? Have they come for Tati? So many men from our town have been conscripted recently. Their absence in the village is felt—lights in windows have gone out all over town.

I know, we all know, that something as small as a knock—the rap of knuckles on wood—could change our lives forever. If the Tsar's army comes for you, they take you for twenty-five years. And we know it means some people might never return.

I wait for the world I've known to crumble, with the scent of chocolate in the air.

"Who is it?"

There's a muffled answer and Tati unbars the door.

A man I've never seen before steps inside. He bows before my father and I see Tati put a hand over his mouth and cry out.

"Yankl?"

But the man doesn't rise until Tati places his hands upon his head and blesses him.

"*Ye'varech'echa Adonai ve'yish'merecha*—May God bless you and keep you . . . " I don't understand why my father says the priestly blessing. He normally only says it on Friday nights with his hands on Laya's head and mine—just after we sing "*Shalom Aleichem*" inviting the angels into our home and before he blesses the wine.

The man lifts up his head and kisses my father's knuckles.

"Yankl!" my father says again. The men embrace. "What brings you here?" Tati asks. "How did you . . . ?"

"It wasn't easy to find you, Rebbe, I'll tell you that much."

Mami takes a step forward and bows her head in his direction. "Can I offer you something hot to drink? I just made *babka*."

"This is Adel, my wife," Tati says to the strange man. And to my surprise, the man looks at her and says, "I remember."

He wears a large cloak that looks like a bearskin, and underneath it, a satin overcoat with white stockings that end in large black boots.

"Please—take a seat." Mami beckons the men to the table as she goes to the kitchen. I can hear her fill the kettle and put it on the fire.

The man sits down at the table and stares at Tati. "It's good to see you, Berman."

Tati grunts. "What brings you all this way, my brother?"

Tati has a brother?

The man starts to sway back and forth at the table as if in prayer. "*Oh-yoy oh-yo-yoy, oh-yoy,*" he chants. "The Rebbe is sick, Reb Berman. He doesn't have long to live."

I see Tati's face go slack, white almost, like he's seen a ghost.

"Here, have a tipple of something." Mami takes out the schnapps and offers both men a glassful.

The man—my uncle?—takes a healthy gulp, shudders, and continues. "We need you to come home. The Rebbe needs you, Berman . . . we all need you. Please come back before it's too late." He takes another gulp of schnapps, then picks up the mug of tea.

Tati shakes his head. "I have to speak to my wife."

"There isn't much time," Yankl pleads. "It may be too late already."

"Then what are you doing here? Leave," Tati growls, and slams his glass on the table.

"Berman . . ." Mami goes to put her arms on Tati's shoulders.

"I said I'd never go back, Adel. You know that."

"You can't send Yankl back out into the cold."

Tati grunts and says, "Will you stay the night?"

Yankl stands up. "No. You're right. I should head back right away. I gave you the message." He shrugs. "What you do with it is on your conscience."

"Get out of my house!" Tati yells.

"Berman!" Mami scolds.

I hear Laya turn over in bed.

Tati grumbles, "*Es tut mir bahng*—sorry," and looks up at his brother. "I'll think about it, okay?"

Yankl walks to the door.

"Yankl, I didn't mean it. You can stay the night. You are always welcome in our home," Tati says.

"It's all right," Yankl says. "I'd best be going back."

"I'll pack you up some food," Mami says, "and a thermos of tea."

He hesitates, then nods.

Mami busies herself in the kitchen, but otherwise there is

silence in the room. The brothers seem to look everywhere but at each other.

"*A bi gezunt*," Mami finally says, bringing him a packed basket. She adds in a low voice, "I'll talk to him. He'll come. Don't worry."

And just as quickly as he'd come, the man is gone.

"Why did you tell him that?" Tati growls when she closes the door.

Mami sits down at the table and takes Tati's hands in hers. "Calm yourself, Berman. You have no choice, and you know that. You must go back to Kupel. You have to pay your respects."

"No choice is also a choice," Tati grumbles. "They never had respect for you, or for me and my choices."

"Maybe he wants to make amends . . . "

"We haven't had word in over a dozen years. They cast us out! I swore to you. I swore to myself that I would never go back. And now they want me back? Me, they said, not you. I won't go."

"Yankl didn't say that," Mami sighs. "You know how I feel about your family . . . but if your father goes to his *oylam*, *chas v'shalom*—God forbid—and you don't make it back there, you'll never forgive yourself."

"And then they'll never let me leave. I'm next in line. You know that. And if they won't accept you, I want no part of it. What—I should leave my wife and daughters to go see a father who never approved of me?"

Mami's long thin hands grip Tati's large ones tightly, her knuckles white. "Yankl wouldn't have come unless the situation was dire. I think you should leave now. Tonight. I'll stay here with the girls." She looks into his eyes and says, "I trust you. I know that you'll come back for us."

"It's not about trust, Adel," Tati says ruefully. "What would happen if you went back to your family?"

Mami shakes her head. "I could never."

"So why is this any different?"

"Because the Rebbe is on his deathbed! Really, Berman?"

"And if Dmitry was dying?"

Who is Dmitry? I wish I understood half of what they are discussing. Everything feels both foreign and familiar all at once, as if these are someone else's parents—but also, as if these are things I've heard them discuss in my dreams.

"It's not the same and you know it. I'm sick of this life we lead," Mami says. "A hovel at the edge of the forest? A *shtetl* full of *nebbishers* who talk behind our backs every chance they get. This town is a dead end. We are on the brink. Maybe this is your chance at salvation. To reclaim all you lost."

"Maybe we should go to your family, then, eh? Reclaim them."

"You know we can't do that."

Tati raises his voice. "So why is this any different?"

Mami starts to cry.

Tati gets up and goes to put his arms around her. "You chose this life. You chose me. Are you saying you regret that choice?"

"No, never!" Mami looks up. "But maybe you can have both. Them *and* me. You have a chance now. You know I never will."

"Adel." He hugs her tightly and sighs. "I will only go if you come with me."

"What? And leave the girls?" Mami's voice is shrill and I hear Laya turn over in bed again.

"If we get there and the Rebbe, my Tati, is willing to finally accept you," he says in a voice that sounds cracked, "*publicly*, then we can come back here, get the girls, and move back to Kupel. But I won't expose them to that kind of spectacle unless I know what my father's answer will be. They must accept you first. That's my condition."

"We can't leave the girls."

"The *kehilla* will take care of them. And anyway, they don't have travel permits. None of us do. I won't take the girls on the road and expose them to that kind of danger. If we are caught, it will mean certain death." Tati rubs his hand across his forehead. "For now, they're safer here in Dubossary."

"Are you *meshugge*? They'll be prey to any man!"

"Liba won't let that happen. She's stronger than she knows."

"Maybe we should tell them . . . "

Tell us what?

"No! We said we'd wait until they got engaged and we'll keep to that. No need to worry them before that. The townsfolk are *mensches*. They'll take care of our girls and keep them safe."

"No girls should be without parents," Mami says.

"Liba will keep house until we return. She's nearly eighteen."

"Which is even more of a reason for us all to go back. What kind of future does she have here? You always say that no one from this town will marry our girls. Well, here's your chance. Liba is almost of age. You can't wait forever. It's time, Berman."

"When the time comes, I will find them worthy husbands. Don't you worry about that."

"When? How old does Liba have to be? You'll wait until she's too old for anyone to want her and then see what's left? Let them come with us. Please?"

My skin suddenly feels cold, coated with pinpricks of ice.

"No!" Tati says. "My girls are more precious to me than rubies and pearls. I won't risk their lives on the roads."

I can tell that Mami's crying in earnest now.

"Adel . . . " Tati's voice is instantly soft.

"No!" Mami cries. "I gave up everything I was—everything I had—for you. I did everything right, and it still wasn't enough. Not here, not there, maybe not anywhere. There's no love lost between me and your family. But it's not like things are all that much better here. I hear what people say. I know how they talk. Please go alone. Do it for me. For us. Get his blessing. Then come back safe and sound and we'll either stay here, or we'll go."

"And what if they don't let me leave? What if I can't come back? What if my father is on his deathbed for months? I can't take that chance. I'll be lost without you. You know how they get into my head. You are my life, *gelibteh*, I can't go without you by my side." He lowers his voice and suddenly sounds nothing like my father. "I don't trust myself when I'm with them."

Mami shakes her head and makes a fist. "And if someone murders the girls in the night, or ravages them, you could live? You're a beast to think to leave them."

"I am a beast," he chuckles, "but I haven't acted like one in many years, and you know that better than anyone." Then he looks at her solemnly. "In times like these, people change. Maybe everything will be different. And if not . . ." I can see my father swallow hard, his jaw working. "You're right. I have a responsibility to my parents. At least to mourn, to say *kaddish* at my father's grave if it comes to that."

"You know . . . if things don't work out . . . there are other places we could go. People speak of America."

"America is a fairy tale."

Mami throws her hands up in defeat. "You're impossible." She shakes her head and sighs. "Fine. I'll come with you."

Tati takes a deep breath and softens his tone. "The girls will be okay. We *will* come back for them, I promise. Adel . . . I know you think that I'm against you in this, but I'm not. It is honestly safer for Liba and Laya to stay here."

Mami seems to make a decision. She gets up and walks across the room. She takes something out from the trunk beneath their bed.

"Adel . . ." Tati whispers.

"Don't stop me, Berman. I need to think. I have to get out of this cabin."